JB CR

CW00494751

Millionaire Mavericks

MICHELLE CELMER
JENNIFER LEWIS
DAY LECLAIRE

MILLS
& BOON

Published in Great Britain 2014
by Mills & Boon, an imprint of Harlequin (UK) Limited,
Eton House, 18-24 Paradise Road, Richmond, Surrey, TW9 1SR

MILLIONAIRE MAVERICKS © 2014 Harlequin Books S.A.

The Oilman's Baby Bargain, The Maverick's Virgin Mistress and *Lone Star Seduction* were first published in Great Britain by Harlequin (UK) Limited.

The Oilman's Baby Bargain © 2009 Harlequin Books S.A.
The Maverick's Virgin Mistress © 2009 Harlequin Books S.A.
Lone Star Seduction © 2009 Harlequin Books S.A.

Special thanks and acknowledgements to Michelle Celmer, Jennifer Lewis and Day Leclaire for their contribution to MILLIONAIRE MAVERICKS.

ISBN: 978-0-263-91204-3
eBook ISBN: 978-1-472-04499-0

05-1014

Harlequin (UK) Limited's policy is to use papers that are natural, renewable and recyclable products and made from wood grown in sustainable forests. The logging and manufacturing processes conform to the legal environmental regulations of the country of origin.

Printed and bound in Spain
by Blackprint CPI, Barcelona

THE OILMAN'S
BABY BARGAIN

BY
MICHELLE CELMER

Bestselling author **Michelle Celmer** lives in south-eastern Michigan with her husband, their three children, two dogs and two cats. When she's not writing or busy being a mum, you can find her in the garden or curled up with a romance. And if you twist her arm really hard you can usually persuade her into a day of power shopping.

Michelle loves to hear from readers. Visit her website at www.michellecelmer.com, or write to her at PO Box 300, Clawson, MI 48017, USA.

One

June

Alexis Cavanaugh was in love with the wrong brother.

She gazed across the candlelit table at the man she had spent the better part of the past week in D.C. with, only half listening as he spoke fervently about Brody Oil and Gas, the company he co-owned with his brother Lance. The brother she was *supposed* to be marrying.

Not that she had expected to fall in love with Lance. The marriage was little more than a business deal cooked up by the Brody brothers and her father, Bruce Cavanaugh, senior senator from her home state of Texas. But hadn't she always done what her father asked of her? Didn't he, as he'd always claimed, know what was best? A marriage to Lance would provide her the financial security and station in society that she'd earned—although other than possess the Cavanaugh name, she wasn't sure what she'd ever done to deserve it.

Not that she didn't find Lance appealing. He was tall and dark and devastatingly attractive—not to mention built like a tank—with a charm that drew people to him. A gentle giant. But he wasn't as refined a man as she was accustomed to. He seemed more comfortable among the roughnecks at the refinery than the shareholders. Mitch, on the other hand, had seemed perfectly at ease with the elite of D.C. They had attended half a dozen parties and fundraisers together—Mitch on his brother's behalf, of course—and he could schmooze with the best of them. He was clearly the brains behind Brody Oil and Gas.

And the brother she clearly was falling for.

So many men treated her like a brainless, witless showpiece. Better seen and not heard. But Mitch listened to her. He *heard* her, and seemed genuinely interested in what she had to say.

She realized suddenly that he was meeting her gaze across the table, a grin on his ridiculously handsome face. A face that had become quite familiar over the past few days. She had memorized every line and curve, the slope of his nose, the sensual shape of his chocolate-brown eyes, the fullness of his lips and sharp set of his jaw. She knew every expression and nuance. And the smile he wore now was an amused one.

"What?" she asked.

"You haven't heard a word I've said, have you?"

He was right. He'd been talking about his business, which obviously meant more to him than anything else, and she had completely zoned out. In her own defense, it was tough to watch those full lips move and not become entranced, not be lulled by the deep tenor of his voice. But that was no excuse to be rude. She was usually an exceptional listener.

"I'm sorry," she apologized.

"I'm the one who should be apologizing. I'm obviously boring you to death. I forget that not everyone is as passionate as I am about the oil business."

"I enjoy hearing you talk about it. I guess I'm just a little tired. It's been a very busy week."

"It has," Mitch agreed, with a smile that was just this side of seductive. "My brother has no idea what he's missing."

Did he feel the same connection, the same longing for her that she had for him? Or was he simply being polite? Was he just naturally flirtatious, like his brother?

"It's late. I should get you back to the hotel."

Just for a moment, she let herself believe that he

couldn't wait to get her back to her room so he could make passionate love to her. The idea both thrilled and terrified her. She had always hoped her first time would be special, and she knew without a doubt that with Mitch, it would be.

But that wasn't going to happen because she was marrying his brother. And shouldn't she save something as precious as her virginity for her spouse? Even if it wasn't a real marriage?

He summoned the waiter and paid the exorbitantly high bill without batting an eyelash. What did she expect when he took her to the most exclusive restaurant in D.C.? Money was obviously of no concern.

He helped her up from her seat and walked her to the door. She took pleasure in the way every head in the room swiveled in his direction. Men watched with envy as their female companions swooned, eyes filled with silent longing.

Sorry, girls, he's all mine. At least until she became officially engaged to Lance. If only she could capture this time and make it last forever. Make a life with Mitch instead of Lance.

The limo was already waiting for them as they stepped out into the hot and muggy evening air, but the soft leather felt cool as she slipped inside. "The Watergate Hotel," Mitch told the driver.

She hoped they would talk more on the way there, but his cell phone rang. He checked the display and told her, "Sorry, but I have to take this."

Though he said nothing specific, it was clear by his tone that the conversation had something to do with the fire at the refinery. She'd heard from her father that the investigation pointed to arson, and though there were no solid suspects, rumors were spreading that Lance's rival, Alejandro Montoya, might be responsible. She couldn't understand why anyone would put so many lives in danger, but having grown up around politics, she'd learned that some people were capable of terrible things.

Mitch disconnected just as the limo pulled up to the hotel. Usually they parted ways in the lobby, as their rooms were in different wings, but tonight Mitch offered to accompany her to her door.

He was just being polite, she told herself. But why now? Why was tonight any different than the last?

The air seemed to sizzle with electricity as they rode the elevator up to the penthouse. More than usual she felt acutely aware of his presence beside her. Or maybe it was just her imagination.

When the doors slid open, he touched her waist to lead her out. His hand felt huge, and warmth seeped through the silk of her sundress, making the skin beneath tingle. She couldn't recall him touching her this way before, and she was sure she would have noticed. When they reached her door, he took the key from her and opened it. She stepped inside and he leaned against the jamb.

"I had a nice time tonight, Lexi," he said. There was heat in his eyes as they searched her face, then drifted lower, to the front of her dress, where, thanks to her very expensive and uncomfortable push-up bra, her breasts swelled over and begged to be noticed. He did notice, and he obviously liked what he saw.

She had never been one to play the seductress, but tonight she was feeling the part. Would it hurt her, for the first time in her boring and proper life, to do something scandalous and wicked? Something just for herself? Who, besides the two of them, would ever know? After years of chastity, hadn't she earned one night of unbridled passion and ecstasy?

She knew without a doubt he would give her exactly that.

"I had a nice time, too," she said, gazing up at him through the fringe of her lashes, wearing what she hoped was a seductive smile. Maybe it was the wine, or the candlelit dinner, but she could feel her inhibitions melting away. "Would you like to come inside for a nightcap?"

Without hesitation he stepped into the room, closing the door behind him. She opened her mouth to ask him what he wanted to drink, but before she could make a sound his arms were around her, drawing her against him. Her nipples tingled almost painfully as they pressed against the wall of his chest and her knees went weak with excitement. Then he lowered his head and kissed her. Her lips parted with a surprised gasp, and he dipped in for a taste.

She expected him to plunder and dominate the way the men did in her favorite romance novels. Instead, his lips were soft and gentle, his touch tender. In spite of having wanted this with all of her heart, she was so stunned she was actually kissing her future brother-in-law that she stood stiff in his arms.

He must have interpreted her reaction as a rejection, because he released her and pulled away. "I'm sorry," he said. "But I've been fantasizing about doing that all night. All *week*."

So had she, and she wasn't going to blow it. She wasn't going to let her fear of the unknown ruin this chance for a night with the man of her dreams.

She grinned her most wicked smile and slid her hands up his chest, wrapping them around his neck. "Then why did you stop?"

This time when he kissed her, he didn't stop. And when he took her to bed, he proved to be everything she had imagined.

And more.

Last night had been the most amazing, terrifying and wonderful night of Lexi's life. She'd had no idea two people could connect—could be in perfect sync—the way she and Mitch had been. She had tried to hide the fact that she was a virgin, but of course he'd figured it out. She'd worried that he might be angry or put off, but the opposite had been true. He'd been so sweet and gentle with her. What could have been a painful, awkward experience had been more beautiful than she had ever imagined possible.

The instant she woke the next morning, cradled in a cocoon of warm silk sheets that still held the scent of Mitch's aftershave, she knew without a doubt that she wouldn't be marrying Lance. She wanted Mitch. And she was sure that if she pleaded her case to her father, he would see that the other Brody brother would be a much better match. As far as he was concerned, it was only the Brody name that was important.

Before she even opened her eyes she smiled to herself and began to imagine what life would be like married to Mitch. How happy she would be because they would love each other. She imagined what their children would look like. They would have a son who would be tall and fit with Mitch's dark hair, olive tones and striking features, and a girl, pretty and graceful with Lexi's creamy complexion and blond hair.

They would have a ceremony in the garden at her father's Houston estate, then honeymoon somewhere warm and exotic. Maybe Cabo San Lucas, or the Bahamas. And if Mitch was agreeable, they could try to conceive while they were there. What better time to get pregnant than on her honeymoon? She had always wanted to be a mother, to have at least three or four children.

Lexi heard movement in the room and realized Mitch was already up. She peered at the clock on the bedside table, surprised to find that it was barely 7:00 a.m.

"Are you awake?" Mitch asked.

She rolled to face him, ready to smile and say, *why don't you climb back in bed and find out,* but he was already showered and dressed, and when she saw the look on his face, her heart sank. Then she realized, of course he would look distressed. He was about to steal his brother's fiancée. Maybe he thought she loved Lance.

She sat up, holding the sheet against her bare breasts. "Good morning."

"We need to talk," he said.

She nodded, barely able to contain her excitement. Here it comes. He was going to tell her he loved her, and beg her to marry him instead of Lance. Of course she would say yes. Then he would undress, and climb back into bed, and she would spend the rest of the morning showing him just how much she loved him. Then everything would be perfect, just like the happily-ever-afters in the romance novels.

His expression somber, he said, "I don't suppose I have to tell you that we've made a drastic mistake."

Wait, what?

A *mistake?*

She had to replay the words several times in her mind, convinced she must have misunderstood.

"No one can ever know that this happened," he continued, his tone grim. "Especially my brother."

He might as well have reached into her chest and ripped out her heart, because that was the way it felt. The fierce, hollow ache was nearly unbearable.

For years she had endured her father's criticism and indifference. No matter what she did to please him, however closely she played by his rules, it was never enough to win his love. Now, once again, she had been rejected by a man whose affection she desperately craved.

Maybe there was something wrong with her, something that made her unlovable.

"Lance is flying in this afternoon to officially propose," Mitch told her. "You have to pretend that everything is fine, and nothing has changed."

How could she act as though everything was fine when she was falling apart? And how could she have been so stupid? Why didn't she see that it was just sex to him? Maybe it was some sort of warped sibling rivalry. Maybe Mitch seduced all of his brother's girlfriends.

Humiliation burned her from the inside out, but she would die before she let Mitch know.

She lifted her nose at him and pasted on a look of boredom. "I don't have to pretend everything is fine,

Mitch. As far as I'm concerned, things are great. You definitely served your purpose."

He frowned. "What purpose was that?"

She racked her brain, grasping for the worst, most awful thing she could possibly say to hurt him as much as he'd hurt her. "A cheap thrill, to cheat my arranged husband out of my virginity. And who better to do it with than his brother. Although I'm sorry to say, I expected better. Your performance wasn't exactly earth-shattering."

Mitch's expression went from one of confusion to ice-cold hatred. She waited for him to shout and berate her, the way her father often did when he was displeased with her. But all he said was, "I should have expected as much from a spoiled and pampered heiress."

No words could have stung more or cut deeper.

He grabbed his wallet from the bedside table. "Meet me downstairs in the lounge at noon," he said, then turned and left without another word.

She sat there for several minutes, feeling sick with grief, but then she began to feel something else. She began to feel angry. How dare he play with her emotions that way. How dare he make love to her and take from her the most precious gift she had to offer—her innocence—then ruthlessly reject her.

Well, she would show him. She would marry his brother and she would make Lance love her. She would be the best wife, the best mother—everything Lance could ever want in a mate.

Mitch would see how happy they were, see how perfect she could be, and he would regret letting her go for the rest of his life.

Two

September

Mitchell Brody had never been one to compromise, but when it came to Brody Oil and Gas, he would do just about anything to ensure its continued growth and success. Even if that meant marrying a spoiled, heartless, manipulative heiress who had a block of ice where her heart belonged.

Bruce Cavanaugh glared at Mitch from behind his massive desk—the desk he boasted once belonged to JFK—in his Houston office, where he sat like a king addressing a lowly peasant. Everything in the room, from the rich furnishings to his many accolades framed and hung on the walls, was designed to intimidate. Mitch would happily tell the overbearing son of a bitch to go to hell, but unfortunately, he and Lance needed his senatorial support. Even more so since the fire at the refinery. If they planned to keep profits up, they needed to expand.

"Your brother has humiliated my family," he told Mitch.

"I know he has, sir. Once more, I would like to express our deepest apologies."

"Rejecting my Lexi for a lowly secretary," he scoffed, as if Kate's profession somehow made her unworthy. Mitch wondered how the senator would feel if he knew that while she was supposed to be planning a wedding with Lance, his precious daughter Lexi had been seducing Mitch instead.

"He was in love with Kate," Mitch said, which seemed to carry little or no weight.

The senator just glared and said, "I don't think we have anything left to discuss, Mr. Brody."

Mitch had never had to grovel in his life, but there was a first time for everything. His brother had damn well better appreciate this. "I'd like you to consider a compromise, sir."

The senator narrowed his eyes. "What kind of compromise?"

"We still need your support, Senator Cavanaugh, and I'm assuming you still want the best for your daughter."

"Your point is?"

"The Brody name can provide that."

"What are you suggesting?"

He had to force the words out. "A marriage between Alexis and me."

He looked wary, but also intrigued, leaning back in his seat and folding his arms over his chest. "Explain."

In other words, kiss the old man's ass, make this worth his while. "I think this arrangement will be in everyone's best interests, Senator. Married to me, Alexis will be set for life financially, and remain in the upper echelon of Texas society."

"And in return?" the senator asked.

"With your senatorial support, my brother and I will expand Brody Oil and Gas and take it to heights our father never dreamed possible."

"I'm sure you can imagine how humiliated my Lexi was when your first arrangement fell through. If I do say yes, what assurances do I have that you won't fall in love with *your* secretary and decide to marry her, instead?"

It annoyed Mitch the way he referred to her as "my Lexi," as though she were a possession, or a commodity. If he really cared about his daughter, would he expect her to settle for an arranged, loveless marriage? Wouldn't he want her to be happy? Or maybe in his mind, wealth and security equaled happiness.

Whatever the man's motivation, it wasn't Mitch's

problem. Besides, as far as he was concerned, Lexi
was getting exactly what she deserved. He should
have realized that the woman under the sweet and
demure exterior was in reality a viper. Not unlike his
mother, who made his father fall in love with her,
gave birth to his sons and then abandoned them.

Lexi had played with his emotions and used him.
Now he was going to return the favor.

"In the first place," Mitch told him, "my secretary
is sixty-eight and married with grandchildren.
Second, I am not a frivolous man when it comes to
my emotions. I'm prepared to do anything for the
sake of my business. I also have a plan to counter-
act any humiliation my brother's rejection caused.
When all is said and done, Lance will be the one who
comes out looking like a fool."

"How will you manage that?"

"With all due respect, sir, I would prefer to
discuss it with Lexi first, to be sure that she's okay
with it."

Senator Cavanaugh silently considered that for
several moments, then he nodded. "I'm inclined to
say yes, but under one condition. I won't force Lexi
to marry you. She must be agreeable to the match,
or the deal is off."

Mitch winced. That could definitely be a problem.
She obviously despised Mitch. He was going to have
to get creative, make her an offer she couldn't refuse.
Perhaps a credit card with no limit and all the depart-

ment store accounts she could dream of. He would give her everything her spoiled and greedy little heart desired. That is, if she *had* a heart.

"Agreed," Mitch said. He rose from his chair and offered the senator his hand. The man's grip was firm and binding.

"One more thing," the senator said, as Mitch turned to leave. "If you hurt my daughter in any way, shape or form, I will crush you and your brother. Understand?"

Mitch nodded, then turned and walked to the door, hoping he hadn't just made the biggest mistake of his life.

Lexi stood in her private bathroom at her father's Houston estate feeling as though she might be sick. She'd been feeling that way every morning lately. Which was what had motivated her to finally take a home pregnancy test. That, and two missed periods. And sure enough, when the little wand was ripe, up popped that little pink plus sign.

She groaned, and dropped her head in her hands. She had always been the perfect, dutiful daughter. The *one* time in her life she'd had the guts to say to hell with what her father wanted and have some fun, this was what happened.

Didn't that just figure?

There was a soft rap on the door and her personal assistant, Tara—the one who had been kind enough to fetch the pregnancy test in the first place—poked her head in. "Well?"

Unable to make herself say the words, Lexi held the results up so Tara could see for herself. "I am so completely screwed."

Tara crossed the room and wrapped Lexi up in a hug. "We'll get through this," she promised. "Everything will be okay."

Lexi rested her head on Tara's shoulder and let herself be comforted for a minute. Tara was the closest thing she had to a best friend. Lexi's father was particular about who Lexi was allowed to befriend. As far as he was concerned, no one was good enough for his little girl. As a result, people believed she was a snob.

And what would they think if she had a baby out of wedlock? Her father would be absolutely mortified. He talked for years about how someday she would marry and give him grandsons to spoil, but this was not part of his carefully laid plan.

"If my father finds out, he'll kill me," she said.

Tara held her at arm's length. "You have options."

Lexi knew exactly what she meant, and shook her head. "Termination isn't an option."

"So, you'll have it?"

"If I do, my father will disown me." Of that she had little doubt. Perception meant everything to him. He would probably accuse her of doing it on purpose, to sabotage his reputation. He would accuse her of not loving or respecting him after everything he had done for her. How many times had she been tempted to ask, *what have you done for me?* Other than shelter her, control her life and treat her more like political leverage than a daughter.

But she would never have the courage to say the words. Despite everything, he was still her father. Without him, she had no one.

"What do *you* want, Lexi?" Tara asked.

That was part of the problem. She didn't know what she wanted. If her father did disown her, cut her off financially, would it be fair to the child to raise it in poverty and shame? But the idea of a stranger raising her own flesh and blood made her heart ache.

This is Mitch's child, too, she reminded herself. Shouldn't he be part of the decision?

As if reading her mind, Tara asked, "What about the father?"

He may have been the biological father, but Mitch had made his feelings unequivocally clear. Their night together had been a mistake, and no one could ever know. "The father wants nothing to do with me."

"Curious," Tara said, looking thoughtful. "Mitchell Brody always struck me as the responsible type."

Lexi's mouth dropped open in surprise. She hadn't told anyone about the night she'd spent with her former fiancé's brother. It would have been too humiliating. How did Tara…?

"I would have to be an imbecile not to have figured it out," Tara told her. "For a week, you talked of nothing else. It was Mitch this and Mitch that. Mitch took me to the Smithsonian and Mitch took me to the most exclusive French restaurant in all of D.C. Mitch and I sat talking for hours. It was obvious you had feelings for him. A woman doesn't hold on to her virginity for twenty-four years, then give it up to a stranger."

That week had been one of the best in her life. She had learned that there was more to Mitch than his serious, and sometimes intimidating exterior. He could be sweet and fun. She'd allowed him to seduce her, and look at the mess it had gotten her into.

"On the other hand," Tara said, "if he was really *that* responsible, he would have used protection."

"He did! That's why I was so hesitant to believe I could be pregnant in the first place."

"Did you use a condom *every* time?"

"Of course we—" She frowned.

Tara mirrored her expression. "What?"

Lexi shook her head. "No, that couldn't be it."

"You had unprotected sex?"

"Only for a minute. It was the middle of the night, and we woke up and he started to…" Her cheeks blushed a brilliant shade of pink. She'd never spoken about anything so personal to anyone in her life. Not even her physician. "But he put a condom on before he…you know…finished."

Tara looked pained. "Sperm can be released before ejaculation. And it only takes one. They teach this stuff in health class, Lex."

But she hadn't had health class. She had been homeschooled by tutors, to spare her the improper influence of other children. And not a single one of those tutors, not even her science instructor, had ever said a word about sex education. Her father would have had a fit. Everything she knew about sex, she'd learned from the romance novels she used to sneak into the house. Lately, she had come to realize that those books offered a somewhat slanted view of what love and relationships truly entailed.

"So, this is my fault," she said. If she hadn't been so naive, she would have known better.

"It's no one's fault. Besides, it sounds like you two had one heck of a night together. Maybe, if there's a chance—"

Lexi shook her head. "There's no chance. He wasn't the man I thought he was."

"Well, he still has rights."

"I know," she said, feeling more confused than she ever had in her life. "I don't know what to do."

"Maybe what you need is some time away to think this through. You've been telling me for months that you'd like to take a vacation. Didn't you mention a trip to Cabo San Lucas?"

The place where she had hoped to spend her honeymoon in marital bliss with Mitch? She couldn't bear the thought of it.

"Too hot," she told Tara.

"Okay, how about an Alaskan cruise?"

She blanched. "As if I'm not nauseous enough."

"I didn't think about that." Tara gnawed her lower lip for a moment, then she brightened. "I know! What about that villa in the Greek Isles that Senator Richardson mentioned? That would be perfect."

Actually, that was an excellent idea. She wanted quiet and seclusion, and no one in Greece was likely to know, or even care, who her father happened to be. But there was still a problem. "What if my father won't allow it?"

"Tell him the humiliation of Lance's rejection is just too much to bear, and you need some time alone."

It was the humiliation of Mitch's rejection that was really killing her, but still, it wasn't a bad idea.

"Make him feel guilty for putting you in this position," Tara said. "It is ultimately his fault that you're going through all this."

Tara had a point. If her father hadn't insisted she marry Lance, Lexi never would have met Mitch. So, in a roundabout way he was responsible, although she doubted he would agree. He would lay the blame solely on her. As always. No matter how hard she tried, she never seemed to do anything right. And though she had never been one to play the pity card, if the circumstance demanded it...

She smiled at her friend, thankful she had someone so supportive to lean on at a time like this, even if she was getting paid handsomely to do so. "How soon can you make the reservation?"

Three

As soon as he left the senator's office, Mitch called his brother.

Lance answered on the first ring. "What did he say?"

"He agreed."

Lance released a breath.

"You're sure you're ready to deal with the backlash?" Mitch asked. "This isn't going to look great for you."

"After the way I humiliated her, I would say I probably deserve it. I'm just sorry that you have to go through this."

"Sorry for what? You were going to make the same sacrifice."

"But I didn't. I went with my heart."

"I'm sure Lexi and I will eventually grow fond of one another," he lied. It was probably more likely they would live completely separate lives. If they didn't kill each other first.

"I just feel guilty as hell making you do this. Now that I know what it feels like to be with someone I love and trust, I want the same for you. I want you to be happy."

"When our company is thriving and we're leaving our competitors in the dust, I will be. Besides, you know I don't believe in love. Life doesn't work that way. Not for me, anyhow." Nor did he want it to. It was tough to betray a man who refused to leave himself vulnerable. No woman would hurt him the way his mother had.

His brother could see right through him. "Not all women abandon their families," he said. "And when Mom did, I'm sure she had her reasons."

Of course she did. Their father was a bastard, emotionally, and at times physically, abusive. But if she loved Mitch and Lance, why leave them behind to suffer in her place? Why not take them with her?

He had no doubt that Lexi was self-centered and spoiled enough to do the same. If she did agree to marry him, he would insist they remain childless. It would be cruel to bring a baby into a loveless shell of a marriage. Sometimes he wished his parents would have spared him the burden of ever being born.

"There is a catch," Mitch told him. "Alexis has to willingly accept my proposal."

Lance let out a low whistle. "Maybe it was my imagination, but there didn't seem to be any love lost between the two of you when I broke the engagement."

Lance had no idea. "He also warned me that if I hurt her, he'll crush us."

Lance chuckled. "The old goat doesn't pull any punches, does he?"

"You're not concerned?"

"Why should I be? I have total faith in you."

Mitch hoped that faith wasn't misplaced. He'd already let his brother down once, betraying him by sleeping with his soon-to-be fiancée. Although it wasn't as if Lance loved Lexi, or thought of the marriage as anything more than a business arrangement. Mitch, on the other hand, had honestly believed there had been a connection between Lexi and him. If he had known that Lance loved Kate the night that he slept with Lexi, he might have asked Lexi to marry him, instead. But she had only been using him.

Ironic that he would be stuck marrying her regardless.

"You can still back out," Lance said.

No, he couldn't. This marriage was imperative. "I've already made my decision. I'm going to call her right now and set up a meeting."

"Suppose you ask, and she says no."

A very likely scenario. But every woman had a weakness. He would find hers and use it to his advantage. "I'll just have to make her an offer she can't refuse."

Though she hadn't yet sought her father's approval, Lexi laid out her clothes for the maid to pack. Her plane departed the day after tomorrow and nothing short of the apocalypse would stop her from being on it. The way she figured it, an emotional meltdown during supper and tearful pleading should bend him to her will.

Her cell phone rang and she checked the display. It was a Houston number that she didn't recognize. Curious, she answered.

"Lexi, it's Mitchell Brody."

Her heart plummeted to her toes at the sound of his voice. "Hello, Mr. Brody," she said in her coolest tone.

"I was wondering if we can arrange a meeting. This afternoon, if possible."

A meeting? What could they possibly have to say to each other?

Fear slithered down her spine. He couldn't know about the baby, could he? Only Tara knew, and she swore not to breathe a word to anyone.

She was being paranoid. Of course he didn't know. Anything he could possibly have to say to her at this point was irrelevant.

"I'm afraid I don't have time," she told him. "I'm packing for a trip. Perhaps we could schedule a meeting in a few weeks, after I return." Maybe by then she would know what she planned to do.

"I'm afraid this can't wait," he said. "It's urgent that I speak with you today. I can be there in twenty minutes."

Though he was the last man on earth that she wanted to see right now, her curiosity had been piqued. Maybe he wanted to beg her forgiveness, tell her that calling their night together a mistake had been a gross error in judgment.

Maybe he was coming to tell her that he loved her. She could at least hear him out, let him grovel a little before she told him to go to hell.

"Fine," she said.

"I'll see you in twenty minutes."

Mitch was at her door in fifteen. When the bell rang, she waved the butler away and answered it herself.

She'd almost forgotten how beautiful he was, how tall and dark and imposing. How delicious he smelled. Some small part of her ached to be close to him, to touch him again, to vault herself into his arms. Probably thanks to the pregnancy hormones that had been wreaking havoc with her emotions the past few weeks.

The easy smile Mitch usually wore was absent. His jaw was set and his expression serious. In fact, he looked almost…nervous. She didn't think men like Mitch ever got nervous.

"Thank you for agreeing to see me," he said.

She folded her arms across her chest. "What was so important that it couldn't wait?"

"Is there somewhere we can speak privately?"

She nodded, and he followed her across the foyer to the study. When they were inside, she shut the door. "Well?"

"First, I want to apologize again for my brother's behavior."

"Don't bother. He did me a favor. We would have been miserable together." She paused, then asked, "How is Lance?"

"Great. Very happy."

"I'm glad. But that isn't what you came here to talk about."

"No, it isn't," he said, looking troubled. "As you probably know, Lance and I are still in need of your father's support."

"Good luck with that." Her father had been furious with the Brody brothers, and still was, as far as she could tell.

"I had a meeting with him today."

Her eyes widened. "He actually agreed to meet with you?"

"I can be very persuasive."

He didn't have to tell her that. Had he not been so persuasive, she wouldn't be in her current dilemma.

"The senator and I have reached an…understanding."

Why did she get the feeling that she wasn't going to like this?

"What kind of understanding?"

"Your father has promised his support if you marry me, instead."

Marry him? After what had happened with Lance, would her father honestly force her to marry the other Brody brother? And why hadn't he said anything to her? Why hadn't he warned her?

"Another business arrangement?" she asked, and Mitch nodded. "Do I have a choice in the matter?"

"In fact, you do. The stipulation was that I have to convince you to marry me."

Her mouth fell open. "He actually *said* that?"

"Essentially, yes."

She could see that the prospect of having to beg Lexi to marry him made Mitch uncomfortable. As it should, after the way he'd used her. Score one for good ol' Dad. And she knew exactly why the senator had agreed to this arrangement. He'd mentioned more than once that he believed Mitch possessed presidential-size political potential. Social status meant everything to him and he would love nothing more than to see his precious daughter serve as first lady to the nation.

Whether or not Mitch was the least bit interested in a political career, Lexi didn't have a clue, and the idea of spending the rest of her life married to someone so coldhearted and manipulative—too much like her father—turned her already questionable stomach.

Yet she couldn't deny that this could be the answer to all of her problems. Marrying Mitch would give her child legitimacy. Although people—her father in particular—might get suspicious when she gave birth to a full-term-size baby two months early. But she could figure that out later.

The real question was, could she stand to be married to Mitch for the rest of her life?

Even if she did decide to marry him, she wouldn't let Mitch off the hook too easily. She was going to make him work for it.

"After the way your brother humiliated me, what makes you believe I would even consider marrying you?" she asked.

"Because I have a plan that will leave my brother looking like the humiliated one."

She narrowed her eyes at him, unable to resist taking the bait. "How will you manage that?"

"It will be leaked that you and I have been secretly seeing each other, and that I seduced you away from my brother that week in D.C. People will be led to believe that you were planning to break the engagement, only Lance did it first, before you had the chance."

"And what will make them believe that? What if they think it's just gossip?"

"My brother and I will have a very public argument to drive the point home."

Reputation was everything to men like Lance and

Mitch, so she couldn't help but feel the slightest bit touched. "Lance would do that for me?"

"We'll do anything for the sake of our business."

So, they weren't doing this for her. They were doing it for their business. Her vindication was just a convenient side effect. She should have known.

Ironically, their so-called plan wasn't that far from the truth. Mitch *had* seduced her, and for a short time she had seriously considered choosing him over his brother.

"Does Lance know what happened?" she asked.

"You mean that night at the hotel?"

She nodded.

"Of course not. As far as he's concerned, this is a total fabrication."

And she could see from Mitch's demeanor that he intended to keep it that way. That would be tough when news of the baby broke. Lance was eventually going to find out.

The truth was, she cared little about her humiliation, and what people might think of her. For the baby's sake, however, she would be a fool to turn down Mitch's offer. A marriage to him would grant the kind of life that the baby deserved.

"My answer is yes," she said. "I'll marry you."

He looked surprised that she would acquiesce so easily. "We should do it soon. I was thinking a small civil ceremony at the courthouse."

The sooner—and the simpler—the better as far

as she was concerned. So much for the extravagant and blissful white wedding she had always dreamed of. "Fine."

"And we should plan a honeymoon. To make it look more authentic."

She thought of the nonrefundable trip she had just booked. "I'm leaving for a seven-day trip to Greece the day after tomorrow. Would that be authentic enough for you?"

He nodded. "That would be perfect."

"I'll have my assistant book you a seat."

"And I'll have mine make the wedding arrangements."

"All right."

"While we're away, I'll arrange to have your things moved into my townhouse."

She hadn't given any thought to the fact that he would expect her to live with him. But of course he would. Married couples lived together. Although the idea of living under his roof made her feel vulnerable. Would he try to run her life, controlling her every move the way her father had? Would she be moving from one prison to another?

And if so, what choice did she have?

Mitch must have read her expression. "You'll have your own room," he assured her. "You'll want for nothing."

Unfortunately, that wasn't true. She wanted something he wasn't capable of giving. She wanted to be loved. She wanted someone to respect and appreciate her for who she was deep down inside. And while he did seem to appreciate what she was doing for him, the love and respect part seemed impossible. Maybe she wasn't worthy. Maybe that was the price she paid for wealth and security. Or maybe the sad truth was, she just wasn't all that lovable.

"You won't regret this," Mitch assured her, which she found terribly ironic, seeing as how she was beginning to regret it already.

"Are you ready for this?" Lance asked Mitch the following evening. They sat across from one another at a linen-draped table in the elaborately decorated dining room of the Texas Cattleman's Club. It was the most public place they could think of for the desired result. If all went as planned, word of what was about to transpire would burn up the town like flaming tumbleweed in the dry season.

"I'm ready," Mitch said.

It was a little hard to believe that this time tomorrow he would be married and on his way to Greece. Twenty-nine was too damned young to be a husband, to be tied down. Not that he or Lexi were thinking of this as a real marriage. It was a business arrangement. One that would no doubt cost him dearly. Both emotionally and financially. That was evident from the astronomically priced wedding ring she'd chosen. Her expensive taste apparently knew no bounds.

A grin kicked up one corner of Lance's mouth. "I'll go easy on you, little brother."

"Don't bother. Whatever you can dish out, I can take." God knows that there were many times he'd gotten a lot worse from their old man. "We have to make this look real, Lance."

"Don't worry, I will," he said, and just like that, the grin faded. Lance assumed a look of pure disgust, and said in a voice loud enough for the entire room to hear, "You son of a bitch."

A hush fell over the room and all heads turned in their direction. No turning back now, Mitch thought.

He held up both hands in a defensive gesture and said in a pleading voice, "Let me explain."

Lance stood so fast his chair flipped backward onto the floor, narrowly missing the table behind theirs. He grabbed his half-full highball glass, rose to his feet and with a flick of his wrist flung the contents into Mitch's face. As the alcohol burned Mitch's eyes and soaked through the front of his shirt, he couldn't help but think, *what a terrible waste of the club's finest whiskey.*

Gasps of surprise filled the silence as Lance stormed from the dining room. Mitch grabbed a linen napkin from the table and wiped his face. With all eyes on him now—most of them friends, neighbors or business associates—he jumped up from his chair and followed his brother to the crowded main lobby, calling, "Lance, wait! I can explain!"

He caught up with him just outside the dining room door. To anyone watching, Lance appeared enraged. *"Explain?* What sort of man seduces his brother's fiancée?"

Mitch heard gasps from the crowd.

"We didn't mean for it to happen," he said, finding it ironic that if Lance had discovered the truth, Mitch probably would have been saying the same thing. Although it would have been a lie. Lexi had admitted to using him to rob her husband of her virginity. Seems the joke was on both of them.

"As far as I'm concerned, you and Lexi deserve each other," Lance spat, and turned to leave. Just as they had choreographed, Mitch grabbed his arm.

The fist came at him so swiftly that, had he not expected it, he wouldn't have had time to duck. As it was, Mitch could only stand there defenseless as Lance's fist connected squarely with his jaw. The blow knocked him backward several feet. He lost his balance and ended up on his ass on the unforgiving marble floor.

Lance shot him one last seething look, then shouldered his way out the door. Mitch's behind ached something special, his jaw stung like a mother and his pride had taken a hit, but the reaction from the patrons told him it had all been worth it. A steady buzz of voices hummed through the lobby and at least half a dozen people were jabbering excitedly into their cell phones. He gave it an hour before the entire population of Maverick County heard the news.

Mitch swiped a hand across the corner of his mouth and came back with a smear of blood. Two employees appeared at either side to help him to his feet, and the hostess handed him a napkin to stop the bleeding.

"I'm all right," he mumbled, shrugging away from their help as though humiliated and distraught. From outside, he heard the squeal of tires and knew Lance was peeling out of the lot, putting the finishing touches on their little charade. And what a show it had been.

He just hoped it was worth it.

Four

With only Tara, Lance, and Mitch's best friend Justin Dupree to serve as witnesses—her father had been called to D.C. on so-called urgent business—Lexi and Mitch said their "I do's" before a county judge the following morning, then drove directly to the airport to catch the first leg of their flight to Greece.

Lexi sat beside her new husband in first class, eyes closed, willing her stomach to settle. Either her hormones were wreaking havoc on her nerves, or her morning sickness had taken a severe turn for the worse. If it was the latter, to hell with having three or four children. This kid could count on being an only child. Up until now, she'd suffered only occasional, mild nausea. Today, she had vomited three times. Once at home, right after she crawled out of bed, once in the ladies' room of the courthouse, and again in the airport bathroom just before their flight boarded. She was beginning to think this trip was a bad idea.

Even worse than marrying Mitch Brody.

"Are you all right?" Mitch said softly.

Far from it. She swallowed back the bile rising in her throat and opened her eyes, grimacing once again when she saw the angry-looking bruise that spanned the left side of his jaw and the nasty gash at the corner of his mouth.

"I'm fine," she lied.

There was concern etched on his face. He folded the newspaper he'd been reading—the financial section, of course—and set it in his lap. "No offense, but you're looking a little green."

How nice of him to notice. "And you're looking black and blue."

He reached up and rubbed a palm across his jaw, wincing slightly.

"I can't believe he hit you. Couldn't he just have pretended to punch you?"

Mitch shrugged, as if it was no big deal. "I told you, it had to look convincing."

Apparently it had. According to Tara, the entire town was buzzing with gossip, and every chance Tara got, she helped out by fanning the flames. In no time, everyone would be convinced that Mitch and Lexi had been having a secret affair. News of the baby would only cement the rumors.

Even though Lexi knew Mitch and Lance had ultimately done it for their business, she couldn't help but feel honored that they had gone to such lengths in part to salvage her honor.

And she thought chivalry was dead.

Despite his casual attitude, it must have been humiliating for Mitch. Or maybe he was one of those men who honestly didn't give a damn what anyone thought.

"I could ring the flight attendant for an ice pack," she offered.

"I'm fine," he said. "Do you need anything?"

She shook her head, which was a mistake because the movement made her stomach lurch. She wished she'd chosen a more casual outfit for the flight instead of the fitted silk suit she'd worn for the ceremony. Something loose and comfortable, like her pajamas.

"You don't look well," he said.

"Thanks."

"That wasn't an insult. I'm concerned."

"I'm just a little airsick. It happens sometimes. And it's kind of embarrassing, so if you don't mind, can we just drop it?"

"Sorry."

After that, they sat in awkward silence. During

their week together in D.C. they had seemingly endless conversations. Most people viewed her as a spoiled and witless debutante, and her father didn't help, perpetuating the rumors by pampering and coddling her. But Mitch had seen past that. He had listened to her, made her feel…special. Now she had no idea what to say to him.

How about something along the lines of, *By the way, did I mention that I'm pregnant with your child?*

She had planned to tell him in the limo on the way to the airport, but she'd been otherwise occupied, trying not to be sick all over the leather interior. She'd decided to wait until they settled into the villa in Greece. She didn't doubt the news was going to come as a shock, but she was sure that when he grew used to the idea, he would be happy to be a father.

As if reading her thoughts, Mitch said, "Maybe we should have a talk about our expectations in regard to our relationship."

She hoped he wasn't talking about sex, because that hadn't been part of the deal. This was supposed to be a business arrangement. She had no intention of being his concubine. "What kind of expectations?"

Her wariness seemed to amuse him. "Not the kind you're obviously thinking of. Our relationship stops at the bedroom door."

"Good," she said, feeling relieved. And strangely enough, a little disappointed.

"What I meant, for example, is that as a part of my business, it's required that I occasionally attend social functions. As my wife, I will expect you to accompany me, and of course I'll do the same for you."

That didn't sound so terrible. "I can do that."

"You'll also be expected to host several parties."

That was something that she was actually quite good at. "Of course."

"And since I'm not particularly fond of seeing my name in the tabloids, or being the source of the latest gossip, I think it should appear to everyone that we're happily married. If word gets out that this is part of a business deal, we'll never hear the end of it. I personally value my privacy."

Personally, she didn't give a damn what people thought. But for the baby's sake, it would be best if they kept up a ruse of wedded bliss, so the child wouldn't feel unwanted.

"As soon as we get back to the states we can start house hunting. Or if you prefer, we could build."

"What about your townhouse?"

"It's too small for our needs."

"If you think so," she said. She had never actually been there, but she couldn't imagine that someone as wealthy as Mitch would live anywhere that could be considered small. Although she couldn't deny that the idea of having her own home was a little exciting. All of her life she had lived in her father's Houston estate or D.C. townhouse. He hadn't even allowed her to decorate her own room, preferring instead to let a professional choose the decor. She had never had a place that was truly hers.

"Of course, you'll be in charge of the household," Mitch continued. "You'll be responsible for the hiring and dismissal of the staff."

"Will I be allowed to decorate?" she asked.

The question seemed to puzzle him. "Of course."

"I won't need your approval for every little thing I do?"

He looked confused. "Is there a reason you should?"

She had just assumed that, like her father, Mitch would deem her untrustworthy or incapable. Or maybe he was just saying these things to lull her into a false sense of security. Maybe he would be an overbearing tyrant.

And maybe you're paranoid.

"Other than the obvious financial requirements, is there anything specific that you expect from me?"

She wasn't sure what he meant by financial requirements. Did he think she would expect him to pay her a salary? "What 'financial requirements' are we talking about?"

"Credit cards, cash. As I assured you, you won't want for anything."

Despite what most people believed, she wasn't the spoiled, pampered heiress they described in the society pages of the paper. Her father had always provided her with a generous allowance for clothing and essentials, but otherwise kept her on a pretty short fiscal leash. He monitored her credit card statements to be sure that she wasn't spending his money on anything inappropriate, and he limited the amount of cash she was allowed. She'd always wondered what it would feel like to be financially independent, to not have someone scrutinizing her every move.

If Mitch did give her financial freedom, maybe this marriage deal wouldn't be quite as miserable as she'd expected.

"Come on," he said. "There must be *something* you want."

Though she was going to wait, he'd left the subject wide open, and she couldn't resist dipping her toes in to test the waters. "What about children?"

"What about them?"

"Well, I know this is just a business arrangement, but I've always wanted kids."

The dark expression that spread across his face chilled her to her core. He shook his head and said, "I think that would be a bad idea."

Oh, this was not good.

Maybe it was the act of conceiving the baby that he had a problem with. Maybe he no longer found her attractive. Their kiss after the vows couldn't have been colder or more formal. Maybe she had been so terrible in bed that first time, he had no interest in a repeat performance.

"If it's the intimacy you're concerned about," she said, "there are other ways—"

"It has nothing to do with that. I feel it would be unfair to bring a child into a loveless marriage."

Her stomach bottomed out. How would he feel if he didn't have a choice in the matter? Would he insist on a divorce? Tell her father the truth about what happened in D.C.? Or even worse, would he disown his child? Then where would she be?

A sense of panic filled her. There had to be a way to convince him, to make this right. "Maybe if we—"

"No," he said firmly, his mouth set in a stubborn line. "There is no maybe. I'll give you anything you want, Lexi. Anything but this."

Just because they didn't love each other, it didn't have to mean their child wouldn't be happy. Her mind worked frantically on a way to make him change his mind.

What if she did everything he asked of her and became the perfect wife? Then would he accept the idea of having a child? But is that what she really wanted? To live a lie?

At this point, did she even have a choice?

Mitch felt slightly guilty for denying Lexi something she obviously longed for, but she would just have to get used to not getting everything her greedy little heart desired. He was sure that no matter how much she thought she wanted children, she had no idea what kind of responsibility it would be. He knew from experience that spoiled debutantes like her didn't have time for anyone but themselves. She would grow tired of the burden, just as his mother had, and walk away. He refused to allow his child to grow up unable to count on the one person who was supposed to provide unconditional love.

They endured the remainder of the nine-hour flight engaged in occasional strained small talk, with Mitch always initiating the conversation. The way she had talked nonstop in D.C., he could only assume that she was now giving him the silent treatment. She probably wasn't accustomed to people not catering to her every whim.

Well, she would have to get used to it. He didn't intend to deny her happiness, but he wasn't about to pamper or spoil her, either. It was time she began living in the real world.

After a brief layover in London, which Lexi spent the majority of in the ladies' room, they boarded a flight for Athens. Lexi fell asleep the minute the wheels left the tarmac and didn't wake until they landed. A limo met them outside the airport to bring them to the port of Lavrio where they boarded the small passenger ship that would take them to the island of Tzia.

Two hours later, and sixteen hours after they left Houston, they finally arrived at the villa where they would spend the next week. About half a mile east, he could see rows of densely built houses that looked like windowed shoe boxes clinging to the steep slope that bordered the village of Loulida, and nothing but open countryside for at least half a mile in every other direction. When Lexi said the area was secluded, he hadn't realized just how alone they would be.

Mitch let Lexi have the top-level master suite and took one of the three guest bedrooms on the ground floor for himself. It was more than enough space for him, and a large sliding glass door conveniently led to the swimming pool, hot tub and pool house, where he guessed he would be spending much of his time. Just off the bedrooms was a spacious living room with a full bar and plush, comfortable-looking furniture. The middle floor held a modern and well-equipped kitchen with an adjoining dining room, while another comfortable sitting room led to the main terrace and the barbecue area.

The interior was a combination of vibrant colors and innovative designs that could have very comfortably housed half a dozen people or more. His preference would have been a place that was smaller, and more intimate. But someone like Lexi would want the biggest and most luxurious lodging available. Although he was a bit surprised that she hadn't hired a full staff to cater to her. She hadn't even arranged for a chef or a maid.

"I think I'll lie down for a while," she said, when he carried her luggage to her room for her. She was still looking a little green, and he couldn't help feeling sorry for her. He had never been one to suffer from motion sickness, but from the looks of it, the last day had been hell.

"Can I bring you anything?" he asked. "Something to eat? A cup of tea?"

"I think I just need to sleep for a while," she said, but looked at him a little funny, as though she couldn't figure out why he was being so nice to her.

That makes two of us, sweetheart. Must be jet lag, or temporary insanity.

"I'll be in my room unpacking if you need me," he told her, then he left her room, closing the door behind him. Something seemed different. Lexi was acting almost…humbled.

He shook his head. It was probably just due to the fact that she was feeling sick. He was sure she would be back to her entitled, narcissistic self by tomorrow.

As he walked to his room he pulled out his cell and dialed his brother, and though it was barely 7:00 a.m. in Texas, he answered on the first ring.

"You're supposed to be on your honeymoon," Lance said.

"I am."

"Then why the hell are you calling me?"

"I just wondered if there's anything new from Darius about the fire. Anything pointing to Alex Montoya."

"Nothing since you left, which was less than

twenty-four hours ago. And if I do hear something, I'll let you know."

In other words, don't call me, I'll call you. "If there are any problems at the office—"

"Mitch, forget about work and enjoy yourself. You're on your honeymoon. Go seduce your wife or something."

"You know as well as I do that it isn't that kind of marriage."

"You're a newlywed, and the way I look at it, that gives you certain rights. Like sex with your new wife on your wedding night. I guarantee you won't be disappointed."

Mitch knew that firsthand, but the question was, how did Lance? Then he realized: Lance must have slept with her when they were engaged.

Lexi certainly hadn't wasted any time hopping from one brother's bed to the next, he thought wryly. Maybe to her, it was just a game. Some kind of twisted challenge. At least Mitch knew for a fact that he had been first. And according to Lexi, that was exactly the way she'd planned it. What she hadn't counted on was Lance dumping her for someone else.

"I felt kind of sorry for her yesterday," Lance said.

"Why?"

"Having only her assistant at her wedding. You would think her father would have the decency to show."

"He's a busy man."

"Too busy to see his only child get married? Would you miss your daughter's wedding?"

No, but then, he wouldn't be having a daughter, or a son. He would just have to be content spoiling the children that he was sure Lance and Kate would have. "I'm sure the senator had his reasons."

"That doesn't make it any less lousy."

Mitch couldn't help thinking she got exactly what she deserved.

After he hung up with his brother, Mitch took a long, hot shower to wash away the travel grit, then collapsed naked between the cool silk sheets. He decided he would sleep for an hour or so, then get up and make them something to eat. But when he opened his eyes again the sun had already set, and the room was dark but for the light in the hallway shining through the open door.

Hadn't he closed the door before he'd lain down? He was almost positive he had. In fact, he *was* positive.

Then he saw a silhouette move across the room. He jerked up on his elbows, groggy and alarmed, but as his eyes adjusted, he realized the form was female. And not just any female.

It was Lexi.

Five

Lexi crossed the room to Mitch's bed wearing a floor-length, low-cut, white silk nightgown that shimmered in the light. Her pale hair lay in soft waves across her shoulders, cascading down to the swell of her breasts.

For a second he wondered if he was dreaming. What reason would she possibly have to be in his room? Was she sick? Or plotting to smother him with his pillow?

"Is something wrong?" he asked, his voice rough from sleep.

"Nothing is wrong."

Relieved, he dropped his head back down on the bed. "What are you doing in here?"

"This is officially our wedding night," she said.

Yeah, so? he thought, unsure of the significance. Then she lifted the gown up over her head and dropped it to the floor. She wasn't wearing anything underneath. Now he knew he *had* to be dreaming. But as she slipped between the sheets beside him, her body warm and soft against his, it was too vivid, too fantastic to be anything but real. Nothing about this made any sense.

"This wasn't part of the deal," he reminded her.

She leaned on one elbow, gazing down at him. In the dim light she looked like an angel, when he knew for a fact she was actually a devil in disguise. "I know."

She laid her hand on his chest, lightly stroking his skin, and his body responded instantly. She was obviously willing, so why couldn't he shake the feeling that something wasn't right? Why did he feel guilty, as though he was forcing her?

"We don't have to," he said, even though he wanted nothing more than to run his fingers through the silky ribbons of her hair and pull her down for a long, deep kiss. He didn't want her to feel as though she owed him, or was somehow obligated.

Uncertainty flickered in her eyes, and in that instant he had never seen a woman look more vulnerable or insecure. Deep inside of him something hard and unyielding softened a bit around the edges. Was it possible that she wasn't as confident and fearless as she liked people to believe?

She pulled her hand away and said, "We won't if you don't want to."

Was she serious? He couldn't think of a single other thing he would rather be doing. He took her by the wrist and guided her hand under the covers to his erection. "Does it feel like I don't want to?"

A smile crept across her face as she wrapped her hand around him and squeezed. The sensation was so erotic he nearly lost it.

"I want you, Mitch," she whispered.

That was all the convincing he needed. He caught her behind the neck, pulled her to him and kissed her.

One second Lexi was lying across Mitch's chest as he tangled his fingers through her hair and ravaged her mouth, and the next she was flat on her back on the bed looking up at him. The change of position was so swift it left her breathless and dizzy. Or maybe it was his kisses that were doing that. She just prayed, as he pressed his weight against her, caressing her skin with his hands and his mouth, that he didn't feel her trembling. She didn't want him to know how terrified she had been that he might reject her. She had no clue how to play the role of vixen, how to be the aggressor, but if she was going to convince him this was a real marriage, if she was going to make him fall in love with her, she had to play the part. What kind of wife would she be if she didn't please her husband sexually? Especially on their wedding night.

Although right now, he seemed to be the one doing all the pleasing, and she had almost forgotten how impossibly wonderful it felt to be close to him. How he made her feel as though she was the most beautiful, desirable woman in the world.

"I thought we were keeping this relationship outside the bedroom," he said, nibbling his way down her throat. On the contrary, it was her intention to keep him in bed as much as humanly possible while they were in Greece.

"Not that I'm complaining," he added. "Just mildly confused."

"We both have needs," she said. "I figure, if we have to be stuck with each other, why not enjoy it?"

He grinned down at her. "Lexi, isn't that supposed to be *my* line?"

"You know what I think?" she asked, and his brow perked with curiosity. "I think you talk too much."

His grin turned feral. "And I like the way you think."

She wrapped her arms around his neck and pulled him to her for a slow, deep kiss. They caressed and touched each other until she felt as though she would go out of her mind. She wanted him inside her so badly, she actually ached.

"Make love to me," she told him. "Right now."

Mitch looked up from the nipple he'd been teasing with his tongue. "I thought that's what I was doing."

"Maybe you could do it a little faster?"

"What's the hurry?"

All she knew was that it felt as though there was a big empty space inside of her that she was desperate to fill. He must have seen the desperation on her face because he opened the drawer on the bedside table and pulled out a condom. At her questioning look he said, "Doesn't hurt to come prepared."

She didn't tell him there was no point, that the damage was already done.

He rolled it on, then entered her with one slow but purposeful thrust. She gasped at the stinging sensation as her body stretched to accept him.

Concern filled his eyes. "Did I hurt you?"

"No," she lied, because it was a good hurt. Since that night at the hotel, she'd had the constant and nagging feeling that something was missing. She had felt…incomplete. Now, with their bodies joined, she finally felt whole again.

She arched up, taking him even deeper inside of her, wrapping her legs around his waist. Mitch groaned and grasped the bedcovers. It gave her a thrilling sense of power to know that he was losing control, and she was making it happen.

He rolled over so that she was on top, straddling him, their bodies still joined. Now that she was up here, she was unsure of what to do. What if she did it wrong and made a fool of herself? What if she was clumsy and awkward, and couldn't satisfy him? "Mitch, I don't—"

"Yes, you do," he said, as though he had complete confidence in her. "Just do what feels good."

She braced her hands on the mattress on either side of him and rose up, but she went too far and he slipped out. She made a noise of frustration, but Mitch didn't seem to mind.

"Don't worry," he said, guiding himself back in like it was no big deal. This time he rested his hands on her hips to guide her. "Take it slow."

She began to move slowly, eyes closed in concentration. At first, she was so afraid to make a mistake, focused so completely on her every move, she wasn't able to let herself enjoy it.

"Relax," he said, arching his hips up to meet her downward thrusts. They slipped into a slow, steady rhythm, and she began to lose herself in the sensation, in the sweet friction, until it began to feel as natural as breathing.

This was the way she wanted to spend the rest of her life. Acting on impulse, living by instinct. Doing things just because they felt good.

"Open your eyes," Mitch said, and when she did, when she looked down at him, she could see that he was barely hanging on.

With his eyes locked on hers, he reached down to where their bodies met and stroked her. Pleasure rippled through her from the inside out and an orgasm that was almost shocking in its intensity locked her muscles. She threw her head back and rode out the sensation, and through a haze she heard Mitch groan, felt him tense beneath her, his fingers digging into her skin.

Limp with satisfaction, Lexi collapsed against his chest, their hearts pounding out a frantic beat together. It just kept getting better and better. She had never felt as close to anyone in her life as she did to Mitch tonight.

This was going to work, she assured herself. Everything was going to be fine. But as he rolled her over and began kissing her, making love to her all over again, she couldn't help feeling like a fraud.

Mitch woke the next morning and reached for Lexi, but her side of the bed was empty. He glanced over at the clock, surprised to see that it was after eight. Jet lag had his schedule all jacked up, because he never slept a minute past 6:00 a.m., even on weekends. He sat up and looked groggily around the room, thinking that maybe Lexi had just stepped into the bathroom, but he could hear the clatter of pots and pans and dishes in the kitchen. He caught a whiff of something that smelled like breakfast, but he knew he must be imagining it, unless she had hired a cook after all.

He rolled out of bed, pulled on a pair of pajama bottoms and walked to the kitchen. Lexi stood by the stove, poking at something in a frying pan with a spatula. On the counter sat a plate with some sort of sausage.

She cooked?

Beside her, the state-of-the-art dishwasher was open and there were actually dishes inside. He didn't think a spoiled heiress even knew what a dishwasher was, much less knew how to use one.

Was it possible that he'd misjudged her?

"Good morning," he said.

She turned to him and smiled a sweet smile that made him believe she was genuinely happy to see him. "Good morning."

She was wearing the silk gown she'd had on last night and her feet were bare. Her hair was pulled back in a ponytail and her face was free of makeup. She looked young and sweet and pretty, but from the neck down, she was all woman. Full and firm breasts, perfectly proportioned hips. He had to fight the urge to scoop her up in his arms and carry her back to bed. Having a little occasional fun was one thing, but they shouldn't overdo it. He didn't want her getting the wrong idea.

"Are you hungry?" she asked. "I made breakfast."

"Starved," he said. They had skipped dinner last night. "Can I help?"

"I've got it. Do you want coffee?"

"I can get it," he said, but she shooed him away.

"Go sit down. Relax."

Ooookay.

He took a seat in the nook by a window overlooking the pool, while she filled a cup that was already sitting by the coffeemaker.

"Milk or sugar?" she asked.

"Black, please."

She laughed lightly and shook her head.

"What?" he asked.

"It's just weird," she said, crossing the room and setting the cup in front of him. "We're married and I don't even know how you take your coffee. I guess this just wasn't the way I imagined my life."

Amen to that. He never imagined himself ever getting married. He would have been happy playing the field the rest of his life. Having relationships on his terms. Living life by his own rules.

She walked back to the stove and he was mesmerized watching her hips sway, the curve of her behind under the silk gown. He couldn't help but wonder if she was commando under there. If so, it wouldn't take much to lift up the gown and pull her into his lap….

He gave his head a shake. He needed to stop with the fantasies and keep his hands to himself.

She scooped scrambled eggs onto his plate, added a few links of sausage and then set the plate in front of him. *"Bon appétit,"* she said, then sat down across from him and rested her chin on her clasped hands.

"Aren't you eating?" he asked.

She shook her head. "I had something when I got up."

He stabbed a forkful of eggs and shoveled it into his mouth…and nearly spit it back out. The eggs were so salty he almost gagged. He forced himself to swallow and chased it down with a guzzle of coffee, but almost choked. The coffee was so strong that if he didn't already have hair on his chest, it would have put some there. He tried to cover the bitter flavor with a bite of sausage, but it was so overcooked and dried out he could barely chew it.

The meal was a total and complete disaster. And one thing was absolutely clear. Lexi *did not* know how to cook.

If he had a choice, he would dump the whole thing down the sink, or do like he had when he was a kid and feed it to the dog. Unfortunately, they didn't have a dog, and she was gazing at him with such a hopeful look on her face, he didn't have the heart to hurt her feelings. He pasted on a smile and said, "Delicious."

He wasn't sure what brought on this sudden attempt at domesticity, but, mind-boggling as it was, he gave her credit for the effort. He forced down every last bite of eggs and sausage, stopping just short of licking his plate clean, and he even asked for a refill on his coffee.

"That was really good. Thanks." He stood to clear his place, but she stopped him.

"You sit. I'll do it."

She cleared away his dirty dishes and set them in the dishwasher. "I was thinking of making lamb for dinner," she said.

If it was even half as bad as breakfast, he didn't

think his stomach could take it. "Why don't you let me cook dinner?"

She frowned. "Why?"

He could see that he was walking a very delicate line here. One wrong step and he would hurt her feelings. "It's only fair that we split the household chores while we're here. Don't you think?"

"But I'm your wife. I'm supposed to take care of you."

That was the part he didn't get. Hadn't they agreed that this wasn't a real marriage? That this was a business deal? This was the last thing he expected. "Why, Lexi?"

The space between her brows furrowed. "Because that's what wives do."

Real wives maybe, not pretend ones. Maybe she had caught a bug and wasn't feeling well, or she was a little off due to jet lag. "You don't have to."

"But I *want* to."

What was he supposed to say to that? You can take care of me in the bedroom anytime you like, but otherwise leave me alone? That was just…sleazy.

It was obvious that a sexual relationship was a really bad idea. And he hoped like hell that this desire for domestic bliss would wear thin. They would get back to Houston and settle into a life of servants and chefs, and live amicable but very separate lives.

"If it means that much to you, you can make dinner," he said.

She sat back down at the table across from him, wearing a smile so full of relief it worried him.

What the hell was going on?

"So, what did you want to do today?" she asked. "We could walk to the village, or hire a car to take us on a tour of the island."

"Actually, I was thinking of just hanging out by the pool."

"Oh. Well, that sounds like fun."

He meant alone. As in, by himself. He hadn't even entertained the idea that she would want to spend the day with him. He figured they would just go their separate ways. But what was he supposed to say? Leave me the hell alone?

This was just too weird.

He rose from his chair and she stood up, too. "I'm going to take a shower."

"And I have to clean this mess. Meet you outside in thirty minutes?"

She looked so eager, so desperate to please him, all he could do was smile and say, "I can hardly wait." But he felt as if he'd climbed out of bed into an episode of *The Twilight Zone*.

Six

When Mitch was gone, Lexi collapsed back down into her chair, dropped her head in her hands and blew out a relieved breath. Talk about stressful. Making Mitch think this marriage was real was going to be a lot harder than she'd anticipated. Especially if he refused to cooperate. She had the feeling that in her attempt to impress him with her domestic skills, she might have overplayed her hand just the tiniest bit.

Thank goodness Tara had answered the phone when Lexi called—considering it had been after midnight, Houston time—and knew how to make scrambled eggs. Although it had still taken Lexi a dozen eggs and six tries to get it right. But part of that was due to the fact that she wasn't sure how to work the electric stove to get the proper heat settings.

It wasn't that she had never wanted to learn to cook, it was just that her father would never allow it. That was what they had servants for. He considered cooking and cleaning beneath her. She was sure it would be fun once she got the hang of it.

There was a leg of lamb thawing on the counter that Tara assured her would be a no-brainer, and tomorrow for breakfast, she might even try something complicated, like pancakes.

She walked to the stove, grabbed the pan of leftover eggs and was about to dump them down the sink when she realized her stomach was feeling marginally settled. She picked up a fork and took a bite, gagged and spit it directly into the sink.

They were awful. Yet Mitch had sat there straight-faced and eaten every bite. Even told her they were delicious. Though she wasn't supposed to have any, she poured herself a splash of coffee and gave it a taste. It was even worse than the eggs.

No wonder he'd suggested that he make dinner. He probably thought she was trying to poison him. She would have to be sure that she made dinner extra special. Maybe then he would think that breakfast had been a fluke and she wasn't completely useless.

She loaded the rest of the dishes and the frying pan into the dishwasher and filled the receptacle with the liquid dish soap she found under the sink, giving the dishes an extra squirt just to be safe. It took her a few minutes to figure out the digital display, but after randomly pressing buttons, she eventually got it running. It was amazing all of the things she didn't know how to do, but she was determined to figure them out. To be the perfect wife. The perfect partner.

However, one thing she definitely had to avoid was sleeping in Mitch's bed. She woke this morning with her stomach in knots, and barely made it to her own bathroom before she vomited. Mitch was bound to get suspicious if he realized she was tossing her cookies every morning. Every day she didn't tell him about the baby she risked making an even bigger mess out of things. But if things went according to plan, by the time she finally did tell him, he would be so happy, and love her so much, he wouldn't even care that she'd kept it from him.

Her baby's welfare depended on it.

Mitch showered, changed into his swim trunks, then headed to the kitchen to grab a soda on his way out to the pool. He stopped short in the doorway when he saw Lexi on her hands and knees, wearing a white beach cover-up, amid an ocean of thick white soap bubbles on the kitchen floor. She was trying frantically to wipe them up with a dish towel, but wasn't doing much more than pushing the suds around, and it was starting to overflow into the living room.

"What the hell happened?" he asked.

Startled, she looked up at him. "I don't know. Something is wrong with the dishwasher."

He looked over and saw that suds were continuing to ooze out from underneath the unit. He slipped and slid his way across the soapy floor and hit the cancel button. "Why didn't you shut it off?"

Only after the words were out, and he saw Lexi's wounded expression, did he realize how harsh he'd sounded. She looked at the dishwasher, then up at him and shrugged helplessly. It was then that he realized, she probably didn't know *how* to shut it off.

Keeping his voice calm, he asked, "How did this happen?"

"I told you, it's broken," she said. "I went to change and when I came back out, there was soap everywhere. You can bet the rental company is going to hear about this."

He had a pretty good idea what had happened, and it was in no way the rental company's—or even the dishwasher's—fault. "What kind of soap did you use?"

"The bottle under the sink," she said, in a tone that suggested he was dim for even asking.

He opened the cupboard and pulled out the soap sitting right in the front. "This one?"

"Yes, that one," she snapped. "Dish soap, for washing dishes."

"That's not for a dishwasher."

She frowned. "What do you mean? It says it is right on the label."

He reached back into the cupboard and extracted a box of granulated dishwasher detergent. "This is for the dishwasher. It doesn't suds up like regular dish soap."

"Oh," she said, pulling her lip between her teeth, looking mortified by her error. Once again, Mitch couldn't help but feel sorry for her. At least she was trying. How could he expect a woman who had probably never washed a dirty dish in her life to know how to run a dishwasher?

"Sorry," she said, her cheeks blushing bright pink.

He shrugged. "It's an honest mistake. No big deal."

She looked helplessly around at the mess she had created, as though she didn't have the first clue how to fix it. And though he felt like a complete degenerate for it, the only thing he could think about was getting her naked, laying her down and rolling around with her until they were both all slippery. Then he would...probably have his head examined.

"Why don't you go out by the pool," he told her. "I'll clean this up."

"It's my mess," she said.

Yes, and he had the feeling that if he left her alone to deal with it, she would only manage to make things worse. Besides, it would be advantageous to both of them if they weren't within mauling distance of each other.

"You're not here to wait on me hand and foot," he said. "You made breakfast, it's only fair that I clean up."

"Are you sure?" she asked, looking relieved for a valid excuse to bail on the situation.

"I'm sure. I'll have this cleaned up in no time."

"Okay." She rose to her feet, her legs all soapy, and tiptoed her way carefully across the floor, so she didn't slip and fall. "I'll see you outside."

No time ended up being over an hour, and he still hadn't been able to get all of the soap residue off the floor. He would just have to warn Lexi to be careful so she didn't slip while she was making dinner.

Though it wasn't noon yet, he felt he'd earned himself a cold beer. He grabbed one from the fridge, put his sunglasses on and headed out to the pool. Lexi lay in a lounge chair on the opposite side, sunning herself. Her eyes were shaded behind dark, designer sunglasses and she was wearing what looked like a very skimpy, pale bikini.

Wait a minute….

He slid his glasses down his nose to get a better look at her, and as his eyes adjusted to the bright sunshine, he realized she was in fact not wearing a pale bikini, skimpy or otherwise.

Lexi wasn't wearing anything at all.

Eyes closed behind her sunglasses, the late-morning sun drenching her skin at a very comfortable seventy-five degrees, Lexi tried to shake off the mortification of failing at the simple task of working the dishwasher. She should have called Tara before she went anywhere near it. She also should have stayed in the kitchen and helped Mitch clean, but she was too embarrassed. And no doubt if she had stayed, she would have done that wrong, too, and looked even more inept than she already did. How could she expect him to take her seriously, to consider her a good wife, if she couldn't even negotiate her way around a kitchen? She would have to make an absolutely perfect dinner.

More than an hour had passed when she finally heard Mitch open the patio door. She peeked through half-closed lids and saw that he was walking in her direction. A shadow robbed the sunshine as he hovered over her. "What the hell do you think you're doing?" he asked, his harsh tone making her jolt with surprise.

Was this some sort of trick question? "S-sunbathing?"

She could see by his exasperated expression that it wasn't the answer he wanted to hear.

"Yes, I can see that," he said. "What I would like to know is why you're naked."

"Technically, I'm not naked. I have bottoms on." More exasperation on his face, so she added, "I don't like tan lines. Besides, everyone in Europe sunbathes topless."

"You're a senator's daughter. I would think you'd know better."

She looked around. "Who's going to see me? We're in the middle of nowhere."

"That's not the point."

Then what was the point? What man didn't enjoy seeing his wife sunbathing topless?

The kind who married his wife for business. One who found her so physically unattractive, the only place he cared to see her naked was in a dark bedroom, where he could pretend she was someone else.

She felt sick all the way down to her soul. She pulled herself up from her chair, grabbed the towel she'd been lying on and wrapped it around herself. "I'm sorry that you find my body so offensive."

"Lexi, that isn't what I—"

"I'll be sure to keep it appropriately covered from now on," she assured him, nose in the air, giving him the cold and bitchy routine so he wouldn't hear the hurt in her voice. She turned to walk away, but Mitch wrapped a hand around her upper arm to stop her.

"I swear you're the most insecure woman I've ever met," he said. "And you're making it really hard for me to do the right thing."

The right thing? What was that supposed to mean? She tried to tug her arm free. "Let go."

Instead, he yanked the towel from around her and scooped her up. She let out a shriek as he flung her like a sack of potatoes over one shoulder and carried her toward the sliding glass door that led to his bedroom.

She wiggled, trying to get loose, but he only held on tighter. "What are you doing?"

"I could tell you that you're beautiful and desirable until I'm blue in the face, but you probably wouldn't believe me."

Okay, so maybe he didn't find her *completely* undesirable.

She pounded on his back with her fists, which was about as effective as hitting a boulder with a feather. "So, you pull a caveman routine instead?"

He slid the door open and carried her into his bedroom. Despite his brutish and uncivilized behavior, a shiver of excitement rippled through her. After all, it had been her plan to keep him in the bedroom as much as possible.

He slid her off his shoulder onto her back on the mattress and knelt beside her, a look of pure mischief in his eyes. "You won't listen to me," he said. "So, I'm just going to have to show you."

Mitch spent the rest of the morning and a good part of the afternoon showing Lexi just how beautiful and desirable he thought she was. And boy, was he good at it. Every time she tried to climb out of bed, he would pull her back in and start convincing her all over again. When she finally insisted she had to put the lamb in the oven or it wouldn't be ready in time for dinner, he reluctantly let her go. She wobbled into the kitchen on spaghetti legs, and every inch of her skin hummed with sexual satisfaction.

At this rate, it wouldn't be long before she could tell him about the baby.

Following Tara's instructions to the letter, Lexi seasoned the lamb shank and popped it in the oven. And though it took a minute of pushing buttons, the oven finally beeped and turned on. She peeled the potatoes and carrots next, then put them aside to add to the roasting pan forty minutes before the lamb was done. Until then, she didn't have much to do, so she went looking for Mitch.

She found him sacked out in a lounge chair by the pool, sleeping so deeply, he was snoring. It looked as though she'd worn the poor guy out. For a second, she considered all the creative ways she could wake him, most using her mouth, but he looked so peaceful, she didn't have the heart.

Instead, she stretched out in the chair beside him to get some sun, but her eyes felt heavy and in no time she drifted into a deep sleep, and had strange and erotic dreams about Mitch. Hazy, disjointed images of bare skin and feelings of intense sexual sensation flooded her. She could smell him, taste the flavor of his mouth and skin. She could feel the weight of his hands touching her, her hair tangled in his fingers, the flex of her muscles as she took him deep inside her body. The strum of sensation on her nerve endings.

Not a strum so much as a loud hum. And the hum grew louder, the sound filling her head until it was more annoying than arousing. A sharp, piercing bleat.

Her eyes flew open and she realized the sound wasn't in her dream. It was coming from the house, through the open door that led to the kitchen…and was that *smoke* she was seeing?

Wide awake now, she jumped from the chair, grabbed her cover-up and tugged it on as she dashed for the house. She was stunned by what she encountered in the kitchen.

Acrid smoke hung in the air, the oven sat open and empty and the pan the roast had been in was sitting in the sink under a flow of water. She could only assume that the black lump was the charred remains of the lamb shank. Mitch stood in the middle of the room in his swim trunks, fanning the smoke detector with a broom.

Oh, God, what had she done this time?

Mitch finally looked over and saw her standing there, watching him. He flashed her a smile and said, "The lamb is done."

After the dishwasher fiasco this morning, there didn't seem to be much point in trying to blame it on the oven. She had obviously screwed up again. Only this time, instead of flooding the house, it looked as though she'd nearly burned it down.

They had made some real progress today, and now

she'd ruined it. She couldn't even imagine what he must be thinking, and she wondered how long it would be before she and the baby were out on the street.

Mitch swung the broom around and, using the handle end, gave the smoke detector a solid whack. It gave one final bleat, then fell silent. Which was even worse than the deafening screech.

She opened her mouth to say something, apologize maybe, but words escaped her.

Mitch walked over to the sink and turned off the tap, looking down at the soggy remains of dinner. "We should probably open a few windows to let the smoke out."

"I'll get the family room," she said, eager to skulk away in shame. This could go one of two ways. He would be completely exasperated with her and make her feel like a total dope, or he would be understanding and sweet, all the while thinking that she was a lost cause.

She honestly wasn't sure which would be more humiliating.

When every window on the main floor was open, she walked back to the kitchen where Mitch was closing the oven and shutting it off. She couldn't tell if he was angry, or just resigned to the fact that he'd married a domestic disaster.

She gestured to the sink, taking a feeble stab at humor. "Was the lamb thirsty, or is this your way of telling me it's too dry for your taste?"

"I couldn't find the lid or fire extinguisher, so this was the only way to douse the flames."

Flames? It had actually been on fire?

Just when she thought she couldn't be more embarrassed, she discovered a whole new level of humiliation. "I don't suppose you would believe me if I said the lamb was supposed to catch on fire."

He cracked a smile.

"So, what did I do wrong this time?" she asked, even though she wasn't sure she wanted to know. She couldn't imagine he would ever let her near the kitchen again, much less cook something.

"The oven was on broil instead of bake."

Which meant what, exactly? She thought meat was supposed to broil. Her confusion must have been obvious because he added, "Bake warms the entire oven uniformly and allows food to cook slower. Broil is a direct flame right over the pan and cooks things much faster. Obviously."

Something she would have known if she'd ever used an oven before.

"I'm sorry I murdered dinner," she said.

He shrugged, again like it wasn't a big deal. "Unless you're a pyromaniac, which I seriously doubt, it was an honest mistake."

She wanted to believe he felt that way, but he had to be realizing how truly useless she was. What would her next honest mistake be? Accidental poisoning?

Maybe there was a reason her father had kept her so sheltered. Maybe he could see that left to her own devices, she was a danger to herself and others.

"I suppose it's obvious that I've never cooked before. Or used a dishwasher."

"Seriously?" he asked, trying to look surprised, but he was a terrible liar.

She shot him a look.

"Okay," he admitted. "I sort of had that feeling."

"I appreciate that you choked down breakfast despite how awful it was."

He shrugged. "It wasn't *that* bad."

"Yes, it was. We would probably both be safer if you cooked from now on."

"What makes you think I can cook?"

"You can't be any worse than me. I should stay as far away as possible from the kitchen."

"How are you going to learn if you don't try?"

"I did try, and I almost burned the house down! I'm useless."

He huffed out an exasperated breath. "What is it with you and this low self-esteem? You are not useless. And if you really would like to learn, when we get back to Texas we'll enroll you in a cooking class."

She shook her head. "No, my father would never allow it. He considers it beneath me."

"Your father isn't the one calling the shots. You're married to me now, and you have a say in your own life."

At first, she thought he was just making fun of her, but then she realized he was serious. Unfortunately, it wasn't that simple. "If he finds out, he'll be furious, and you still need his senatorial support."

"Let me worry about that."

He would risk his relationship with her father just so she could have a couple of cooking lessons? She narrowed her eyes, still not sure if she could trust him, wondering if this was some twisted game to him. "You're serious?"

"Yes. Very serious." He folded his arms across his chest and leaned against the counter. "Out of curiosity, what else has your father kept you from doing?"

She considered his question for a minute, then said, "It would probably be easier to tell you what he *did* let me do, since it's a far shorter list."

Mitch shook his head. "My father could be a real bastard, but I'm beginning to wonder if I didn't have it so rough, after all."

It was the first time he had ever said anything to her about his family. Of course, she had never really asked. "What did he do to you?"

"Suffice it to say, the slug to the jaw I took from Lance was nothing in comparison."

"Your father *hit* you?"

"On a regular basis. But it sounds worse than it was. I got over it."

Why did she get the feeling he really hadn't?

"So, what are we going to do about dinner?" he asked.

She looked over at the sink, at the remains of the lamb shank. "Don't look at me. I'm not going anywhere near the stove until I get those lessons."

"In that case, why don't we get dressed and go into the village?"

That sounded like the perfect solution to her. "Give me fifteen minutes."

Seven

What the hell was wrong with him?

Mitch walked with Lexi down the dirt road to Tzia, the local village, wondering what the hell he'd been thinking today when he carried her into his bedroom. So much for treating this marriage like a business deal. But when she'd accused him of finding her repulsive, and he realized she actually meant it, that she wasn't just manipulating him, the hurt look she wore had done something to his brain. What choice did he have but to show her how wrong she was?

And what was all that crap about cooking lessons? Where the hell had that come from? He didn't care if she could cook or not. But again she had looked so helpless and dejected. He couldn't help but feel sorry for her. Which was probably exactly what she wanted. But there was a small part of him that kept wondering, what if it wasn't an act?

She'd reached for his hand as they left the villa, and what was he supposed to do? Refuse to hold it? Tell her he didn't think it was appropriate? They *were* married. He could feel himself getting sucked into…something, although as genuine as her feelings seemed to be, he couldn't shake the suspicion that she had ulterior motives. They had agreed this was going to be business and nothing more, and he was determined to stick to that. As soon as they got back to Texas. He figured by then they would have gotten this nagging sexual attraction out of the way and would both be sick of each other.

At least he hoped so.

They reached the village just before sundown. As they passed under the arch leading inside, the beauty of the architecture stunned him. They strolled down cobbled streets lined with shops, crowded bars, and outdoor cafés. There was even a gallery whose front window boasted the works of famous Greek artists such as Tsarouhis, Fasianos, and Stathopoulos.

After some browsing, they chose a quiet café at the north end of the village and sat outside under a thick blanket of stars. He ordered an ouzo and though he tried to convince Lexi to try it, she opted for a bottled water, instead. In D.C., she had always had a glass or two of wine with dinner.

"Are you sure you don't want something to drink?" he asked after the server left the table.

"I'm sure."

"Wine or beer?"

She smiled, a warm breeze blowing the hair back from her face. "Why, are you planning to get me drunk?"

If he'd learned one thing in the past couple of days, it was that he didn't need the aid of alcohol to have his way with her. They ordered their food, both choosing authentic Greek favorites, but when it came, Lexi just picked at it.

"You don't like it?" he asked.

"No, it's good. I'm just not very hungry."

As far as Mitch could tell, she'd barely eaten anything since they left the U.S., and maybe it was his imagination, but she looked thinner than she'd been that night in D.C. He didn't remember her collarbones being so pronounced and her cheeks so hollow. He knew she was insecure, but would she drive herself to the point of anorexia? Or what if she was sick? Something more dangerous than airsickness and jet lag?

"Is something wrong?" he asked.

His question seemed to surprise her. "No, why?"

"You've hardly eaten a thing since we left Texas. Are you sick?"

There was the slightest pause before she smiled and assured him, "I'm fine, really." But he couldn't escape the feeling that she wasn't being completely honest with him. Although, what reason would she have to lie?

By the time they finished eating, most of the shops had locked their doors and the bars looked overcrowded and smoky, so they headed back to the villa with nothing but the full moon to light their way. The air had cooled and it was so silent, Mitch could hear the thump of his own heart.

Once again, she reached for his hand and rather than fight it, he twined his fingers through hers.

She surprised him by asking, "Did your father hit Lance, too?"

His father wasn't a subject he liked to discuss, but in all fairness, he had been the one to bring it up earlier. "Lance, me, our mother—until she'd had enough, packed her bags and left."

"Your mother left without you?"

"As Lance likes to say, she had her reasons."

"My father never hit me, but in a weird way I wish he would have."

"No, you don't."

"At least then I would know that he felt *something*. After my mom died he just…shut down. I did everything I could to make him happy, everything he ever asked, but I still felt invisible."

If what she said was true, maybe she didn't have the spoiled and pampered life after all. Maybe she was just as bitter and confused as everyone else. Or maybe she was one hell of a good actress. Either way, this conversation was getting a little too personal. She needed to understand that when they got back to Texas, things would change.

But what if she didn't understand that? What if, God forbid, she thought she was falling in love with him? He knew how it was for women like Lexi. They decided on something they wanted and went after it with a vengeance, all pistons firing. Right up until the second they got bored and found a new toy to amuse them.

"We should probably talk about how things will be when we get back to Texas," he said.

She gazed up at him, her skin luminous in the moonlight. "What things?"

"Us. Our relationship."

"Okay."

"I just think I should be clear about a few things. I'm a very busy man, and I like to do things, to live my life, a certain way. You should know that I don't intend to change."

She nodded silently, but he had the distinct impression he'd hurt her feelings. If he had, he was sorry for that, but it was important they were both clear on the way things would be.

"As we agreed before, this is a business deal. Nothing more."

"Of course," she said, but he could swear there

was a slight waver in her voice. An edge of disappointment. Maybe she really believed things had changed. Well, that wasn't his problem.

Then why did he feel so damned guilty?

She was silent the rest of the walk home. When they walked in the door, he expected that they would go their separate ways, to their own beds, but she stunned him by keeping hold of his hand and leading him to his bedroom. The sex was so passionate and intense, for a while he almost forgot that it wasn't real. As she lay naked beside him, her body curled around his, the idea of this ending seemed almost inconceivable. But he had never been one to mistake sex for affection or love. When she tired of the arrangement and pulled her inevitable disappearing act, he wouldn't be sorry to see her go.

Though Mitch's words stung and she seriously considered giving up, Lexi chose to disregard what he'd said about their marriage and forge ahead with her plan.

They spent the better part of the next six days in bed, or in various other places, having sex. And when they weren't climbing all over each other, or collapsing with sheer exhaustion, they sunned themselves by the pool or went for walks and explored the shops in the village. Sometimes they just talked about his work, or their families. There was so much about him she didn't know—and wanted to learn.

As the days passed, she slowly began to realize that not only did she have real feelings for Mitch, she was almost positive she was falling in love with him. But since she had never been in love before, she couldn't be one hundred percent sure. She only knew that it had to be something very special, and she didn't doubt that he was feeling it, too.

Since that night walking back from the village, he hadn't said a word about the marriage being just business. Instead, he'd shown his affection for her in a hundred little ways.

She was confident that in a week or so, if all continued to go well, she would be able to tell him about the baby. Then she could finally stop feeling as though she was walking on eggshells, constantly conscious of everything she said and did.

She could finally relax and be happy.

Their last night in Greece, she lay beside Mitch, listening to his deep, heavy breathing as he slept, knowing she should get up and go to her own room, but feeling too lazy to move. She always waited until he was asleep to slip away. As much as she would have loved to spend all night with him, she was still getting sick every morning. Soon though, he would know about the baby, and she could stop hiding. But for now, she really needed to get up.

Five more minutes, she told herself, letting her eyes drift shut and cuddling up against Mitch's side.

When she opened her eyes again, sunshine was

pouring in the windows. Mitch was behind her, his breathing slow and deep as he slept, but one part of his anatomy was already wide awake.

As she was considering the most pleasurable way to wake the rest of him, she felt a familiar lurch in her stomach. She broke out in a sudden cold sweat and a wave of nausea overwhelmed her. Swallowing back the bile rising in her throat, she slid out of bed as quietly as possible and pulled on her nightgown. There was no time to make it to her own bedroom. She had no choice but to use Mitch's bathroom. She reached the commode just as her stomach violently emptied. The spasms were so intense, she was convinced she would look down and find an internal organ or two floating around. When she was finished, her entire body felt limp and shaky. She sat on the floor and rested her face against the cool tile wall.

"Are you all right?"

Lexi's eyes flew open. Mitch was standing in the doorway, wearing only his boxers, his hair mussed from sleep, concern etched on his face. Damn it! She should have shut and locked the door.

"I'm fine." She reached over and flushed the commode, but it was obvious that she'd been sick.

"No, you're not." He grabbed a washcloth from the towel bar and soaked it with cool water from the tap. He wrung out the excess and handed it to her. She wiped her face with it, feeling the nausea beginning to pass. She would be completely fine in an hour or so.

He reached over to feel her forehead, but she held up a hand to stop him. "I don't have a fever. I'm okay."

"What's going on?" he asked.

"Must be something I ate," she lied, and she could see he wasn't buying it.

"I know something is wrong. You've hardly eaten anything all week, you've lost weight, and every morning you look pale and exhausted. I want the truth."

He knew. She could see it on his face that he'd already figured it out for himself. Or at least suspected. She had the feeling that her saying the words was a formality at this point.

Maybe this was a good thing. The longer she put it off, the harder it was going to be, right? The more it would sound like a lie. And he didn't look upset, exactly. More concerned than angry, so maybe it would be okay.

She took a deep breath, blew it out, and finally said the words she had been holding on the tip of her tongue for more than a week. "I'm pregnant."

"Pregnant?"

She could not have prepared herself for the look of dumbfounded shock on his face. Whatever he might have thought was wrong with her, pregnancy had clearly never crossed his mind. And if his reaction was any indication, everything would *not* be okay.

"You didn't think to mention this before?" he asked, his voice low and quiet, but she could see that he was ready to explode. And could she blame him?

He'd said it himself, he didn't want to bring a child into this. Had she really thought a week of fantastic sex was going to make him change his mind? Make him fall madly in love with her?

She felt as if she might be sick again.

"I only found out for sure a few days before we left," she said, knowing it was a pathetic excuse. "I was waiting for the right time to tell you."

"That's what this has all been about, hasn't it?"

"All what?"

"The cooking and the cleaning. The sex. Did you think you could manipulate me?"

Her heart sank. What was she going to tell him? No? Lie to him again? She had done that, just not in the way he thought. Not so sneaky and underhanded. "It wasn't like that, I swear. I wanted you to see that I could be a good wife."

He looked so disgusted with her, so…violated. "I didn't marry you so I could have a wife. I only did it for your father's support."

And that was her life in a nutshell. She was only as useful as her political connections. No words could have cut deeper or stung more.

"Does Lance know?" he asked.

Lance? Why would he think that she would go running to his brother? "No, of course not."

"And he never can," Mitch said.

His words took her aback. What the hell was that supposed to mean? How could he not find out, eventually? Did Mitch expect her to give the baby up, or even worse, terminate? Was he that cold and heartless, or so arrogant that he believed the choice was his alone?

What did his brother have to do with this, anyway? This was between her and Mitch. "Who cares if Lance does find out? What's he going to do about it?"

The veins at his temple pulsed. "You can't mess with people's emotions that way, Lexi. He and Kate are happy. Something like this could tear their marriage apart. I refuse to let that happen."

How could she and Mitch having a child ruin Lance's marriage? This didn't make any sense. "What are you asking me to do, Mitch?"

"We'll raise the baby as mine," he said.

Then it dawned on her. Their odd and confusing conversation suddenly made sense. He thought it was Lance's child. Lance, who she had barely kissed, much less slept with. It had never even occurred to Mitch that the baby was his.

Did he honestly believe that she would jump from Mitch's bed right into his brother's? Did he really have such a low opinion of her?

Obviously, he did. This past week, all the time they had shared, it meant nothing to him. He was using her for a good time, because he apparently believed that was all she was good for.

Her stomach lurched and she had to fight to keep from vomiting again. How had she gotten into this mess? Married to a man who considered her a garden-variety slut, one who jumped from one brother to the next as casually as she changed shoes. Even if she did try to tell him the truth, she doubted he would listen, or believe her. Or care.

She had been hoping they might have a real marriage. Not just hoping, but longing for it. She desperately wanted someone to really see her. To love her. But it was clear that Mitch would never be that man. He could never respect or love her, and all the pretending, all the seducing in the world would never change that. It would never alter the preconceived notion he had of her.

First rejected by her father, then by her husband. As long as she lived, she would never trust any man ever again.

Using the wall for support, she pulled herself to her feet. She swayed unsteadily for a second, then straightened her spine and faced Mitch. "If you'll excuse me," she said, brushing past him, but he grabbed her by her upper arm to stop her.

"From now on, I would appreciate it if you kept your hands to yourself."

She lifted her chin and met his eyes, so he wouldn't see how humiliated and cheap he'd just made her feel. "The truth is, you were hardly worth the effort. Looks like I married the wrong brother."

She could see that her arrow had hit its mark, but for some reason it only made her feel worse.

She yanked her arm free and stalked from the

room. She was stuck with a man who was arrogant, coldhearted and just plain mean.

On the bright side, she could spend the rest of her life making him as miserable as she was.

Mitch watched Lexi strut from the room, feeling more betrayed and disillusioned than he ever had in his life. He'd honestly believed that they had connected, that the dynamics of their relationship had shifted. He'd let himself consider that their marriage might be more than a business deal. But it had all been an act. She had used him.

How could he have been so foolish? How could he have let his guard down when all along he knew the kind of woman that she was? Because he had been thinking with something other than his brain, that's how.

Alexis Cavanaugh was a spoiled, heartless viper and that would *never* change.

At least now he knew why she had so readily agreed to marry him, and he was thankful that she had. Lance and Kate were happy and he refused to let Lexi's selfishness—her lack of concern for anyone but herself—ruin that. For all he knew, she might have conceived on purpose. Maybe she felt she needed a bargaining chip, a way to guarantee her marriage to Lance, but he had broken the engagement and married Kate. Mitch could only imagine what Lexi's next move would have been had he not offered to marry her, instead. Blackmail, maybe? Extortion?

He wondered what the senator would think if he knew what his daughter had been up to. Of course, for all he knew, she learned this sort of behavior from him. But Mitch couldn't let himself forget the old man's threat. *If you hurt my daughter, I'll ruin you.* He didn't have a choice but to make this work. For the company's sake.

She was his wife, God help him, and he was going to raise his brother's child the way he would his own, with the best of everything. He had never imagined being a father, especially at his age, but he didn't seem to have much choice. He had no reservations about running a multimillion-dollar company, but the responsibility of shaping a child's life terrified him. Probably because his own father had done such a bang-up job with him and Lance.

When Lexi grew bored and left them, which he had little doubt she would eventually do, he would reject everything he had learned from his own father and be the best single parent possible. He owed the kid that much. Someday, when the time was right, he would tell Lance and the child the truth, but until then, no one but he and Lexi would know.

That wasn't even the worst part. To keep up the ruse, so Lance didn't suspect the truth, Mitch and Lexi had no choice but to make their marriage look like a real one.

Eight

The trip home was the longest and most miserable in Lexi's life. It was raining as they boarded the ferry to the mainland and the ride was a choppy one, launching her already questionable stomach into turmoil. The first leg of their flight was delayed due to weather and they missed their connecting flight. They were stuck in the London airport for six hours waiting for the next available departure, and when they finally took off for Texas, the flight was so turbulent she spent most of it in the bathroom in a scene straight out of *The Exorcist*.

The entire time, Mitch didn't say a single word to her.

When they reached Houston, she was so relieved she felt like dropping to her knees and kissing the ground. She just wanted to go home and crawl into her own bed. But as they were climbing into the limo, Mitch reminded her that all of her things had been moved into his townhouse and that was her home now. On the bright side, he didn't seem any happier about it than she was. Her misery wasn't as hard to swallow when she knew he was right there with her.

Located on a golf course in what was by far the most affluent neighborhood in Maverick County, Mitch's townhouse was anything but small. The front door opened into a foyer and spacious living area. It smelled of furniture polish and faintly of Mitch's aftershave. The decor, to her surprise, was very homey and welcoming. Not what she would expect from a house occupied exclusively by a man.

There was a formal dining room and enormous kitchen with every modern device known to man. On the countertop sat a huge bouquet of flowers, two champagne glasses and a bottle of sparkling fruit juice chilling on ice. Beside it was a note penned in Tara's handwriting that read, *Congratulations and welcome home!*

At Mitch's questioning look, she said, "It's from Tara, my assistant."

He gestured to the nonalcoholic drink. "I guess it's safe to say she knows you're pregnant."

"She's my best friend. I tell her everything." Well, almost everything.

"That's sad," he said.

"What? That I tell her everything?"

"No, that you have to pay someone to be your best friend."

How did he always manage to hit the rawest nerve? But she refused to let him know that he'd hurt her feelings. She lifted her nose at him and said, "That's a little hypocritical coming from a man who had to buy his wife."

She braced herself for a sarcastic comeback, but instead, the hint of a smile tipped up the corner of his mouth, catching her off guard.

"Your room is on the second floor," he said. He backtracked through the house to where he left her bag by the stairs. He grabbed it and started up, and she followed him.

"Dry cleaning is picked up and dropped off Mondays and Thursdays. It will be your responsibility to see that it's left on the porch."

"Fine."

"I have a cleaning service in Monday, Wednesday and Friday."

"What about a cook?"

"I'm not home enough to warrant it. I usually eat out or order in. But if you want to hire someone, I won't object. And of course when we move, we'll need a full-time staff." He led her to the first room on the left. As far as she could see, there were three other bedrooms.

It was a typical spare bedroom, with gender-neutral furnishings and decor, but Tara had placed several of her things from her bedroom at her father's estate around the room. Photos and keepsakes mostly, as well as her books.

She peered into the walk-in closet and saw that Tara had also arranged all of her clothes and shoes, and in the bathroom she found her makeup and toiletries.

Mitch stood in the doorway watching her. "Is it satisfactory?"

It was more than adequate, but she said, "I suppose, if this is the best you can do."

He folded his arms across his chest. "Well, the master suite is larger, but then, you would have to share it with me."

Like *that* would ever happen. "Where is your room?"

"Why? Are you planning another midnight visit?"

"Actually, I need to know so I can avoid it."

He flashed another wry grin. "End of the hall on the right. The third floor is the den and my office. I would appreciate it if you didn't go up there."

Which meant that would be the first place she investigated.

"Just up the road is the community center. There's an exercise room and tennis courts. There's also a pool, although I'll warn you that bathing suits are not optional. Unless you want to get yourself arrested."

"Don't worry, I'll only walk around naked inside the house."

He didn't look as though he believed her, which would make actually doing it all the more fun.

"I'll need a space for Tara to work."

"She can have the room across the hall. I'll call my real estate agent so we can start house hunting."

She still didn't see the need for anything bigger than this, but he was the one paying the bills, so who was she to argue? "I'd like to unpack and change, and I have a few phone calls to make," she told him.

"Okay," he said, but he didn't move. At her questioning look he added, "Oh, did you want me to leave?"

"Please."

"I should probably check in with my girlfriend, anyway. Let her know I arrived home safely."

She wondered if he really did have a girlfriend, then figured he probably just said he did to annoy her. If he cheated on her and her father found out, Mitch could kiss his support goodbye. She smiled sweetly and said, "You mean the girlfriend who needs occasional reinflation?"

He smirked. "I'll be unpacking if you need me," he said as he left, closing the door behind him.

She sat on the bed and looked around. She would have to thank Tara for setting up her room. It made her feel a lot less like an interloper.

She turned on her cell phone and found she had half a dozen messages from her father and two from Tara. Since she wasn't quite ready to face her father yet, she called Tara first. They hadn't spoken since before the kitchen disaster—she'd been too embarrassed to admit how she had botched Tara's seemingly simple instructions.

She dialed and Tara answered on the first ring. "Welcome home! Did you see your surprise?"

"I did, thanks. And thank you for arranging all of my personal things."

"I'd love to take credit, but that was your husband's idea."

It was weird enough when she thought of Mitch as her husband, but to hear someone else say it felt like the final nail in her coffin. "That must have been before he decided he hates my guts."

"Oh, my gosh! What happened? I thought things were going really well."

"They were. He didn't even seem to care that I completely botched breakfast, flooded the kitchen, and nearly burned the house down making dinner. And the sex? Amazing. Everything was great, right up until the second I told him I'm pregnant."

"Oh, no, Lex. Was he really that upset?"

"I don't think it was the baby so much as the fact that he thinks it's Lance's."

"He what!?" she shrieked, obviously outraged. "You told him the truth, right?"

"There didn't seem to be much point. I doubt he would have believed me. He apparently thinks he knows the kind of person I am. I figure, why shatter his illusion?"

"Oh, Lex, I'm so sorry."

"I guess the worst part was that I thought for the first time in my life, someone really saw me, you know? I thought he cared." Lexi was mortified to realize that she was welling up. Enough of this. She had to pull herself together.

"Maybe if you told him the truth—"

"There's no point now. I can never trust him again."

"You're going to have to tell him eventually."

Yes, but for now, she would make him suffer a bit. Make him as miserable as she was. "Could we talk about something else?"

"Sure, Lex," she said, sounding hurt. Why did it feel as though whatever Lexi said or did, it was never right?

They talked briefly about setting up a temporary office for Tara in the townhouse, and then she called her father.

In lieu of hello, he snapped, "Why didn't you call? You should have been home hours ago."

It was on the tip of her tongue to say, "Hi, Dad, nice to talk to you, too." But she had never had the courage to speak to him that way. One wrong move and he might shut her out completely. Stop calling altogether.

"Our flight was delayed due to bad weather," she said. "We just got home."

"Well, I was concerned."

Just not concerned enough about her to come to her wedding, or call her while she was in Greece.

"Would a call have been too much trouble?" he asked sharply.

She could have asked him the same thing, but of course she didn't. "No, Daddy. I'm sorry."

That took the edge off his tone. "How was your vacation?"

"Greece was wonderful." It was the company she could do without. Although she couldn't deny that they'd had several very good days.

"You, Mitch and I will be meeting for dinner tomorrow evening at the Cattleman's Club," he said. *Demanded,* really.

"I'll have to ask Mitch if he's available."

"If he wants my support, he will be. Seven o'clock. Don't be late. I'm flying in from D.C."

He was flying all that way just to have dinner? She wondered what she and Mitch had done to deserve that. "We'll be there."

They disconnected and she set her phone down. She should probably give Mitch the good news.

She changed into a T-shirt and cotton capri pants, then went looking for Mitch. She started to walk toward his bedroom, then changed her mind and decided this would be the perfect time to snoop upstairs. She tiptoed quietly so he wouldn't hear her, and what she saw as she reached the top took her breath away. The entire floor was one large, open room. At one end was Mitch's office, which consisted of a slightly cluttered desk, file cabinet and bookshelves lining one wall. Across the room was a media center with a huge flat-screen television and a whole cabinet full of electronic equipment. Not to mention a wet bar. Everything was dark polished wood with comfortable-looking chocolate-brown leather furniture. One hundred percent male.

She crossed to his office area, running her fingers across the back of his chair, wondering if she should take a peek inside his desk. Just to annoy him, of course.

"I should have known I would find you up here."

She turned to find Mitch standing at the top of the stairs, arms folded over his chest.

"I thought we agreed you wouldn't come up here."

She shrugged. "I believe you issued an order. I never agreed to it. This is nice, though. Very macho."

"Is there a particular reason you're up here?"

To annoy you. "I was looking for you."

"Really? Because I told you I would be in my room, unpacking."

"I must have forgotten."

"What did you want?"

"To warn you that my father has invited us to dinner at the Cattleman's Club tomorrow night at seven."

"I'll have to check my schedule."

"That's what I told him. He said that if you want his support, you'll be there."

"Well, then, I guess I'll be there."

"That's what I told him."

"My brother left me a message. He said that Kate would like you to join her for a welcome-to-the-family lunch on Thursday."

"Family?"

"She is your sister-in-law."

Oddly enough, Lexi hadn't even thought about that. She had a family now—someone other than her father, that is. But she couldn't help wondering if it would be weird going out to lunch with the woman who had stolen her fiancé. "I'm not sure if that's a good idea."

His expression darkened. "You think you're better than her?"

"Of course not! Kate seems wonderful. I just thought it might be awkward."

"Fine, I'll tell Lance you don't want to go."

"I didn't say that. I'll go, okay?"

He shrugged, as though it didn't matter either way to him, yet she had the distinct feeling it did. "She said to meet her at the Cattleman's Club café at one."

She nodded, wondering how she was going to get there. If she asked Mitch to send a car for her, he would probably just accuse her of being spoiled. Unfortunately, her father had never allowed her to learn how to drive. Having his driver take her everywhere was just another way for him to keep track of her every move. Maybe Tara could drive her. And maybe, if she asked Tara nicely enough, she might teach Lexi to drive. She was twenty-four years old. It was high time she began asserting her independence.

"I talked to the real estate agent. We have a 10:00 a.m. appointment tomorrow. He said he has several properties to show us."

"That was quick."

"I called him last week and told him we'd be looking. The state of the economy being what it is, he said if we decide to buy, there's a huge selection right now. Building new would take considerably longer."

She shrugged. "Whatever you want. As long as I'm free by four."

"Why?"

"I have an appointment with my gynecologist."

His expression darkened. "Speaking of that, I think it would be best if we kept the...*situation* to ourselves."

She was tempted to tell him that the *situation* had fingers and toes and a beating heart, but she didn't see the point. He obviously wasn't ready to acknowledge the life growing inside of her. "Fine."

"Also, I think it would be best if people are led to believe that we're happy."

She pursed her lips. "Then maybe we should forget those cooking lessons and get me some acting lessons, instead."

"You don't give yourself enough credit. In Greece you had me snowed."

That's because I wasn't acting, you moron, she wanted to shout. But what good would it do? His mind was made up about her and she would never forgive him for it, so they were more or less at an impasse.

"Define happy," she said.

"I think we should act like newlyweds, show each other affection."

She narrowed her eyes at him. "How much affection?"

"I'm not suggesting we publicly maul each other. I'm talking about little things like holding hands, and maybe occasionally smiling at each other."

"But no kissing," she clarified. Not that she didn't enjoy kissing him. Quite the opposite. Every time his lips touched hers she got so hot her brain short-circuited. If that happened she might do something stupid, like sleep with him again. And because he did amazing things to her body, she knew once wouldn't be enough. If she slept with him too many times, she might begin to forget how awful he was.

"No kissing," he agreed.

Good.

So why did she feel disappointed that he hadn't put up at least a tiny fuss?

His cell phone rang and he looked at the display. "It's Lance. I have to take this."

"I'll be in the kitchen getting something to eat."

She brushed past Mitch and headed downstairs, hearing him call after her, "The fire extinguisher is in the pantry."

Smart-ass. She should burn the place down just to spite him.

"Welcome home," Lance said when he answered. "Did you get my message?"

"Yeah. In fact, I just talked to Lexi. She'll meet Kate for lunch." He didn't mention that Lexi hadn't looked all that thrilled with the idea. Mitch knew that she and her father looked down on people of Kate's past station in society.

"I'm glad," Lance said. "Kate is pretty excited about having a sister-in-law."

"Seriously?"

"The truth is, she credits Lexi for us finally getting together. If I hadn't planned to marry Lexi, Kate probably never would have quit, and I would still be walking around with my head in the clouds, not realizing how important she is to me."

That was an interesting way to look at it.

"Speaking of marriage," Lance said, "how was the honeymoon?"

"It was okay," Mitch told him, which wasn't a total lie. It had gone pretty well, right up until the moment Lexi showed her true colors. Unfortunately, if Mitch was honest about how truly miserable he was, not only would Lance feel guilty as hell, he might want to know why. It would be best for everyone involved if even Lance believed Lexi and Mitch were happy.

"Just okay?" Lance hedged.

"Better than okay," Mitch said. "I think this just might work out."

"I'm glad to hear it," he said, sounding relieved.

Mitch wasn't yet sure how he planned to handle the news of Lexi's pregnancy. Lance wasn't stupid. He would do the math and realize when she'd conceived. Mitch would just have to admit to his brother that he and Lexi slept together in D.C. He could lie and say they were drunk, claim they had been so out of it they had forgotten to use protection. He just hoped Lance wasn't too pissed at him, although Mitch wouldn't blame him if he was.

But that could wait a while, at least another month or two, until Lexi started to show.

"Any news about the fire?" he asked his brother.

"Whoever set it knew what they were doing. Darius hasn't been able to trace a thing."

"What does he think about Montoya? Is he even capable of pulling something like that off?"

"If he is, we'll find out."

Mitch couldn't help wondering if Lance was so determined to pin the fire on Alex Montoya that he would wrongly accuse an innocent man. "What if it wasn't him?"

"He's the only one with motive."

"We don't know that for sure, " Mitch countered.

"Hey, by the way," Lance said, "Darius asked that we meet him at his office next Wednesday evening."

"Did he say what for?"

"He said we had some business to discuss, but he wouldn't say more than that."

"Does it have something to do with the fire?"

"I don't think so."

"Sure, I'll be there." He was sure that by then he would need a night away from his wife—if they hadn't already killed each other.

Nine

The following morning Mitch and Lexi drove to the real estate agent's office to begin looking at houses. And though she still felt like death warmed over from a bout of kneeling to the porcelain gods, she put her best face on. The agent, Mark Sullenberg, was a friend of the family, which meant she and Mitch had to act happily married.

Unfortunately, he was really good at it.

There was barely a minute when he wasn't touching her, either holding her hand or casually draping his arm across her shoulders. He was so good, so charming and sweet to her, she started to forget they were only playing a role. It made her think of that week in D.C. and how perfect it had been, how naturally they had connected, which in turn made her feel depressed and lonely, because she knew she would never feel that way again.

She just prayed they would find a house soon, so they could go back to hating each other. But after looking at half a dozen homes, they hadn't found a thing either of them even remotely liked. They were all ultramodern in exclusive gated communities with lots of BMWs and luxury SUVs in the driveways. And they all looked the same. Lifeless and boring. By the sixth house, she could see that Mitch was getting frustrated and she was beginning to think that building new might be their only option.

"Can you show us something different?" Mitch asked Mark. "Something a bit more…"

"Traditional," she finished for him.

"Exactly," he said, looking surprised that she'd nailed it right on the head. "Something with some character."

"There is one property that recently came on the market," Mark said. "It's just outside of Maverick County. A renovated plantation house. The only problem is that it's located on ten acres of land, and you said you wanted to look in more of a suburban setting."

"How big is it?" Mitch asked.

"Fifty-five-hundred square feet. It used to be a horse farm, so there's a barn and stables."

That caught Lexi's attention. Her uncle on her

mother's side had kept horses when Lexi was a child. Though she had always wanted to learn to ride, her father would never allow it. Too dangerous, he'd decided. But her uncle would let her brush the horses and help feed and water them. The idea of owning a horse or two thrilled her.

She glanced over at Mitch, thinking she would reduce herself to begging if that was what it took to make him agree to at least look at it, but he appeared as intrigued as she was.

He shrugged and said, "Couldn't hurt to look at it."

They piled back into Mark's car for the twenty-minute ride, Lexi feeling uncharacteristically excited. For some reason, she had a really good feeling about this one.

"I'll warn you that it's a little run-down and overgrown," Mark told them. "When the owner died, there was a dispute with the will so it's been sitting empty for a while. It has a lot of potential, though."

They pulled off the road into a long, tree-lined driveway. He hadn't been kidding when he said it was overgrown. It would take a lot of work to get the yard in order. But Lexi couldn't keep her eyes off the house itself. It was…amazing. A huge, white Greek revival with pillars and balconies and black shuttered windows. She could just imagine herself in the evenings sitting on the long front porch drinking lemonade and watching the sun set, or playing with the baby in the shade of the trees.

She knew without a doubt, this was the one. This was home.

Mark pulled to a stop and they all climbed out. As he'd done before, Mitch took her hand, lacing his fingers through hers. But this time it was different. This time he really held on, as though he was brimming with pent-up excitement.

"It was built in 1895," Mark told them, "and completely remodeled about thirty years ago. It's a little rough around the edges, but an excellent investment."

She and Mitch stood there for a moment, side by side, hands clasped, gazing up at the remarkable structure. Lexi didn't know about Mitch, but she felt as though this was meant to be. As if, for the first time in her life, she'd finally come home.

"So, what do you think?" Mark asked.

"We'll take it," they said in unison, then looked at each other, startled that they were in complete agreement.

Mark laughed. "Wow, how's that for a consensus? You haven't even seen the inside."

"Well, then," Mitch said, giving her hand a squeeze, "let's see it."

Lexi knew at this point that it was only a formality, but they followed Mark up the porch and through the front door. The interior was a bit shabby and outdated, the kitchen and bathrooms in particular desperately needed updating, but all Lexi could see was the potential. Mitch must have felt the same way. When they concluded the tour he told Mark, "Let's write up an offer," and when they got back to the office to fill out the paperwork, instead of bidding low, he offered several thousand above the asking price.

Though she didn't let it show, she felt almost giddy with anticipation. They were buying a house. A house whose renovations she would help plan, and whose rooms she would decorate however she chose. She could hardly wait to get started.

She had never felt so...*alive*. As though an entirely new and amazing world was opening up to her.

"I'll submit this right away and hopefully we'll hear something in the next day or two," Mark told them as they were leaving. "I'll be in touch."

Though she was practically bursting with excitement when they were in the car on the way back to the townhouse, Lexi tried to hide it. An automatic defense mechanism she'd learned from dealing with her father. If he knew something was important to her, he would use it against her as leverage. A true politician.

Then Mitch asked, "So, you liked it?"

She could no longer contain herself. She blurted out, "I knew I wanted it the second we pulled into the driveway. If I had every house in the world to choose from, that's the one I would have picked."

"It's going to need a lot of work. It'll probably be months before we can move in."

"I would be happy living in it just the way it is."

He shot her a sideways glance. "The interior is a disaster. We're going to have to gut it and start from scratch. The renovations will go much faster if it's unoccupied."

Although she would be happy moving in there today, he made a good point. Especially with the baby coming. The sooner it was finished, the better.

"I'll start calling contractors today," he said.

"Shouldn't we wait until we know for sure that we got it?"

"Don't worry," he said, his tone a little smug. "We'll get it."

There were definitely advantages to being married to a man who was used to getting what he wanted.

"I'd like to get a horse or two," she said, prepared for an instant argument.

But Mitch said, "We could do that." Then he added offhandedly, "It would be a good atmosphere for raising kids."

It was the first time since she'd told him she was pregnant that he'd acknowledged the baby. She wondered how he would react when she told him the truth. Would it change his feelings for her? Make him dislike her a little less?

Probably not. Knowing Mitch, he would be even angrier, and hold it against her for the rest of her life. It would probably be in her best interest to at least wait until they had signed a mortgage to tell him the baby was really his. Just in case.

"Did you want to go to my appointment with me today?" she asked, unsure of what his reaction would be, and wondering how she would feel if he refused.

He was quiet for a moment, eyes on the road, then asked, "Do you want me to?"

She realized that yes, she did. Even though he didn't know it yet, this was his baby and he shouldn't miss out on anything. From the first pre-natal visit to the birth, she wanted him to be there for every minute of it.

He hates you. He thinks you're selfish and spoiled.

But if she denied him this opportunity, wouldn't she be proving him right?

Before she could talk herself out of it, she told him, "I want you to."

"Then I'll come," he said.

He reached over and turned the radio on to a country-western station, ending the conversation, yet she couldn't help but feel as though they had made some sort of progress today. Although progress toward what, she wasn't exactly sure.

The doctor's appointment wasn't at all what Mitch had expected. In fact, he hadn't known quite *what* to expect.

He figured they would take her temperature and blood pressure, which they did, and she was asked to pee in a cup. Typical doctor-visit stuff. What he hadn't been expecting was the internal exam.

Though he'd seen Lexi intimately on more than one occasion, and his first instinct was to do or say anything to annoy her, this just didn't seem the place, so he turned his back while she stripped from the waist down and got up on the table.

Even though the process went quickly, he gained a whole new respect for what women had to endure during a routine exam. Between all the poking and prodding and the giant cotton swab the doctor used for God only knows what, he felt grateful to have outdoor plumbing.

Then the doctor pulled out a piece of equipment that looked a lot like some recreational sex apparatus. It was long and narrow with a cord coming out one end that was attached to a monitor.

"This is an internal ultrasound," the doctor explained. "So we can get a better idea of the baby's development."

Lexi looked a little nervous so Mitch took her hand.

As the doctor inserted it, she gasped and said, "Cold," then winced a little as he made adjustments. Suddenly, up on the monitor popped a hazy black-and-white image.

"There's the fetus," the doctor said, pointing to a white area on the screen. "And these are the arms and legs."

Mitch didn't see anything but a fuzzy blob at first, but as the doctor gestured to the different body parts, it began to take shape. With its oversize head and stubby appendages, it looked more alien than human.

"This flutter is the heartbeat," the doctor told them.

"Can we hear it?" Lexi asked.

He turned the volume up and the rapid whoosh of the baby's pulse filled the room.

Mitch had never even considered being a father, and here he was listening to his baby's heartbeat, looking at its tiny form on a monitor.

Lance's baby, he reminded himself.

In a way, he felt as though he was stealing something invaluable from his brother, an opportunity to see his child develop. But he was sure that Lance and Kate would eventually have children and he would experience it all with her. This might be Mitch's only chance.

"Everything looks great," the doctor told her. "I'll see you in a month."

When they were back in the car and on their way home, Lexi sat so quietly gazing out the window that Mitch began to think maybe something was wrong. He couldn't help but ask, "Are you okay?"

"Seeing the baby, hearing the heartbeat. It suddenly seems so...*real*."

She looked so dazed and bewildered he wondered if the weight of the responsibility was finally sinking in. Wouldn't it be ironic if, now that he'd finally begun to accept the situation, she changed her mind and decided not to have it?

"You say that like it's a bad thing."

She looked over at him, surprise on her face. "No, of course not! I just…" She shrugged, then shook her head. "Never mind."

"Tell me," he said.

"You'll just make fun of me."

"I promise I won't make fun of you."

She studied him for a moment, as though she wasn't quite sure she could trust him. Finally she said, "I guess I'm just a little…scared."

He didn't think Lexi was scared of anything, and was surprised that she would admit it to him, of all people. "Scared of what?"

"Being a bad parent. What if I do everything wrong?"

It was on the tip of his tongue to say, "You probably will." But he didn't have the heart to knock her down when she looked so vulnerable and unsure of herself. She was opening up to him and he couldn't use that against her. Besides, there was always the very slim, one in a million chance that she would be a good mother and stick around. Maybe he should give her the benefit of the doubt.

So she would only disappoint him later? What was the point?

"You'll do the best you can," he told her, wishing he actually believed it, but Lexi seemed to buy it because she smiled.

A minute later, he pulled into his driveway and cut

the engine, but when he looked back over at Lexi she was frowning.

"What's wrong now?" he asked.

She turned to face him, looking almost nervous. "Mitch, there's something I need to tell you. Something you should know."

He had no idea what she was going to say, but he had the feeling he wasn't going to like it. "What?"

She hesitated, lip wedged between her teeth. Then she said, "About the baby…"

"What about it?"

"I thought you should know…"

She looked so nervous, he started to worry something was really wrong. "What are you trying to say?"

After another pause she finally said, "I just wanted to say thank you for coming with me today. For being a part of this."

And here he'd thought it had been something important. Half a dozen snarky comebacks were just dying to jump out, but instead he said simply, "You're welcome. Now, we better get inside and get ready or we'll be late for dinner. I get the distinct feeling your father isn't one to tolerate tardiness."

She smiled and nodded. "That's a fairly accurate assumption. I love my father, but to be honest, the sooner this evening is over and he flies back to D.C., the better, as far as I'm concerned."

Well, that was one thing they could agree on. So, why did he get the feeling there was something else? Something she wasn't telling him?

Ten

When Lexi and Mitch arrived at the Cattleman's Club to meet her father, her goal was to get in, eat dinner, and leave as fast as humanly possible. Which was odd because in the past she had cherished every moment her father would spare her. It seemed that lately she was no longer so desperate for his time or his approval. But Mitch needed his support, so she would be on her best behavior.

"Are you ready for this?" Mitch asked, holding out his hand for her to take.

She laced her fingers through his. Another few hours of pretending they were madly in love? She could hardly wait. At least now when he touched her it didn't feel so…unnatural. In a way it was kind of nice, even though she knew deep down that he hated her, or at the very least disliked her a lot.

"This way," the hostess said, gesturing toward the dining room door. They followed her, and as they entered the room, it took a few seconds for Lexi to process what she was seeing. Tables full of familiar people all smiling at them, balloons and streamers everywhere and a banner draped across the back wall that announced in huge block letters, *Congratulations Mitch and Lexi*.

Everyone shouted, "Surprise!" and the room erupted in laughter and applause.

She heard Mitch mumble, "Oh, shit," and thought, I couldn't have said it better myself.

Lance and Kate stood close to the door, beaming. He stepped forward and shook Mitch's hand.

"What did you do?" Mitch asked him.

"Don't look at me, bro. This was all Kate's idea. I couldn't talk her out of it."

"You had to have a wedding reception," Kate said, flush with excitement. She hugged Mitch, then pulled Lexi into a warm and affectionate embrace, and Lexi was so stunned she almost forgot to hug her back.

"But it wasn't just me," Kate said, nodding toward the door. "Your assistant was a huge help."

Lexi turned, and realized Tara was standing just off to one side of the door. She hadn't even seen her when they walked in.

She flashed Lexi a feeble smile and said, "Surprise."

She was the only one in the room who knew what a disaster the marriage was. No wonder she looked so apologetic.

"So, were you both surprised?" Kate asked.

Lexi nodded and Mitch said, "To quote the great Chevy Chase, if I woke up tomorrow with my head sewn to the carpet, I wouldn't be more surprised than I am now."

The room burst into laughter.

Someone handed Lexi and Mitch each a flute of champagne from a passing tray, and she realized everyone in the room already had their own glass.

Lance held his up in a toast. "To my little brother and his wife. May you live a long and happy life together!"

"Hear, hear!" everyone chanted, clinking their glasses together, and Lexi had no choice but to pretend to take a sip. As she studied the sea of faces before her, she couldn't help noticing that the one she had been expecting to see wasn't there. Her father.

Tara must have read her mind because she leaned close to Lexi and said, "The senator's secretary called a while ago to say he'll be a little late."

Didn't that just figure? He skips her wedding altogether and shows up late for the reception? She wondered why he bothered to show up at all. But she didn't have much time to think about it as a constant flow of friends, relatives and club members stepped forward to hug them or shake their hands and give their best wishes. Darius Franklin and his fiancée Summer Martindale, Kevin Novak and his wife Cara, Mitch's best man Justin Dupree. Even Sebastian Huntington and his daughter Rebecca were there. And those were just the people she recognized. She had no clue Mitch had so many friends.

A too-real wedding reception for a fake marriage. Did it get much worse? Lexi couldn't help thinking that this just might be the longest night of her life. But as the champagne flowed and the music played, she discovered herself getting caught up in the festivities. Mitch never once left her side, and if he wasn't holding her hand or draping an arm around her, he was touching her in some way.

Dinner was served around eight and halfway through the meal, Kate started to clink her glass with a fork, and then everyone joined in. Lexi had been to enough wedding receptions to know that it meant she and Mitch were supposed to kiss.

Mitch looked at her apologetically because he knew as well as she did that they had to make this look real. She held her breath as he cradled her face in his hand, leaned forward and laid a kiss on her that curled her toes and turned her brain to mush. The guests applauded, and she heard a couple of wolf whistles. After that, it seemed as though every five minutes the clinking started, and Mitch would be forced to kiss her yet again. Not that he seemed to mind, and she couldn't deny the man did fantastic things with his mouth.

He'd had several glasses of champagne with dinner, then after dessert, switched to whiskey. The more he drank, the more relaxed he became, and the more relaxed he became, the more affectionate he seemed to be. By the time they had their first dance together, he nearly had her convinced they were madly in love. The song playing was a slow one and he pulled her so close, gazed so tenderly into her eyes, she thought any minute he might drag her to the nearest broom closet.

"When we walked in here I thought this night was going to be a disaster," he said. "But I have to admit, it hasn't been so bad."

She'd thought the same thing, but she was actually having a great time.

"You might have to drive us home tonight," he warned her. "I think I may have had a few too many."

That could be a problem. "I can't."

He frowned. "You haven't been drinking, have you?"

"Of course not! What I mean is, I really can't. I never learned how to drive."

His eyes widened. "You're kidding."

She shook her head.

"Let me guess. Your father wouldn't allow it."

"It would have made it more difficult to keep me

under his thumb. I had a driver who took me wherever I needed to go."

Mitch shook his head in disgust. "No offense, but the more I learn about the senator, the less I like him."

His irritation stunned her, but she realized it was a nice change to have someone to defend her. "I can ask Tara to drive us."

"I'll call a car," he said. "And the first chance we get, I'm teaching you to drive."

"Seriously?" First cooking lessons, now driving? He was being almost too nice and understanding. Probably tomorrow, when he was sober, he would come to his senses and change his mind.

"Speak of the devil," Mitch said, gesturing toward the door with his chin.

She turned and saw that her father had arrived. He was watching Lexi and Mitch dance, and he didn't look happy.

"Is it my imagination," Mitch asked, "or does he look really pissed off?"

"It's not your imagination." She couldn't help wondering what she'd done this time, because when he looked like that, it was usually her fault. "I should go talk to him."

"You want me to come with you?"

"Maybe you'd better give us a few minutes alone." The last thing she needed was for her father to berate her in front of her husband. Not that she thought it was possible for Mitch to have a lower opinion of her than he already did, but why take a chance?

She crossed the room to where her father waited, forcing a smile, and said, "Hello, Daddy."

She hadn't expected a warm greeting, but she also hadn't expected him to clamp a hand around her upper arm and pull her to an unoccupied corner. He had never been one to get physical.

"What's the matter with you?" he said under his breath, but she had no idea what she'd done.

"I—I don't know."

Before the senator could respond, Mitch appeared at her side. He held a hand out for him to shake and her father had no choice but to let go of her arm.

"Senator Cavanaugh, I'm so glad you could finally make it." He was all smiles but his words had bite. He put an arm protectively around her shoulders and asked, "Is there a problem?"

"Yes, there's a problem. Lexi looks awful. Her skin is pale and she's obviously lost weight."

"You think so?" Mitch asked, looking down at her.

"I know my daughter, Mr. Brody, and I know something isn't right."

Sudden fear gripped her. With that invaluable senatorial support in mind, what if Mitch decided to break down and tell her father the truth? Instead, he looked at Lexi with one of those sizzling smiles and said, "She looks damned good to me." Then right in front of her father, he lowered his head and brushed his lips against hers, so soft and gentle and sweet that her knees went weak.

He eased back, and with his eyes locked on hers said, "Excuse us, Senator, but I'd like to dance with my wife."

Her father's stunned expression as Mitch took her hand and led her away gave Lexi far more satisfaction than it should have. When they were back on the dance floor, he said, "What the hell kind of man tells his daughter she looks awful at her wedding reception?"

"I probably looked happy."

"Isn't that the point?"

"I think it makes him feel threatened because when I'm happy about anything, he always says or does something to sabotage it."

"He's your father. He's supposed to *want* you to be happy."

Lexi shook her head. "The entire time I was growing up he talked about how he wished he'd had a son, but my mom died before they had the chance. He never said he resented me for being born a girl, but it was obvious he felt that way. As I got older, he started to talk about me getting married and giving him lots of grandsons. Like he only saw me as a baby-breeding machine or something."

"I guess that explains why he was so anxious to marry you off."

"Exactly." But he didn't want a grandson so badly

that he would tolerate her being an unwed mother. If she had a boy, she honestly wouldn't put it past him to try to take the baby and raise it himself.

"Is he still looking at us?" Mitch asked.

She looked past his shoulder and saw that her father was holding a drink and talking to Sebastian Huntington, but his eyes were on Lexi and Mitch.

"Yes, he's still looking."

A devilish smile curled the corners of Mitch's mouth and she was sure that any second he might sprout horns. "Then let's give him a good reason to feel threatened."

Before she could ask what he planned to do, he lowered his head and locked his lips with hers, kissing her so passionately, so deeply, she could swear she felt him hit her tonsils. She might have been embarrassed but her brain had ceased to function the instant his lips touched hers. When he finally pulled away, she was breathing hard and gripping his suit jacket with both hands.

"How did he like that?" Mitch asked, looking a little breathless himself.

She looked over just in time to see her father walk out the door. "Apparently he didn't, because he just left."

"Good riddance."

She looked up at him and smiled. "Thank you for rescuing me."

"You owe me big time," he said. "And I would be willing to accept sexual favors as payment."

She opened her mouth to speak, but before she had the chance he said, "Relax, I'm just kidding."

Oddly enough, she'd been about to ask, *What would you like me to do?* Instead she said, "Not that it wasn't fun to see my father knocked down a peg or two, but if you want his support you should really be careful what you say to him. He likes to play hardball, and he enjoys a good fight, but not at the expense of his pride."

"If getting his support means kissing his ass, I'm not sure I want it anymore."

Her breath caught in her throat. If Mitch didn't want her father's support, then why would he stay married to her? And if he left her, what would she do then? Crawl back to her father and beg him to take her in? What choice would she have?

"Of course, if I blow this, Lance will probably kill me," Mitch continued. "So, I don't really have much choice."

The surge of relief she felt was so complete she nearly collapsed. She couldn't help but feel she'd just dodged a bullet.

Mitch wasn't usually much of a drinker, but he had figured the more intoxicated he was, the less inclined he would be to attack Lexi the instant they stepped in the front door. And what a brilliant plan *that* had been. While he had managed to keep his hands to himself, he'd been lying in bed awake for the past hour staring at the ceiling with a boner that just wouldn't quit. But what did he expect when he spent half the night with his hands all over her and the other half with his tongue down her throat?

On the bright side, they seemed to have everyone at that party convinced that they were happy as clams and having the time of their lives.

He rolled over and the sensation of the sheets sliding against his hard-on was almost enough to set him off. He could always take care of matters himself, but how sad was that? Very, considering he had a gorgeous wife just down the hall and he couldn't make love to her.

Couldn't or wouldn't? He was the one making the rules. He had told her that their marriage wouldn't be more than business, and he was beginning to think that as far as dumb moves went, that just about topped them all.

He couldn't help but wonder if Lexi was lying in her bed, staring at the ceiling, feeling as sexually frustrated as he was.

He heard a noise coming from the first floor, the screech of the kettle whistling. He sat up in bed. Though normally boiling water wouldn't cause him alarm, he knew Lexi could find a way to turn even making tea into a disaster of biblical proportions.

He jumped out of bed, threw on his robe, and headed down to the kitchen to stop her before she set something on fire. What was she doing up at 1:00 a.m. anyway?

When he got to the kitchen, the flame under the kettle was off and Lexi was opening and closing cupboards. She was wearing that same long silk gown she'd worn in Greece, and all he could think about was getting her out of it.

"Looking for something?" he asked.

She spun around, startled. "What are you doing here?"

Her breasts swelled enticingly against the sheer fabric and he could see the rosy outline of her nipples. Maybe it was his imagination, but her chest looked fuller than it had just a week ago.

"Last I checked, I live here," he said. "What are *you* doing?"

"I couldn't sleep, so I came down to get something to drink."

"Were you looking for something?" he asked.

"Herbal tea," she said. "Sometimes it helps me sleep. I thought I might make a cup. Do you have any?"

"In the narrow cupboard above the coffeemaker." He watched, mesmerized once again by the sway of her hips under that silk as she crossed the kitchen and opened the cupboard. "Top shelf in the back."

She stretched for it, but even on her tiptoes she wasn't tall enough. She turned back to him and said, "I can't reach it."

He knew even before he took a step that he was going to regret this, but he couldn't stop himself. He crossed the kitchen, caging her into a corner, and to his surprise, she didn't object or try to move to one side. She smelled fantastic and she was giving off enough pheromones to bring a football team to its knees.

Resting one hand on the counter beside her, he reached up with the other to grab the box of tea bags. He told himself that getting this close to her without an audience was a bad idea, but the message was getting scrambled in his hormone-drenched brain. Instead of backing off, like he should have, his body was telling him to move closer.

Lexi's breathing sounded labored and he could feel her trembling. He wasn't sure if she was scared or excited, or a little bit of both.

"We shouldn't be doing this," she said, but she didn't try to stop him, didn't push him away.

"I know. But I get the feeling we're going to, anyway." He didn't just get the feeling, he knew for a fact.

She opened her mouth to speak, probably to tell him to back off, but since that was the last thing he wanted to hear, he lowered his head and kissed her instead. With his tongue in her mouth she wasn't able to do much but moan. Which was exactly what she did. Her arms went around his neck and she tunneled her fingers through his hair. If she'd been planning to stop him, she had obviously changed her mind. At this point, they were both too far gone to turn back, and he only felt slightly guilty for using her this way.

Wasn't it Lexi who had said that they both had needs, and suggested that since they were stuck with each other, why not have a little fun?

At that moment, he couldn't think of a single reason he shouldn't take her advice.

"Tell me you're not wearing panties under this," he said, gripping the silk in his hands.

She gave him a fiery smile. "Why don't you look and see?"

He pulled it up over her head. Nope, no panties. And damn did she look good naked.

"How about you?" she said, eyeing his robe. "Are you wearing anything under there?"

He grinned. "Why don't you look and find out?"

She undid the belt and shoved the robe off his shoulders, smiling when she realized he wasn't. For an instant, he considered carrying her up to his bedroom, but honestly, he didn't think he could wait that long. He wanted—needed—to be inside her. It hadn't even been a week since they'd last made love, but it felt like years.

Not love, he reminded himself. This was sex.

He lifted her up and set her on the counter. Without hesitation she hooked those long, shapely, perfect legs around his waist. He was inside her, buried just as far as he could go, before he even thought about using a condom.

But why bother? It wasn't as though he could get her more pregnant than she already was, right?

He wanted it to last, but she was so hot and wet and tight. The sensation of skin against skin had him hovering on the edge of a precipice, struggling to keep his balance, but Lexi was moaning and writhing and sinking her nails into his back. Then she gazed up at him with a look that was caught somewhere between shock and ecstasy, and her entire body started to tremble. Her muscles contracted around him and he couldn't have held back then if his life depended on it. He came so hard his knees nearly gave out and he had to grab the edge of the counter to hold himself up.

Lexi clung to him, her forehead resting on his chest, breathing hard. "We really shouldn't have done that."

"No," he said, his own breath coming in short rasps. "We probably shouldn't have."

He could always say the alcohol had impaired his judgment. What was her excuse?

She lifted her head and gazed up at him. "Now that we have that settled, you want to do it again?"

Eleven

Lexi woke the next morning at six-thirty and immediately felt that something was different. Something
other than the fact that she was in Mitch's bed and
she was curled up against his side while he slept
soundly.

She lay there for several minutes, trying to put her
finger on the change, then realized she didn't feel
sick. She should be bolting to the bathroom by now,
losing last night's dinner.

She lay there for another minute or two, sure that
any second it would hit her, and still nothing.

Maybe she had to move a little, jostle her
stomach, to get the ball rolling. She untangled herself

from Mitch's arms and slowly pulled herself into a sitting position, waiting for that overwhelming wave of nausea, for the cold sweats and the abrupt rush of bile to her throat. Instead she felt something else in the pit of her stomach. She felt...*hungry*.

She usually couldn't choke anything down until closer to lunchtime, yet here it was not even seven and she was famished.

The doctor had told her chances were good the morning sickness would ease up, but she'd had no idea it would end so abruptly.

Mitch touched her back and in a groggy voice, asked, "Are you okay?"

"I think so." She had warned him last night, when he refused to let her get up and sleep in her own room, to expect her abrupt departure from bed.

He peered up at her through sleepy eyes, his hair adorably mussed. "Should I get you a bucket?"

She gave him a playful shove, even though she liked that he was worried about her. "I don't think that will be necessary. I actually feel pretty good. Like I could eat breakfast." Which meant he would have to make it since he'd asked that—until she started those lessons—she please not cook anything. Although she had managed to boil water last night without incident.

He looked over at the clock and groaned. "It's too early to eat."

"Don't you have to get up and get ready for work, anyway?"

"Since someone kept me up half the night, I was planning on sleeping in and going in late."

"*I* kept *you* up?"

"You were insatiable. I feel so...used."

She wasn't the one who kept dragging him back under the covers every time she tried to go back to her own room, or kiss her awake when she would start to doze off from sheer exhaustion. "You just keep telling yourself that," she said. "But we both know what really happened."

He grinned up at her. "Since you're not sick, how would you feel about it happening again, right now?"

She huffed impatiently, and said in her best exasperated voice, "I suppose breakfast can wait."

When he finally let her out of bed it was closer to lunchtime. She showered and dressed, and when she went downstairs to the kitchen to find him, he was fixing them something to eat. She had expected him to be in a suit, ready to go to the office, but he was dressed in casual slacks and a polo shirt.

"Don't you have to go to work?" she asked.

He shrugged and said, "They'll manage without me one more day. Besides, I promised you a driving lesson."

She had just figured, since he'd been intoxicated at the time, that he would have forgotten about the driving lessons. The thought of actually getting behind the wheel of a car, especially with Mitch watching, had her heart skipping a beat. "Maybe we shouldn't."

"How else will you learn?"

"What if I do it wrong?"

"You probably will at first, but that's all a part of the learning process."

"What if I do something terrible, like run us off an overpass or something?"

"I promise I'll keep you on solid ground until you get the hang of it."

She chewed her lip, wondering what she could say to talk him out of it without sounding like a total chicken.

Mitch reached over and took her hand. "Have a little faith in yourself, Lexi, and you'll do just fine."

That was the problem. She had been taught to believe that she couldn't do things on her own, but he was right. She had to stop being so afraid of everything, so willing to depend on other people. It was time she started living her life, and not just sitting back and watching the world pass by around her.

She took a deep breath and blew it out. "Okay. Let's do it."

"After we eat, we'll take you out for your first lesson."

At least this way she didn't have to ask Tara to do it.

Mitch's cell phone rang and he unclipped it from his belt to answer it. "Hey, Mark, what's up? Did they accept our offer?"

Lexi's heart jumped when she heard the real estate

agent's name. She held her breath while Mitch listened quietly, his expression hovering somewhere between curiosity and concern. He'd all but said he would do anything to get the house, but what if the owners changed their minds and refused to sell it?

"I understand," he said. "I'll talk to you later." He hung up and clipped the phone back on his belt. "That was Mark."

As if she hadn't already figured that out. "What did he say?"

"He heard from the seller."

"And?"

A slow smile spread across his face. "They accepted the offer. The house is ours."

Lexi screamed and threw herself into his arms. She had been so afraid that something would go wrong, she hadn't let herself hope it would really happen. Now she was so excited she could barely contain herself.

Mitch laughed and hugged her back. "I guess I don't have to ask if you're happy."

"I am," she said, resting her head against his chest, squeezing him tight. For the first time in a long time she was really, really happy.

Something had happened last night. When he took her hand and they walked into that party, something in their relationship had changed. She was sure of it. They could say that this marriage was nothing more than a business deal, but she knew it wasn't true. He was the man she'd spent that amazing week with in D.C., the one she had fallen in love with. And despite a few rocky patches, she knew that deep down she had never really stopped loving him. And he loved her, too, even if he hadn't said so.

"We close in a week," he said.

"We?" she asked, looking up at him.

"It's your house, too."

Her house. The idea made her almost giddy with excitement.

Everything was perfect. Even better than perfect.

Except for one thing. She still hadn't told Mitch the truth.

Lexi had assumed her lunch at the Cattleman's Club café would be just her and Kate, but when Tara dropped her off at the club and the hostess led her to the table, she saw that they were being joined by Summer Martindale, Cara Pettigrew-Novak, Alicia Montoya, and Rebecca Huntington.

Lexi wondered if she was walking straight into the lion's den. Kate had been incredibly sweet the other night at the party, but what if that had been an act? What if she resented the fact that Lexi had been engaged to her husband and she'd lured her here to humiliate her?

Kate saw Lexi approaching and rose from her chair, a huge smile on her face, and said, "Hey, sister-in-law!" Then she proceeded to wrap Lexi up in one of those warm and affectionate hugs.

Well, that was unexpected.

"Sit down," Kate said, gesturing to the empty seat beside hers. "I think you know everyone here."

As she sat, the women smiled and greeted her warmly, and Lexi began to think that maybe this would just be a friendly lunch with the girls after all. Which for her would be a totally new experience. She hadn't been allowed to have many friends or associate with people who weren't the top shelf of society—she couldn't have contact with anyone who could be a potential danger to her father's political aspirations. He never would have approved of a friendship with someone like Kate, a lowly assistant, or a dancer like Cara. In fact, there wasn't a single person at the table, besides Rebecca Huntington maybe, whom he would deem acceptable. And for the first time in her life, she didn't care what he thought. Lately, the past couple of days especially, she'd been feeling rebellious and independent, and she *liked* it.

A waitress appeared at their table to take Lexi's drink order. Lexi saw that everyone else had an alcoholic beverage, and boy did she wish she could have one, too, but she ordered an iced tea instead. For a second, she worried someone might question her choice, but no one said a word.

"We try to meet at least once a month," Cara told her, "so we can discuss all of the latest gossip."

Lexi wondered if she had ever been the topic of conversation.

"Today we're also celebrating," Summer said, and all heads turned her way.

"What are we celebrating?" Alicia asked.

Summer held out her left hand, so everyone could see the enormous diamond ring and diamond-encrusted wedding band she was wearing. "Darius and I eloped!"

Excited squeals and congratulations followed.

"I'm so jealous!" Rebecca said. "It seems as though everyone is getting married but me."

"Marriage is hard work," Cara said, then added with a smile, "but well worth it when you finally get the gears running smoothly."

The waitress brought Lexi's tea and set a basket of fresh bread and rolls on the table. Lexi was absolutely famished—the last few days it seemed as though she was constantly eating—so she dove right in and grabbed a roll.

"What's the latest with the refinery fire?" Rebecca asked Summer, and Lexi couldn't help noticing that everyone glanced at Alicia. At first she wondered why, then remembered that it was Alicia's brother Alex who was being looked at for the arson.

"Is Darius any closer to finding out who did it?" Kate asked.

Summer shrugged apologetically. "He doesn't say too much about his work."

"I know what everyone thinks," Alicia said. "But Alex would never hurt a soul. He didn't set that fire."

"I believe you," Rebecca told her. "Alex is a good person," Lexi noticed that the woman looked at Rebecca with surprise. "Based on what I've heard, I mean," she added, blushing slightly.

"What about the rezoning in the Somerset district?" Kate asked. "I heard Alex was behind it."

"He is, because someone had to do something to pick up revenue. I know that no one wants to believe it, but the town is in trouble," said Alicia. "With Alex's help, I'm working on a project to create an 'Old Towne' tourist attraction downtown. It will bring jobs and add tourist revenue to the city, not to mention preserve history, which, as curator of the museum, is important to me."

"Sounds like your life lately has been all work and no play?" Cara asked with a strange smile on her face.

"Well, not *all* work," Alicia said cryptically.

"Did you meet someone?" Rebecca asked excitedly.

Alicia flashed them a smile. "Maybe."

"Girlfriend, are you holding out on us?" Summer asked.

"Let's just say I'm afraid I'm going to jinx it. But I will say that I have a date this Friday. He said he wants to take me somewhere special."

"You have to come to Sweet Nothings," Rebecca insisted. "A special date deserves sexy underwear."

Alicia laughed. "I could spend my entire salary in your store, Becca."

"You're one of those people who can eat anything and still stay pick thin, aren't you?" Cara said. Lexi was surprised to find that Cara was talking to her, and mortified when she realized why. While everyone had been chatting, Lexi had almost wiped out the bread basket by herself.

"Sorry," she said, setting down the roll she'd been devouring. She could feel her cheeks turning pink. "I skipped breakfast."

"I just have to look at food and my butt gets bigger," Rebecca said.

"I hate to think what I'd look like if I weren't dancing all the time," Cara said.

After that, Lexi was careful not to draw attention to herself. She ordered a salad with the dressing on the side, then only ate half, even though she was hungry enough to eat three times that much. Maybe the next time they met—if she was even invited next time—she would be able to tell them about the baby.

It was getting to the point where she *had* to tell Mitch the truth. She had almost said it the other day after they found the house, but she'd chickened out at the last minute. She knew, though, that it was time. She'd begun to believe that now he would be thrilled to learn that the baby was his. Because even though he hadn't said it out loud yet, Lexi was convinced that he loved her. He showed her every day in a hundred little ways. Most of them in the bedroom.

Though she knew better than to mistake sex for love, she was sure that this time it was different.

The alternative was no longer an option.

Twelve

Mitch found it ironic that when he had agreed to meet at Darius's office, he'd figured he would be thankful for the time away from his wife, when in reality, he would much rather be at home with her. For a self-proclaimed workaholic who loved his job above all else, he'd been taking a lot of time off since they got back from Greece.

At first he tried to convince himself that it was just the sex, and then he told himself that he felt guilty leaving her alone, or was worried that she might try to use the stove and burn his house down. But now, as he sat in the conference room of Darius's security firm with Darius, Lance, Kevin and Justin, he couldn't deny that he simply missed her company.

As hard as he tried to tell himself that she was a spoiled, heartless brat who cared about no one but herself, her actions said he was way off base. If what she'd told him about her father was true, and after seeing the senator in action he was pretty damned sure it was, it was a miracle that Lexi had any self-esteem at all. He now believed that she hadn't hopped from his bed to his brother's as some sort of vendetta, but because she was desperate to be accepted and loved. She *deserved* to be with someone who could love her. But Mitch didn't do love.

In a few weeks, he'd gone from thinking that he was somehow superior to her, a better human being, to thinking that he just didn't measure up. But he had to stick it out for the baby's sake, the niece or nephew growing in her who deserved to be raised by family, not some stranger.

"So, when is this meeting going to start?" Kevin asked Darius.

"As soon as the last person I invited gets here." No sooner had the words left his mouth than the conference-room door opened and Alex Montoya walked in.

In an instant, Lance was up and out of his chair. "What is he doing here?"

Alex shot Lance daggers with his eyes.

"I asked him to come," Darius said. "As a Cattleman Club member, this concerns him, too."

Mitch sat up in his chair, in case he needed to hold his brother back, but after a tense moment, Lance took his seat and Alex found a chair on the opposite side of the table. Mitch didn't like Alex, but he gave him credit for having the guts to show his face.

"I called you all here," Darius said, "because I have suspicions that someone may be cooking the club books."

"Are you suggesting that someone is embezzling from the club?" Justin asked.

"That's exactly what I think."

"What led you to think that?" Kevin asked.

"When I set up the new billing system for Helping Hands, something strange happened. The club cut us a check for expenses, but it was made out to Helping Hearts. I called the office and talked to Sebastian Huntington and asked him to fix the error. I just assumed he'd used the wrong name, but he said that he'd sent the wrong check by accident."

"I didn't know there was an organization named Helping Hearts," Mitch said, although admittedly, he didn't pay much attention to the club's finances.

"I didn't either," Darius said. "But I was curious so I did a bit of research, and after some digging, I found that Helping Hearts doesn't exist."

"As club members we have the right to examine the books," Alex said, looking as concerned as the rest of them.

"I suppose you think you should be the one to investigate," Lance snapped back. "How do we know you're not the one behind it?"

Alex glared at him. "First you call me an arsonist, now you accuse me of theft? Perhaps you would like to blame me for the stock market crash as well."

"I know," Darius interrupted, before fists started flying, "that it can't feasibly be someone in this room. Only a member higher up in the ranks could pull this off."

"Like who?" Kevin asked.

"I'm not ready to point any fingers yet. And Alex is right, we need someone to examine the books. I think that person should be Mitch."

Suddenly all eyes were on him. "Why me?"

"I can handle setting up a simple billing system," Darius told him, "but you're the financial whiz kid of the group. If anyone would be able to spot discrepancies, it's you."

"I agree," Justin said.

"I do, as well," Alex agreed, which earned him a sharp look from Lance.

Kevin added his vote. "Me, too."

"So it's unanimous," Lance said.

Mitch wasn't sure if he was comfortable with this, but it seemed he didn't have much choice. "And if I find something?"

"We'll demand an audit from an outside firm. According to the bylaws, the club has no choice but to comply."

"I'm still having a tough time believing someone would steal from the club," Kevin said.

"So was I," Darius assured him. "I never would have come forward with this if I wasn't sure. You'll keep us posted, Mitch?"

"Of course."

The meeting broke up after that, Alex wisely being the first one to leave. On his way out, Justin asked Mitch, "You want to head to the club for a drink? Watch some soccer?"

Normally, Mitch wouldn't have hesitated to spend a few hours with his best friend, but he didn't feel right leaving Lexi alone. Besides, he had promised they would talk about contractors and the renovations they wanted to make on the house. "I can't tonight," he told Justin.

"Have to get back to the old ball and chain?"

Mitch didn't justify that with a response, he just shot Justin a look.

Justin laughed and shook his head. "Damn. I never thought I'd see the day when Mitchell Brody settled down."

"You could be next," Mitch said, which only made Justin laugh harder.

"I wouldn't advise holding your breath. Now that you're tied down, that just means more available women for me."

Leave it to Justin to rationalize it out like that. Although it surprised Mitch to realize it, he didn't miss playing the field. Maybe later that would change and he would begin to feel restless. But for now he was quite content being a one-woman man.

When Lexi answered the knock at the front door, the last person she expected to see standing on the porch was her father. As far as she knew, he was supposed to be in D.C.

"Daddy, what are you doing here?"

"I need to speak with you," he said, entering without waiting for an invitation.

"Of course," she replied, stepping aside. Maybe he was here to apologize for the way he'd acted at the party.

He gazed around the foyer looking unimpressed. Probably not big or grand enough for him. "Is your husband here?"

"No, he had a meeting." She gestured toward the kitchen. "I was just making myself a cup of tea. Would you like one?"

"You're making it? Does your husband not even have the decency to hire a housekeeper?"

She shrugged. "It's not a big deal. In fact, I sort of like doing things myself for a change."

He shook his head. "It's even worse than I thought."

Clearly that apology wasn't going to happen. "What's worse than you thought?"

"Your life. What Mitch has reduced you to."

Reduced her to? On the contrary, it felt as though

she had been introduced to a world she never knew existed, with opportunities and possibilities she had never dreamed of. "I'm fine, Daddy. Really."

"Nothing about this is 'fine.' After the degrading display the other night at the party, I've decided not to give the Brody brothers my support."

Her heart sank. "You can't do that."

"I can and I will. I still can't believe the way he was groping you. Do you have any idea how it looked to everyone else in the room?"

"Probably like we were a newlywed couple so madly in love we couldn't stand being apart."

"Well, the charade is over, so there's no need for you to stay here any longer. Pack your things and I'll take you home."

She didn't want to leave. "You promised them your support."

"I also told him that if he hurt you, I would crush him."

She began feeling a little frantic. Her father was being completely unreasonable. "But he *didn't* hurt me."

"He sullied your reputation, which is even worse, as far as I'm concerned."

"Reputation is more important than my happiness? I love Mitch."

He spit out a rueful laugh, and regarded her as though she were the village idiot. "You can't possibly be that naive. He only married you for my support."

The lengths he would go to, the things he would say to make her feel bad about herself, knew no bounds. But she knew exactly what this was about, even if he wouldn't admit it. It had nothing to do with reputation or Mitch's behavior at the party. He only wanted her to leave Mitch because she wanted to stay. He wanted control of her life back. Married to Mitch, he could no longer manipulate her. But this time she didn't have to listen to him. "You really can't stand it, can you?"

"Stand what?"

"To see me happy."

He scoffed. "That's ridiculous."

"Then why would you say something like that to me? I say I love Mitch and you accuse him of using me?"

"I said it because it's true. You know that I've never believed in coddling you."

"How do you know Mitch hasn't fallen in love with me?"

He shook his head sadly, as though she were even more pathetic than he realized.

"Do you believe I'm that horrible?" she asked. "That unlovable?"

"I didn't say that. But he isn't right for you."

"A month ago you seemed to think he was."

"Well, I was wrong."

If he couldn't accept that Mitch loved her, that was his problem, not hers. Mitch was going to be furious when he found out that her father had reneged on their deal, but she was pretty confident that he wouldn't hold it against her.

"Charade or not, I can't end the marriage."

"Why not?"

She shouldn't say it, but as soon as she told Mitch the truth everyone would know anyway. "I'm pregnant."

"Pregnant?" The anger disappeared and to her surprise, a look of wonder overwhelmed his face. "I'm going to be a grandfather?"

She had expected him to be furious. But it made sense that he would approve now that he was getting something he wanted out of the deal. And he had always wanted a grandson.

She smiled and nodded.

"That's...incredible."

"We had even discussed naming him after you," she said, even though they had done no such thing. They didn't have a clue what the baby's gender would be, much less what they planned to name it.

But he seemed to buy it because he beamed with pride. "I suppose a divorce *is* out of the question now, but we can figure out a way to make it work."

She smiled, thinking it was time to go for the throat. "You can start by giving Mitch and Lance all the senatorial support they need."

His smile faded. "I can't do that."

"You will if you want to see your grandchild."

He was so stunned that for a moment, he didn't seem to know what to say. It was the first time she had ever seen him rendered speechless and she enjoyed every second of it. When he found his voice, he asked, his tone soaked in disbelief, "You would use your own child against me?"

She sighed. "If I have to. Of course, I have plenty of other things I could hold against you."

"What things?"

"Things that could make your life very difficult when you're trying to get reelected."

The color leached from his face. "Did you just threaten to blackmail me?"

She sure as hell did. For the first time in her life she stood up to him and it felt wonderful. She flashed him a "Bless your Heart" smile. "Daddy, blackmail sounds so…uncivilized. Up on Capitol Hill I believe they call it extortion."

"I can't believe you would do this to me."

She shrugged. "I guess you could say that I learned from the master."

She waited for the anger, for him to explode, but to her surprise, it didn't happen. He just stood there, perplexed, as though he simply could not grasp what had just happened. That his compliant little girl had finally grown a will of her own. God knows it was about damned time. Then the front door opened and Mitch walked through, the vestiges of a cool early-autumn breeze following him inside.

"I thought that was your car outside," he said to her father as he walked right past him without shaking his hand or anything, pulling Lexi into his arms and kissing her. "Sorry it took so long, sweetheart."

Long? He'd barely been gone an hour. She had assumed "meeting" meant maybe twenty minutes of business followed by a few hours of drinking and bullshitting with the guys. Sort of like her lunch with Kate, but with more profanity and testosterone.

"Daddy stopped in to say hello," she told him. "Wasn't that nice?"

He obviously knew something was up, and he played along, saying in a Southern drawl that she had never heard him use before, "Why, yes it was. Can I get you a drink, Senator?"

"Unfortunately, he was just leaving," Lexi said. "But thanks for stopping by, Daddy."

Looking shell-shocked and confused, her father mumbled goodbye and let himself out of the house. As soon as he was gone, Mitch turned to her and, the drawl gone, asked, "What the hell just happened?"

Thirteen

Mitch lay in bed several hours later, Lexi against his side, her body warm and soft. He couldn't stop smiling. "I wish I could have seen the look on his face when you threatened him. That must have been priceless."

"I keep waiting to feel guilty. I never dreamed of saying something like that to him. Instead, I feel…liberated."

"I don't mean for this to sound condescending, but I'm proud of you," he said, and he could feel her smile.

"I'm proud of me, too. And I don't think you ever have to worry about losing his support. It's a real possibility that he won't ever speak to me again, though."

"How do you feel about that?"

"Not as bad as I expected. In a way, I kind of feel relieved. I don't need him anymore." She was quiet for a moment, then said, "Mitch, there's something I need to tell you. Two things, actually."

He rolled on his side to look at her. "What?"

"First, I lied to you. I said something really awful that wasn't true."

He frowned. "What?"

"It was the morning after we slept together in D.C. I thought…" She paused and bit her lip.

"You thought what?"

She took a deep breath. "I was so naive. I woke up, and I thought that you were going to beg me to marry you instead of Lance. I thought you…loved me. And you have no idea how long I'd waited for someone to feel that way about me. But the first thing you said that morning was that sleeping together had been a mistake. I was crushed. I lashed out and said the most awful thing I could think of."

"That you used me?"

She nodded.

In an odd way he was relieved, and at the same time it disturbed him. Not because she lied—he understood why she'd done it, and couldn't really blame her—but because she had just cemented the fact that he had totally misjudged her.

"I know we had barely spent a week together, but I loved you, Mitch. And I think…I think I still do."

He knew what she wanted, what she desperately

needed, but as much as he wanted her to be happy, he couldn't bring himself to lie to her. "I care for you, Lexi. I really do. I just can't…"

She rolled onto her back, but not before he saw her face fall, her happiness crumble. "I understand."

"It's not you. It's me."

She shrugged. "You don't have to explain."

He waited for her to get angry, or to cry. To do something. But she just lay there quietly and he felt like the world's biggest heel. She deserved better than this. Better than him. She should be with someone who loved her. Who was capable of love.

"What else?" he asked.

"What do you mean?"

"You said there were two things you had to tell me."

"Oh," she said softly, turning away from him to lie on her side, pulling the covers up over her shoulder. "It wasn't important."

He considered pushing the issue, but figured maybe he was best off not knowing. He lay awake for what felt like hours, marinating in his own guilt and self-loathing.

When he woke in the morning and reached for Lexi, she wasn't there. He got out of bed and pulled on his robe. He figured Lexi was downstairs in the kitchen making tea, but he found her in her bedroom, packing. She was leaving him.

He was more disappointed than surprised. "Going somewhere?" he asked.

She turned to him, looking tired and sad. "Good morning."

He doubted that. "You don't have to do this."

"Yes, I do."

He had half a mind to beg her to stay, to swear that things would change, but that would just be cruel and selfish. The best thing he could do for Lexi was let her go.

"Are you going back to your father?"

"God, no. I would never give him the satisfaction."

"Good. He doesn't deserve you. And don't worry about money. I'll see that you and the baby are set for life."

"I appreciate that, but I can't spend the rest of my life with other people always taking care of me. I need to do this on my own."

"Where will you go?"

"Tara said I can stay with her until I'm on my feet."

He was tempted to insist that she stay with him, at least until the baby was born. By then, the house would be ready and she could stay there. But if she needed to prove something to herself, he wasn't going to stop her. Maybe she would realize how hard it was to be on her own, and come back to him.

But Lexi was tough, and he had the feeling she would be just fine. He would miss her, and always care about her, but the truth was she deserved a better man than Mitch Brody, and he hoped someday she would find him.

* * *

Lexi had never been so humiliated in her life.

Her father had been right all along. Mitch didn't love her. He "cared" for her, which she was pretty sure translated into caring about her father's senatorial support. Just as her father had warned her.

She could be a bitch about it and see that her father did everything in his power to crush them, but she just wasn't the vindictive type. After all, it wasn't Mitch's fault that Lexi had fallen in love with him. She had done that herself, creating her own fantasy world. Mitch had told her time and time again that their marriage was just business, but she hadn't listened.

"You have to tell him the truth," Tara said, handing her a steaming cup of tea. She took a seat in the armchair across from the couch where Lexi sat. "It's his baby. He deserves to be a part of its life."

"I will tell him. Eventually."

"When? After the kid is out of college?"

"After I get back on my feet, when I don't need his help." Which might be a while considering she had no job skills, no driver's license and all she'd had the will to do the past four days was sit curled up on the couch in Tara's condo, feeling sorry for herself.

The prospect of supporting herself and the baby was beyond overwhelming, but she was determined to figure out a way.

"He's going to have to pay child support," Tara said.

She knew that was inevitable. He would insist, because that's the kind of man he was. But she wasn't ready to accept his help. Not yet. Although at this point, there was no way he would be anything but furious with her when he found out the baby was his, and he would be completely justified. She should have told him the truth that day he assumed the baby was Lance's, whether he believed her or not. At least then she could say that she'd been honest. But she had procrastinated and put it off and painted herself into a tiny little corner that she had no hope of getting out of unscathed.

When all was said and done, everything was her fault. She had made this mess, done this to herself, and she was the only one who could fix it.

But right now, she just wasn't ready.

Mitch sat in his office, staring out the window, finding it impossible to concentrate on his work. Since Lexi had left him, he hadn't been able to think straight. Hell, he'd barely been able to function. He just couldn't stop thinking about her, *missing* her. He'd stripped his bed and pillows, even sprayed air freshener, but he could still smell her, still feel her presence in the room. He couldn't drive his car without picturing her behind the wheel, so adorably nervous, but determined to learn. He couldn't walk into the kitchen without remembering the night they had made love there.

He had lost all interest in buying the house. Part

of what had drawn him to it was her excitement, the thought of them being a family. Now there didn't seem much point in leaving his townhouse, even though he was miserable whenever he was there.

She had been indelibly ingrained in every part of his life, and he couldn't help wondering if this feeling he was having, the crushing ache, the longing he felt every time he thought of her—which was pretty much all the time—meant he loved her.

"Why don't you just call her?"

Mitch turned to find Lance standing in the doorway, arms folded across his chest. He sighed and asked, "Is it that obvious?"

Lance grinned. "You look just like I felt when Kate left me. And trust me when I say, if she loves you, she'll forgive whatever you did."

Lance was a good brother. He had always been there to protect Mitch, had always taken care of him and supported him no matter what. He owed him the truth. He'd already waited too long. "Come in, and close the door."

Lance did as he asked. "What's going on?"

"Lexi is pregnant," he said.

Lance laughed. "Already? You two sure didn't waste any time."

"It's not what you think. The baby...it's not mine."

He frowned. "What do you mean, it's not yours?"

"She's more than three months."

"Three months? That would mean she got

pregnant…" He trailed off, so Mitch finished the sentence for him.

"Right around the time you two were engaged."

He shook his head in disbelief. "Son of a bitch. All that time I felt so guilty for going behind her back with Kate, and she was cheating on *me?*"

His brother could not be that dense. "She wasn't cheating on you, you idiot. The baby is yours."

Instead of looking shocked or humbled, or even angry, Lance laughed and said, "No, it isn't."

He must have been in some serious denial. "Yes, Lance. It is. She told me herself."

"Then she was lying."

"How can you know that for sure?"

"Easy. Because I never slept with her."

"What?"

"I only kissed her once and believe me when I say that it wasn't all that red hot for either of us."

"Then why, on my honeymoon, did you tell me that if I slept with her it wouldn't be a disappointment?"

He shrugged. "A guess. It wasn't, was it?"

"Of course not, but…" This didn't make any sense. "Why would she tell me it was you if…?" Realization hit him with a force that knocked the breath from his lungs. "Oh, shit."

He must have gone white as death, because Lance asked, "Jesus, Mitch, what's wrong?"

How could he have been so stupid? "I'm an ass, that's what's wrong."

"I'm sorry, but you've completely lost me."

Despite what he'd believed at first, he knew without a doubt that Lexi hadn't been capable of hopping from Mitch's bed to Lance's. And that could only mean one thing.

"It's mine," he said, and at his brother's confused look added, "The baby. Lexi is having *my* baby."

"Then why did she tell you it was mine?"

"She didn't. When she told me she was pregnant, I just assumed it was yours."

Lance looked more confused than ever. "I thought you said she was three months. How could it be yours?"

Mitch dropped his head in his hands. He had no choice but to tell Lance the truth. He looked up at his big brother. His protector. "There's something I have to tell you. Something I should have told you months ago."

"What?" Lance asked.

"Remember that week I spent with Lexi on your behalf?"

Lance nodded. "Of course."

"That last night, before you proposed, we... I slept with her." Mitch waited for the impending explosion.

"I'm not an idiot," Lance said calmly. "I saw the way you two acted after the D.C. trip. I kind of figured something happened."

Mitch couldn't believe that Lance knew, or at least suspected, this entire time. "You're not mad?"

"It wasn't a real engagement."

"But you're my brother. You were going to marry her."

"But I didn't. If it would make you feel better, I could punch you again. Although it looks like you're doing a pretty fair job of beating yourself up."

"I deserve worse, believe me."

"Let me get this straight. She told you she was pregnant, and you just automatically assumed it was mine?"

He nodded.

"So, what you were saying to her was that you believed she slept with you, then turned around and hopped in the sack with your brother?"

Mitch pinched the bridge of his nose. "Yeah, pretty much." Lexi must have been furious. Not to mention humiliated.

"Why didn't she just tell you the truth?"

"She probably thought I wouldn't believe her."

"Would you have believed her?"

"Probably not."

"I hate to say this, Mitch, but you are an ass."

He wanted to be furious with Lexi for not telling him the truth, for lying by omission, but the only person he could muster any anger for was himself. All of this, this entire jumbled-up mess, was his fault. Yes, Lexi had lied about using him, but he had spent a week wining and dining her, and yes, seducing her, only to turn around and say it was a mistake. Could he really blame her for being hurt and lashing out? If he had known her better then, he would have realized she wasn't capable of what she'd claimed. She would never use anyone.

Ironically, if he had been honest with his brother from the start, he would have learned the truth and they could have avoided this entire mess.

"What I still don't get is *how* she got pregnant," Mitch said.

His brother smirked. "You don't really need me to explain that to you, do you, Mitch?"

Mitch sighed. "I know *how,* I'm just not sure when it could have happened. We were careful."

Lance shrugged. "Birth control has been known to fail."

"I think… I think I love her."

"You think?"

No. He *knew* he loved her. It was the only explanation for how miserable he was without her. He rose from his chair. "I have to go see her."

"It's about time."

Mitch grabbed his jacket and headed for the door. Then he remembered there was a slight hitch to his plan. He had no idea where she was.

Lance must have read his mind because he said, "She's staying at her assistant's condo." Mitch looked confused. "Wives are an excellent source of information."

Hopefully, Mitch would be finding that out for himself. He was going to ask Lexi to marry him, and this time they were going to do it right.

Fourteen

The doorbell rang, and since Lexi was home alone and not expecting anyone, she peered out the front window to see who was standing on the porch. Her breath caught and her heart started to hammer a million miles an hour when she saw that it was Mitch.

What could he possibly want?

He must have come right from work because he was wearing a suit. He glanced her way and though she dropped the curtain, she wasn't fast enough. He saw her.

Damn it!

He knocked on the door and called, "Come on, Lexi, I need to talk to you."

She was going to shout back that everything they needed to say had been said, but it was a lie. Instead, she unlocked the door and pulled it open. "What?"

"I finally figured it out."

"Figured what out?" she asked, stepping aside so he could come in.

"When it happened."

She shut the door and turned to him. "When what happened?"

"When you got pregnant."

His words nearly stopped her heart. She hoped he didn't mean what she thought he meant. "W-when?"

"The third time, in the middle of the night. For a few minutes we didn't use a condom. Am I right?"

Stunned, she asked, "How did you…?"

"I figured it was time to tell my brother the truth. Imagine his surprise when he found out that he was having a child with a woman he never slept with."

She chewed her lip. "I never actually said—"

"That you slept with him. I know."

"I was going to tell you—"

"But you didn't trust me," he finished for her. "I get it. I was an ass."

Huh? What was he saying? "You're not angry?" Lexi asked.

"How can I be angry at you when this entire mess is my fault?"

What? This was her fault. "This whole thing started because I lied and said I used you."

"Lexi, this whole thing started because *I* told *you* we made a mistake, because I didn't want to admit that I was falling in love with you."

He *loved* her?

No, of course he didn't. She knew exactly what this was. Now that he knew about the baby, he wanted them to be together. Or maybe he was worried that he and Lance would lose the senator's support. Either way, it was obvious he would say anything to get his way, even if that meant lying about loving her.

"Aren't you going to say anything?" he asked.

"Like what?"

"Hell, I don't know, maybe something like, you love me, too?"

"I won't stay with you just for the baby's sake."

"I don't recall asking you to. This is entirely selfish. I want you to stay with me for my sake. Because I love you."

"If you're worried about losing my father's support, I'll see to it that you don't."

"This has nothing to do with that. As far as I'm concerned, he can take his support and shove it where the sun don't shine."

"I don't believe you. It's the only reason you married me."

"Maybe it was," he admitted. "But it's not why I want to marry you now."

"We're already married."

"I know, but I was thinking that it would be nice if we had a big wedding, did it right."

"No. What would be nice is a neat and tidy divorce."

He folded his arms across his chest. "You still honestly think I'm doing this for your father's support?"

"Among other things."

"You don't believe I love you?"

She shook her head.

"Okay," he said. "I guess I'm just going to have to prove it to you."

Good luck with that.

He pulled out his cell phone, dialed a number and put it on speaker.

"Who are you calling?" she asked. If she wouldn't believe him, did he think she would believe someone else?

"Senator Cavanaugh's office," she heard her father's secretary say.

"It's Mitch Brody, could I speak with the senator? It's urgent."

"One moment, Mr. Brody." She put him on hold.

"What are you doing?" she asked.

"They say actions speak louder than words."

Oh, no. He wouldn't.

Her father came on the line, his tone exasperated. "What do you want, Brody?"

"Hello, Senator, I just wanted to tell you to take you support and sh—"

"Mitch!" she screeched. She snatched the phone away from him and snapped it shut. "Are you crazy?"

"No. I love you."

His phone immediately began to ring, but Lexi ignored it. "Why would you do that?"

"How many times are you going to make me say it? It isn't about the baby, and it's not about the senator. You could be carrying the postman's baby and I would still love you. And my business, my life, means nothing if you aren't in it."

Would he say all that if he didn't really mean it? If he didn't love her?

"You love *me?*" she asked.

"Yes, *you*. You know, we really have to work on this self-esteem issue you have."

She bit her lip and nodded, afraid that if she said anything, she would burst into tears. Mitch must have realized, because he pulled her into his arms and held her. She could hardly believe it was real— that after everything they had been through, this was actually going to work out.

"You know, you could say it, too," he said.

She smiled up at him. "I love you, Mitch. I've known since that week in D.C. that I wanted to spend the rest of my life with you."

He gazed at her, his eyes so full of love and affection she had to swallow back a sob. He caressed her cheek and said, "I can hardly wait for us to be a family."

Tears slipped from the corners of her eyes and he brushed them away with his thoughts.

"Those better be happy tears," he said.

She grinned up at him. "Absolutely."

He grinned and kissed the tip of her nose. "We had kind of a bumpy start, I guess."

"A little," she said, but she knew that from now, it would only get better.

* * * * *

THE MAVERICK'S VIRGIN MISTRESS

BY
JENNIFER LEWIS

Jennifer Lewis has been dreaming up stories for as long as she can remember and is thrilled to be able to share them with readers. She has lived on both sides of the Atlantic and worked in media and the arts before she grew bold enough to put pen to paper. Happily settled in New York with her family, she would love to hear from readers at jen@jenlewis.com. Visit her website at www. jenlewis.com.

For Anne, Carol, Jerri, Kate, Leeanne and Marie

One

Who on earth could be calling at this time of night?

Alicia Montoya reached out from under the covers and groped for the phone on her bedside table. She squinted at the green numerals on the clock.

2:07. *What the heck?*

She lifted the phone to her ear.

"Hello?"

"You're okay. Thank God."

"Who is this?" Her sleepy whisper was barely audible.

"Hi, beautiful."

Oh, boy. His rich, deep voice flowed into her ear and started to awaken parts of her she'd never even known she had until she met Rick Jones. "Hi, Rick."

"I'm so glad you're fine."

Alicia glanced at the clock again. "I was fine until the phone woke me. Didn't I tell you not to call me at home?"

She wondered if her brother Alex had heard the phone. Probably. She was a deep sleeper so it may have been ringing for a while.

Pretty much nothing could happen in the Houston-metro area without her brother being aware of it. Any minute now he'd come barreling in to see what was going on.

"Sweetheart, are you sure you're not married?" Rick teased her relentlessly about her insistence on keeping their relationship secret.

If you could call it a relationship. They hadn't actually kissed yet, but they'd held hands once. That counted, right?

"I'm most definitely not married." She laughed. "Not even close. But I told you my brother is insanely overprotective. Believe me, you do not want him to know you're calling me at two in the morning."

"Why not? You're a grown woman. You can do whatever you want at two in the morning." His tone suggested there were some delicious things they could be doing together at this very moment.

Alicia wriggled under her warm sheets. What would it be like to have Rick right here in bed with her? To run her fingertips over his hard chest or through his silky dark hair?

She had no idea what that would be like, and if Alex learned about Rick, she wouldn't get a chance to find out.

"Trust me on this. It's better if he doesn't know about you. Why are you calling me in the middle of the night, anyway? To torment me with the sound of your sexy voice?"

She smiled in the privacy of darkness. She'd never met a man she felt so comfortable around. With Rick, she could relax enough to tease and flirt. To just...be herself.

"Actually, I was calling to see if you're okay. I'm watching TV and there's breaking coverage of a big fire in Somerset right now. It's hard to tell what's going on in the dark but it almost looks like El Diablo."

"What?" Alicia wondered if she was dreaming. "Our ranch is fine."

Still, fear pricked through her and she slid out of bed onto the cool wood floor. "Hold on, let me look out the window." She hurried across the room and pulled back the thick curtains.

"Oh, my God." Her hand flew to her mouth. An orange glow pierced the darkness.

The flashing lights of emergency vehicles moved along the drive through the ranch, and even through the insulated glass she heard the throb of a helicopter circling overhead.

"It's on fire! The barn! Oh, no, the animals are in there—" She darted across the dark room to the closet.

"I'm coming over."

"No, please don't." Panic flashed through her as she tugged on jeans under her nightshirt. "Whatever's going on, you coming here will make it worse. I have to find Alex. The calves...." She struggled to pull on a pair of boots. "I've got to go."

"Please, let me come."

"No, Rick. Not now. I'll call you as soon as I can." She hung up the phone.

"Alex!" She called out into the hallway of the big ranch house.

A light shone downstairs, and Alex's bedroom door stood open. "Alex, are you here?"

No answer.

She dashed down the stairs two at a time and ran to the front door. She opened it to the smell of smoke and the wail of sirens.

A mass of heaving flame engulfed the barn roof and lit the darkness all the way to the house. "Alex!"

Alicia took off running across the lawn that separated the house from the barn. She could see figures moving, running in the eerie glow from the fire. Shouting mingled with the roar of flames crackling, wood splintering and water gushing from hoses.

"Alex, where are you?" Fear made her voice crack.

Alex was always at the center of everything. She knew with every cell of her body that he was inside that burning barn.

Heart pounding, she raced toward the fire. He might be bossy and overbearing, but he was also the best brother and the warmest, most caring man in the world.

He'd raised her since their parents died and managed to scrape and struggle to provide a good life for them—a wonderful life, now that he was so successful.

A figure rushed up to her in the dark and she recognized one of the ranch hands. "Diego, have you seen Alex?"

"He sent me to wake you. He said to make sure you stay inside the house until he comes."

"He's okay?"

Diego hesitated. "He's trying to rescue the calves."

"Oh, no! I knew he was in there. We have to get him out." She started running to the barn.

Diego grabbed her sleeve. "Miss Alicia, please. Alex wouldn't want you near the fire."

"I don't care what that stubborn fool wants. I've got to get him out of there."

She wrenched her arm free and took off running again. She wasn't the Our Lady of Fatima senior track champion for nothing.

She heard Diego behind her, pleading for her to stop, protesting that Alex had personally entrusted him with her safety and that if he found out—

"There he is!" She saw him emerge from the vast doorway on one side of the barn, driving a herd of calves in front of him.

The young cows were confused and ran in all directions—even trying to get back into the burning barn—as the workers tried to shove them out into the safety of the darkness.

Alicia ran into their midst and grabbed hold of the collar of the calf nearest her. "Come on, princess, you don't want to go back in there." She tugged it away from the doorway.

The hot glow of flame brightened the inside of the barn and seared her skin like noonday sun. Cinders whirled in the smoky air, and ash pricked at her eyes. Every instinct told her to run far, far away.

But she turned to see Alex heading back inside. She gave the calf a slap on the rump to drive it out and plunged for the doorway, toward Alex.

"Alejandro Montoya! You get out of that burning barn or I'll—"

Alex wheeled around. "Alicia, you shouldn't be here. I told Diego—"

"I know what you told Diego, but I'm here now and you need to get out of this barn before the roof collapses. The whole ridgeline is on fire!"

He frowned and glanced back into the barn. "I'll just check to make sure they're all out."

"No!" She grabbed the front of his shirt. His face was almost black with soot but his dark eyes gleamed with purpose.

Desperation made tears spring to her eyes. "Don't risk your life!"

"We've got them all out!" A voice shouted from the darkness. "I counted. All forty-five calves are safe."

"Thank God." Alex grabbed Alicia and threw her over his shoulder in a fireman's lift that knocked the breath from her lungs.

Alicia fought the urge to kick and protest his overbearing reaction. But he was running from the barn, so at least she'd got him heading in the right direction.

"You need to get back in the house and stay there until I come for you!" he shouted as he set her down on her feet a safe distance from the barn.

"I'm not a child, Alex. I can help."

"Nothing's going to help save the barn." Alex winced as a sidewall gave way and the roof started to lean to one side, like a ship keeling over in rough seas.

"It was here before the house. It's over a hundred years old. It's been home and shelter to thousands of animals, and now…" He shook his head.

Alicia bit her lip. She knew how much every inch of this ranch meant to her brother. He'd sweated and saved and worked so hard for it.

Buying El Diablo had been a crowning moment in

both of their lives. The proof that despite all the odds stacked against them, they'd made it and were going to be fine.

She looked back at the barn, now a heaving mass of bright flame. "What happened?"

"We don't know. The fire came out of nowhere. Thank heaven we have smoke alarms that woke Dave and Manny in the apartment above it. They called the fire department, but the building was already going up by the time the first truck arrived."

A tall man strode toward them. Reflected flames illuminated his police badge and the handcuffs glinting at his waist.

"This way, please." He gestured to the driveway where a host of different emergency vehicles winked and flashed their lights in the orange half-light. "We need you all in one place."

"I'm the owner," Alex said. "I need to protect my animals."

The tall policeman squared his shoulders. "Everyone must be interviewed for the investigation."

"What do you mean, investigation?" Alicia squinted through the firelit darkness.

"It's early yet, but the fire marshal thinks this fire was deliberately set. They found empty gas containers near where the blaze started."

Alicia bit her lip. *Who would do this?*

Alex stood up for himself, and as a result he'd made some enemies, but who could hate him—or her—enough to destroy the ranch?

"Arson?" Alex's voice rumbled like a train. "If I find out who did it I'll—"

"Please, sir. Come this way. We have to take a statement from everyone, and I need your cooperation."

Alex blew out a snort of disgust and took Alicia's hand. "Whoever did this will pay."

She kept her mouth shut. No use arguing with him at a time like this. Better to get him out of danger and focus on getting through this awful night.

They picked their way across the grass. An ember landed on Alex's shirt and Alicia slapped it out with her palm.

A strange thought occurred to her. "Didn't Lance Brody's place have a fire recently?"

"There was a blaze at Brody Oil and Gas, yes. That swine had the nerve to accuse *me* of setting it. As if I would stoop to something like that." He clucked his tongue.

She frowned. "If Lance Brody really thinks you burned his building, could he have done this as revenge?"

She could tell by the look on Alex's face that he'd already thought of this. The rivalry between Alex and Lance Brody went back all the way to Maverick High School, where they'd jostled for position on the soccer team. The last thing she needed was to fan the flames of that rivalry.

"I'm sure it wasn't him." She waved her hand in the smoky air. "I don't know why I just said that. Why would a successful businessman get involved in a criminal act?"

"They have paid flunkeys to do their dirty work," Alex growled. "I wouldn't put anything past Lance Brody, or his brother, Mitch. I've been a burr under their saddles for years. Maybe this is their way of trying to push me out of town."

He turned to the barn, where the roof had now collapsed and flames licked out of the hayloft windows.

His eyes flashed with a mix of anger and pain. "But no one's going to run me off El Diablo, and whoever did this will regret the day they were born."

At lunch the next day, Alex paced back and forth across the dining room at the ranch, his burger growing cold on the plate.

"Alicia, it's not safe for you here right now. If someone's out to get me, who knows what they'll try next. You can stay with El Gato."

Alicia looked up from her plate as goose bumps spread over her skin. "I'll be fine here. Besides, you need someone to look after you."

She pointed to his plate with her best schoolmarm expression. "Eat your food."

"I'm serious, 'Manita. It's not safe."

"Staying with Paul 'El Gato' Rodriquez is what's not safe. I know you won't hear a word against him, but everyone knows he's involved in drug trafficking."

Alex grunted as he slid into his chair. "They just don't like to see a Latino make a lot of money. You'd be shocked if you knew how many people think I'm involved with drugs or guns or something. They don't think we can make money the old-fashioned way like they do."

He took a bite of his hamburger. "That's why joining the Texas Cattleman's Club was such a big deal for me. When I'm there, I'm one of them, a member of the club. They have to smile at me and act polite, even if they'd really prefer to see me hang." He grinned. "I love that."

Alicia hated the way her brother still felt like an outsider, even now that he was one of the richest men in the area.

"You were accepted into the Texas Cattleman's Club because you're a man of honor and an upstanding member of Somerset society. You *are* one of them."

"That's one of the many reasons why I love you, sis. You have such great faith in the human spirit." He winked as he took a sip of soda. "But you're still not staying here. El Gato can protect you from anything."

"I'm sure he can. He's probably got nine millimeters stashed in the trunk of his car, but frankly that kind of 'protection' makes me nervous."

"He's one of us. When the going gets tough, sometimes it's better to stick with your own."

"I don't consider a suspected criminal to be one of 'my own' in any way."

"You know what I mean. When you come from the barrio, you see the world a little differently."

"You're talking as if I didn't grow up in the same house as you." Alicia bristled. She hated when her brother treated her like a kid. "I was there, too, remember? I know what hard times are like, and I'm more than glad to have left them behind. You need to get rid of that chip on your shoulder," she said, still trying to figure out how to change Alex's mind. "I could go stay with one of the neighbors."

Alex narrowed his eyes. "I don't trust those people. Not right now."

"How about Maria Nunez? You've known her as long as I have. You let me sleep over at her house when we were in school. I'm sure she won't mind me staying a few nights."

He grunted. "I always suspected that Maria of having a wild streak. Still, her parents are good people. Does she live at home?"

Alicia laughed. "No. She's twenty-six years old, remember? She has an apartment in Bellaire. Very safe area."

"If she's not married, she should be at home with her family." Alex took a swig of coffee.

"It's not the nineteenth century anymore, Alex. Deal with it. I'll call her right away. If she says no, then I'll go to El Gato, okay?"

The lie tingled on her tongue for a second, since she had no intention of going anywhere near Paul Rodriquez and his crew of scary henchmen, even if he was Alex's oldest friend.

Alex clucked with disapproval. "Stubborn."

"Sensible." She smiled sweetly. "You know I am. Don't you trust me?"

Her heart fluttered as she realized he had every reason not to.

"All right, you can stay with Maria. You are sensible, and I'm very proud of you. I love you like crazy, 'Manita, you know that?"

"I do, and I love you, too, you big bear of a brother." She rounded the table and gave him a kiss on his thick head of hair before going upstairs, heart pounding.

Alicia closed her bedroom door carefully before picking up her phone.

She hadn't even dared add Rick's number to her favorites, in case Alex happened to pick up her phone and notice a new number there among her old friends from school.

Anticipation mingled with anxiety made her fingers twitchy as she dialed.

It rang only once.

"Hey, beautiful." That soft, seductive voice.

A smile spread over her face. "What if I'm not looking at all beautiful right now?"

"Impossible. You can't help it," he said, making her feel warm all over. "I saw on the news they put the fire out and that no one was hurt. What a relief."

"Tell me about it. We rescued every single calf, only a few scrapes and cuts on them. The barn is gone, though. Nothing left but soggy blackened wood. And there was a six-month supply of good hay in there that we'd put up for the winter."

"I'm sorry to hear that. I hope it was insured."

"It was, but the barn is irreplaceable. It was one of the first buildings in Somerset. A true historic landmark. I was hoping to get it preservation status, but I guess I can forget about that now." She sighed. "It could have been much worse. If the wind was blowing harder, the house could have caught fire."

"I wish I were there to give you a hug."

"Trust me, I could really use one."

"Then since you won't let me set foot on El Diablo, you're going to have to come here to get one."

Adrenaline flashed through Alicia. How could she ask this delicately? Or even indelicately? "Can I spend the night with you?"

A beat of silence made her pulse throb, but it was followed by a rushed, "Of course." His enthusiasm almost made her laugh.

"Wow, that sounded bad, didn't it? It's just that Alex

doesn't think it's safe for me to stay here. The police think the fire was set deliberately and he's worried the arsonist will come back to finish the job. He wants me to go stay with an old school friend of his, but I don't like the guy."

"I don't want you near any guy except me. And in case you didn't know, my suite at the Omni has four bedrooms."

"You're kidding."

"Not even a little. Pack your bags and come on over."

"My car was parked behind the barn. It pretty much melted."

"No sweat, I'll come get you." She could almost hear him panting like an excited puppy.

She smiled. "I don't think so. If Alex sees your car, it'll ruin everything. I'll ask him to drive me to the Texas Cattleman's Club. That way he won't suspect anything and you can pick me up there. I could be there by four this afternoon."

"I'll meet you outside."

Alicia frowned. It might be nice to hang out at the club a while. She wouldn't mind showing her new beau off to her friends. But maybe he'd just want to get her bags back to his place.

Or get *her* back to his place.

A naughty smile snuck across her lips and her body tingled with anticipation. She'd be all alone with Rick in his hotel suite, and she had a feeling that tonight would be a night she'd never forget.

"Great, I'll meet you by the front door. See you then."

She hung up the phone, downright jumpy with excitement.

She'd recently bought some sexy lingerie at Sweet Nothings in anticipation of becoming more intimate with Rick. She had it hidden away in the back of her dresser drawer so Alex wouldn't stumble across it while looking for something.

Now hopefully she'd finally get a chance to put it on—and watch Rick take it off.

Justin pressed the button to raise the roof on his Porsche convertible. He wasn't sure Alicia would appreciate the wind in her hair.

Like every inch of her that he'd had the pleasure to see so far, her dark hair was silky smooth and perfectly groomed.

And he was looking forward to seeing a lot more of her now that he'd have her all to himself, in his suite, for days—and nights—on end.

He'd like to see desire flare in those big brown eyes, and run his eager hands all over her glowing olive skin.

A wicked grin spread across his face.

Then he wiped if off.

Cool your jets. First of all, Alicia was traumatized by the fire at the ranch she shared with her brother. She needed his support, not his hands pawing all over her.

Second, she had no idea who he really was.

He cursed and tapped his fingers impatiently on the wheel as he waited at a traffic light.

Why did he have to call himself Rick Jones when he met her?

Sure, he used the name often, but usually for making hotel reservations or when he met someone who had "gold digger" written all over her. There were definitely

times when being Justin Dupree—of *those* Duprees—
was a serious liability.

Once people knew he had more money than God,
they treated him differently. And he was tired of the
society press tailing him like a bloodhound, looking for
more stories for their gossip columns. Thanks to them,
he now had an embarrassing reputation as a playboy
that was really only half-deserved.

Okay, maybe three-quarters. But that was all in the
past.

He was thirty now and more settled. He wasn't so
excited about partying all night. Lately, he wanted to
spend quality time getting to know a woman before he
slept with her.

Take Alicia. How many dates had they been on?
Maybe eight, and he still hadn't slept with her.

Or even kissed her.

He blew out a breath. The light turned green and he
honked his horn to get the car in front of him moving.
Eight dates and not even a kiss on the lips? That was
ridiculous. And he wasn't entirely sure how it had
happened, either.

There was something so perfect about Alicia, so
pure and sweet and gentle, that he never quite felt right
about asking her back to his place. She was the kind of
girl you'd send flowers to, the kind whose parents you'd
chat with when you picked her up at her house. The
kind you'd buy a corsage for on prom night.

Except that they were both adults and her parents
had been dead for years. Why did Alicia Montoya turn
him from a hardened ladies' man back into an eager and
apprehensive schoolboy?

He wove through traffic on the beltway and took the exit for Somerset. Alicia Montoya was something else, and he didn't mind waiting for the chance to weave his fingers into her soft hair.

"I'm not Rick Jones." How hard was it to just say it?

One snag was that Alex knew him. He'd used the alias partly so he could ask Alicia about Alex and maybe dig up some useful information about him for Mitch and Lance Brody. If he actually did go to El Diablo, Alex would recognize him from the club.

And then there was Alicia herself.

Usually once he told a girl he was actually Justin Dupree, she laughed off the deception and fawned all over him, thrilled to be dating the notorious shipping heir instead of some regular guy.

Alicia though…

He let out a low whistle. He suspected she wouldn't take the deception lightly. She'd gone to a convent school, for crying out loud. She carried white linen handkerchiefs in her purse. Her French-tipped finger-nails did not look like they'd ever been anywhere Mother Superior wouldn't approve of.

Did he really want to blow his chance of feeling those luscious, manicured nails rake down his back?

No. He didn't. Which was why he wasn't going to mention the little name issue just yet. He'd wait until the drama of the fire blew over. Until he'd held her in his arms and whispered sweet nothings in her ear.

Until he'd made hot, wild love to her all night long.

Then he'd tell her.

Two

Alicia paced under the elegant awning outside the Texas Cattleman's Club.

Bees buzzed around flowers blooming in the carved-stone planters. Sunlight glistened on the polished-marble walkway and flashed off the brass accents on the door as members came and went, waving hello and stopping to commiserate about the fire.

Alicia tried to act normal, as though she wasn't about to embark on possibly the biggest "first" in her life.

She'd never spent the night at a man's house before. She'd never…

She'd never done a lot of things, and she hoped to rectify that, starting tonight.

The hushed sound of a powerful engine made her glance up. Rick pulled up in front of the awning and leaned out of the driver's seat of his silver Porsche.

The sun shone in his tousled dark hair. "How do you manage to look more gorgeous every time I see you?" He cocked his head and fixed his bold blue eyes on hers.

Alicia blushed. She had gone to a little extra effort with her appearance today. She wanted everything to be perfect.

She gestured to her luggage. "I tried not to pack too much stuff. Just some clothes for work and a few casual things."

Like the pretty lingerie she'd bought last week.

He stowed her bags in the trunk. Black tailored slacks clung to his powerful thighs and a well-cut polo shirt emphasized the width of his shoulders. Was it fair for a man to be so dangerously handsome?

She could hardly believe he was interested in her.

"Do you want to go in?" She gestured to the front door. Cara was inside and she'd love to see the look on her friend's face when she got an eyeful of Rick.

Although she'd met him at the club, she wasn't sure if he was a member. The couple of times she'd mentioned his name to friends, she'd drawn blank stares.

He hesitated and glanced at the double doors that led into the wood-paneled sanctuary. "I'd actually rather get back to the hotel. I have a business call coming. Nothing major, it won't take long."

"Oh, no problem. Let's go then." She tried not to let her disappointment show.

Of course he had business to conduct. She wasn't exactly sure what he did, but judging from the car he drove and the fact that he had a four-bedroom suite at the Houston Omni, it must be pretty darn important.

She couldn't expect him to put his whole life on hold because she needed a place to stay.

At the Omni, the bellhop removed Alicia's bags from the trunk and she felt strangely weightless as she watched them disappear across the glistening marble floor of the lobby.

No turning back now.

Not that she wanted to. Rick was so thoughtful and sweet. He squeezed her hand as they walked to the bank of elevators.

She squeezed back, trying not to let her nerves show. He had no idea this was new for her. That she'd never spent the night with a man before.

Or, in fact, ever had sex.

At age twenty-six.

How shocked would he be if he knew? At this point, it was such a humiliating secret, she even kept it from her girlfriends. Only Maria—who she'd stayed close to since high school—knew the terrible truth.

When Alicia had asked permission to use her as an alibi for her stay at Rick's, Maria had been so excited she could barely get words out. "Who is he?" she asked. "Is he cute? I'll only lie for you if you promise to go all the way!"

Alicia had laughed off Maria's exhortations, but being a virgin at twenty-six was no laughing matter.

She flashed Rick a smile as he pressed the elevator button.

She wasn't even quite sure how it had happened. One minute she was a teenager telling boys she wasn't that kind of girl, the next she was looking in the mirror wondering where her so-called youth went.

Now she'd found the right man to finally initiate her into womanhood. Rick was perfect. Almost too perfect, in fact. She knew Alex would be suspicious of him.

But then Alex was suspicious of everyone.

"Be it ever so humble…" Rick winked as he slid the keycard into the lock.

"Oh, my." Alicia's jaw dropped as the door opened to an elegant interior, lush with fine fabrics and gleaming antiques. "This is a hotel room?"

"Not really. It's more of a furnished apartment with all the amenities. Not too many apartment buildings come with room service, and with all the traveling I do, it's nice to have everything taken care of."

"I guess if you don't have a wife to take care of you, a hotel staff is the next best thing." She smiled, looking around the luxurious environment.

Rick's silence made her turn.

Alicia bit her lip. A wife? What on earth was she thinking? Now he'd suspect her of auditioning for the role.

"And I guess you don't have to worry about mowing your lawn." She tried to push the conversation forward, to distract from her gaffe. "But you probably wouldn't anyway."

Duh! Rick Jones had probably never mowed a lawn in his life. Men who hung out at the Texas Cattleman's Club had "people" for that.

She and Alex were probably the only members who weren't born with silver spoons in their mouths. Another reminder that she was out of her element here in Rick's luxurious penthouse.

"Which bedroom would you like? We're on the

corner so each one gives you a different view of the city."

He ushered her into a large room with gold draperies, an elegant sleigh bed and a panoramic view west over the Galleria area.

"Gee, I don't know if this is fancy enough for me." Alicia grinned.

"I see what you mean. And really, the morning light is better from the east."

He guided her out the door. Pleasure shivered through her at the feel of his hand at the base of her spine.

They entered a room with a large four-poster bed laden with embroidered pillows. Elegant white draperies fluttered slightly in the air-conditioner breeze. The view across the treetops of Memorial Park—all the way to the shimmering skyscrapers of downtown Houston— was breathtaking.

"Then again, sometimes it's annoying being woken up too early."

Gentle pressure from his palm sent heat snaking through her belly. She allowed him to ease her out the door.

The third bedroom had a Japanese flavor with willow-green draperies and images of cranes and lilies on the wall.

The bedpost and furniture were crafted from elegant bamboo. A bubbling fountain ornamented one corner of the bright space.

The view looked down on a wooded bend in the river—a strangely wild vista for this part of the world— and added to the impression of a lush retreat.

Alicia smiled. "Pretty! I like this one."

"Make yourself at home. You can stay as long as you want. And I mean that quite literally. I have the suite reserved for the next two years."

She laughed. How much money did this guy have? This suite probably cost ten thousand dollars a night. "Hopefully, my brother will let me come back home before then, but I appreciate the offer."

Rick's striking blue eyes fixed on hers. "Now, dinner. I usually have it sent up from the hotel restaurant, but we could go out if you prefer."

"I don't want to put you to any trouble."

"If you insisted on me cooking it myself, I think we'd both be in trouble, but as long as professionals are involved, it's no trouble at all." A naughty dimple appeared in his left cheek. "Let me get you a menu."

He slipped out of the room, leaving Alicia to catch her breath.

Her heart pounded under her pale-blue blouse and her high heels sank into the soft carpet.

Houston lay at her feet like a rug unfurled, the sun setting over the trees and rooftops casting a soft glow over the delicate furnishings of the lovely bedroom.

Tonight was the night. By tomorrow morning she'd be a woman in every sense of the word.

Rick appeared in the door with the menu, startling her out of her thoughts. "If you don't like anything on the menu, we can talk to the chef. He's a pretty cool guy. He knows I'm wild about lobster so he saves the best ones for me."

"I love lobster." Alicia looked up. "I always feel guilty eating something that can live so long, but they're too delicious."

"Done." Rick snatched the menu from her fingertips, which tingled as his hand brushed against them. "And your visit here definitely calls for champagne."

They ate in the suite's formal dining room. Champagne sparkled in crystal flutes as candlelight illuminated the details in the wood-paneled walls, and cast shadows across the white, linen tablecloth.

The chef had prepared them an array of different sauces for the lobster and some creative and colorful salads.

The champagne tickled her nose and she was careful to take only the tiniest of sips so she wouldn't get tipsy. She didn't want to miss a single minute of tonight.

Rick leaned forward. "Does Alex have any suspects for the fire?"

Guilt speared Alicia as she realized she'd totally forgotten about Alex and the fire. "I don't think so, but there was a suspicious fire at the Brody headquarters a while back and they had the nerve to blame Alex, so being a guy, he's decided the Brodys might be responsible."

For a moment, she thought she saw a shadow flit across Rick's face. He picked up his glass and took a sip. "I'd think you'd be friends with the Brodys. They're members of the Cattleman's Club."

"Yes, but Alex and Lance have this dumb rivalry dating back to high school. I'm glad it's not medieval times or they'd be challenging each other to jousts. Typical macho silliness."

"So, you don't believe Lance Brody set the fire?" His expression was strangely serious.

"Of course not. Why would a successful businessman want to burn down our barn? That doesn't make any sense at all."

She hesitated. "Alex does have some enemies, though. No one who'd really want to hurt him, but he's trodden on a few toes over the years."

"Haven't we all? It's part of being successful."

She sighed and nodded. "And he rose so far so fast, it put some people's noses out of joint. Did you know Alex used to be the groundskeeper at the club?"

"You're kidding me." His look of genuine shock made her wonder if she shouldn't have told him.

Did Alex want people reminded of his humble beginnings?

"Not for long. Just during part of high school and college. He used to mow the lawns after class. Once his import-export business took off, he quit and he's never looked back."

"I had no idea." Rick raised a brow. "Alex sounds like quite a character."

"He's an amazing man."

"And I guess he doesn't think any guy is good enough for his baby sister." A smile lifted one side of his mouth. "Is that why you won't let me near the house?"

Alicia laughed. "He's overprotective. It drives me nuts. I know he's only like that because he cares about me, but come on—I'm twenty-six!"

He leveled a serious blue gaze at her. "Maybe you should get your own place."

"Oh, I've thought about it, but as far as Alex is concerned, a girl doesn't leave home until she goes to live with her husband."

She blanched. Once again she'd managed to raise the specter of marriage. That spooked most guys right out of the room. "It's a Mexican thing. We're very traditional. You learn to work around it."

At least some people did. Maria had lived on her own for three years.

Maybe I'm just the lamest wimp on earth.

She fished inside her lobster claw, hoping he'd change the subject.

Was he crazy to want an affair with Alicia? Alex Montoya was not someone to tangle with.

Lord knew he put enough distance between himself and his own interfering relatives. Did he really want to get involved with a woman whose brother hovered over her like a shadow?

Justin watched her probe into the red depths of her lobster claw like a surgeon with a scalpel.

She looked up. "What?"

"I've never seen someone eat a lobster with such meticulous precision."

"I like to enjoy every delicious morsel." She smiled and popped a tender piece into her mouth. Like everything else in Alicia's world, her plate was perfectly ordered, not a lettuce leaf out of place.

"You're very detail-oriented."

"I'm a museum curator. We're probably the most detail-oriented people on earth. Except maybe for mail-service workers. But at least we don't have to worry about going postal."

She shot him an infectious grin, then returned to surgery on her lobster.

"I didn't know you were a curator. You must be very accomplished to hold that position at your age."

He'd been impressed and intrigued when she told him she worked at the museum, but for some reason he'd assumed she gave tours or taught classes there. It didn't occur to him she was running the show.

"Oh, I wouldn't say that." A delicate blush darkened her cheeks. "I'm just passionate about my work. The Somerset Museum of Natural History was just getting started when I joined as an archivist. The original curator left for a job at the Smithsonian, and I kind of stepped into the role."

"I'm ashamed to admit I've never been to the museum. What kinds of artifacts do you have?"

"It's an interesting mix. Most of it came from a huge private collection started almost a century ago. Dinosaur bones, fossils, meteorites, that kind of thing. We have some Native American artifacts from a different private collection. My focus has been on objects unique to the Houston area, and in particular to Somerset. This region has some interesting history. People seem to forget that when they talk about knocking down old buildings to put up a strip mall."

Justin's ears pricked up. "You mean the redevelopment of downtown Somerset?"

"Exactly." Alicia tossed her head, which made her thick dark hair swing over her shoulders, golden highlights sparkling in the candlelight. "That would be a travesty."

Interesting. He'd heard rumors that Alex had blocked the redevelopment of a key area that could have meant a big windfall to a couple of club members, including Kevin Novak. "Wouldn't redevelopment be good for the local economy?"

"That's what some people say, but our downtown area is one of the most well-preserved main streets in Texas. The architectural style is unique. Come on, have you ever seen corbelling like the fascia of the old town hall?"

Justin laughed, impressed by her command of architecture. "I can honestly say I haven't." Longhorn cattle with brass horns jutted out beneath the metal roof of the grand old building—Texas-style gargoyles. "I admit the aspirations of the town's founders were writ large in those buildings. It does have its own charm."

Alicia nodded, passion shining in her dark eyes. "And that would all be lost if they were bulldozed to make way for more generic big-box stores. It's like the stuff I see in my job. Once upon a time, that fossil was just another boring insect or fish or leaf. Now it's the only one of its kind that's survived to the present day. A unique glimpse into another time that enriches our understanding of the world around us and its history."

"I've never heard that perspective before." He frowned. "I suspect most people would rather have a dry cleaner closer to home or a Mega Mart where they can get cheap groceries."

"I'm not saying those things aren't important, but downtown Somerset is too special to let it be lost forever. There are plenty of bland, ugly buildings that can be torn down instead." She flashed a wicked grin. "I'd be happy to give them some suggestions."

"Maybe you should."

Justin frowned. He was getting a very different impression of the Montoya family than the one he'd formed based on idle gossip.

He'd assumed her brother stood up to block the redevelopment because he had his own profit-making agenda for the area. Now it almost seemed like he'd stalled the new development to make his history-buff sister happy.

This was not the fearsome and dangerous Alex Montoya of local legend.

Justin sipped his wine and peered at Alicia through narrowed eyes. "What would you do with the downtown?"

"I'd love to see it become a tourist attraction. Some of the buildings are ideal for upscale retail, or for quaint bed-and-breakfast accommodation. I don't think many people in the Houston area have any idea how beautiful Somerset is. It could become popular as a weekend getaway, and that would bring business and tax revenue to the town without destroying its unique charm."

"I'd hire you to do that in a heartbeat."

"Shame you can't." Her luscious lips turned into a smile that heated his blood. "Or can you?" Her brows lifted. "You haven't told me what you do."

Oh, I'm just heir to the largest shipping operation in the western hemisphere.

He wasn't at all sure how she'd react. But if he told her, he'd also have to confess that he was Justin Dupree, not Rick Jones.

"Nothing very interesting. Pushing papers around."

She cocked her head, which made her earrings sparkle in the candlelight. "Didn't you have an important phone call to make?"

"A phone call?"

"At the club, you said you couldn't stay because you had a phone call?"

"Oh, yes."

His little white lie to explain why he couldn't go inside. Once you started with this stuff it was hard to stop.

Still, he didn't want anyone to greet him with a hearty "Hey, Justin" until he'd had a chance to dig himself out of this hole he'd gotten into.

"I forgot about that call. But no matter. The world will continue to turn on its axis."

"I'm sorry to be a distraction. I don't want to get you into trouble."

Her look of concern touched something inside him.

"You are the best distraction I've ever encountered and I'd face all kinds of trouble to spend an evening with you. Tell me more about the natural history of Somerset. Were there dinosaurs around here?"

The sparkle in her eyes made him lean forward so he could enjoy their glow. "Absolutely."

Alicia was sure Rick's eyes would glaze over when she told him about the dig she'd helped out on last summer. Instead, his interest seemed to deepen with each detail she revealed.

Those intense blue irises stayed fixed on hers as she described each bone they unearthed, and how they had preserved and stored them for reassembly at the museum.

If she wasn't mistaken he seemed...fascinated.

The candlelight flickered over the hard planes of his handsome face while he asked intriguing questions and actually *listened* to her answers.

Which only increased the turmoil of excitement in her stomach. How could anyone be this wonderful?

He'd said he pushed papers for a living, but his tan suggested time spent outdoors and the athletic cut of his body belonged to a man of action. There was clearly more to discover about Rick Jones.

But everything she'd learned so far had her dangerously close to falling in love with the man.

Her dessert fork clinked against her glass as she set it down too hard.

They'd known each other less than three weeks. She had no intention of actually falling in love with him or anyone else. But you didn't have to be in love to kiss.

Her mouth twitched at the prospect of pressing her lips to his. His mouth was wide, mobile, with a way of lifting slightly higher on one side than the other like he had a naughty secret.

"I have a secret." His words took her by surprise, as if he'd spoken her thoughts aloud.

"You do?" Her pulse quickened.

"I had something made for you." His blue eyes twinkled.

Alicia stared at him. "What?" She hoped it wasn't freaky lingerie with slits in strange places. Maybe now she'd discover the dark side of Rick Jones. There had to be something horribly wrong with him, didn't there?

Rick reached into his pocket, which really set her heart pounding.

Of course it's not a ring, you idiot. He barely knows you. Stop watching so many old movies.

He pulled out a jewelry box.

He laughed at her expression. "Don't panic. It doesn't bite." That wicked dimple deepened as he handed her the box over the remains of their pecan pie.

Alicia took it with shaking fingers and tried not to look like he'd just given her a stick of dynamite. She flipped the lid.

A single blue gem attached to a fine silver chain sparkled against white velvet. A bold five-pointed star shone through the glittering facets.

"Texas topaz! Oh, my goodness, it's lovely."

The sparkly stone was almost the same haunting blue as Rick's eyes.

"I found the stone years ago on a trip into the Texas Hill country. The rock-hound friend I was with couldn't believe I found a gem like this on my first try. I never knew what to do with it."

He glanced down at the box in her hand. "When you told me you worked at the natural history museum, I knew I'd been saving it for you. I had it cut at a place downtown."

"Julie's Gems? Julie's been my biggest supporter in saving the historic buildings."

"That's the place." He grinned. "And I noticed you wear blue a lot. It kind of matches the dress you have on."

Alicia tried not to melt into a puddle on the floor. "You are without a doubt the most thoughtful and generous man I've ever met." She couldn't keep emotion out of her voice. "It's beautiful. Let me try it on."

"I'll help you." He rose and rounded the table.

Alicia stood, smoothing out the skirt of the simple silk dress she'd changed into for dinner.

She did wear blue almost every day. It had always been her favorite color.

She lifted the single flawless gem out of its box and dangled it on the pretty chain. Pleasure and anticipation tingled through her as Rick moved behind her.

His spicy and intriguing scent wrapped around her, and she could feel the heat of his skin through their clothes. His fingertips brushed hers as he took the delicate necklace, and Alicia suppressed a shiver of delight.

He lifted the delicate chain around her neck and fastened the clasp.

"Let me see." With a deft movement of his hands he spun her gently toward him. Their eyes met and a flash of something passed between them.

Pure lust, probably.

Not being experienced, Alicia couldn't put a name to any of the sensations pouring through her.

Only inches separated her from Rick and as they stood facing each other, the space between them seemed to crackle with energy.

Rick held her gaze. "Magnificent." His eyes rested not on the finely cut gem, but directly on hers, as if the compliment was intended for her rather than the jewel.

Alicia's lips parted, but no words came out. Instead, she stared at Rick's lips, issuing a silent invitation for them to join hers.

Their mouths met in an instant, lips crushing together as their arms slid around each other. Alicia heard a slight moan issue from her mouth as the warm, firm pressure of Rick's kiss sent a wave of pleasure rippling to her toes.

Their tongues touched, tentative and gentle, asking a sensual question.

Rick's broad hands closed around her waist, firm and steady. Her fingers reached up into his silky dark hair as their kiss deepened. Her breasts crushed against his chest, nipples hard with desire as he pulled her tighter into his embrace.

His thin polo shirt separated her from the taut muscle of his chest and suddenly she longed to strip off the layers of clothing between them. To feel his skin against hers.

Rick pulled his lips away slowly. The sensation hurt. She'd longed for this kiss and waited and hoped.... And now it was over. But the ache of longing hadn't diminished. It throbbed—stronger—deep inside her.

Alicia drew in a sharp breath. "Thank you."

"For the kiss?" Rick tilted his head, bemused.

"For the necklace." Heat rose up her neck. "But the kiss was lovely, too."

And hopefully, just the beginning. Would he invite her into his room to spend the night? She hoped so, but how could she make that clear without being forward?

She'd spent so much time trying to keep boys' hands away from anything below her neck that she had no idea how to encourage Rick in that direction now that she was ready.

"It's late," Rick murmured.

"Yes." Hope flared in her heart.

They stood, arms entwined, lips inches apart. In her high heels she was almost his height, and if she dared she could reach up and kiss him again right now.

"I think we should go to bed." Rick's eyes glittered like sapphires.

"Oh, yes," breathed Alicia. "I agree." Her belly contracted with excitement.

"Let me show you to your room."

She tried to keep a goofy grin off her face as they

walked across the candlelit living room and into the hallway that led to her room.

Rick's hand at her waist guided her gently, sending awareness trickling along her nerves. The rough silk of her dress chafed against her nipples even through the expensive bra she'd worn.

Tonight's the night.

Alicia tried to keep her breathing steady as he opened the door and ushered her inside.

She'd left the room spotless and perfectly organized—just in case. No makeup scattered on the dressing table or pantyhose spread over the chairs. She'd even turned the sheets back and opened a sachet of lavender into a little dish to add a fresh, floral scent.

She shuddered slightly as Rick pulled her closer and pressed his lips to hers. She rubbed against him, startled and thrilled by the hard length in his pants. Heat flooded her limbs and she wondered if it would be indecent to start unbuckling his belt while she still had control of her fingers.

But he pulled back and rubbed her cheek with his thumb. "Sleep tight, my beauty. I'll see you in the morning."

As the door closed behind him, Alicia fought the urge to scream with frustration.

What's wrong with me?

Three

Justin leaned back against the closed door of his bedroom and cursed the lust that roared through his body like fire. He was hard as any rock in the Texas hills. His muscles ached and throbbed with the urge to pull Alicia closer. To undress her and lick every inch of her warm, silky body. To make her cry out in hunger and desire as he pleasured her all night long.

A low groan escaped his mouth and echoed in the still air of his bedroom.

Thank heaven he'd still managed to behave like a gentleman.

Alicia came to him looking for sanctuary, not seduction. She was shaken by the fire and by the strange accusations of arson flying through the rarefied air of Somerset. It was his duty to comfort her and make her feel safe.

He shook his head as if that might dislodge the

lustful thoughts rambling around his brain. It wasn't her fault she was built like a sex goddess, with curves that could bring a grown man to his knees.

He marched across his room and flipped on the jets in the shower.

Cold.

The sound of her own cry woke Alicia with a start.

She sat upright in bed and searched for the familiar digital face of her clock.

Instead, the stiff tick-tock of an antique carriage clock reminded her that she wasn't at home. In the darkness she had no idea what time the strange clock read.

Sweat pricked her brow and images from her nightmare crowded her mind. The embroidered bedcover clung to her like the rich lace of the dress she'd been wearing in her dream.

A wedding dress.

Standing at a kind of altar—or was it outdoors?—she watched as handsome men in suits and evening dress approached, bearing gifts and smiling.

Some of them looked familiar, like Remy, the exchange student from France she'd dated (very) briefly her sophomore year of college. And Lars, the boy from Minnesota who'd made the mistake of challenging Alex to a game of tennis when he came to pick her up.

Others looked new, unfamiliar, each handsome and smiling and staring at her with the heat of passion in his eyes.

Until a fierce growl erupted out of the night—wait, wasn't it day?—and sent each suitor scurrying into the distance, passion forgotten.

Stop! The silent words had scratched at her throat. *Wait! Don't leave me here all alone.*

Please?

A sob rose in her throat and tears behind her eyelids. The growl filled the air around her again, and she turned, frightened of the monster who'd chased away so many strong men.

But the monster was also a man. Tall and broadly built, his dark eyes filled with...love.

Her brother, Alex.

"Oh, Alex, why do you have to be so suffocating? Let me be. Let me live!" The words rattled in her brain as the first tears flowed.

She realized she'd woken up at the exact moment in the dream when she'd looked down at her hands. They'd been gnarled and spotted with age. Wrinkled and ringless. The hands of an old woman.

She glanced at them now in the dark, relieved by their smooth, familiar outline in the reflected glow of moonlight through the crack in the curtains.

In the dream they'd been different.

She startled awake as the horrible truth of the dream sank in: she was still a virgin. An eighty-year-old virgin.

A racking sob heaved her chest. *Why me?* What was so wrong with her? Sure, she wasn't the most beautiful woman in the world, but ordinary women managed to marry and have children. Or go on dates.

Or even go all the way.

Just once!

She'd been so sure she'd break her losing streak tonight, that Rick would finally pop the rather wizened cherry she'd been keeping secret for years now because it was so horribly embarrassing to be still a virgin.

Twenty-six, for crying out loud! She was probably the only twenty-six-year-old virgin in the entire state of Texas. Or the whole United States.

Maybe even the whole world.

A wail escaped her lips as she collapsed back on to her pillow. At that moment, light streamed into the room as the door was flung open. Rick stood in the doorway.

"Alicia, what's the matter?" His voice rang with concern.

"I...I...I..." *I want to make love to you.*

Did she want him to know that she was a freak? A grown woman who'd never been kissed below the neck? Who'd never seen a man naked, or felt his hands on her bare skin?

Tears streamed down her face.

Rick approached the bed. "Don't cry, Alicia. I know last night was a horrible shock. But at least no one was hurt. They'll rebuild the barn and they'll catch the criminal who set the fire."

Through her fog of tears she felt his fingers caress her tangled hair. But she didn't want comfort. She wanted breathless passion.

She thrust out her arms and wrapped them around his neck, then crushed her mouth against his. Parted in surprise, his lips hesitated a moment before joining in the kiss.

Rising to her knees, she pressed her body against his through her long nightgown. Her nipples hardened against the bare muscle of his chest. The stubble of his cheek was a sweet balm to her fevered skin.

Don't stop! She tightened her grip around him, determined not to let him escape.

"Alicia." He managed to free his mouth for a second to gasp her name. "I'm not sure this…"

She fumbled with the strings of his pajama pants, unsure how her hands had found them, but intent on getting them undone immediately.

"Sweetheart, it's okay." Rick flinched as her hand brushed against his rock-hard erection.

She yanked on a string, but the knot was tight and she couldn't work it loose. Still jerking at it with one hand, she raised the other to tug down the shoulder strap of her nightgown.

The thin satin tore easily and she pulled down the gown to bare her breast. Cool night air tightened her nipple.

"Touch me," she pleaded, still tugging at his pajamas.

Rick lifted a tentative palm to her bare breast. She shuddered hard as he brushed her nipple.

"Alicia, I don't know if this is a good idea." She heard him swallow. "You seem a little…overwrought."

With a burst of elation she pulled open the knot holding his pajamas closed and started to push them down over his hips.

"Really, I think we should slow down." His pulsing erection and husky voice contradicted his words. "How about…a cup of tea?" he croaked.

Alicia froze. "Tea? What is it about me that makes you think of *tea* at a moment like this?" Suddenly, fierce sobs racked her body. "What's wrong with me? What's *wrong?*"

Her words rang out into the silent air of the hotel room and bounced back at her off the polished surfaces.

"Nothing's wrong, Alicia. You've just had a long day and you need some sleep."

"Sleep is the last thing I need." Her voice quavered as she readied herself to make her terrible confession.

Rick's eyes were midnight-blue in the scant light that streamed through the half-open doorway and outlined the ripped muscle of his neck and shoulders.

"I need *you*." Alicia drew in a shuddering breath. "I'm a virgin."

Justin almost fell off the bed. "You're kidding me."

"Would I kid about something like this?" Alicia's big brown eyes glittered with tears.

"Wow. I mean, that's amazing." His erection throbbed.

"It's not amazing, it's depressing." She picked up the torn section of her nightdress and held it over her bare breast. "I can't figure out what's wrong with me."

"Absolutely nothing is wrong with you. You're the most beautiful woman I've ever met. You're the sweetest—"

"I don't want to be sweet!" Desperation flashed in her eyes. "I want to be wild."

Rick glanced down to where his fierce arousal jutted beneath his untied pajama string. "I think you're well on your way."

"You're shocked."

"In the best possible way." He lifted a thumb and brushed away the tear that ran down her cheek. It broke his heart to see her so sad. "It's a very erotic revelation."

She blinked, her lashes wet. "It is?"

"Absolutely. It means you've never tasted the most

intense sensations in the whole world, and you're about to experience them for the first time."

Her eyes widened. "I am?"

"Absolutely." He leaned in and pressed his lips to hers. They parted, warm and yielding. His tongue flicked into her mouth and he felt her shiver in response.

Gently, he pushed aside the hand covering her breast and replaced it with his own. Her nipple peaked beneath his palm, and sent a flash of heat straight to his groin.

He stroked her nipple with his thumb as he pulled back from the kiss. Her tears had vanished, leaving her eyes bright and curious.

"That feels good," she whispered. She bit her lip, suddenly shy.

"Excellent." He lowered his mouth to her breast and blew. The nipple tightened in response.

"Ooooh," she murmured, arching her back.

He licked a circle around the areola and drank in her rich, feminine scent as he tasted the honeyed silk of her skin.

She rocked against him when he took her nipple in his mouth and sucked. Then he slid the second strap of her nightgown over her shoulder and placed his palm on her other lush, full breast.

Under his fingers, her heartbeat was rapid with excitement.

The soft fabric of her lace-edged nightgown—appropriately virginal—slid down to her waist and he kissed her belly.

His own arousal was excruciating. Everything down there was so sensitive the mere touch of Alicia's manicured hand could send him to another dimension. He really shouldn't be so turned on by her innocence, but something about it was insanely hot.

Gently, he pushed her back against the pillows where she'd so recently tossed and turned in anguish. Her smooth hair splayed on the pillow like a halo. A smile flickered across her full lips as her eyes closed.

She obviously felt safe with him.

Little did she know he was not Rick Jones, the man she trusted with her virtue.

Guilt snaked through him and knotted up with the lust that had overtaken every synapse. He certainly couldn't tell her *now,* while they were locked in a sensual embrace.

Her first.

He slid one hand under her sensational backside and lifted her hips enough to pull her nightgown to her thighs and down over her shapely legs.

"Are you cold?" he whispered.

"Not even a little," she said through a smile. Her thick lashes flickered open and she reached up her arms. "Come here."

He hesitated. While not exactly romantic, a condom was still a necessity. "I'm aching to, but first I have to get something. Don't move a single muscle. Do you promise me you won't?"

"I promise." A slight frown played over her smooth brow.

Rick climbed off the bed and sped to the bathroom and back in record-breaking time. He was half-afraid Alicia would come to her senses and refasten the lock on her chastity belt.

Relief washed over him when he saw her still lying

there, a goddess glazed with moonlight, staring up at him with hungry eyes.

He rolled the condom over his hard length and climbed on to the bed next to her. His hand played over the curve of her hip and her soft belly. She bucked as he slid a finger between her legs and touched the sensitive flesh there. Already hot and slick, she was aroused and ready.

He suppressed a moan of anticipation. He couldn't wait to be inside all that lush heat and enjoy the deep closeness with Alicia.

It's her first time, take it slow.

He drew in a breath and kissed her belly as her fingers ruffled his hair. Her skin quivered as he moved his fingers over her aroused and swollen flesh. Carefully, he parted her legs and lowered his mouth, greedy for the taste of her.

He groaned at the feel of her moist warmth against his mouth. He ran his tongue over her soft folds and she shuddered in response. "Oh, my," she moaned.

A grin crossed his lips as he repeated the gesture. It had been many years since he'd first discovered the unique and tantalizing joys of sex for the first time, but it was a wicked thrill reexperiencing them through Alicia.

Her hips writhed, and she pressed herself against his mouth, begging for more. He licked and sucked until he felt her throb, hot and willing.

Layering kisses over her belly and breasts, he rose over her. He feathered a single, soft kiss on her cheek. "Are you ready?"

She nodded, eyes shut tight as a lascivious smile played over her sensual mouth.

Careful and slow, he guided himself inside. A

breathy groan escaped his mouth when he sank into the hot, tight sweetness of her.

Alicia let out a tiny cry and his eyes flicked open, but instead of pain, her expression spoke of sweet relief.

"I'm free." A broad smile lit her beautiful face.

"And this is just the beginning."

He buried his face in her neck as her hips rose to meet him, drawing him deeper. He built a rhythm and Alicia rode it with him, rising and falling, her breath coming faster and her sweet sighs building to urgent moans.

Celibate for so long, her body was rigged with explosive desire and ready to blow.

And right now, so was his.

Not yet, he pleaded with himself. He couldn't remember feeling such intense and urgent arousal. *It's her first time, make it last.*

Alicia pressed hurried kisses over his face and shoulders, nipping and licking. Her hands pressed his hips to hers, deepening the connection until he could hardly stand it.

Her moans now ended in fevered shrieks, each driving him closer and closer to the brink of insanity.

Suddenly, her fingernails dug into his back. "Ohhh.... Ohhh...."

She shuddered hard as the first waves of her orgasm hit her. The fierce contractions of her untried muscles gripped him and he climaxed with her, riding the waves until they both washed up, sweaty and breathless, on the rumpled shores of her bed.

Eventually, he managed to crack his eyes open. Alicia lay sprawled against the fluffy pillows, hair damp with perspiration.

Her skin glowed golden in the half-light and her chest rose and fell in unsteady gasps.

"Goodness," she breathed.

"I'm not sure goodness has anything to do with it." He winked. "But it's kind of fun, don't you think?"

Alicia let out a laugh that filled the air like sweet music. "Yes!" she shouted. "It's magnificent. Is it true? Am I really no longer a virgin?" Her eyes, wide with humor and excitement, glowed in the darkness.

"You are officially deflowered."

"Thank goodness!"

Justin laughed. "Some women treat their virginity like a prize."

"And I used to be one of them—more fool me." Her pretty white teeth shone in her smile. "Seriously, I'm happy for women who want to have sex for the first time with their husbands, and I'm sure that works great if you marry at...oh, eighteen, but waiting until you're twenty-six? I wouldn't wish that on anyone."

She blew out a hearty sigh. "Did you know that in the Middle Ages they thought prolonged virginity could turn a woman's skin green?"

"Sounds like the ploy of some young swain to get the key to his love's chastity belt."

Her bright gaze filled his heart with joy. "Sex is healthy and normal, not some weird sinful activity that should only be done in the dark while you hold your nose."

"I couldn't agree more." He kissed her soft cheek.

"All those years I was told to keep my legs crossed, *or else*. I didn't know any better."

"Isn't that the whole point of convent school?"

She giggled. "Pretty much, yes. Though it's also a good place to learn how to smoke and drink so that no one smells it on your breath."

"You smoked?"

"No, of course not. I'm the original Goody Two-shoes, remember?"

He cocked his head, then gave her nipple a swift suck. It formed a hard peak. "I'm not so sure."

"Oh, you have no idea what a relief it is to get that millstone off my neck. I feel like a regular person now. I can walk down the street without wondering whether people somehow *know* I'm different."

"I hate to break it to you, but you're definitely not a regular person." He pressed a kiss to her lips. "For one thing, you're dangerously beautiful, so most men are probably afraid to come near you. It takes an especially arrogant one like me to get up the nerve."

She laughed, her full breasts bumping against his chest in a way that made him hard all over again.

"For another, you're brainy as well as beautiful, which is doubly intimidating." He narrowed his eyes. "Except to a genius like myself."

"So modest."

He grinned. "You're anything but ordinary and a run-of-the-mill guy would never cut it for you."

She released a soft, sweet sigh. "Lucky thing I met you, then."

Alicia's radiant, dark eyes shimmered with joy. He'd put that joy there, and it gave him almost as much of a thrill as having sex with her.

There was something truly special about Alicia. She

took pride and pleasure in everything she did, with the result that being around her made a man want to be a better person.

He certainly wanted to be a better person.

Better than a guy who'd give a woman a fake name.

Justin blew out a breath. He *really* wished he'd had a chance to tell her before they'd had sex.

What kind of a cad took the virginity of a woman who had no idea who he truly was?

And she had no clue he was good friends with her brother's longtime rivals. That alone was cause for a big blowup.

He shoved a hand through his hair. He hadn't planned it this way at all.

"Kiss me." Alicia's sweet command blew his labored thoughts from his brain.

He kissed her, enjoying the softness of her mouth and the caress of her hands on his back.

He'd never met a situation he couldn't charm his way out of eventually. He'd figure out the perfect moment to tell her, and everything would be fine.

She'd probably find it funny.

Wouldn't she?

Four

Alicia had trouble opening her eyes. This room was much brighter than her bedroom at home.

It must have been a dream.

A glance to the side confirmed that she lay alone in bed.

But why did her body feel so…strange? Her limbs were heavy, and her breasts seemed more tender than usual. Her lips tingled and so did her…

Goodness. Alicia clutched the covers around her.

Maybe it wasn't a dream.

She turned to look at the pillow beside her in the king-size bed.

The fluffy goose down wrapped in snow-white Egyptian cotton bore the unmistakable indent of a head.

Had she really slept with Rick?

She remembered a dream about being an eighty-year-old virgin.

But she also remembered a second dream.

A glorious dream where Rick kissed her and licked her, his hands roaming over her body until he entered her and drove her to heights of wild pleasure.

Sense memory throbbed in the muscles deep inside her.

Alicia drew in a deep breath as a secret smile spread across her mouth. *It was real.*

But where was Rick?

She pulled on a flowered silk robe and checked her hair in the mirror. Wild, in a sensual kind of way. She fluffed it with her fingers, then opened the door into the hallway.

Bright morning sunlight filled the space. Then she saw the note on her door.

Morning, beautiful, I've gone to a meeting. I'll be back by eleven so don't go anywhere, <u>please</u>—Rick.

His underlined *please* made her laugh. He really wanted her.

If memory served her correctly, he'd enjoyed last night every bit as much as she had. She could almost hear his urgent moans and feel his hot breath on her ear.

A shiver of longing rippled through her and she prayed eleven o'clock wasn't too far away. A peek at the clock in her room answered her prayer. Thank goodness it was Saturday, otherwise she'd have slept through half a morning's work.

Her cell phone rang on the dresser in the bedroom and she hurried to answer it. Her heart pounded and she hoped it was Rick.

"Halloooooo," Maria said.

Could she really give her friend the scoop she'd be sure to insist on?

"Hi, Maria, how are you?"

"Very formal, hmm. Does this mean you were up late last night reading theological philosophy with Mr. Rick Jones?"

Alicia cleared her throat. "Something like that." She was glad Maria couldn't see her guilty smile.

"So, did you guys figure out how many angels can fit on the head of a pin? I've been struggling with that one for years."

Alicia laughed. She could totally picture Maria's raised brow. "We figured about forty, as long as their wings were folded."

Maria tut-tutted. "Come on now, Alicia. Stop playing with me. Did you, or didn't you?"

Alicia hesitated, glanced over her shoulder, then whispered, "We did."

"I knew it!" Maria's joyous whoop almost deafened her. "Well, this calls for a celebration. Want to meet me at T.J.'s for lunch?"

"Actually, Rick's just gone to a meeting and he'll be back by eleven."

"And let me guess. You'd rather have lunch with some new hunk than with your oldest and dearest friend?"

"Well…"

"You'd better! You know I'd ditch you in a second for the right guy."

They both laughed. It was so true.

"Now that we've established that I have no principles, you'd better tell me all the details so I don't rat you out to Alex."

"Alex! Oh, my gosh, I totally forgot about him. He's all alone at the ranch." Guilt pricked her like a needle.

"All alone? You've got at least ten different employees living there."

"You know what I mean. Who'll make him breakfast?"

"He's a big boy. I'm sure he can pour himself a bowl of Wheaties."

"What if the arsonist came back? I've got to call him."

"Not until you tell me more about last night."

"Maria! I'll tell you all about it another time. And believe me, I really appreciate you covering for me, otherwise nothing would have happened at all."

"Okay, okay, but one thing before you cut me off." Maria had stopped teasing and her voice was filled with concern. "I know I joke around a lot, but this Rick Jones better treat my very best friend like a princess or he's going to have me to answer to. Did he make it wonderful for you?"

Alicia nodded, then realized her friend couldn't see. "Oh, Maria, it was more than wonderful. He was so gentle, so tender. It was…beautiful."

"Phew." Maria laughed. "Well, then enjoy your day with him and wish him all the best from me. And give me a call if you want to come up for air."

Alicia shut off her phone and caught sight of her face in the bamboo-framed mirror on the dressing table. Her goofy grin almost made her laugh.

Then she remembered Alex, and her grin vanished.

She punched in his number and waited while the phone rang, cold anxiety trickling through her.

"Hey, 'Manita. How's Maria?"

Alicia gulped. "She's great. How are things at the ranch?" Her voice sounded nervous and false. She hoped he wouldn't press for details about Maria. She didn't want this lie to get any more elaborate.

"No more trouble. The vet's been out to check the animals and the insurance guy was here. The police have interviewed all the workers, but I don't think they have any leads yet."

"I'm coming home, then."

Even as she said it, her entire body screamed *no*. She wanted to stay here, with Rick.

"No way. You stay with Maria. We still have no idea who's behind this, so there's no way to predict what they'll do next. I've got enough problems already. I don't want to have to worry about my baby sister being in danger."

Alicia's relief mingled with stone-cold guilt. "Are you sure you're okay? Did you eat breakfast?"

"I'm not an invalid."

"Did you eat breakfast?"

"I wasn't hungry."

"Alejandro Montoya, you'd better go make yourself something—"

"Stop fussing. Maybe it's better I learn to do things for myself, otherwise how will I manage when you leave to get married?"

His teasing tone told her he was joking. He probably didn't think she'd ever leave to get married. And until this morning, she'd worried the same thing.

But now everything was different.

She fingered her blue topaz necklace and let her smile return. "All right, don't eat anything, then. See if I care."

Her reflection in the mirror revealed red lips and flushed cheeks. Her eyes were glassy and her hair—

well, her hair needed work. "I'll call you later and you can reach me on my cell if you need me."

She hung up the phone. How shocked Alex would be if he knew what she'd been up to last night. If he knew that—right now—she was waiting for her new boyfriend to return.

Her lover.

Finally.

Justin marched up the walkway into the Texas Cattleman's Club. Things were getting too complicated for his taste and he intended to do a little untangling. At least as much as he could without making Alicia run for cover.

"Good afternoon, Mr. Dupree." The doorman nodded to him. "Mr. Brody's waiting for you in the library."

"Justin!" Mitch rose from a leather club chair near the carved-stone fireplace as Justin entered, his dark eyes shining with amusement. "You've been hard to find lately."

"Busy. We're in the midst of a deal. I'm wearing a suit right now because I just signed a contract. Saturday morning, can you believe it? But the guy's heading back to Athens this afternoon."

His tall friend narrowed his eyes. "That's not the only thing keeping you tied up. I saw how well you hit it off with Alicia Montoya."

Justin just smiled.

"Did you dig up any dirt on her brother?" Mitch asked.

Guilt trickled through Justin as he eased himself into

a chair. He wished he'd never volunteered to get information about Alex from Alicia.

Both Mitch and his brother, Lance, suspected Alex of the sabotage at Brody Oil and Gas, but because of the longtime enmity between Lance and Alex, there was no way they could approach him without things quickly escalating to a confrontation. It happened every time Lance and Alex got near each other.

"Pretty suspicious that a fire broke out on the Montoya place, don't you think?" Mitch asked.

"They don't know who's behind the fire at El Diablo. The police are looking into it but there are no suspects yet, from what I hear."

"Do you think it's possible that Alex set the fire to divert suspicion from himself about the fire at our refinery?"

"Why would he destroy his own property?".

"For the insurance money." Mitch took a sip of whiskey. "That old barn was begging to be burned down. He probably had it insured for twice its value."

"Alicia said it was a historic building. One of the oldest in Somerset."

"Maybe they wanted to clear the way for a state-of-the-art setup. Alex has some of the finest breeding cattle in the entire state of Texas these days. He always was a competitive son of a bitch." Mitch signaled to the bartender to bring a drink for Justin.

"I don't think he's behind it."

Mitch looked at Justin closely. "Who else could it be?"

Justin leaned back in his chair. "It's got me stumped. But I'm starting to think that the fires are somehow tied into the missing funds Darius discovered. Have you finished the unofficial audit yet?"

"Not yet," said Mitch, "but I'm close."

"Look, Mitch, from what Alicia's told me, the refinery fire doesn't sound like something Alex would do. He's a legitimate businessman."

"One of his best buddies is Paul Rodriquez. Don't try to tell me 'El Gato' is legit."

"No, El Gato has 'drug cartel' written all over him, but he and Alex Montoya aren't business partners. They're old friends or something. Alex has an import-export business, and from the sounds of it, he's making money at the ranch, too, with those big-ticket bulls he's breeding."

A wry smile lifted one side of Mitch's mouth. "Are you falling for Alicia Montoya?"

Justin took a gulp of whiskey. "I'm telling you what I've learned. The Montoyas seem like decent and up-standing people. I think we've all been too hasty in our judgment of Alex."

Mitch took a swig from his own glass. "He slammed the brakes on redeveloping downtown and ruined Kevin's deal. One of the councillors told me he was so persuasive that he almost single-handedly talked the city council into rezoning the area for historic development. I can't figure out if he actually wants to redevelop it himself, or if he just couldn't stand to see someone else make a buck doing it."

"Alicia's heavily involved in the preservation of the downtown area. She says it's one of the few authentic and picturesque main streets in the state. She's working on a committee to turn it into a tourist attraction."

"*Downtown* Somerset as a tourist attraction? I

suspect you're thinking with a part of your body other than your brain."

"Why not? If you look past the cheesy signage and faded paint, there are some beautiful buildings there. I think she's absolutely right to want to preserve Somerset's history. We already have enough strip malls in the Houston suburbs."

"It's hard to argue with that." Mitch peered into his glass. "As I get older, I'm starting to take a more serious interest in the future and what will be here when my own children grow up."

Justin's eyes widened. "Are you and Lexi already talking about children?"

Mitch smiled slyly. "We've done more than talk about it. We're expecting."

Justin almost choked on his drink. He'd been shocked to his boot heels when Mitch said he was getting married. Mitch was always the last man standing at the bar and the first to run from any sign of a woman wanting commitment.

Apparently Alexis Cavanaugh—now Alexis Brody—had worked some kind of magic spell on him.

"That's great. Congratulations."

"You're pole-axed." Mitch's smile broadened into a grin.

"Totally."

"I don't blame you. I used to laugh at the whole idea of love and marriage, let alone family. But let me tell you, when you meet the right woman, your whole world changes."

Justin blinked. He'd certainly been looking at things differently since he met Alicia. Lying about his

JENNIFER LEWIS   63

name, for example. He wasn't going to do that again—ever.

"With Lexi, did you just…know?"

Mitch blew out a sigh. "It was a bit more complicated than that. You know the story. It started out as a business arrangement with Senator Cavanaugh. She was supposed to marry Lance. When Lance ruined that plan by marrying Kate, I figured I'd marry Lexi myself. Then I fell madly in love with her."

"Sounds like a real fairy tale—Texas style." Justin raised his glass and laughed.

"I'll drink to that. You're next, bro. I have a feeling." Mitch's dark eyes narrowed. "And from the way you're defending the Montoya family, I'm beginning to wonder if you've already met your lady. I bet Alex wouldn't mind his sister marrying into the illustrious Dupree clan."

"Yeah, except for the fact that the Brodys are my best friends. He doesn't know I'm seeing her."

"She's keeping you as her dirty little secret?"

"Something like that."

"Well, watch your back. There are strange things going on all around us."

"Too true. If the Brody brothers can settle down and get married, almost anything can happen."

"Fires are burning, bro. Fires are burning. Sometimes they start right here." Mitch tapped his chest with a knuckle. "When that happens, there's no way to put 'em out."

The click of the lock made Alicia jump to her feet. She'd had plenty of time to shower and style her hair and put on one of her favorite dresses—which just happened to match the necklace Rick gave her.

And if he were to look underneath her dress—an event she fervently hoped for—he'd find a pretty lace bra and panties in a contrasting shade of pale blue.

"Alicia." Rick's warm, masculine voice sent a shiver of awareness through her.

"I'm here." She hurried out into the hallway, heart pounding.

Rick stopped, as if struck motionless by the sight of her. He looked devastatingly handsome in a stylish, dark gray suit. His hair was tousled and his blue eyes sparkled with fascination.

He held out a bouquet of fat pink roses. "I bought these for you." He frowned. "But I want you holding me, not a bunch of roses." He glanced around for a surface to put them down on, then set them gently on a hall table. "Much better. Now my hands are free."

Alicia's body shimmered with anticipation as Rick took a bold step toward her. Her eyes closed as he wrapped his strong arms around her and gave her a tender kiss on the lips.

Pleasure crept over her like the sun's heat. Her nipples thickened against the stiff fabric of his suit. And hidden, secret parts of her—parts she'd never been fully aware of—now throbbed with desire.

He grew hard against her, and she instinctively pressed her hips against his erection, delighting in the arousal that flared between them.

"Damn, I missed you so much." His voice was rough.

"You were only gone for a couple of hours."

"Way too long. Let's not do that again anytime soon." He pulled off his slim dark tie with two fingers and unbuttoned the collar of his white shirt to reveal his bronzed neck.

On impulse, Alicia slipped her fingers into the collar of his shirt, against his hot skin.

Rick kissed her nose, which made her smile. Her fingers—without checking back to her brain—unbuttoned the next button on his shirt, and the next, while her other hand slid over the rippling muscle of his pecs.

The scent of him drove her half-crazy. The fine wool of his expensive suit mingled with the musky aroma of sexually aroused male—an inviting combination of civilized and primitive.

She raked her nails over the front of his crisp shirt, down past his sleek, leather belt, to the thick bulge beneath it.

Rick groaned as she wrapped her hand around his rigid length through his pants. She held him, tight, while she let her other hand rest on the firm curve of his athletic backside.

He grew harder still when she freed her hands to pluck at his belt buckle.

Her breath came in unsteady gasps as desire pounded inside her like a drum, heightened by Rick's obvious excitement.

His hands roamed over her silky dress, strumming her nipples and exploring the curve of her waist.

At last, she freed the leather from the buckle and tugged down the zipper. His erection throbbed against her hand and made her shiver.

Without ceremony, she shoved down his pants and

pressed herself against his thick arousal. She couldn't wait to feel him inside her.

Rick lifted the skirt of her dress and slid a bold hand inside her panties. Hot and slick, she writhed against him.

"Take me now. Right here," she breathed, hardly aware of her own words.

Rick's erection throbbed again. He pulled a condom from his jacket pocket, ripped it open with his teeth and rolled it on. Then he tugged her panties to one side and entered her.

Alicia cried out at the intense sensation, then gripped Rick so her scream wouldn't make him back away.

Rick cupped her buttocks and lifted her up to him until her back arched and she took him as deep as she could.

"Oh, yes, just like that. It feels so good," she murmured, rocking against him.

Sensation swirled through her, and colors flashed behind her eyelids. She clung to Rick, her fingers clutching his rapidly dampening shirt.

She hadn't even given him time to remove his jacket. A burst of laughter accompanied the thought.

"What's so funny?"

"Me," she said on a groan as she writhed against him. "I couldn't wait for us to get undressed. I wore pretty underwear and you didn't even get to see it."

Her breasts felt swollen and deliciously sensitive against their lacy prison.

"Let me have a look," rasped Rick.

Keeping the steady rhythm, he raised a hand and tugged down the front of her dress.

"Nice." He flashed a dazzling blue gaze that made her heart leap. "Sometimes it's more fun to do things out of order."

She gasped as he lifted her feet off the floor and strode for the living room, still hard inside her.

Without missing a beat, he eased them both down onto a green silk chaise lounge.

Alicia's eyes squeezed shut as he thrust into her, but not before she had time to take in the restrained elegance of the setting: expensive antiques, fine china and crystal, delicate watercolor paintings.

What they were doing here seemed so *wrong*.

In the best possible way.

She wriggled under him, enjoying the sound of her own pleasured moans. "Oh, yes, Rick, again. Do it again." She clutched him to her as he rode her until every nerve and muscle of her body hummed with sheer bliss.

Just when she was about to lose all control—

He stopped.

Completely stopped. No movement at all, except their chests rising and falling against each other as their breath came in ragged gulps.

She tried to lift her hips but the sheer weight of his muscled body made it impossible.

Almost growling with frustrated desire, she opened her eyes, and saw his dangerous baby blues staring at her. A wicked smile slid across his mouth.

"What?" she gasped, her body sprung like a catapult and desperate for release.

"Good things come to those who wait," he whispered.

Alicia wiggled, which had no result but to make her

more agonizingly aroused. When she was about to scream, he started to move again.

Oh. So. Slowly.

Only the tiniest movements at first. Incremental. Just enough to drive her that little bit closer to the brink of insanity.

He slid—very gently—in and out, the stroking motion creating an extraordinary sensation.

Then he picked up speed.

Alicia moaned and cried out with relief as she built toward her climax. The pressure intensified, growing and gathering inside her like a huge storm cloud ready to explode and drench the whole state.

Her orgasm crashed over her like a clap of thunder, sucking the breath from her lungs and throwing her back against the chaise lounge with a howl of exuberant release.

Rick's own climax shook him like a jackhammer and he cried out as he collapsed on top of her.

It was some moments before she managed to draw enough breath to speak. "What was that? What were you doing?"

"Have you ever heard of the G-spot?"

"I think I read about it in *Cosmo* once."

"Well—" a naughty grin lifted one side of his mouth "—now you know what it does."

She lay splayed over the chaise, her head hanging slightly off one end so her hair brushed the floor. Rick held her on to the silk surface with a firm arm, or she might have fallen limply to the carpet.

Alicia blinked. "G-spot, huh?" Her muscles still throbbed with stray contractions. "I wonder what evolutionary purpose that serves."

Rick chuckled. "The natural historian at work. Isn't pleasure reason enough for it to exist?"

"I suppose." She pressed a thoughtful finger to her lips. "I could see how once you've experienced that, you'd keep coming back for more, which would likely ensure the survival of your genes in the next generation."

"Unless you're using a condom." Rick traced a line on her belly with his finger. Her muscles shivered in response.

"So true. In that case, you have to admit you're doing it just for fun."

They both chuckled. Then Alicia's stomach grumbled.

"Hey, did you have breakfast?"

"No. I confess. I was distracted by my other appetites." With some effort, she lifted her head up onto the chaise. "And I even berated Alex for not eating properly this morning. I'm such a hypocrite."

Rick's playful expression faded. "You spoke to Alex?"

"Yes. I wanted to make sure everything was okay at the ranch."

"Did you tell him you're here?"

"No." She shifted onto her elbow. "It's better he doesn't know, especially with so much going on. He'll just worry, then overreact."

"And I'll be challenged to pistols at dawn for assailing your virtue."

"Exactly." Alicia sighed. "Why go looking for drama? Let's at least wait until they find out who set the fire. Then he'll have some other man to direct his hostile energies toward."

Five

"Where are we going?" Alicia asked as Justin pulled onto the freeway. They'd changed their clothing after the impromptu tryst, then headed right out in search of lunch.

"Downtown Somerset."

He could feel her curious gaze on him. "Why?"

"Because I want to see it through your eyes." Since he was now striding around town defending her plan to preserve the old buildings, he wanted to know more about what he was trying to save.

And more about the lovely Alicia.

Her gaze darkened. "What if Alex sees us?"

He managed not to laugh. "Is he likely to be hanging around downtown Somerset on a Saturday afternoon?" For someone so smart, she was more than a little paranoid.

"Well, no, but..."

"So stop worrying. If we run into him you can say I'm a visiting professor of natural history," he said, knowing full well that if they did run into Alex, she wouldn't be the only one who had some explaining to do.

She chuckled. "There is no such thing. Besides, you don't look like a professor." She eyed the pale blue shirt he'd changed into. "They don't usually wear Prada."

"Me, either. It was a gift from one of my aunts."

"She has good taste. I like the color."

He smiled. "I know. That's why I wore it. See? I'm getting to know you, bit by bit. And so far, I haven't found a bit I don't like."

"All this talk about biting is making me squirm." She wriggled in her seat, inadvertently pulling her simple white dress tight across her full chest.

Justin suppressed a groan of arousal. "Please, don't talk about biting and squirming while I'm driving. It could be dangerous."

Alicia let out a little growl. The lascivious gesture sent a ripple of lust straight up his spine. He couldn't wait to see more of her wild side.

Alicia crossed her sleek, tanned legs, giving him a flash of inner thigh.

The sensation in his crotch was getting to be pretty unbearable. "Tell me where to park," he said as he pulled off at the exit. The hum and buzz of Houston subsided as they entered the peaceful, tree-lined streets of historic Somerset.

Victorian houses sat gracefully amidst large lawns and mature trees. A kid rode by on a bike, like something out of the 1950s.

"That house is a Stanford White." She pointed to a stunning Beaux Arts "cottage" he'd never noticed before. "He was a famous nineteenth-century architect who—"

"Was murdered by the husband of a woman he had a scandalous affair with."

"You've heard of him," she said with surprise and delight in her eyes.

"I had one of the most expensive educations money can buy. Despite that, I managed to pick up a few facts along the way. It's a beautiful house."

He'd stopped the car and they sat with the engine humming. "The detail is incredible. You'd never see that kind of elaborate molding on a house today."

"And just two years ago it was condemned. The roof was damaged during a storm and the city wanted to tear it down. That's when I joined the Somerset Historical Society and we raised money to have it restored."

Pride showed on her beautiful face. "It sold for two million when it was finished, and the owner loves it so much, she lets us give tours as a fundraiser."

Justin was intrigued. "How did you get interested in architectural history?"

"I always loved to look at beautiful houses." She glanced up at the steep eaves and shimmering multi-paned windows. "When I was a little girl we lived in a tiny house in the barrio. The roof leaked and the foundation was half-rotted, but my parents didn't dare ask the landlord to fix anything in case he tried to raise the rent. My parents saved every penny they had because they couldn't wait to move out of there and buy their own home. The American dream, you know?"

She laughed, but her laughter was tinged with sorrow. "They used to talk so much about that house they dreamed of—the sunny windows it would have with views of a grassy backyard, a big kitchen with rows of shining copper pots. Alex wanted his own bedroom so he could put up shelves for his collection of model airplanes."

For a second, her eyes filled with tears. "I don't suppose they ever came close to having enough money for a down payment. My dad was killed in an accident where he worked and after that my mom just struggled to make ends meet. No one talked much about buying a house again. Except Alex." She smiled. "He always said you have to dream big, no matter what. Even after our mother died, he kept saying that."

"He's right." Emotion rose in Justin's chest.

How he wished he could turn back time and give Alicia's family the house of their dreams. The most pressing financial problem his parents ever faced was finding new tax loopholes to exploit.

He slid his arm around her shoulder. "Your parents would be so happy to see you and Alex at El Diablo."

"Oh, I know." Her eyes brightened. "My mom used to clean houses all over Somerset and El Diablo was one of them. She took such pleasure in polishing all the lovely quarter-sawn oak trim and buffing the brass doorknobs." She stared out the window, as if lost in the past. "I know this sounds silly, but when we were there—she used to take me along when school was out because she couldn't afford a sitter—we'd pretend it was all ours. I used to dance down those corridors and pretend one of those pretty bedrooms with the chintz curtains was mine, and that I had a closet filled with fine clothes."

"And now you do."

"Yeah." A broad grin settled across her face as she turned to him. "Funny, isn't it?"

"It's totally awesome," he said, meaning every word of it. "I guess the American dream is alive and well in Somerset." He squeezed Alicia and she nuzzled against him.

Something kicked inside his heart. A fierce longing to give Alicia the world—or at least the most beautiful house in it.

Where did that come from?

"So, there are more of these old gems in Somerset?"

"Oh, yes. It developed as a suburb for wealthy Houstonians, so nearly all of the buildings are special in some way. Look at this one."

She pointed to a quasi-gothic stone structure across the street. "The owner fell in love with a medieval abbey in Somerset, England, and had it brought here brick by brick and rebuilt as his home. It even has some of the original stained glass inside. I gave a tour of it last year through the museum."

"You're a busy woman."

"Keeps me out of trouble." She flashed him a grin.

"Until now." He grazed her neck with his teeth. Desire flashed through him, and he realized they were still idling on a busy street. "But let's save that energy for later."

"Sounds like a plan. Can we stop by Julie's Gems so I can rave over her work on the necklace you gave me?"

"Sure thing." He couldn't hide a pleased grin as he pulled back on to the road, heading for Main Street, the focus of Alicia's preservation efforts.

He hoped they wouldn't run into anyone who'd greet him as Justin. On the other hand, if they did, maybe it would be the hand of fate at work.

Alicia showed him a hidden alleyway behind Julie's Gems where his car barely fit into the single parking space. "You need more parking around here," he muttered with a raised brow.

Alicia shrugged. "Or more people need to start using public transportation." She winked. "It's better for the earth."

"This is Texas, sweetheart."

"So? Miracles can happen." She smiled sweetly and marched ahead of him up the neat alley. Her heels clicked authoritatively over the cobblestones. The way her backside jiggled slightly inside her flimsy white dress almost deprived him of his senses.

Miracles can happen.

With Alicia around, he had a feeling almost anything could happen.

"I can't wait to thank Julie for the work she did on this topaz." She opened the door. "I think it's the loveliest gift I've ever had."

Justin followed her into the store and greeted Julie. "It was a hit."

"I knew it would be." The bubbly jeweler hurried from behind the counter and gave Alicia a hug. "But you didn't tell me it was for one of my favorite people."

Justin shrugged. "I didn't know you two knew each other."

"Alicia knows everyone in Somerset," said Julie, tossing her red curls. "And we all adore her."

Alicia flushed sweetly.

Julie stared at the topaz glittering on the delicate chain around her lovely neck. "And that is some very fine craftsmanship, if I do say so myself. Though I do have to give some credit to Rick for bringing me such a perfect stone. I don't believe for a minute that he dug it up himself." She shot him a wry glance. "But he certainly has an eye for a fine gem."

Justin chuckled. "I was with an experienced rock hound. Otherwise I probably would have tossed it back into the soil."

Julie narrowed her eyes at Alicia. "Do you believe a word of this?"

"I do." Alicia's sweet smile and words of affirmation filled Justin's chest with warmth.

Until he remembered that she had every reason to be wary of him.

Would she believe his story about the stone if she knew he wasn't Rick Jones? He'd used the fake name here, too, as he often did when he didn't want the media sniffing after him.

He'd gotten so tired of stories and innuendo— *Shipping Heir Commissions Jewels for Mystery Sweetheart*—that subterfuge was second nature to him now.

Would Alicia have treated him differently if he'd introduced himself as Justin Dupree?

For all he knew, Alicia had never heard of the Duprees. She'd figured out by now that he was well-off—a four-bedroom penthouse hotel suite let that cat out of the bag—but she hadn't asked where the money came from.

She seemed to genuinely enjoy his company and showed no interest in plumbing the depth of his pockets.

Most girls would be fingering the sparkling bracelets—or rings—by now, in the hope that he'd offer to buy her another, but Alicia was far from the velvet-lined cases, chatting enthusiastically with Julie about her plans to restore the downtown area.

"Julie did a lot of the restoration on this storefront herself."

"I live in the apartment above it, too," Julie said, gesturing to the patterned tin ceiling. "I love everything about this area. I'm so glad it's not going to be bulldozed and turned into a parking lot."

"At least not if Alex and I can keep stalling the developers." Alicia sighed. "Some people don't think about anything but money."

"I wish there were more people like you and your brother, who don't mind standing up to the powers that be."

Alicia chuckled. "We've been doing it our whole lives, so we're not going to stop now. And once people start to see what downtown Somerset can be, they'll all jump on the bandwagon and congratulate themselves for coming up with the idea."

Julie laughed. "She's the eternal optimist."

"Yet another reason why she deserves only the best. And she also needs some lunch, rather urgently. Julie, would you care to join us?"

"Heck no." Julie crossed her arms. "You two need to be alone. And you need to get out of here before all the chemistry in the air starts turning my gems pink."

Alicia giggled, which made her full breasts bounce

against the white fabric of her dress. Justin tried to ignore the heat rising in his groin.

He shot Julie a grin. "Thanks again, Julie. You're a gem."

"Yeah. I hear that all the time." She crossed her arms over her chest and shot him a knowing smile. "If you dig up any more AAA quality rocks, you know who to call."

Her wink told him she still didn't believe his story—which was in fact the gospel truth. As usual, he didn't care in the least whether she believed him or not. He'd never been one to sweat other people's opinions—until he met Alicia.

"I thought we'd go to Tea and Sympathy for some lunch," he said in her ear as they left the shop. The honey scent of her skin made him want to bury his face in her neck, but he managed to restrain himself.

"Perfect." She flashed a pearly grin. "They make smoked salmon and cucumber sandwiches to die for."

"I hope no one will have to die." He couldn't resist grazing his hand down her waist and over the lush curve of her backside as he ushered her under the striped awning over the tea shop.

"Outside or inside?" He nodded at the wrought-iron tables and chairs that lined the slate sidewalk.

"Definitely inside." She glanced up and down the street like a fugitive. "I know it's very unlikely Alex is anywhere near here, but…" She shrugged. "Humor me, please?"

"I'd do anything for you."

The words rattled around his brain as he followed her into the darkest corner of the café and pulled out her chair.

He couldn't remember having feelings like this for

a woman—ever. Usually all his devotion went into the family business, and his free time was spent blowing off steam.

Right now, steam thickened in the air between him and Alicia. It hovered over the white, cotton tablecloth and wound around the wooden chairs. Wisps licked around their fingers as they both reached for the crystal pitcher of water in the center of the table, and their fingers—almost—touched.

His palms prickled with the urge to run over the silky curves of her body. To strip off her soft white dress and watch her skin bead with perspiration as he drove her to new heights of bliss.

This steam was a delicious torment, and he had no desire to blow it off at all.

"Can you believe this storefront was originally built as a tea shop?"

"I can. Our ancestors were mad about tea. I hear they started a war over it once."

Alicia smiled. "The Boston Tea Party happened at least a hundred years before this area was developed. Still, it's reassuring to think that some things have stayed the same. We think we're so advanced with our laptops and cell phones, but deep down, we enjoy the same things our ancestors did."

He'd finished pouring water for both of them and she picked up her glass and took a sip. "Has your family always lived in the Houston area?"

An edge to her voice told him she was becoming increasingly curious about him. As well she might.

"Actually they're not from the Houston area at all. They settled outside New Orleans at the end of the

Pleistocene Era and they're still there today. Well, my mom is. My dad died three years ago."

"I'm sorry to hear that." Sorrow filled her big brown eyes.

"It was a merciful release. He'd been sick for a long time. That's when I took over running the family business."

"What kind of business is it?" She leaned forward.

"Transportation. Did you see they have crumpets on the menu?"

"Rick! You're so mysterious. I'm beginning to be quite suspicious of you. What type of transportation?"

"Ferrying goods from place to place. Container shipping. Very unglamorous, I'm afraid."

He glanced at the printed menu, hoping she'd drop the subject.

Duprees and shipping went together like tea and crumpets. Yes, she had to find out who he was eventually, but he'd prefer to have it happen someplace private, as he expected her reaction might be…dramatic.

"I think it sounds intriguing. So, you import and export goods from all over the world? That's what Alex does."

"Other people import and export them—people like Alex—and they pay money to bring their goods on our ships. We just get the goods from A to B. We used to run everything out of New Orleans, but back in the fifties we moved most of our operations to Houston, which is why I work here."

He tapped his menu. "Hey, they've got quails' eggs. I haven't eaten those in years. I'm definitely having that. How about you?"

Alicia's eyes narrowed. Apparently, she was hip to

his desire to change the subject. "I'll have the egg salad. They make it English style with a dash of curry powder."

"A flash of heat just where you least expect it."

"Exactly." Her plump lips slid into an enticing smile. "I know I'm feeling flashes of heat in all kinds of places I never expected."

Justin leaned forward. "And we've only begun to explore your erogenous zones."

He'd much rather think about Alicia's erogenous zones than the illustrious Dupree clan.

Her eyes widened and she glanced anxiously around the café.

"Don't worry. No one can hear us." He should know. He was used to keeping his affairs private. He'd learned the hard way.

They gave their orders to the friendly waitress, then Alicia leaned in close. "Is your mother lonely now that she's a widow?" Concern filled her beautiful eyes.

Justin startled at the deeply personal question. "Oh, no. She's not the lonely type. Always busy with charitable activities, friends, that kind of thing."

"I'm glad to hear that. I always think it must be so hard to lose your spouse once your children have grown up and left home. Suddenly, you're all on your own."

He stared at Alicia for a moment. His mother probably had never been all on her own in her whole life.

There was a staff of five just inside the house, and at least another ten on the estate. Not to mention that his mother was a blur of motion. When he was little, he used to resent that she never invited him to sit on her lap for a story, the way mothers did in books. She was far too busy for that.

Over time, he got used to it. Maybe that's why he didn't get all misty-eyed over the idea of family life. He'd never really had any. His father was at work all the time, or off participating in manly sporting pursuits.

Quite possibly having affairs as well.

His parents' relationship was anything but romantic. He couldn't imagine how they'd managed to conceive him. Perhaps some aristocratic breeding process involving frozen semen.

"She must wish you lived closer." Alicia tilted her head with sympathy.

"Oh, I'm not so sure. I'd been away at school almost since I'd learned to read. If she was desperate to clutch me to her bosom, she'd have done it a long time ago."

"You didn't grow up at home?"

"Sure, I was there until I turned eight, or so. Then they decided it was time to get serious about my education. I did come home for vacations, though."

"That's horrible! I've never heard of such a thing."

"It's a family tradition. I went to the same school my father attended. The family estate is out in the country so there wasn't really a school for me to go to there."

Not unless he'd attended the local public school— over his mother's dead body. He suppressed a snort. The idea of a Dupree having a normal childhood was quite laughable.

"Would you do that to your child?" Her face was tight with alarm.

"I don't know. I've never thought about it."

"Never? Do you not want children?" She'd pulled

back from the table, almost seeming to put distance between them.

"Sure I do. I think." He frowned. He truly had never thought about it. "I mean, everyone does, sooner or later."

Alicia stared at him like he'd grown alien antennae. "You're thirty years old and you haven't given a moment's thought to starting a family?"

"I'm busy with work." Was that so odd? His crowd didn't talk much about settling down.

Well, not until lately. Suddenly, it was all the rage.

Alicia must think he was some depraved party animal who never looked beyond that evening's festivities. He frowned. "You're right. It is strange. I guess I never met someone who made me think about it."

Until now.

The words hung in the air between them.

"You're used to being alone." She bit her lip. "For all I complain about Alex, I admit I've never really wanted to live alone. I'm used to having my family about me, small as it is."

"I could see how you worried about him being alone even for one day. I think that's sweet."

What would it be like to have someone care that much about you?

He'd been expected to fend for himself from a young age. Part of becoming a man. Or becoming a Dupree. It had never occurred to him before that those two things were different, that you could be a man without being a distant, patrician father who wouldn't kiss his son good-night in case it made him "soft."

"I think there's a lot to be envied and admired about the close relationship between you and Alex. Kind of makes me wish I had a sister I could smother." He shot her a mischievous smile.

"Much as I complain, I know he just does it because he cares. He's a big softy, really, underneath the gruff exterior. I bet you guys will get along great once you get to know each other."

"If you ever allow us to meet, that is," he teased.

The waitress set down their lunch and he watched as Alicia took a bite out of her egg-salad sandwich. She chewed thoughtfully.

"You know what? Maybe it is time for you guys to meet."

Justin froze.

"I mean, we've already been…intimate." Her lovely complexion darkened a shade. "So, he can't exactly forbid me to see you."

"He might just insist we marry before sunset."

Alicia giggled. "You're so right. My honor is at stake." She took a sip of water and flushed even darker. "But don't worry. I don't expect you to marry me just because you've claimed my virtue."

She was embarrassed, but turned on at the same time. Her dark eyes glittered and her lips and cheeks were flushed. Alicia Montoya was apparently much more interested in making wild and passionate love than in securing a big rock for her finger.

There was something very reassuring—and totally hot—about that.

She leaned in. "Come to think of it, I pretty much threw my virtue at you."

"You sure did." His voice was husky, and his pants uncomfortably tight. "Lucky thing I'm a good catch."

"I was so upset when you didn't try anything."

"It practically killed me not to. I had to take a cold shower that night. But after all you'd been through with the fire and the suspicion of arson, I didn't want to take advantage of you." He grinned at her. "I had no idea you were downright desperate to be taken advantage of."

He raised a quail's egg to his mouth and flicked his tongue over it for a second before popping it in.

Alicia's eyes flashed. "I've got a lot of lost time to make up for."

"About ten years, I'd say. We'd better get cracking right after lunch. I'm going to take you to one of my favorite places."

Six

Rick turned the car down a gravel drive and under the scrolled-iron arch leading to the Houston Bay Yacht Club.

Alicia's eyes widened. "I've heard of this club."

She patted her hair. She'd insisted on having the top down so she could enjoy the breeze—now she regretted the rash gesture.

"Whatever you've heard, it's not all that bad."

"Oh, stop it. This is probably the most exclusive yacht club in the world. Don't some of the crowned heads of Europe dock here?"

"Sure. Loads of kings and queens milling about. But we'll do our best to avoid them." He shot her a grin. "I come for the sailing, not the socializing."

"I guess that makes sense if you're in the shipping business."

"A container ship has virtually nothing in common

with a racing yacht, except that they both float on water."

"That's a big thing. I've never been on a boat before."

She wasn't sure if she was excited or terrified at the prospect of floating out on the ocean.

"Really?" Rick turned to her, eyebrows raised.

"I've never been on a cruise, or in a canoe, or even in a rowboat at the park. You probably think that's pretty funny."

Manicured flower beds lined the drive, which ended at a small parking lot hosting an extravagant collection of luxury vehicles.

"I think it's great." Rick's smile broadened as he pulled into a space between an SUV the size of a WWI tank and a vintage Bentley. "Another of life's grandest experiences awaits you."

He jumped out and hurried around to open her door. She couldn't help smiling at the chivalrous gesture. "And I'd be delighted to show you the ropes, literally and figuratively."

"That sounds kinky."

"Good, it was meant to."

He guided her out of the parking lot and up some stone stairs toward an imposing clubhouse. But instead of leading her to the door, he took her elbow and ushered her around the side of the building, through a small garden, and down two more flights of steps to the marina.

Alicia gasped at the sight of all those white boats bobbing like corks in the bright afternoon sun.

"Choppy today," said Rick cheerfully.

Alicia's stomach contracted.

"Always makes it more exciting. Unless I'm trying to clock my best time, then it ticks me off."

"You race?"

"Absolutely." The light glinted off his dark hair as he squinted into the sun. "It's a true rush to race someone else using only the power of the wind to propel you. That's when you learn what you're made of."

Alicia glanced about, suddenly aware of her heeled shoes. "What if I find I'm made of something that melts?"

He slid his arm around her waist and hugged her close. "Don't worry, I'll lick you all up if you melt." His hot whisper made her ear tingle.

"You're so bad!" She tapped his arm, which didn't budge from around her waist.

The sturdy warmth of his muscled embrace buoyed her confidence. "Hey, I always brag about how much I like to try something new. Here I am. Show me the ropes, sailor man."

They walked through the marina, past rows of gleaming yachts and speedboats, ranging in size from the tiniest dingy to luxury cruisers with brass-trimmed decks that looked like you could host a party of a hundred on them.

Rick waved at two tanned preppy types winding a coil of rope on the dock of one of the boats, but he didn't introduce her.

Alicia glanced back at the clubhouse. Sun gleamed on the slate roof and illuminated the stone planters overflowing with yellow flowers. She was curious to see what the place looked like inside.

Maybe Rick just wasn't into the social aspect of

things. Or maybe she wasn't the type of girl he'd show off to his friends.

A chill swept through her. She wasn't some waspy princess with an Ivy League degree and a pedigree dating back to the Mayflower.

Her heels clicked loudly on the decking. Rick marched ahead of her, the muscle of his shoulders flexing under his shirt, past millions of dollars worth of ocean-going hardware.

She couldn't shake a sudden, powerful feeling that she didn't belong here.

"Nearly there. I dock at the end of the marina so I can get in and out without getting stuck behind a bunch of Sunday sailors."

And maybe he wanted to get her on to the yacht and out of the club before anyone could figure out that she wasn't one of them.

Oh, Alicia, you're being silly! Why look for the negative in this beautiful moment?

So what if he wasn't going to marry her and take her home to Mom?

She wasn't here for that. She was here to enjoy a beautiful afternoon with an exciting and thoughtful man, and to have a good time. Not to worry about what was and wasn't going to happen between them in the future.

"There she is." He beamed and pointed at a long, sleek white boat with red sails furled against a tall mast. The letters TITAN III were emblazoned on the side in red.

Alicia looked warily at the shiny white deck. "What happened to Titans one and two?"

"Oh, they're out there in little pieces somewhere.

Luckily, I'm a strong swimmer." A dimple appeared in his cheek as he surveyed her, laughter in his blue eyes.

"You're joking."

"Yes, I'm joking. I sold them when something better came along. I'm fickle like that."

And you'd do well to remember that, young lady, and not get carried away thinking about happily-ever-afters.

Her main goal—humiliating as it was—had been to shed her embarrassing virginity and have a good time doing it. If their relationship continued a bit longer and they had more fun together, so much the better.

Right?

"Ready to board?" He lifted an arm to help her up to the ramp that connected the boat to the dock. "You'll want to take your shoes off when you get on deck. It can be slippery as the boat kicks up some spray once we get going. But don't worry, there's a rope to hang on to."

"Great," managed Alicia, taking tentative steps up the stamped-metal ramp.

She could swim, thanks to lessons under the stern command of Sister Benedict, but she'd never swum anywhere except a chlorinated pool, with no waves or undertow whatsoever.

On the deck, she removed her shoes and handed them to Rick, who stowed them in a cubby.

"Take a seat over there."

Alicia looked. The closest thing to a seat was a slippery-looking ledge. She sat down on the sun-warmed surface while Rick started unwinding rope and unfurling the sails. He tossed her a life jacket and she donned it with some relief.

"I love to come out here," he said cheerfully.

"There's no better way to shake off the petty concerns and stresses of the business world than to set out to sea with wind in your face."

The wind whipped the pale cotton of her dress against her skin, where it clung to her curves. Sunlight glistened off her legs and toasted her bare feet, while the water sparkled all around them.

Beautiful.

Finished with the sail, Rick unwound the rope tying them to the dock and pushed away from the ramp.

Alicia watched, riveted, as he guided the yacht out into the bay using the tiller and movements of the sails, and a lot of taut and tanned muscle. The memory of those strong arms around her made her belly quiver as she saw him work.

He was a very capable man with a surprising array of talents. She couldn't help glowing with pride that of all the women in the world, he'd chosen to spend the afternoon with her.

What did it matter if he didn't want to introduce her to his yacht-club buddies?

They were probably boring anyway.

She turned her face to the sun and let it warm her. She'd been spending too much time holed up in the office lately. It was time to embrace new experiences and strike out in bold new directions.

Even if they were a little scary.

Since his was almost the last boat in the whole marina, they were soon leaving the club behind and heading out into the flat gray expanse of Houston bay.

Alicia's nerves tingled as they went farther and farther away from dry land. She couldn't see the opposite shore, so they seemed to be heading out into the wild blue yonder.

Rick pulled two frost-covered bottles of lager out of thin air.

"Refreshments." He grinned and flipped the tops off with a bottle opener. The glass felt cool and wet against her rather sweaty palm. "To adventure."

Alicia raised her bottle and clinked it against his. "And new experiences."

He took a sip, then leaned close. "Especially those of a sensual kind." His breath warmed her neck and made her shiver with pleasure. Their lips joined in a kiss that sent energy sparking through her.

"What are we doing?" she gasped, breaking the kiss. "We might get sucked out to sea."

"Anything could happen." Rick cocked his head. "And you might find you like it."

"You're such a tease." She sipped her chilled lager.

"What makes you think I'm teasing? Have I steered you wrong yet?" He nodded to his strong hand that guided the boat with the tiller.

"Well, no." A smile tugged at her lips. "I've been having a fantastic time with you."

"So you should be starting to trust me by now." Something flickered in the blue depths of his eyes. "At least a little bit."

"I apparently trust you enough to go out in a boat with you, so who knows what's next?" She looked about her, taking in the varied horizons—both industrial and pastoral—of Houston bay. "Tell me, can you get in your boat and go literally anywhere?"

"You mean, to the Bahamas, or Mexico?"

She nodded.

"Absolutely. All you need is enough water to drink and some food for the journey. No gas required." He grinned. "But it helps to know where you're going to dock. You usually can't just pull up on a beach unless it's a deserted island."

"Oooh. I like the sound of a deserted island. Nothing but palm trees, a crystal-clear lagoon…" She cocked her head. "And maybe an undiscovered tribe with a complex and interesting culture to explore."

"Always working, I see."

She shrugged. "What can I say? I love my work. And I tend to get on well with people so hopefully I could persuade them not to shrink our heads."

Rick guffawed. "I suspect traveling with you would be a real adventure."

"You should try it sometime."

"I think I am." His blue gaze rested on her face and she felt a wave of energy flow between them. "And so far I like it very much."

Alicia's heart squeezed. The time she'd spent with Rick could already be counted among the best hours of her life.

Was it possible that he felt the same way?

Could there be a real future between them?

As if in answer to her question, he took her hand in his. Their palms pressed together, their fingers wound into each other.

Rick turned to stare out over the prow. "I've spent a lot of my life chasing adventure. Always thinking that happiness was on top of the mountain, or just past the rapids, or around the next bend."

He turned back to her and met her eyes. "I think I've been looking in all the wrong places."

Alicia swallowed. She could almost hear the blood thundering in her veins as they sat, entwined, heading out into the unfamiliar wind and water of the bay.

What a dramatic turn her life had taken in the past week.

The fire seemed almost inconsequential compared to the seismic shifts in her inner and outer landscape.

Overnight—literally—she'd gone from being a "good little girl" plodding through her uneventful existence to being a sensual woman taking life by the horns.

Or by the tiller. "Can I have a turn steering?"

"Of course." His grin revealed that he loved her take-charge attitude. "Come sit up here and take over."

She eased herself into position and grasped the long, white handle that extended down into the belly of the boat.

She was surprised to find she had to work quite hard just to keep it steady. A quick jog to one side made Rick chuckle.

"The more you move it around, the slower you go."

"So, I guess you need strapping muscles to go fast enough for a race."

"Doesn't hurt, but it all comes with practice. Including the muscle."

Alicia's biceps muscle was beginning to feel like it might burst into flame, but she held the tiller steady as the boat plowed in a straight line through the steely water. "Wow. I like this."

She felt Rick's gaze on her face, and became aware of her chin tilted in pride and enjoyment.

"I like you liking it."

He pulled on a rope and did something with the sail that turned it slightly. The yacht moved faster over the water.

The wind whipped her hair behind her head and plastered her dress to her body.

"I feel like I'm flying!" Her words were almost lost in the wind.

"Yeah." Rick grinned. "Isn't it great? And flying's not so bad, either. I have a light aircraft I fool around in, too."

Alicia laughed. "Is there anything you haven't tried?"

Rick met her gaze with those soulful blue eyes. "Yeah. A lot of things. Some of them I never thought I'd want to try."

Like marriage.

And children.

The words flew past her, unspoken, but communicated as loudly as if he'd shouted them into the wind.

Alicia blinked, her chest tight. Maybe she was just imagining this whole relationship in her head. She really shouldn't get carried away. He was her first, but she certainly wasn't his.

Not even close.

So what made her think she'd be his last?

Rick moved close to her. He slid his arm around her waist while she did her best to hold their course steady. "You're going to make me wobble," she protested, as he leaned in to nibble her ear.

"A little wobbling might be interesting." He peered mischievously down the front of her life vest. "See if you can hang a left. There's a nice open spit of land on the far side of the bay."

Alicia pulled the tiller to the left, only to find the boat jag sharply to the right.

"Oops. Forgot to tell you that you turn it whichever way you don't want to go. Tiller Toward Trouble. So, if you're running from Jaws, you point the tiller at him and you'll take off in the opposite direction.

"I should point the tiller toward you," she teased, wrestling with the handle.

"Quite possibly. But I'd just chase faster." He shot her a wicked grin.

Alicia was both exhausted and exhilarated when they arrived back at the marina. She was also drenched with sea spray and cautious exploration confirmed that her hair was wild as Medusa's. "I must look a fright," she murmured, trying to catch her reflection in a shiny metal plate on the ship's deck.

"You look ravishing. In fact, I'm tempted to ravish you right now."

Rick's dark hair was tousled and shiny from the wind and spray. His eyes shone with excitement that mirrored her own.

"I'm tempted to ravish you right back," she whispered, casting a surreptitious glance at the grand clubhouse. "But I suspect we should wait until we're somewhere more private."

As they drew closer, she saw a crowd had gathered on the elegant balcony that faced the bay. "They're having some kind of party."

"There's always a party going on here. Those poor

people must not have decent homes to go to." He shook his head with pity. "I prefer a more *private* party."

The flash of heat in his eyes caused a rush of warmth between her legs.

"I think it's a barbecue."

No one looked that dressed up. She saw the two preppy guys in polo shirts and cargo shorts that they'd passed on their way out to the boat.

"They have them every Saturday."

"Looks kind of fun." She was still new to this life-styles-of-the-rich-and-famous thing, and sometimes it was a blast just to see a new place and meet some new people.

Again she noticed a strange flicker of darkness in Rick's eyes.

Then his usual teasing expression returned. "I'm afraid I'm not willing to share you with anyone right now." He growled slightly, so that only she could hear. "I've managed to keep my hands off that gorgeous body all afternoon and I can't wait a moment longer."

His hands left the tiller and appeared to move toward her of their own accord, which made the boat stray off their careful course into the marina.

"Watch out!" she called, grabbing the handle, as they drifted dangerously close to a gleaming mon-strosity with yellow sails. "It's probably not hard to do a million dollar's worth of damage around here."

"Too right." He grinned, suddenly back under control, and steered *Titan III* into the forest of shiny masts with their colorful sails furled. "Glad I have you here to keep me on track. How did you like your first time out on the water?"

"I loved it."

Energy still danced through her, sparked by the exhilarating experience of steering the fast craft through the open water, harnessing the power of the wind.

"Then you'll come out again?" He raised a brow.

"I'd like to."

She'd more than like to, and not just because she'd discovered the fun of sailing. She wanted to spend more time with Rick. It was a relief to know that he already wanted to make plans beyond this weekend.

"Fantastic. I think next time we'll sail right out of the bay, into the gulf. What do you think?"

Anticipation trickled through her. "I think I'm ready."

Right now she felt ready for anything. Her quiet, humdrum existence of going to work and spending evenings with Alex seemed a distant memory.

Rick lashed the boat to the dock and helped Alicia back onto dry land.

"Oooh, I feel a bit wobbly," she gasped, as she attempted to keep her balance on the unmoving wood of the dock.

"That's what happens once you get your sea legs. It feels downright unnatural to stand on solid ground."

He moved close to her and slid his arms around her waist. He smelled heavenly: salt and sea air, mingling with his warm male scent.

Their lips met in a steamy kiss, and her hands slid around his waist to enjoy the muscles of his back through his rumpled cotton shirt.

When they pulled apart, she was breathless and wobbly. "I'm not sure that helped."

"Sorry." Rick shrugged and winked. "I guess we'd better get you home so you can recover in bed."

The flash of desire in his eyes suggested she would not be recuperating alone.

Heat crept through her. Then she hesitated. "I don't know. Maybe I should go back to the ranch and see what's going on."

"No way." Hands on hips, Rick made a show of barring her way. "The only place you're going is the penthouse suite of the Omni. Any other plans will have to wait."

Before she had a chance to protest, he slid one arm around her waist and the other behind her legs and swept her off her feet.

Alicia shrieked as he lifted her into the air. "You can't carry me!"

"Just watch me." He marched along the dock, a grin creasing his handsome face.

"I'm not that wobbly. I can walk, really." She tried to wriggle free, but she only rubbed against his hard chest, which made her pulse quicken.

"You give your sea legs a rest. You'll need your strength." His smile revealed even, white teeth. "Trust me."

Seven

The tray of fruit from room service was a work of art. Sliced peaches, plump berries, lush slabs of pineapple…but Alicia had no appetite for food.

"Champagne?" Rick popped the cork without waiting for her reply.

"Sure." She tried to sound calm, though her eyes were probably wide as saucers.

They'd showered—separately—and while she'd donned a soft, silk robe after drying off, Rick had marched into the living room wearing…nothing at all.

His body was tanned a deep nut brown from the waist up. Clearly he devoted ample time to leisure rather than sitting hunched over a desk all day.

His legs were paler, but sturdy and muscled. A spreading line of dark hair accentuated the ripped muscles of his chest as he held out the glass.

Alicia took it, trying not to stare.

"One of us is overdressed," he murmured, as he poured a second glass.

His dark hair curled, still damp, over his forehead, hanging almost to his piercing blue eyes.

"Moi?" she managed, taking a sip of champagne.

She'd never thought of herself as especially self-conscious about her body, but the idea of stripping off her robe—it was still broad daylight, after all—made her belly clench.

"Toi."

"You speak French." Another surprise.

"Of course, I…" He hesitated, and a shadow passed over his brow. "I learned it in school."

He turned and walked across the living room, then pulled down the shade. They were so high up that no one could possibly see in, except perhaps from a helicopter, but she was touched that he considered her modesty.

The champagne sparkled over her tongue and the sight of his toned body heated her insides. While his back was turned, she undid the knot at her waist and slipped the robe down over her shoulders.

He walked to a second window and pulled the blinds. "Alicia, I have something to tell you—"

He turned, then stopped and stared, openmouthed. "Oh, Lord."

She'd let her robe fall to the floor and stretched out on the chaise like a Victorian courtesan. "Yes?"

"I…I…" His voice was a husky groan. "I can't seem to form a sentence."

"Then don't." She lifted a finger and beckoned.

Rick's chest rose as he inhaled deeply and walked across the floor, champagne glass in hand.

He knelt on the floor next to the chaise, and feasted on her with his eyes.

"The only reason people look at art is because they don't have a view like this to admire." His words caressed her ears as his hungry gaze heated her skin.

She writhed a little, exploring her newfound sensuality.

He didn't even have to touch her. Just being close to him made her insides shimmy and dampened her private, female places.

Her breathing quickened as he leaned closer. "You drive me crazy," he whispered into her neck.

"It must be my razor-sharp intellect," she teased. His intense arousal was shockingly visible—and only heightened her own fierce desire.

"Yeah, that, too." His eyes roamed over her breasts and belly, and along the length of her thighs.

Under his admiring gaze she felt deliciously sensual—beautiful—seeing herself for the first time through another's eyes.

The ordinary body that got her from A to B and stayed mercifully healthy and strong regardless of how many late nights she worked, had suddenly transformed into a garden of pleasure that begged to be explored.

Rick reached out his fingers slowly, as if afraid they might get burned. He held them above her waist, so close that she could feel his heat.

She lifted herself a fraction until her skin met his palm. His eyelids slid closed and he let out a sigh.

Then his hand started to roam. Over her hip and

along the full curve of her thigh. A seductive smile played on his lips as he slid an inquisitive finger in between her legs. "It's hot in there," he whispered.

"Burning hot," she breathed, as her hips jolted under his touch.

"I'd better do something about that." He lowered his head. "We don't want to set off the smoke alarms."

He pressed his wet mouth to her hot flesh and sucked.

Alicia's back arched and she moaned as sensation snapped through her. She reached for him, threading her fingers into his thick, damp hair and writhing under his mouth.

Already, the tension built inside her and she got that heavy, throbbing feeling that she was almost ready to explode. "Wait!" she cried. "Stop."

Rick stopped, eyes open and glowing.

"It's my turn."

A smile tilted the corner of his mouth when Alicia slid out of her prone position and pushed him gently down on the chaise.

She inhaled deeply and took his hard length in her hand. His erection throbbed, alive and sensitive, as she lowered her lips over its tip and savored a man for the first time.

Salty and silky, the taste only fueled her raging appetites. She took him into her mouth and sucked, enjoying the low groan that told her he loved this every bit as much as she was. She wrapped a hand around the shaft and caressed it while she licked the tip.

He touched her breasts—careful and cautious as a curator—while she explored and enjoyed his arousal.

When she couldn't stand the spiraling increase of tension, she slowly pulled her mouth back. "I'd like to go on top," she whispered, blushing.

"I'd love that." Rick's throaty enthusiasm gave her the encouragement she needed. Didn't he always? She was so lucky to have found a man she could trust with her embarrassing innocence.

They rolled on the condom together, then she climbed over him on the wide chaise and took him— slow and careful—into her hot, moist depths.

"Oh, my," she heard herself moan, as his hard length stroked ultra-sensitive nerve endings deep inside her. "I think I found the G-spot again."

Rick's chest shook in a silent laugh as she moved just enough to spark sensation that made her gasp. Somehow the feelings were even more intense and overwhelming in this position. Every move she made sent shockwaves of pleasure shooting through her.

She lifted her hips and slid back and forth, glad that she didn't have to pretend to be knowledgeable or cool or even capable—that she could enjoy the brand-new experience with the wide-eyed excitement she felt.

She discovered that if she kept him deep inside her, but rocked back and forth slightly, the sensations spread right though her crotch and up into her belly in a flush of pleasure. "Oh, my," she said again, conscious of her naive delight.

"I think you've found your clitoris," rasped Rick, his eyes squeezed shut as she writhed over him.

"Really?" A smile spread across her lips. "I can see why they make such a fuss over it."

Throbbing and pulsing seemed to have taken hold of

her down there, and she stopped thinking and gave herself over to the primal enjoyment flooding her mind and body.

She moved her hips in rhythmic motion until Rick's hands on her waist increased the speed and intensity and they reached an explosive and noisy climax together.

Alicia collapsed onto him, damp with perspiration and gasping like she'd just run a race.

Rick held her in his arms and stroked her hair. "You're amazing, wonderful, beautiful, sexy, brilliant and totally hot," he breathed, his chest heaving against hers.

Something leapt inside her. His words sounded so…heartfelt. Not like flattery or a meaningless compliment.

Rick Jones made her feel desirable and appreciated.

"You, too," she said with a grin. "And I'm so glad we're making up for all my wasted time."

"It's my pleasure." His words tickled her ear. "More pleasure than you can imagine."

She laughed and wriggled against him. "Well, since you've been gracious enough to initiate me into the delights of my own sensuality, I'd like to do something for you."

"I think you just did," he whispered, stroking her cheek.

"Something more…traditional."

"I'm not sure there's anything more traditional than sex. None of us would be here without it."

Alicia opened her eyes and met his humorous blue gaze. "You're so right, but none of us would be here without food, either. I'm going to cook for you."

"You don't have to do that."

"I know, I want to. I *love* to cook." She growled the words against his cheek. "It's a bit of a passion for me."

"You certainly are a woman of passion." He nipped at her neck.

A ripple of pleasure filled her. It was true! She actually was a woman of passion—after all these years of waiting to experience simple pleasures most people took for granted.

What a thrill—not to mention a relief—to find that she was as capable of passion as anyone on the planet.

"Cooking was probably my first love. Unlike other things, I learned it at a very young age and I've been practicing for a long time."

Rick shifted positions until they lay on their sides, facing each other. "The suite does have a kitchen…somewhere. It might be behind one of the doors at the end of the hallway. I never go down there."

Alicia mock-slapped his biceps. "You're terrible! You really never cook at all?"

"I'm ashamed to say I never do." He lowered dark lashes and pretended to look sheepish. "I'm totally dependent on room service for basic survival."

"Poor baby." She shook her head. "Because, let me tell you, a five-star chef has nothing on home cooking that's been made with love."

Rick's eyes widened slightly.

Alicia gulped.

Did she have to say the word *love* like that?

It was one thing saying she loved to cook, quite another to say she'd cook for him *with love*.

"I cook for all my friends," she stammered. "I love hosting dinners."

In other words, it doesn't really mean much at all.

Which wasn't true.

Rick had opened up something inside her, unlocked some hidden place she didn't know even existed. Maybe it was just sex—or passion—and all the new feelings they created in her, but she felt far more for him than she could express in mere words.

"I'm honored to be counted among your friends."

She blushed, sure he could see right through her.

His placid demeanor didn't hint at his emotions. Was he trying to tell her he just wanted to be friends? Or that any embarrassing slips of the tongue on the subject of *love* would be daintily glossed over?

Her chest grew tight. "What's your favorite kind of food?" Her voice sounded a little too high.

"I suspect it's your favorite thing to cook, whatever that is."

"Then let me surprise you."

Justin looked down to find his plate totally empty, just like the serving dishes of green and red curry, and the sticky rice noodles Alicia had served with them.

All that remained of the meal was the basil garnish and a satisfied feeling in his stomach.

"You're a goddess."

Alicia flushed. "It's nothing."

"Hardly. And you did surprise me. I wouldn't have expected Thai food."

"You thought I'd make something Mexican." She lifted a brow.

"You see right through me. I should have known you could never be predictable."

"I make some killer Mexican dishes, too." She smiled and crossed her arms. The topaz he'd given her sparkled at the top of seductive cleavage nestled in a silvery-white blouse.

Alicia Montoya literally glowed with confidence and sensuality. Everything about her was perfect.

And she'd just made what was hands down the very best meal he'd ever eaten.

"It's the fresh chilies." She leaned forward. "That's what makes both Thai and Mexican food really sing. One of these days I'm going to grow them myself. Maybe when I finally get my own place."

"What keeps you from moving out right now?"

"Alex."

"I'm sure he'd survive without you."

"One day he'll have to." A shadow passed over her brow. "At least I hope he will. I don't want to live with my brother for the rest of my life."

Maybe you could come live with me. The words hovered somewhere behind his teeth, until he grabbed a glass of dry white wine and washed them down his throat.

What was he thinking? He'd never asked any woman to live with him. He didn't even want male roommates, which was one of the reasons he lived all by himself in a huge hotel suite.

He liked his space. His freedom.

Didn't he?

Alicia rose and took both their plates. He grabbed them from her hands. "Let me take those." His voice came out a bit gruffer than he'd intended. "You've done enough."

"Oh, don't be silly. What are you going to do with them?" Her eyes sparkled. "You probably don't even know how to run the dishwasher."

"I could learn."

Alicia laughed. Still, he insisted on carrying the plates into the kitchen.

There were a lot of things he could learn. How to cherish the woman who brought a ray of bright, warm light into his life and heart. How to sustain a relationship beyond a month—something he'd never really wanted to do before. Heck, maybe he could even learn how to cook if those wicked hot chilies were involved.

He could even figure out how to have a very different relationship than his parents. And be a real father to his own children.

Children? Now he was truly getting ahead of himself.

He let his eyes drift to Alicia's lush, black-velvet-covered backside as she strode down the hallway just ahead of him, carrying the serving dishes.

Beautiful. And hot.

But so much more. Alicia had clearly obtained great pleasure from making this meal especially for him. She'd put thought and effort into every detail of the preparation and presentation. She'd made a simple dinner truly special.

This was the kind of woman he could imagine sharing all kinds of new experiences with. Maybe even sharing a life with.

His chest constricted. *One step at a time, Justin Dupree. First you need to tell her your real name.*

"Where are you going on your trip?" She turned to confront him with a bright, trusting smile.

"Hong Kong. Meeting with some dock officials."

"Sounds like fun." She entered the small but well-equipped kitchen where she'd made her magic.

"You should come." He meant it.

She laughed. "I have to work, remember? Even though my job doesn't pay megabucks, it means a lot to me. And I have people counting on me."

"Of course. I'll be back on Friday. We could spend next weekend together."

She didn't turn, but he saw her cheek lift in a smile, a smile that spread across the room to him.

Okay. He'd tell her next weekend.

He didn't want to spoil their perfect time together tonight and leave her with a bad taste in her mouth. Next Friday night he'd invite her over, give her something special from Hong Kong to sweep her off her feet, then 'fess up about his little white lie.

Yes. Much better.

He put the dishes into the dishwasher. "See, you can teach an old hound dog new tricks." He grinned, then slid his arms around her waist. "Now, where were we?"

Alicia had noticed a familiar car in the driveway, so she wasn't surprised to see a familiar face in the kitchen of El Diablo when she let herself in.

"Hi, Darius." She shook his hand.

"Hi, Darius?" Alex cut in. "You go away for the weekend and forget about your own brother?"

He walked toward her, his broad grin belying his accusation, and gave her a big bear hug. "I missed you like crazy, 'Manita, but I survived, see?"

"I do see." She kissed his cheek. "How are things going? Do the police have any leads?"

"Nope. That's why Darius is here."

Alicia knew him as another of the Texas Cattleman's

Club's newest members, the owner of a prominent security firm. The tall, dark-skinned man projected an air of effortless confidence. She also knew him as one of Lance Brody's best friends.

"He's looking into all the angles to see if we can figure out what's going on."

"And to make sure it doesn't happen again." Darius had a laptop open on the large island in the center of the kitchen. "Right now it looks like someone out there wants to frame Alex."

"But didn't they find gas cans?"

"Yep. Mine," said Alex. "From the tractor shed. I hadn't used them in months, so someone took them out and filled them, then brought them back here and set the fire."

"That's insane. Who could have done it?"

"No idea." Alex shrugged. "We don't lock the gates here, so anyone can come in and out."

"Anyone *could have* come in and out," corrected Darius. "We're going to put in a security camera and a keypad at the gate so that everyone will have to enter a code to come in and all activity will be recorded."

"I feel like a prisoner in my own home," growled Alex.

"It's for your own safety. And Alicia's." Darius typed on the keyboard. "We're going to set up a security camera near the barn, too."

"You can't be too careful," said Alicia with a shiver. A total stranger had stolen onto the ranch to wreak havoc and cast suspicion on Alex. "Do they still think you set the Brody fire?"

"They do. Lance Brody told Darius that someone saw my truck at the scene."

Alicia looked at Darius, who said nothing.

"That's ridiculous. There must be hundreds of trucks like yours in the Houston area," she said.

"I know. But if someone wants to believe I'm an arsonist, they'll trump up phony evidence any way they can."

"Why would anyone want to frame you?" Fear curled in her chest at the idea that someone would want to get Alex in trouble.

"There are plenty of people around here who'd be glad to see the back of me. Some folks are just bent out of shape that a kid from the barrio can own one of Somerset's finest ranches and become a member of the prestigious Texas Cattleman's Club."

"I admit we still have no leads," said Darius. He closed his laptop and looked up. "But we'll find the culprits of both fires and make sure they're convicted of their crimes."

"And I have faith that you'll find the truth."

Darius extended his hand, and after the slightest of pauses, Alex shook it.

Once the door had closed behind Darius, Alex strode back into the room.

"Alex, I'm surprised you'd have Darius Franklin do this, given how close he is to Lance Brody."

Alex shrugged. "He's the best man for the job, even if he doesn't choose his friends wisely. I trust him." He leaned in close to Alicia. "You look…different."

Alicia's face heated. "What? How on earth would I look different?"

"You're…glowing. Or something. I don't know. It's strange."

"I got a lot of sleep while I was there." Alicia blushed at her lie.

"Nice necklace." His dark eyes fixed on the topaz glittering at her neck.

Alicia's hand flew to it. "Thanks. Julie's Gems." She hoped he'd assume she'd bought it for herself.

"Pretty."

"I missed you."

"I missed you, too, 'Manita. I'm glad it's safe for you to come home. With Darius on the case, I feel we're close to finding out who did this."

"And why. That's the weirdest part."

"Human motivation is a strange thing. You think you know someone, then…" He threw his hands up in the air. "Be careful who you trust, that's what I always say."

He picked up an apple from the large fruit bowl in the center of the island and took a bite. "At least we can always count on each other."

"Absolutely." She uttered the word with conviction, while guilt and anxiety roiled in her stomach.

What would Alex say if he knew she'd spent the weekend with a man?

She longed to talk about Rick—she was overflowing with joy and excitement and hopeful anticipation. But better not to tell Alex, especially right now when he was so suspicious of everyone and everything.

She'd better go spill her guts to a girlfriend instead.

The airy indoor-outdoor café at the Texas Cattleman's Club bustled with a lunchtime crowd. Alicia was pretty sure she could air her confidences without being overheard.

And she sizzled with anticipation at the prospect.

Since joining the club, she'd grown close to Cara Pettigrew-Novak. They were friends years earlier while Cara's marriage to her college-sweetheart husband, Kevin, had slowly fallen apart, and she'd been thrilled to see them recently mend their broken bridges and get back together—apparently happier than ever.

She waved from her table as she caught sight of the statuesque blonde in the doorway. Cara waved back and weaved through the elegantly set tables toward Alicia.

They rose to kiss. "Oh, my goodness, you're positively radioactive," exclaimed Cara. She tucked her curly blond hair behind her shoulders and sank into her seat. "I can't wait to hear about the man who put that gleam in your eyes."

Alicia let out a wistful sigh, unable to stop a goofy grin from creeping over her face. "He's amazing."

Cara poured them both a glass of sparkling water. "I can tell, without you even saying a word. More details please!"

Alicia glanced around as if Rick might walk in at any moment and hear her bragging about him.

"Well, you remember the night I met him, when you were here at the club for Lance and Kate's reception. We just spent the most amazing weekend together," Alicia said.

"What does he look like?" Cara raised a slim, blond brow.

"Oh, tall, dark, handsome. Nothing special." Alicia blushed a little.

"Sure." Cara winked. "And I bet he doesn't have a muscle on his whole body."

"He is rather nicely built, even by your standards." Cara owned a chain of dance studios and always looked ready to compete in the Olympics. "Not to put too fine a point on it, he's perfect." Alicia sipped her water and the bubbles sparkled over her tongue.

"Oh, I'm not sure any man's perfect."

"Come on, you got back together with Kevin after all those years apart."

"Kevin certainly isn't perfect. He's pretty damn wonderful, though." A smile spread across her lovely face. "And I still love him like crazy."

"I know. I admit I used to be horribly jealous of you two. You were so lucky to meet the right man in college."

"Uh, hello? I almost divorced him. We've spent more time apart than we have together over the past few years. And part of the problem was that we found each other too early on. He wasn't ready to settle down, not really."

"I guess you're right. Good things come to those who wait."

"Something I've never been very good at, unfortunately." Cara waved to the waiter. "Why waste time reading the menu? Let's just have a hunk tell us what's good."

Alicia had noticed that the waiters at the Texas Cattleman's Club tended to be dashingly handsome. Their long white aprons gave the place an air of a refined European bistro.

A gorgeous young man with cropped dark hair approached the table.

"Could you tell us what's really sensational today?" asked Cara with an innocent smile.

"The red snapper is so fresh it's almost swimming. And the sauce made the chef cry. It's served on a bed of locally grown organic vegetables."

"Sold." Cara slapped her menu closed.

"Oooh. Me, too. And a Diet Coke."

"No wine?" Cara raised a brow. "I'll have a glass of pinot noir."

After the waiter had disappeared, she leaned toward Alicia. "I can't believe you're going to drink soda with a meal like this."

"I don't like to drink at lunch. Makes me tipsy."

"As long as there are no *other* reasons..." Cara narrowed her eyes.

Alicia gasped. "Absolutely not." She raised her hand in a three-fingered brownie salute. "On my honor." Then she paused as a chill swept over her. "At least I hope not."

"Please tell me you've been taking precautions."

"Yes. Of course I have."

It was time for her to get serious about contraception. Maybe take the pill or something. She'd never even needed to think about it before. Although they'd used condoms, she knew they weren't all that reliable.

"You don't sound too sure."

"Can we change the subject?" Alicia squeaked, as a flush crept up her neck.

"No way. Not until you tell me more about the man who has you glowing like a nuclear accident. Tell me his name again? I can't remember it."

"Rick Jones."

"Jones?" She pursed her pretty mouth. "I don't think I know anyone with that name. Which is funny, when you think about it. I guess he's not a member."

"I don't think so. I've mentioned his name a couple of times and no one seems to know him."

"How odd that you met him here, then. I suppose he must have been here as a guest. What does he do?"

"Something in shipping. He's in Hong Kong right now on business."

"There's big money in shipping."

"I kind of got that impression. He lives in a hotel suite."

She laughed. "That's one way to avoid cleaning and cooking."

"Yes. He's totally unembarrassed about his inability to do either."

"I guess he saves his energy for other pursuits." Cara lifted a brow.

Alicia felt her face heat up. "You're absolutely right. And he sails, too. We went out on his yacht."

"A yacht!" Cara clapped her hands together. "I love it. Was it one of those huge things with a full-size kitchen and a staff of ten?"

"No, a slick racing yacht with barely room to turn around."

"Really?" Cara frowned and put down her fork. "Have you ever met Justin Dupree?"

Alicia racked her brain. "Nope. Don't think so."

"He's a member so you'll run into him sooner or later. He's heir to some vast shipping empire. Absolutely rolling in it, or so they say. And he's into yacht racing, too."

"Weird. I guess those pursuits aren't all that unusual around here."

"Not if you're loaded to the gills." Cara rolled her

eyes. "I'm glad it's not him, though. He's a serious skirt chaser. I'd be giving you some stern warnings."

"Well, I honestly have no idea what Rick is like when I'm not with him. We've only spent time alone so I haven't actually met any of his friends." She sighed. "He's so gorgeous he must have women falling all over him."

"But he has eyes only for you."

"So far." Alicia smiled. "He's been unbelievable. I'm not very…experienced." She cleared her throat, unwilling to admit exactly how inexperienced she was. "And he's been so thoughtful and caring."

"He sounds like a keeper. Has he met Alex yet?"

Alicia stopped, her glass suspended in the air. "Not yet."

Cara laughed. "You're afraid, aren't you?"

"Of course not! Alex is perfectly reasonable."

"Oh, come on! He tried to stop you from seeing *me* when we were first friends. He thought I was fast or something, because I did a lot of dancing and cheerleading."

"He's very traditional." Why did she always feel such a strong urge to defend Alex?

"Traditional? He's downright Neanderthal when it comes to protecting you. Still, if you need a buffer there when you tell him about Rick, I'll be there for ya. We could even get together right here in the café. Nice and informal."

"I don't think so." Alicia winced. "I only just started dating him. I don't want to freak him out. Not yet, anyway." She giggled. "But if things continue the way they've been going so far, I may well take you up on your offer."

"I'm glad to hear it. You deserve to meet someone fabulous."

"I agree." Alicia raised her Diet Coke and clinked it against Cara's wineglass. "To romance."

The snapper smelled sensational when it arrived, borne by the equally delicious waiter.

She took a bite. "I can see why the chef cried. Then again, since I met Rick everything seems…brighter, richer, more flavorful. Is that crazy?"

"Absolutely. Sounds like love."

"Oh, it can't be love. Like I said, we only just met. We've had a few dates, and I spent one weekend with him."

"Sometimes that's all it takes. Where is his suite?"

"The Houston Omni, near the Galleria. It has views all over Houston—it's incredible."

Cara paused. "The Omni? I'm pretty sure that's where Justin Dupree lives. I went to a wild party there a couple of years ago. You could see all of downtown from his living room." Her friend's face turned serious. "Are you sure it's not him?"

Alicia shook her head, perplexed. "His name's Rick. Of course it's not him."

"I don't know, Alicia. He's a shipping heir, tall, dark and handsome, races yachts and lives at the Houston Omni. Don't you think that's a bit too much of a coincidence?"

Alicia frowned. "That is odd."

"I have a weird feeling it's the same guy."

Cold fear skated down Alicia's spine. "Why would he change his name?"

"I can't even begin to imagine." Cara frowned. "You

know what? There's a picture of Justin Dupree in last month's *Vanity Fair.* Let's go look at it and you can tell me if he looks anything like your Rick. They've probably still got a copy in the library."

Eight

The library's stone fireplace and gleaming black and white floor always gave Alicia the sense of being in a grand castle.

Today, she felt like she was heading for the execution block.

Couldn't Cara just let her enjoy her first-ever chance to brag about a hot date?

Now a creepy mystery cast a shadow over her glorious weekend with Rick.

Or at least she thought he was Rick.

Cara riffled through a stack of magazines spread over a low shelf while Alicia stood nearby.

Doubts skated around her mind, bumping into faith that it was all a silly misunderstanding. Hopefully Justin Dupree—whoever he was—would look nothing whatsoever like Rick.

"There he is." Cara stabbed the shiny page with a fingernail, then handed it to Alicia.

Her red snapper turned into a lead ball in her stomach when she saw the picture: Rick, gorgeous in black tie, with both arms wrapped around the impossibly slim waist of a smiling blonde in a barely-there dress.

She scanned the caption: "Shipping Heir Justin Dupree Squires Mila Jankovich to Blake Foundation Gala."

Her rib cage turned into a vice, tightening over her heart. "It's him," she breathed. "I can't believe it. Why would he lie to me?" Tears already hovered in her voice.

"I don't know, sweetie, but we'll find out." Cara slid an arm around her back.

Alicia's initial shock was quickly morphing into anger. "Why didn't he want me to know who he is? I noticed he didn't introduce me to anyone at the yacht club." She frowned and put the magazine down on a table. "And now that I think about it, he wouldn't come into this club with me, either. Now I know why." She blew out a breath. "It might have been awkward if one of his buddies slapped him on the back and said, 'Hey, Justin!'"

"It is odd. He's a member here, though he doesn't come all that often. I guess he travels a lot. Or maybe just hangs out at the yacht club, instead."

"You know him?"

"I've met him. He's friends with Mitch and Lance."

"Mitch and Lance *Brody?*" Alicia's eyes widened.

Cara smiled. "Do you know any other Mitch and Lance combos?"

Alicia's body grew cold. "Mitch and Lance think Alex set the fire at their refinery. They hate him."

A nasty possibility occurred to her. "Do you think

they could have sent Justin my way to dig up information about Alex?"

Cara stared at her, blue eyes wide with confusion. "I can't imagine they'd stoop to something like that. I admit I don't know Justin all that well, but I'm sure he's too busy to get involved in intrigues." She squeezed Alicia's hand. "Oh, sweetie, I know how much he meant to you."

"Believe me, I am eternally in your debt." Her voice sounded as calm and cold as she felt. "I'm glad I found out now and not after he'd had more fun at my expense."

"I'm pretty sure Kevin knows him. Maybe he can shed some light on the whole situation."

Humiliation burned in Alicia's gut. "Please don't tell Kevin. Or anyone." She glanced over her shoulder and was glad to find the library empty. "It'd be so awful if everyone knew. Or if Alex found out."

Ugh! She'd trusted her own instincts for once, followed her pathetic, girlish heart, and look what happened.

She blinked to keep tears from springing to her eyes.

"Hey, here's a crazy idea." Cara reached into her bag for a tissue and offered it, but Alicia shook her head. "Why don't you *ask* him?"

"Ask Rick? I mean, *Justin?*" She snorted. "I wouldn't even know how to address him when he picked up the phone." She shook her head. "I'd rather die than give him another chance to lie to me."

Her spine grew rigid as she realized the extent of his deception. "We spent the whole weekend together— literally every hour—so he had ample time to tell me who he really is if he was ever going to. Which apparently he wasn't."

"It doesn't make any sense."

"The only way it makes sense is if he wanted to keep me separate from his real life. A bit on the side." She glanced back at the glossy issue of *Vanity Fair.* "Why does that woman look familiar?"

"She's a model." Cara waved a hand as if to dismiss her. "Does some fashion stuff and a bunch of Revlon ads. Very overexposed."

"Great. His real girlfriend is a supermodel. I guess I should feel bad for her, too." The tears threatened again. "I want to go home."

"Listen, Alicia, that picture means nothing. Just because he took some girl to a gala does not mean he's engaged to her."

"Then why is he wrapped around her like a tortilla?" She shrugged her clutch bag higher under her arm. "It doesn't matter anyway. It's over between us."

"Oh, sweetie. Maybe there's some perfectly reasonable explanation."

"Yeah. Maybe he was abducted by aliens and they sent him back to earth with a new identity." She cocked her head.

"I said a *reasonable* explanation."

"When you come up with one, give me a call."

"I'm so sorry." Cara's pretty face was taut with distress. "I wish I wasn't the bearer of the bad news."

Alicia gave her a hug. "You're a true friend. A lot of people would have let me go on seeing him because they didn't want to make waves. I'm very grateful. I just need to go home and have a good cry."

Justin couldn't understand it. He'd called Alicia when he landed in Hong Kong and left a message on her cell.

No response.

Okay, so some people had trouble with international dialing codes. He called back first thing the next morning, which was early evening in Houston.

No answer. Left another message.

Now, three days later he'd left at least six messages and had yet to hear a word from her.

He loosened his tie and stretched out in the leather chair at his hotel desk.

Not talking to her was driving him mad. If he couldn't enjoy the feel of her soft body against his, he at least wanted to hear her warm, sensual voice over the phone. He missed her with an ache that tightened his muscles. He couldn't remember ever hurting this badly for a woman.

Alicia was so different from all the other women he'd dated. Self-possessed and calm, she didn't try to impress him by bragging about her accomplishments. Instead, he had to tease them out of her.

She was thoughtful and caring, as evidenced by the lovely dinner she made for him. Ever since, he'd been longing to try his hand in the kitchen so he could make something for her and return the gesture.

In addition to being brilliant and kind, she was also smoking hot between the sheets—and anywhere else they happened to be when the mood struck.

And fun. Sailing with her had been a blast. He could tell her first taste of speed had given her an appetite for more. She'd be a great racing companion, with her no-nonsense, practical attitude and her sunny approach to life.

She was a great companion, period. And he wanted

to spend a lot of time with her. Possibly even the rest of his life.

Justin blew out hard. Suddenly everything looked different. Traveling wouldn't be an end in itself if he had Alicia to come home to. He wouldn't need to blow off steam by partying and jumping off mountains anymore.

He could think of far better ways to unwind—in Alicia's arms.

His phone lay on the desk, its shiny black surface an affront. He wanted to pick it up and call her again, but there was such a thing as coming on too strong.

Not something he'd ever thought about before.

Usually he was the one hoping someone would back off. He generally tired of women before they tired of him—right around the time they started hinting at something permanent.

That sent him off in a cloud of dust.

Justin frowned.

Maybe Alicia needed to cool off a little after all the time they'd spent together.

When he got back he'd bring her a big bunch of flowers, deal with the awkward business about his name, and start over again.

He leaned back in his chair. Only three more days. He could handle it.

"You've been working late all week." Alex frowned at Alicia as she came through the door at the ranch late on Friday evening. Her usual glow had noticeably dimmed and she seemed rushed and tense.

"Busy. We're gearing up for a visiting exhibition,

which involved stripping down the big gallery and packing all the pieces away. Today the walls went up, but they still need painting."

She marched into the kitchen and threw her big leather bag on the island. "And I've got a bunch of phone calls to make about the plans for downtown."

"No wonder you look tired." He crossed his arms over his chest. "But usually you love all that stuff. You hate having too little to do. Is something else going on?"

She blinked, and if he wasn't mistaken, she swallowed. "Nope. Nothing." She bustled over to the fridge and started unloading storage containers onto the island.

"Alicia...." He said her name in the singsong way that drove her crazy. "I don't believe you."

"Don't then." She opened up a container and sniffed.

Alex frowned. She hadn't actually snapped at him, but that's what it felt like.

Something was definitely going on. His first instinct was to collar his baby sister and make her 'fess up. But his urge to protect Alicia sometimes threatened to drive a wedge between them. He held himself in check. She was a grown woman, and entitled to some privacy.

He wasn't going to say a single word.

Not yet, anyway. If she was still moping by Monday he wouldn't be able to restrain himself.

The phone rang, and instead of moving to answer it like she usually did, Alicia started spooning leftover casserole into a baking dish.

"I'll get it," he said. She did too much around here. Who was he to assume it was her job to answer the phone, anyway?

"No." Her sharp answer made him stop in his tracks. "I will."

But instead of picking up the phone on the wall in the kitchen, she hurried down the hall to the den.

And she didn't pick it up there, either.

Alex stuck his head out the kitchen door in time to see her crouch to read the caller ID. Instead of picking up the handset, she pushed the button to send the message straight to voice mail.

Curiosity overtook him. Like a *vaquero* stealing up on a runaway calf, he crept down the hallway.

With her attention fixed on the machine blurting its greeting in her friendly voice, Alicia didn't even see him.

"Alicia, it's me…uh…Rick. I've been calling your cell all week but there's no answer. I know you told me not to call you at home, but I'm worried about you."

Cold shock settled into Alex's stomach.

Alicia was seeing someone. Or not seeing him. Apparently, she was avoiding this *Rick's* phone calls.

This man was bothering her. Pestering her.

Rick who? He didn't know any Rick. He was nervous about her being around those moneyed hotshots at the Texas Cattleman's Club, but so far she hadn't shown a peep of interest in any of them.

Or so he'd thought.

He sucked in a deep, silent breath. Alicia stood watching the phone, arms crossed and eyes narrowed.

"I don't know what's going on, but I had a wonderful time with you and I'm really looking forward to seeing you again. I'm back in Houston and you know where to find me. So, call me, okay?"

The machine clicked off. Something in Alex clicked into the *on* position. "Who the hell was that?"

Alicia wheeled around and gasped. "What are you doing listening to my phone calls?"

"Since when did you start keeping secrets from me?"

Tears welled in her big brown eyes. "Since I started wanting a life of my own." Anger and pain rang in her voice. "But I haven't been doing a very good job of it, so go ahead and yell at me."

She stormed past him down the hallway and back into the kitchen. She shoved the casserole dish into the microwave and punched the numbers with uncharacteristic drama.

Alex fought the urge to yell.

His natural instinct to go ballistic was an "opportunity," according to the corporate management book he'd been reading lately. An opportunity to become more...approachable.

He drew in a measured breath. "Would you like to tell me what's going on?"

"Not really." She swiped at a tear with her wrist, and turned to pull the lid off a container of day-old rice.

When Alicia stopped cooking and started reheating leftovers, something was very wrong.

"What did this Rick do to you?" He managed to keep his tone even.

"Nothing. Nothing at all. It doesn't matter." She slammed open a kitchen cabinet and retrieved two dishes with a loud clatter.

"Alicia Montoya, I know you better than I know myself and I don't think I've ever seen you this upset. Now you want to lie to me and tell me everything's okay?"

She stopped dead, hands frozen in midair with their plates.

"I don't want to lie to you, Alex." She turned, slowly, and set the plates on to the island. "I don't ever want to lie to you, or to anyone else."

She took a deep breath and tucked a strand of hair behind her ear. Then she lifted her chin and looked him dead in the eye with an expression he'd never seen before. "I spent last weekend with him."

A fist closed around Alex's heart. "At his house?"

"In a hotel."

Alex's lungs couldn't hold air. This sleazebag had taken his baby sister to a hotel? Probably some lowlife motel filled with hookers and junkies and… "Where can I find him?"

Alicia pursed her lips with distaste. "And you wonder why I didn't tell you about him?" She crossed her arms over her chest. "You treat me like a little kid. You *made* me sneak around. I would have liked to tell you about him and see if you know him and ask you what you think, but because you turn into a raging beast at the thought of me dating a mere mortal, I couldn't."

Alex frowned. Was this true?

She'd dated. He remembered those sorry losers who came to the house over the years.

He'd made sure to let them know that Alicia was not just any girl they could grope and fondle and tell their friends about. Maybe he had scared a few of them off.

"You deserve the best, 'Manita."

"I know you only want to protect me, but it's too much. I'm twenty-six and I need to make my own mistakes." Her stern demeanor wavered. "And I just made one, but it's okay. I learned from it, and I'll know what to do differently next time."

Alex worked hard to keep his breathing steady. The urge to pummel someone—namely this Rick—made his blood pump fast and hard. "I'm glad you learned from your mistake." Good. His voice sounded nice and calm.

"We went out a few times and I really liked him." Her eyes shone with pleasure. Which was like a fist of very unpleasant feeling to Alex's gut.

"He was sweet, considerate." Her expression hardened. "So, after the fire, I decided to go stay with him."

"You lied to me."

"I did. There was enough drama already. I didn't need to make more, for either of us. I just wanted to spend the weekend with a man I'd grown to like." A frown furrowed her pretty forehead. "But he turned out to be a totally different man altogether."

Adrenaline flashed through Alex. "Did he hurt you?"

"No! Nothing like that at all. But he's not right for me. That's all that matters." Her gaze implored him not to pry further.

He stepped forward and took her in his arms. She softened and let him hug her.

"You be careful with those rich boys at the club. Those kind of men eat girls like you for breakfast."

"I know. I wasn't planning to date one of them. It just happened. But it's over now. Can we leave it in the past?"

"Sure, 'Manita. Just one of those things."

Rick. The name didn't ring a bell. He'd put out feelers though. By this time tomorrow he'd know who'd made his baby sister cry. And then he'd figure out what to do with him.

* * *

Justin scanned the café at the Texas Cattleman's Club. No sign of Alicia. He poked his head in the game room. Still nothing. He was about to go explore the library, when a hand on his arm stopped him.

"Justin Dupree, I presume." Cara Pettigrew-Novak fixed him with a steel-blue gaze.

"At your service, ma'am."

"Just checking, because I thought you might be someone called Rick Jones."

Justin frowned. "I've been known to use that alias on occasion." He arched his brow.

"So I hear. You used it on my friend Alicia."

"Where is Alicia? Is she okay?" Urgency sparked through him.

"She's fine, no thanks to you. Why did you give her a fake name?"

Was that why she wouldn't return his calls? He knew she wouldn't like it, but he was pretty sure it wouldn't be a deal breaker. Not after they'd shared so much together.

"I use it all the time. Keeps the press off my trail."

"Alicia isn't a journalist."

"I know that, now."

"Did you ever think she was?" Cara tilted her chin.

"No. I didn't." He narrowed his eyes. "What exactly is going on? Does Alicia know I'm Justin Dupree?"

"She does."

"How?"

"I told her." She crossed her arms. "I thought she should know. Don't you?"

"Yes, of course. I was planning to tell her." Why was

he having this conversation with Cara, when he should be talking to Alicia? "Is she here?"

"Nope. Haven't seen her. I hear someone broke her heart."

Justin gulped. "She was upset?"

"Really, really upset."

"Damn." His chest tightened. "I've got to explain."

"That you didn't want the press on your trail?" She chuckled. "I'm not sure that will go over well."

"That I wanted to tell her because I...because she..." *Because I've never met anyone I care about so much.* "Where is she?"

"At home, I imagine. El Diablo." She leaned close. "It was cruel, you know, giving her a fake name so she wouldn't know she was being seduced into bed by one of the foremost ladies' men in all Texas."

"Cara, you exaggerate." He tried to make light of her barb. "And I didn't seduce her. At least I don't think I did. It was mutual. And why am I telling this to you?"

"I told her she should give you a chance to tell your side of the story. I assured her there was probably a perfectly reasonable explanation. So far, I haven't heard one, but..." She shrugged her slim shoulders. "She didn't seem very interested."

"I've got to go see her." He reached into his pocket for his car key.

"You'll recall that she lives with her brother." Cara tilted her head, waiting for his reaction.

"Alex Montoya. I'm sure he'll be reasonable."

She laughed. "He can be, under the right circumstances—which these definitely aren't." She patted his arm. "Listen, I don't know you that well, but you seem like an okay guy. At least that's what Kevin, Lance and Mitch say."

"I'm honored."

"And Alicia was pretty smitten with you before I clued her in to your little deception. I hope you two manage to work it out."

"Me, too."

The gate to El Diablo was locked, and Justin had to use the intercom to request admittance.

"Name?"

He thought for a second. "Rick Jones." That's what she'd expect him to call himself.

With relief, he saw the gate swing open, and he drove in.

Cattle grazed in fenced pastures on either side of the long curving drive that led up to the grand old house. Alex Montoya had done well for himself—and for Alicia—especially considering their humble background.

Alex was a smart man. Hopefully not one to jump to rash conclusions, or hold a grudge.

Yeah. Right. He and Lance had one of the longest-running grudges in local history.

He parked in the turnaround in front of the house and stepped out. Before he'd reached the shady porch, Alex emerged from the front door, his dark, intense eyes set in a fierce glare.

His deep voice boomed through the air. "Since when do you go by the name Rick Jones?"

"Is Alicia at home? I need to speak with her, Alex."

"She doesn't want to see you." Alex took the steps two at a time, until he was standing chin to chin with

Justin. Alex's chin, however, was several inches higher than his. "You can leave now."

"I'd appreciate the chance to talk with her."

"That won't be possible." The taller man's eyes narrowed. "Do you always use a fake name with women that you plan to use and cast aside? Nice girls who don't have blue blood so they're ripe for the plucking?"

Alex's eyes flashed. He grabbed Justin by the shirt, knuckles digging into his chest.

"It's a bit more innocent than that. I get hounded by the paparazzi so sometimes I resort to—"

"If you didn't sleep with so many damned heiresses, the paparazzi wouldn't be interested in you," Alex hissed right in his face. "If you come near my sister again, I'll, I'll… I don't know what I'll do, but let's not find out."

He removed his fist from the front of Justin's shirt and looked at it as if it had a mind of its own.

"Your sister means a lot to me." He held his head high. "She's a very special person."

"You think I don't know that?" Alex cocked his head and stared hard at Justin. "My sister is too good for someone who associates himself with the Brody brothers." His voice took on a tone of polished steel.

"Mitch Brody and I have been good friends for a long time, and I know his brother Lance, too. They're good men, Alex."

Alex leaned in until Justin could smell the testosterone rolling off him. "Did they put you up to this?"

"Of course not. I happened to meet Alicia at the club, we struck up a conversation and became friends." Which was the truth. Justin had volunteered to get information on Alex for the Brodys; they hadn't asked him to. The thought of it now made him feel sick. How could he have even considered doing that to Alicia?

"Do I look like I was born yesterday?" Alex's hands looked like they were itching to wrap themselves around Justin's neck.

"Alicia is a beautiful and intelligent woman. I don't need an ulterior motive to be interested in her. As I've tried to explain, I care for her very much. The name thing was a misunderstanding. Entirely my fault. If you'd just let me speak to Alicia for a few minutes, I'm sure—"

"Get off my ranch!" Steam was about to start rising out of Alex's dark hair. "If you don't leave now, I'll have my men tow your car—and you—to the gates."

"Alex." Alicia appeared behind him in the doorway. "It's okay. I can handle it."

Justin's heart surged. "Alicia, I can explain."

"Go back inside, 'Manita. He's leaving."

Alicia came down the steps in faded jeans that hugged her spectacular legs and a simple denim shirt. Ravishing. "Alex, I said I can handle it. I'm not a baby."

Her eyes met Justin's and energy crashed between them. Hope swelled in his chest.

"I've been burning to tell you my real name, but the time never seemed quite right. I'm mortified that you found out and I promise to make it up to you."

Alicia strode past Alex, boot heels firm on the hard ground. "Get in your car. I'll ride to the gate with you."

"Maybe we could sit somewhere and talk."

Alicia ignored him, rounded his Porsche and opened the passenger side.

"'Manita, I don't think you should—" Alex's interjection was cut off by Alicia slamming the car door shut.

Justin turned his back on Alex and got in on the driver's side. He turned to look at her. "I missed you," he said softly.

"Start the engine." She stared straight ahead.

He hesitated for a second, then turned the key. "Cara told me what happened."

"Yes. I felt like a real ass."

"I'm so, so sorry. I never meant for you to find out from someone else."

He wasn't embarrassed by the pleading tone in his voice. Part of him was just grateful and relieved to be sharing a space with her again.

"Drive." She nodded to the gearshift. Justin reluctantly shifted into Drive and started along the driveway. "I don't want to see you again."

"Alicia, you don't mean that."

"Trust me—and me, you can trust, I'm pretty straightforward, unlike some people—so trust me, I mean it with every bone in my body."

"I use the name Rick Jones all the time. I'm registered at the hotel under that name."

"You registered with a fake license and credit card?" She cocked a brow.

"Well, no. They do know my real name, but officially, on the books, I'm Rick Jones."

"But they have the privilege of knowing your real name. A privilege I was not granted." Her voice was silvery and cool, not the warm caress he remembered. "Even after we slept together."

"I wanted to tell you since the beginning. I tried several times but…"

"But what?"

He shoved a hand through his hair. "I guess I knew all along that it would be a big deal to you. Once I got to know you, that is. I could tell that you'd consider even a minor fib to be a huge deception."

"You were right about that. And I'd hardly consider lying about your identity to be a minor fib."

Despite him driving as slowly as the car would go, they were dangerously close to the gates. Kidnapping her was tempting, but definitely not a good idea under the circumstances.

"What can I do to make it up to you?"

"You can't. As I said, I don't wish to see you again. Since we're both members of the Texas Cattleman's Club, there's no way we can avoid each other completely, but I see no reason for anything beyond a polite greeting in the future."

She held her head with the dignity of a queen. Strange how someone could look so regal when dressed like a cowgirl, but that was Alicia Montoya. A woman of many dimensions, each more fascinating and compelling than the last.

If he told her he loved her, would that melt her hardened heart?

He cursed the thought even as it occurred to him. If he told her right now she'd think he was toying with her.

"Could I take you out on my yacht again, as a friend?" He didn't try to cajole or sweet-talk her. She'd loved sailing though, he could tell.

"No. You can stop right outside the gates. I'll walk back in."

"Alicia, you're making too much of this."

"That's your opinion. As you've already admitted,

you knew it would be a big deal to me so you deliberately continued to conceal the truth. I told you all kinds of confidences."

She turned to look at him, finally, eyes filled with tears. "I told you about my childhood, and my family, and all our private hopes and dreams. And you chose to disrespect me by keeping the truth from me, so it wouldn't interfere with all the hot sex we were having."

A fat tear fell and rolled down one lovely cheek.

Justin's heart ached to bursting. He longed to reach out and touch her, but he knew that would propel her from the car.

"It wasn't just about sex." His voice was gruff. "You mean a lot more to me than that. I truly enjoyed every minute we spent together. I was afraid of spoiling it, yes. I figured the longer we spent together and the more you got to know me, the less of a big deal it would be when I finally told you. I almost gave it away when you noticed I spoke French—my family is originally from France and we've always spent enough time there to become fluent. I was about to turn and tell you everything, but there you lay, naked and resplendent, and the words withered on my tongue because I didn't want to drive you away."

A tear rolled down Alicia's other cheek. She did nothing to brush it away. "I trusted you. I came to you asking for help. You knew I was innocent—dangerously naive, even—and you took advantage of that. Why didn't you tell me you were friends with the men who are trying to frame my brother for arson? Or that you already knew my brother? How could you keep that from me?"

"I didn't think it—"

"I don't even want to know." She shook her head. "After what's happened between us I could never trust you again, and I don't intend to try."

"But—" Panic surged through Justin as she reached for the door handle.

"Please, don't come to El Diablo again. You won't be welcome here."

"I'll call you, after you've had some time to think."

"No. Don't call, don't visit, don't write." She turned a cold, dark gaze on him. "I'll be polite when I meet you in company, but don't for a single second think that it means I've forgiven you."

She swung her long denim-clad legs to the ground, then slammed the door.

It couldn't have hurt more if she'd slammed it right on his heart.

Nine

Justin heaved his clubs back into his locker. He'd whacked a ball around all eighteen holes of the Texas Cattleman's Club golf course, and it hadn't helped a bit. His muscles stung with energy and his legs itched to run.

He couldn't stand still, or sit, or sleep when every fiber of his body ached to be with Alicia.

"Hey, Justin!" Kevin Novak strode into the locker room, blond hair windblown, hauling his own clubs. "I hear you're in the doghouse with my wife."

"Yeah. The girls have closed ranks against me." He shut the locker door. "Can't say I blame 'em though. I'm guilty on all counts."

Kevin pulled out his driver and wiped off the end with a cloth. "I can see the advantages of having a double identity. You could get up to all kinds of tricks and no one could pin it on you." He winked. "Sounds fun."

"That's all in the past. I don't want to play tricks on anyone, but old habits die hard and all that. Rick Jones is dead. I killed him myself. I stand before you and everyone else as Justin Dupree."

"The only man crazy enough to pursue Alex Montoya's sister."

Justin walked over to Kevin. "Alicia is the most incredible woman I've ever met. I'd walk through fire for her."

"I'm sure her brother would be happy to arrange that." Kevin raised a brow.

"Yeah. Can't blame him though. If I had a sister I'd probably feel the same way."

"Do you think she'll ever forgive you?"

"She won't give me a chance to get close to her. She was here this morning and barely acknowledged me." He let out a long sigh. "I've closed billion-dollar deals with my archrivals in the business world, but I can't even get her to look my way."

"You need a plan." Kevin settled his humorous blue gaze on him. "And I think I have one. Why don't Cara and I invite you and Alicia to dinner? Then you'll be on neutral turf and you can talk things out."

"Alicia would never agree."

"She will if we don't tell her you'll be there."

"She'll leave when I show up."

"No, she won't. She and Cara are good friends, and Alicia's very polite and thoughtful. I don't think she'd blow off a dinner someone else spent time preparing."

"You might be onto something there. But will Cara go for the idea?"

Kevin put his clubs in his locker. "Cara's got a soft spot for you. She thinks you're ready to settle down and enjoy some wedded bliss."

"She does, huh?"

"Hey, I screwed things up between Cara and me because I wasn't ready for family life when we first got married. I put all my energy into making money and almost lost the truly important things no amount of money can buy. I've been given a second chance and I feel it's my duty to help another lonely man find the way to his woman's heart."

"Kevin Novak, a romantic. Now I've seen everything."

"I just know how good it feels to enjoy life with the woman you love."

"I hear you. I'd do almost anything to get back in Alicia's good graces."

"How about Saturday?" Kevin shut his locker.

"If you think this crazy idea will work, then I'm game."

A small knot formed in Alicia's stomach as she rode in the elevator up to Cara and Kevin's apartment in downtown Houston. She was eternally grateful to Cara for alerting her to Justin's deception, but how much had Cara told her husband? She'd begged Cara to keep the embarrassing truth secret, but married couples probably shared everything.

She'd always hoped to have a marriage with no secrets. Or even just a relationship.

Anger trickled through her when she thought about how Justin Dupree had duped her. He'd taken something from her—trust—and it would be a long time, if ever, before she got it back again.

"Alicia!" Cara greeted her with a kiss at the open door. "Come in, we're so pleased you could come."

"Alex didn't want to let me out of the house." Alicia gave Cara her jacket and walked into the chic, modern space. "He's hovering over me more than ever. I think he'd like to rip Justin Dupree limb from limb."

"Yikes." Cara made a face. "Still, I think it's adorable how protective he is."

"I wish he'd find someone else to protect." She sighed. "Though I can't say I blame him. Apparently, I need protecting."

"You do not. It was a silly misunderstanding. Justin's really sorry."

"And how do you know? You haven't talked to him, have you?"

"Well, actually—" Cara reddened. "Come in and have a drink."

"You didn't, did you?" Alicia grabbed her arm, panic surging inside her. The idea of people sitting around whispering about her humiliation made her want to curl up into a ball. "Please, tell me you didn't say anything."

"Sweetie," Cara squeezed her hand, "I know you want to forget about the whole thing, but I think that would be a terrible waste."

"What do you mean?" A bad feeling crept over her. "What are you up to?"

"Come into the living room." Cara tugged her by the hand. "I made my world-famous cheese puffs."

"You know I can't resist those." Alicia forced a smile to hide a growing sense of dread. "The apartment is lovely." She might as well attempt to be polite.

"Thanks. We're both counting the days until our house in Somerset is ready. They should break ground next month."

Cara pulled her through a double doorway into a large living room. Candlelight glowed on a low table in front of the inviting black sofa and classical music rose from hidden speakers.

"Hi, Alicia." A deep, familiar voice rose from somewhere as hidden as the speakers.

Alicia stopped dead, gripped by panic.

Justin came into view on the left side of the room, holding a tumbler. She tried to focus on his glass so she didn't have to meet the gaze of those intense blue eyes.

She gulped. "Cara, what's going on?"

"Kevin and I wanted to have a couple of our good friends to dinner." She tugged on Alicia's hand, but Alicia remained rooted to the spot. "White or red wine? Or would you prefer something else?"

I'll be polite when I meet you in company.

Could she follow through on her promise?

"Justin." She nodded. Then she swept past him. She did not take his offered hand or even look him full in the face. It was the best she could do for now.

Every fiber of her being screamed for her to run straight out the door, but what would that accomplish? This was the first day of the rest of her life—as the woman tricked by Justin Dupree. She might as well get used to it.

Though she wasn't going to forgive Cara and Kevin anytime soon. She'd eat dinner, be as cordial as she could manage, then go home and lock herself in her bedroom for the rest of the weekend. "Red, please."

"Great. It's a wonderful Malbec Kevin brought back from Argentina. And help yourself to my cheese puffs." Cara practically danced across the room.

Alicia moved slowly to a black leather chair. She wasn't sure she could eat a cheese puff without throwing up, let alone an entire dinner.

But if Justin expected her to turn and run, he was wrong.

"How was your week?" That soft, warm voice, with a touch of grit, crept over her.

"Fine, thanks." *No thanks to you.*

She scanned the room. Cara's inventive touch was visible in colorful accents and a bright, contemporary painting that lit up the wall.

She'd bet the whole place was black and white when Kevin lived here by himself. Cara shone a ray of bright light into everyone's life. It was a shame she'd never accept an invitation here again. She forced a smile as Cara handed her a glass.

"To new beginnings," said Cara gaily. When her toast was met with an awkward silence, her bright expression faltered. "Mine and Kevin's. We're happier than we've ever been."

"That's great." Alicia raised her glass. "I'm thrilled for you." Her words rang a little hollow, and the wine splashed in her glass as Justin moved closer to join the toast.

She shrank as his arm neared hers, though she let him clink his glass against hers. It was only polite, after all.

"Dinner will be ready in a couple of minutes. Let me go check on it." Cara hurried away to the kitchen, leaving Alicia in her chair with Kevin and Justin standing right over her.

"So, Justin, entering any yacht races this month?"

"The season's winding down but I might squeeze in one more if I'm in town the last week of the month. Depends on a few things."

Alicia could swear she felt Kevin glance down at her, but she kept her eyes firmly fixed on her glass.

"Alicia, have you ever been sailing?"

Kevin's question made her voice catch in her throat. She cleared it, but before she could speak, Justin cut in. "Alicia came out on my boat with me last week. She's a natural sailor."

"Did you enjoy it?" Kevin smiled at her expectantly.

Had Justin put him up to this? Her neck prickled with irritation.

"It was an interesting experience. I'm not sure I like drifting out in the middle of nowhere. I suspect I'm a landlubber at heart." She smiled pleasantly, though it felt more like a grimace.

"Nonsense! You took to the water like a mermaid." Justin's voice trickled into her ears again.

"A flattering comparison but I'm far more comfortable with feet than a fishtail."

She was damned if she'd meet his gaze. She stared at a point to the left of his head, so Kevin might think she was actually looking at him. There was no way she'd put herself at the mercy of those dangerous blue eyes and much-practiced charm.

"Some sports take a while to get used to," continued Kevin bravely. This little reunion must have been Justin's idea. Wasn't having her body at his mercy all weekend enough? "You really should give it another try."

"No, thanks." She sipped her wine and fixed a non-committal smile on her face. "I think I'll stick to tennis."

"We should play doubles some time." Kevin leapt enthusiastically on her suggestion.

"That would be lovely," she said. "I'll tell Alex to dust off his racquet. He used to be on the school tennis team and I'm sure he'd love to play again."

Ha! Take that, conspirators.

"Dinner's ready!" called Cara from the kitchen. "Alicia, could you give me a hand with the dishes?"

"Sure," she said with relief. She excused herself and dove for the kitchen.

"Sorry," Cara said quietly. "It seemed like a good idea at the time."

"Justin set this up, didn't he?" whispered Alicia.

"I think it was actually Kevin's idea. Rather romantic. It's not often you get two guys putting their heads together to hatch a plan to hook a girl."

"Oh, I bet it's far more common that you'd imagine. Except that romance is not usually the aim." Alicia raised a brow.

"You're really not going to give him a chance, are you?"

"Nope. Would you like me to carry the salad?"

"Sure." Cara handed her a large majolica dish piled high with fresh vegetables. "People can change, you know."

"You mean, like Kevin?"

"Exactly. Men are slow to mature. Kind of like a fine wine."

"Or a baby elephant."

Cara laughed. "You're awful."

"Yeah, and I have every right to be." She pushed past Cara and out into the dining room. A wide doorway opened into the living room, and through it she glimpsed Kevin and Justin enjoying what looked like a casual conversation. How on earth was she going to survive an entire meal at the same table with that snake?

She deliberately sat next to him so that she wouldn't have to look at him. The table was large enough that she wasn't assaulted by his male scent, though it certainly was annoying having that low, seductive voice level with her ear.

Kevin brought out steaming bowls of fresh pasta, and Cara spooned spicy red sauce over them.

"How's the new exhibit coming along?" asked Justin, once they were settled.

Alicia stiffened. "Fine. We're unpacking the boxes on Monday."

"What's it about?" Kevin asked, pouring white wine for all of them.

"A traveling exhibition from the Smithsonian about changes in the environment."

"You mean, like global warming?" She felt Justin's bright gaze scorch the side of her face.

"Not really." She took childish pleasure in her negative answer. "Ancient changes. Oceans that became deserts, forests turned to stone, that kind of thing. We have some striking fossil samples to put on display, and three interactive video programs. I have school groups booked solid for the entire month."

"That's wonderful!" exclaimed Cara. "I know you've been trying hard to lure schools to the museum."

"Museums are about the living, not the dead," Alicia repeated her mantra. "And I'm thrilled, to be honest. It was a big deal getting the board to agree to host this exhibit and I'm hoping it's the start of a new era for the Somerset Museum of Natural History."

"I'm sure it will be. Here's to new beginnings!" Cara lifted her glass.

"I think you already said that, hon." Kevin leaned in and laid a kiss on her cheek. "But it's a nice thought, anyway."

"All right, I'll rephrase." Cara tossed her long blond curls. "Here's to new beginnings for things that got off to a lousy start in the first place."

Alicia pretended to sip her wine, but didn't. She was superstitious that way.

Besides, her relationship with Rick—*Justin*—got off to a fabulous start.

It was the part that came next which stank.

Kevin leaned in. "Justin, how was Hong Kong?"

"Busy, as usual. I had a lot of meetings but I didn't go out much. I couldn't wait to get back home." Again, his gaze warmed Alicia's cheek.

"I've slowed down on the traveling myself. Things that seem fun when you're right out of college definitely lose their luster as you gain maturity."

"Especially when you have a lovely woman to come home to." Justin's wistful tone almost crept under her skin.

Then it occurred to her she might not even be the woman he was talking about. She'd learned a few things about Justin Dupree since she'd found out the truth, and none of them was too flattering.

"How is Mila Jankovich?" The words shot out of her mouth.

How embarrassing that she even remembered the name from the social pages. Unfortunately, it was burned on her brain in flaming scarlet letters.

A stunned silence followed her question. Now it was really awkward that she didn't turn and look at Justin, since everyone was staring at her. She speared a broccoli floret and lifted it to her lips, though her stomach had contracted shut.

"I don't know." Justin spoke softly. "I haven't seen her in a while. I think she still lives in New York."

"Alicia and I saw a picture of you with her in *Vanity Fair*," explained Cara. "Is it true that she barely speaks English?"

"Her English isn't bad. She has a funny Canadian accent because she learned from an exchange student who came to live with her in the Ukraine. She's actually a lot nicer than she looks when she's not giving that supermodel stare for one camera or another, but she and I were never more than casual companions."

"So you never dated?" asked Cara, like a journalist who reasks a question that's just been answered. Alicia knew what her friend was doing on her behalf, but mostly still she wished she'd never mentioned Mila's name.

"I took her to a couple of social events. A friend of mine runs her agency and he wanted her to be seen with the 'right people.'" He chuckled. "Kind of scary that I'm the right people, but I didn't mind since they were charity events I'd have gone to anyway." He paused and

Alicia felt her skin burn again. "There's someone else I'd much rather have taken."

The awkward pause stretched on for a full thirty seconds, while Alicia forked individual peas from the inside of a mange-tout. She was done being a sucker for Justin Dupree's notorious charms.

"Great puttanesca sauce, sweetheart." Kevin kissed Cara on the neck and she blushed.

"It's delicious," chimed Alicia, glad the conversation had turned neutral again.

"Thanks. I've never made it before. I wasn't sure about the capers but I think they really add a zing to it."

"It's perfect," said Justin. "Best food I've eaten all week."

"I'll go start getting dessert ready." Cara rose from her seat with obvious enthusiasm. Alicia was about to run after her to offer help, but Kevin was quicker. He tracked her out of the room like a shadow.

"Alicia…" His deep, seductive voice made Alicia's back stiffen.

"Yes, *Justin?*" She picked up her water and took a sip. She didn't dare drink any more wine in case she became susceptible.

"Don't you think this is a little silly?"

"Me sipping my water?"

"You refusing to look at me." If she wasn't mistaken, she heard an edge of unease in his voice, different from his usual confident banter.

"Don't flatter yourself. I'm not refusing to look at you. I just have better things to look at."

She cast about the table for something to fix her eyes on. The cut-glass carafe filled with salad dressing worked.

"Are you *afraid* to look at me?"

"Afraid? Why on earth would I be afraid?"

"It just seems odd that you won't meet my eye. I'd think you'd at least want to give me a stony glare or something."

"Why, would that be exciting for you?" She twirled her wineglass between her fingers. "I think you've had enough fun at my expense, don't you?"

She rose from her chair and headed for the windows. The penthouse apartment had wide French doors that opened onto a balcony with a view over Houston. She tried the stainless steel handle and it opened easily.

Phew. Alicia stepped outside and inhaled the cool evening air.

The setting sun glistened on thousands of glass windows, making the city glitter like a mosaic. No doubt other people down there, in all those cars and houses and apartments, were suffering. Her petty concerns were nothing compared to some of the real problems people had.

All she wanted to do was forget about Justin and get on with her life. Which had been perfectly fine before she met him, thank you very much.

"Alicia." His voice came from the doorway behind her.

"That's my name. At least we're in agreement on that."

"I'm so terribly sorry about what happened." His voice was gruff with emotion.

Alicia's breath caught in her lungs. Something told her not to blurt out a snappy comeback.

"If I could turn back the clock to our first meeting and introduce myself as Justin Dupree, I'd do it in a heartbeat."

"Except that then my friends would have warned me against you." She tilted her head to the evening breeze, trying to cool her flushed face. "I'd never have gone to stay the night with a notorious womanizer."

"I know. That's one of the many reasons why...why I love you."

The words took a split second to sink in. Then Alicia's brain spat them out. He didn't love her. He just couldn't stand not to have someone eating out of his palm. He wanted to charm her and get her back on his good side, so he wouldn't have any embarrassing unfinished business with her.

She fixed her gaze on the distant purple horizon.

"I do, you know." He moved closer. "Love you."

Her heart squeezed. "You don't. You barely know me."

"I know you enough to see that you are a rare and amazing woman."

"Well, I'm not." Her voice shook slightly. "You only want me now that I'm not available, so you've painted a fantastical picture of me in your head. I'm a quiet, rather dull museum curator, with—as you know only too well—almost no experience with the opposite sex." She sniffed. "I'd hardly call that amazing. And there's nothing rare about me."

"Trust me, there is." His voice drew closer. "You are the only—and I mean *the only*—woman who's been horrified to find out that I'm actually Justin Dupree. I started using a fake name because when I introduced myself as Justin Dupree, women would start pawing me and hanging on my every word like I was Einstein. When I was a kid I enjoyed female attention, but after a while, I got pretty tired of wondering whether a woman was genuinely interested in *me* or if she just liked my family name and all the millions that came with it."

"What a cross to bear."

"I know." He laughed. "It does sound ridiculous. Not many people have the luxury of complaining that they have too much money and too many women fawning over them."

His body heat radiated through her clothes as he moved closer. "But it hurts when people don't see you. When all they see is the name and the money and everything that can do for them. And if you're surrounded by people like that, your life starts feeling pretty empty, no matter how busy you are."

Her skin prickled at his nearness. Any minute now, she expected him to slide his arms around her waist in the proprietary manner that only a few days ago she'd found so charming.

But he didn't.

"You're not like that, Alicia." He hesitated, and she could almost feel his breath on her cheek. "You're not at all impressed by money or power or the trappings of prestige. You judge everything according to your own exacting standards. I realized that pretty fast and I knew I'd made a mistake in giving you a false name. I planned to tell you the truth, but then the fire happened and I didn't want to upset you when you had plenty to be upset about already."

Alicia wanted to snark, *How thoughtful.* But the words stayed on her tongue. It was thoughtful. He could easily have blurted out the truth. What did he have to lose?

Her in his bed?

He hadn't actually tried to get her into bed at all. He'd kissed her good-night and hustled away to his own bedroom. She was the one who dragged him into bed.

"I love you, Alicia." His soft voice crept over her like light from the last rays of the sun.

His words were so…heartfelt. They bypassed her anger and humiliation and touched something inside her.

"I know we haven't spent very much time together, but I've lived long enough to know something good when I see it. And what we have is very, very good. I can talk to you about anything. You're curious and enthusiastic. You truly appreciate the world around us, and the people in it." He paused, and drew in a deep breath. "You bring magic into every day and I'd like to spend the rest of my life with you."

Alicia's heart nearly stopped. *What did he just say?*

Adrenaline flashed through her, making her hands twitch. She couldn't possibly ignore him anymore. Even if it was just an act, he'd gone too far.

She turned, slowly, to face him. She found his handsome face taut with emotion. His deep blue eyes shone with passion and—as she knew it would—his imploring gaze sent a ray of tenderness right to her heart.

His arms hung by his sides, but she could see from the

set of his shoulders that he itched to wrap them around her. "When I was in Hong Kong, I couldn't think of anything but coming home to you." He looked into her eyes. "All the things I used to like—going out to clubs, hanging out with friends, even taking a boat out on the water—nothing seemed fun without you there to share it."

Alicia blinked. Something like hope bloomed in her chest. She was starting to truly believe him.

Then common sense splashed her brain like cold water. "But we've only been on a few dates. Maybe you're just...attracted to me." She didn't dare believe it was more.

Though she had to admit that she'd been all but convinced he was "the one" before she found out about his name.

He tilted his head and a wry expression appeared on his face. "I know what attraction feels like. My reputation as a ladies' man is no secret, and I admit there's some fire behind that smoke. But what I feel for you is very different. It confused me, to be honest. I've always avoided emotional commitments. I never wanted a serious relationship." His blue gaze darkened and the force of it threatened to knock her off her high heels. "But with you, I want so much that I don't even know where it ends. I don't want it to end, ever."

She felt his hands at her waist—tentative at first, then firmer as her body yielded instantly to his touch. A deep sigh escaped her as she melted into his arms and their lips met. The kiss exploded through her, sending energy all the way to her fingers and toes.

Oh, Justin. His real name filled her mind, with the

knowledge that he really was still the sweet, fun, exciting and caring man she'd spent that blissful weekend with.

The name was different but nothing else had changed.

She held him close, her fingers pressing into the muscle of his back and her head angled to his kiss. Justin's arms wrapped around her and crushed her to his hard chest.

She'd tried so hard to push all thoughts of him from her mind, to forget all the dreams and hopes she'd enjoyed and reimagine her future without him in it. Now, in his arms, all the joy and anticipation and excitement came flooding back.

And the desire. Her nipples tightened against his firm muscle and heat flooded her belly. Her body throbbed with arousal and her fingers itched with a sudden urge to unbutton his crisp pale blue shirt and tug it off.

But they were outside on a balcony, illuminated by the glow of the setting sun.

"Justin," she breathed, tugging her lips from his with considerable effort.

A smile lifted his mouth and lit his eyes. "You used my real name."

"You're still…you."

"I certainly hope so." His perplexed expression almost made her laugh.

He was the same man she'd fallen in love with. And yes, it was love. Otherwise it wouldn't have hurt so badly when she tried to tell herself it was over.

"Rick Jones, Justin Dupree—they're just names." She bit her lip. "Maybe I made too much of the difference."

"I never intended to deceive you. I just wanted to meet you as…a man. Not as someone with a price tag and a list of expectations attached."

"Well, Justin Dupree, I guess it's nice to finally meet you." She reached out and pushed his hair back off his forehead. "You're pretty cute, you know?"

"Thanks." His adorable, dimpled smile weakened her knees a little further. "You're not half-bad yourself. But it wasn't your gorgeous face or your breathtaking body that I missed."

"No?" She lifted a brow.

"Nope." He shrugged. "I missed talking with you. I missed your smile, and the way your eyes sparkle when you're excited. I missed your laugh, and the way you sigh when something moves you."

Alicia swallowed hard. His emotion showed in his voice, and in the lines of his handsome face. Oh, boy. She was falling for him all over again. And how could she not?

She put her hands on her hips. "You didn't miss my body at all?"

Justin cocked his head. "Okay, maybe I missed it a bit."

"You didn't miss my kisses?" She narrowed her eyes.

He looked sheepish. "I'd be lying if I said I didn't."

"And you're never going to lie to me again, are you?" She leveled a hard stare right at those baby blues.

"Never." He said it slowly, enunciating each syllable. "On my life, I will never lie to you again."

Tears welled in her eyes, but she tried to blink them back. "I lied, too, so I could be with you." She wiped away a tear that spilled out. "So, I know how it happens. I lied to my brother, who I love more than anyone."

Except maybe you.

"Did you ever tell him you came to stay with me, instead?"

"I did. He was mad, but he got over it. I think he knows he was trying too hard to protect me, and it backfired."

"And I was trying too hard to make you like me, and that backfired, too."

Alicia inhaled a shaky breath. "I do like you, Justin Dupree." She blinked and he reached out to wipe away her tear. "I like you very much."

His smile threatened to break into a grin.

Joy swelled inside her. "I think I might even be able to look past all that embarrassing wealth and notoriety you're saddled with."

"That's big of you." His grin broadened. "Not many people could be so open-minded."

"I even like your name—Justin—it has a nice ring to it."

"Justin and Alicia. It's a stylish combination, don't you think?" His gaze sparkled with warmth.

Alicia nodded, emotion flooding her chest. A sudden image of the letters *J & A* etched on a wineglass, or embroidered in linen napkins, snuck into her brain.

Get a hold of yourself, she thought.

But she really didn't want to. Right now she wanted to let go. To shed all the doubt and fear and insecurity that had plagued her, and revel in the sweet joy of this perfect moment.

Except that they were on a balcony. At someone else's apartment.

"We really should go back inside. Cara and Kevin are probably wondering what happened to us."

Justin laughed. "They might think you pushed me off."

"I'm still pretty mad at you." She pursed her lips. "But I think I can get over it. I know from my brother's experience that sometimes life can be a pain in the butt when everyone has an opinion about you before they meet you."

He nodded. "It's annoying when people start out with a cartoon version of you in their heads, and you have to work to show them there's a real person in there, too."

"Yeah. Poor Alex." She grinned. "And poor you, too." She pressed a kiss to his lips, which sent a ripple of desire shivering to her toes.

"Would you have dated me if you knew I was Justin Dupree?"

"No way." She shook her head. "I've got a reputation to protect."

"You'd have known your carefully guarded virginity was in mortal danger."

"True." She pretended to look thoughtful. "So in fact, maybe I would have chased after you myself. And then you'd have wondered if I just wanted you for your money and your fancy name."

"I'm not sure I would have cared, in your case." He kissed her. "I'd have just counted myself lucky."

Alicia leaned her head against his chest, enjoying his natural male scent and the steadiness of his strong body. "We do have something really good together."

She glanced up, taking in the strength of his chin and his chiseled cheek. "Whoever you are."

His chuckle shook them both. "I'm glad you're not holding my double identity against me anymore."

"Guess it proves you can get used to anything. Though if I call out 'Rick!' while we're making love, you have no one to blame but yourself," she teased.

He growled and nipped at her cheek. "If you're calling out while we're making love, it's all good as far as I'm concerned." He tightened his arms around her. "I missed you so much."

"I missed you, too," she confessed. "I tried like heck not to. That's why I was so mad at you. I couldn't get you out of my mind."

"That's because we're meant to be together." His fingers caressed her back, heating her skin through her thin dress. "Alicia, I want to ask you something, and you don't have to give your reply right away. You can think about it for a day, a week, a month, as long as you want. I have to ask though, or I'm going to explode."

She swallowed. "Sure." Fear zinged in her stomach. "Go ahead." What could he ask after such a preamble? Her heart beat in terror and anticipation.

He pulled back a fraction, so she could look up into his face.

The last bronze rays of light illuminated his features, and emotion darkened his gaze. "Alicia Montoya, I love you and I want to spend the rest of my life with you. Will you marry me?"

Ten

Justin held his breath. He didn't think she'd say yes, but for some crazy reason he had to ask anyway.

Patience had never been a virtue he could brag about. And he wanted Alicia to know that she wasn't just another woman to him, but the woman he wanted to spend the rest of his life with.

Alicia's big brown eyes filled with tears. "I love you, too, Justin." She said his name deliberately, but with warmth, as if she accepted his name and the real him that came with it.

She blinked, teardrops glittering on her long, dark lashes. "I know you don't need an answer right away, and that the sensible thing to do would be to wait. We could date for a while, get to know each other. But—" She inhaled sharply. "I've never met anyone like you. Not because you're rich and influential and all that other stuff, but because you're thoughtful and caring and you really appreciate the opportunities life offers you, and you live each day to the fullest." She swallowed and blinked again. "And I would like to marry you."

"Yes!" Justin lifted her up in the air and she shrieked. Her body felt featherlight in his arms as he spun her around. Joy and excitement surged through him and he kissed her with force. "We'll have a fantastic life together."

"Are you psychic?" she asked, laughing.

"No, just smart." He grinned. "And so are you, so you know I'm right."

"You're not very modest though, are you?"

"Not at all." He shrugged. "Sorry."

Alicia narrowed her eyes. "There is one thing you must do, before we can marry."

Uh-oh. The serious look on her face sent a shard of alarm to his gut. "What?"

"You must ask my brother for permission." Mischief sparkled in her stern gaze.

"What if he doesn't give it?" Justin cocked his head.

"You have to convince him to give it." A naughty smile crept across her sensual mouth. "Old-school style."

"Oh, boy." Justin frowned. "So, I have to promise to give him a herd of cattle for your hand in marriage or something?"

She winced. "It better be a good herd, with some prize bulls. And make sure you tell him he has to give me away at the wedding."

"Hmm." He chewed his lip. "I might need to add some wagons loaded with gold bullion."

"I'm sure you'll think of something." She grinned. "You're good at talking people around."

"I'm certainly glad I managed with you." He stroked her back, enjoying her softness through her delicate dress. "I didn't want to spend the rest of my life missing you and being miserable. Kevin told me how lost he felt without Cara all those years."

Alicia gasped. "We'd better go back in."

They unwove their arms from around each other. Alicia straightened Justin's shirt collar and he removed a smudge of mascara from under her eye with his thumb.

He took her hand and stepped back through the French doors. No sign of the apartment's owners. The door to the kitchen still closed and no dessert on the table.

"Kevin? Cara?" Alicia walked past him. "We're back and we have some news."

Cara and Kevin came out of the kitchen. "We were wondering what you two were up to," said Cara. "We wanted to give you some privacy."

Alicia tucked her hair behind her ears. "We went out on the balcony."

"Well, I'm glad no one got pushed off." She glanced from one to the other.

"We made up," said Alicia with a shy smile. "In fact, we more than made up."

"We're getting married," said Justin, unable to keep a proud grin from spreading across his face.

Cara let out a shriek and tore across the room to Alicia. She kissed her hard on both cheeks. "That's wonderful!" She grabbed Justin and kissed him, too. "I'm thrilled for you both!"

Kevin beamed. "I don't think Cara was ever going to forgive herself if you two didn't get back together. She's done nothing but mutter about how she should have kept her damn mouth shut. So, you've made my wife happy as well as your future bride."

"She'll be my bride as soon as I can convince her brother to give her away."

"Oh, boy." Kevin grimaced. "Better wear a bullet-proof vest when you go ask."

"Alex isn't that bad," protested Alicia. "He's just a little overprotective."

"He's a lot overprotective." Cara grinned. "I wish I could be a fly on the wall at that meeting."

Justin's steady nerves were a point of pride, so he didn't at all like the way his finger shook slightly as he pressed the buzzer at the gates of El Diablo.

He'd called to set up a meeting with Alex, but his messages had gone unanswered. Alicia had simply shrugged and told him Alex wasn't great at returning calls, so he should stop by the ranch.

He could swear she had a gleam in her eye at the time. She wanted him to prove his love for her.

Well, damn it, he would.

The intercom crackled to life and a voice grunted, "Yeah?"

Alex. Apparently, he took personal charge of the security system.

"Alex, Justin Dupree here." He went for authoritative confidence. "I'd like to talk to you about Alicia."

To his surprise, the iron gates started to swing open.

So far, so good. Justin piloted his Porsche inside. The

hair on the back of his neck prickled a bit when he glanced in the rearview mirror and saw the gates swing closed behind him.

Calm down. He's your future brother-in-law. If this Brody thing ever gets settled, you might even be friends one day.

He wondered if Alicia was home. Perhaps she was watching secretly from one of the windows.

She'd refused to move in with him until they were formally engaged, so he was pretty sure he wouldn't see her in his bed again until he got Alex on his side.

The big barn was being rebuilt and the sidewalls were already framed. A tall figure strode out from the construction site, sleeves rolled up over powerful forearms and a grim expression on his hard-edged face.

Justin pulled the car to the side of the drive and climbed out. "Alex, good to see you."

"I wish I could say the same. Still, we're shorthanded here raising the roof. Come this way."

Justin's eyes widened as Alex disappeared back into the wood skeleton of the barn.

Anything it takes, baby, I promise. Whatever Alex made him do, Alicia was worth it.

With his next breath, he followed him in.

"Got a greenhorn here," bellowed Alex. "But he's light so he can climb up to the rafters."

Justin swallowed as he glanced up to the high sill where the roof would rest. He could see the trusses stacked at the far end of the barn frame, with a crane ready to hoist them into place.

"Whatever you say, boss," said an older man at the controls of the crane.

"Wear this." Alex flung a scuffed yellow hard hat at Justin, and he caught it and put it on. "There's a ladder up at this end where the first truss will be raised. You steady on your feet?"

"Sure am."

Alex's stern face betrayed no emotion as he tossed Justin a pair of worn leather gloves and a spirit level. But he could swear he saw a twinkle of evil in his eye.

Justin scaled the tall aluminum ladder leaning against the frame. He'd climbed masts higher than this out on a heaving ocean. Still, he hadn't had a man who hated him at the tiller that time.

At the top of the ladder, he stepped up onto the sill. "What's the plan?"

He saw the first triangular truss rise off the ground, lifted by the crane. It swung slowly toward him. Three other men climbed up into position around him.

"They'll get the ends," said Alex. "You line up the middle of the truss with the sill and check it for plumb. When it's right, Joe will nail it down."

Great. As long as the truss didn't knock him to the ground, he might survive to enjoy marriage to Alicia.

He steadied himself on the sill, which happily was almost a foot wide.

Alex must know about his plans with Alicia. If he didn't he wouldn't have let him in here. This was a test. If he passed, he'd be home free.

Or at least that was a good thought to keep in mind as the heavy truss floated through the air toward him. As it moved within reach, Justin grabbed the truss and helped settle it in position at his feet, while the guys at both ends did the same.

He checked it for level. "It's dead on."

Pneumatic nailers fixed it into position with loud thunking sounds. "One down, twenty-nine more to go." Alex looked up with a grin. "Though for the next one, you'll have to move out along the center beam."

Justin looked down at his feet where a long span stretched to the next support column. He lifted his head high.

"No problem."

Alicia was worth it.

He wasn't surprised to see her standing nearby when he finally climbed down from the barn frame nearly five hours later. They'd raised thirty trusses to form the biggest roof he'd ever seen in his life.

She came across the lawn toward him. "Great job, guys! Come on in the house and have something to eat."

Justin glanced down. His light blue shirt was drenched with sweat and a layer of fine sawdust coated his entire body. Alicia clearly didn't mind though. Her big dark eyes sparkled with…triumph?

Apparently, he'd done something right.

"The barn looks fantastic. It's going to be nice to have all that extra space for the calves."

"You're right, 'Manita. I know you were sad about the old barn burning, but this one will be a lot more useful."

"I'm glad Justin was able to help."

He caught sight of her grin before she turned back to the house.

Inside, he found the kitchen table piled high with freshly made tortilla fixings. Alicia snapped the lids off two cold beers and set them down.

"Come help yourselves." She handed them each a plate. "I have to run down to the post office before it closes. Eat up, and I'll be back in a few." She gave Justin a knowing look as she marched past him. *Now's your chance,* the look seemed to say.

"Help yourself. You earned a good meal," grunted Alex. "You're stronger than you look."

"I enjoyed it." He wasn't entirely lying. "I never did any construction before. It's eye-opening to see how things go together."

"A well-constructed building can last a thousand years. Even a wood building, as long as it doesn't burn down."

A brief silence settled in the room as they loaded rice and chicken onto warm tortillas.

Justin glanced up. "Are the police any closer to finding out who set the fire?"

"You don't think I did it?" Alex lifted a dark brow. "That seems to be the word around town."

"People are scared of what they don't understand. They start flinging accusations about."

"People like your friends Mitch and Lance Brody?"

"I think you all know that none of you are involved in any of this." Justin spooned some guacamole on to his plate.

"Lance Brody outright accused me. Darius told me he was going around telling people someone saw my truck at the scene."

"I'm sure the fire upset him and he started grasping at straws. I told him myself I was sure you didn't have anything to do with it."

Alex stared at him for a long moment. "You did?"

"Sure. The way Alicia talked about you, I knew you'd never be involved in something like that."

"Alicia talked about me?" Alex's grim expression softened into surprise.

"She talks about you a lot. She really looks up to you."

"Huh." His grunt contained more emotion than he probably intended to reveal.

"The problem is, if you didn't set the Brody fire, and the Brodys didn't set your fire, then who's wandering around Somerset carrying chemical accelerants?"

"And why?" Alex frowned.

"Someone who has a bone to pick with both you and the Brodys."

Alex snorted. "What in the heck do I have in common with the Brody brothers that would make someone come after both of us?"

Justin picked up a fork from a pile of gleaming cutlery. "Well, one thing occurs to me. You're all fairly new members of the Texas Cattleman's Club."

"What does that have to do with anything?"

"Honestly, I have no idea." Justin shrugged. "But something strange is going on—the fires, the money missing from the club's accounts—and I have a feeling it's all connected somehow."

"Do the Brody brothers still have me at the top of their list of suspects?"

"I doubt it, but I confess I haven't seen 'em in a while. There's only one person I want to spend my free time with these days." Justin spooned sour cream onto his tortilla.

"I suspected as much." Alex picked up his beer and headed for the door. "Let's sit out back."

"Out back" was a wide, shady veranda with potted daisies and an expansive view of the back forty. Or the back four hundred, which is what it looked like. Sturdy cattle grazed as far as the eye could see.

Alex eased himself into a wooden chair, and Justin took the bench beside him.

"I love your sister." There, he'd said it. "We got off on the wrong foot, but she knows I care about her and she's prepared to forgive me and look to the future." Justin inhaled the cool evening air. "I'm hoping you're willing to do the same."

"That's a lot to hope for." Alex took a hearty bite of his rolled tortilla.

"I've asked her to marry me, and she said yes, but only on the condition that you'll give her away."

Alex stopped chewing. "You asked her to *marry* you?" He stared. "You only just met."

So she hadn't told Alex. She'd trusted him to sort things out on his own. Her faith in him warmed his heart still further.

"It doesn't take a lot of time to know you've met the right person."

His dark eyes narrowed. "You gave her a ring?"

"Not yet. I wanted to get your permission first. Alicia's old-fashioned." He couldn't help smiling. "That's one of the many things I love about her."

Alex still looked as if someone had smacked him with a two-by-four. "You actually proposed marriage? And here I thought you were just hoping to take her out on a date again."

"Alicia and I want to be together. We're both adults. Why waste time?"

"You caught me off guard." Alex blew out a long breath. "I was pretty impressed you were prepared to frame a barn just to win a date with her."

"I'd frame a barn for the chance to see her smile."

"I'm beginning to believe you would." Alex frowned. "Our parents got married after only one evening together. They just knew." He shook his head. "I guess it works that way sometimes."

"I didn't think I'd ever fall in love, but then I'd never met someone like Alicia."

Alex put down his plate. "Alicia's used to a certain lifestyle." He leaned forward. "I've worked hard to provide it for her."

"I can guarantee she'll have everything she wants. I own a good-size shipping company and we—"

"I know, I know." Alex's frown deepened and he stared off into the distance. "Damn, I hate the idea of losing Alicia to another man." He turned to Justin. "That sounds bad, and I don't mean it like that, but she's my baby sister." He picked up his plate again and took a giant bite of his tortilla.

Justin did the same, and they chewed in silence for a moment. Then he took a deep steady breath. "Will you give Alicia away at our wedding?"

Alex looked up at the horizon. The sky had turned mauve and cast an eerie glow over the fields of cattle. "I know you've got a lot of money, but Alicia needs more than that." He fixed his gaze on Justin. "She's tough on the outside but soft and gentle inside. If you break her heart I'll…" The look in his eyes said it all.

"I'll cherish her and treat her with respect and love. I promise you that." Justin swallowed.

Hope surged in his chest as he saw Alex's expression soften.

"Then I give you my blessing." He turned to Justin. His stern features showed some of the pain he'd no doubt experience at losing Alicia from his daily existence. "And yes, I'll give her away. But if you don't treat her right, you can count on it that I'll come take her back." Alex glared for a second, striking alarm into Justin's heart. But then he simply said, "Congratulations, brother-in-law."

Justin's chest ached with joy. "I appreciate your trust. I promise you I'll earn it every day."

Justin extended his hand and Alex shook it with a quick nod. "I believe you will," Alex said.

"You'd better both go have a shower and clean up," said Alicia, as she stepped through the French doors out on to the patio, looking radiant as a sunrise. "Because we're all going out to celebrate."

"Were you listening the whole time?" Alex cocked his head.

"No, I really did go to the post office. But I heard the important parts."

Her shy smile made Justin's heart leap.

Then she turned to Alex and took his hands in hers. "And I'm very glad you're going to give me away at my wedding. You've always been the most important man in my life, and everything I am today, I owe to you."

Justin watched her brawny older brother tear up.

Alex pressed a kiss to Alicia's forehead. "You're the best sister a brother could hope for and I wish you all the happiness in the world. The two of you are welcome to live at El Diablo, by the way. I don't like the idea of my baby sister living in sin at a hotel."

"Alex! It's the twenty-first century. They don't call it living in sin anymore."

"I call a spade a spade. Even if you are getting married."

"If I listened to you, I wouldn't be getting married. I'd have gone to stay with that sleazy El Gato." She did a mock shiver. "Luckily, I decided to trust my own instincts for once."

She smiled at Justin. "I'd be happy to live with you wherever you are."

"As long as there's a ring on your finger," growled Alex.

"Speaking of which…" Justin reached into the back pocket of his pants and pulled out a small ring box. He turned to face Alicia, then lowered himself slowly to one knee. He wanted to do it the old-fashioned way—even in front of her brother—because he knew she'd like that.

"Alicia Montoya, will you be my wife?"

"Oh, Justin." Her hands flew to her mouth as tears glazed her eyes. "How thoughtful!" Her voice wavered. "And yes, I will be your wife."

He flipped open the small, white velvet box. Inside shone the most spectacular diamond he'd been able to find in the entire Houston area. It was nearly four carats and glittered like the Gulf of Mexico.

"Oh, my goodness." Alicia's eyes widened.

Justin pulled the ring from its satin bed and slid it onto her finger.

"Oh, Justin, it's so beautiful!" Alicia admired the sparkly gem on her finger.

"I had it set in platinum since I notice you prefer silver jewelry."

"It's perfect." She looked up at him, eyes shining with tears. "You're perfect."

"Oh, I'm a long way from perfect, but with you by my side I'll be the best I can be." He grinned, almost delirious with happiness. He turned to Alex. "And I have no intention of keeping Alicia prisoner in a high-rise hotel. I think we should buy a house in Somerset—perhaps one with a tennis court, since I know Alicia likes tennis."

"And a pool," said Alex with a serious expression. "She likes to swim and it gets hot in the summer."

"What about a lake?" Alicia's eyes sparkled with humor. "For you to sail on?"

Justin laughed and had to stop himself from pulling her into his arms.

"I think a sweet little house with a nice little garden would be just fine," she said. "And the sooner we get married, the less time I'll be living in sin."

She tilted her head and looked up at Justin. "Could we get married here at El Diablo? That would mean a lot to me. If it's okay with Alex."

"Of course," both men replied instantly. They glanced at each other and a half-smile formed on Alex's face.

"I can tell we're going to be a very happy family," said Alicia with a smile. She looked at Justin shyly. "And maybe our new house can have some extra bedrooms, in case our family gets bigger."

Justin's chest swelled almost to bursting. "I can't wait."

"Then you guys better shower and change so we can go celebrate our engagement."

"Great idea," said Justin. "Where shall we go?"

Alicia smiled and admired her ring. "Why, the Texas Cattleman's Club of course. Where else?"

* * * * *

LONE STAR SEDUCTION

BY
DAY LECLAIRE

To my new family at Desire™,
and all the wonderful authors who contributed to
THE MILLIONAIRE'S CLUB series. Many thanks.

One

It was inevitable.

Rebecca Huntington knew it was only a matter of time before her path and Alejandro Montoya's collided. In this case, literally. Stepping from the brilliant Texas sunlight into the elegant interior of the Texas Cattleman's Club, she walked straight into his arms.

He caught her. Of course, he caught her. He had the reflexes of a cat, no doubt thanks to his years on the soccer field. For one brief, insane second her body gave, imprinting itself against his like a bittersweet memory. How many years had it been since they'd made love as though there were no yesterday, no tomorrow, only this moment of endless joy? She'd thought she'd found the love of a lifetime. Instead, he'd taken her innocence and ended their relationship with breathtaking cruelty, something it had taken her years to get over. And here she was, back in his arms, shades of that long-ago love affair haunting her still.

"Excuse me." His voice caressed her, the passage of years having deepened the slight Latino intonation, making it even more delicious than when they'd dated. "If you'll let go of me, I can leave."

Part of her wanted to cringe and pull away. But she refused to allow him the satisfaction of seeing how much he could still affect her. She released her grip on him—why in the world were her hands grasping his crisp, white shirt?—and held her ground.

The sunlight streaming in through the open doorway hit him square in the face, leaving hers in shadow. She could only be grateful for that fact when she saw the expression in his rich brown eyes—one of acute dislike, bordering on loathing. She didn't understand it, had never understood how their affair could have gone so hideously wrong. Nor could she understand why every part of her responded to him as though they were still one.

He towered over her five-foot-six frame by a full eight inches, though she managed to gain a small advantage with three-inch heels. High, sweeping cheekbones emphasized his deep-set eyes and framed a straight nose and full, sensuous mouth. She'd lost herself in that mouth, one skilled in the art of giving a woman pleasure beyond description.

She didn't dare let him know how deeply he'd affected her. Somehow, someway, he'd use the information. And it wouldn't be to her advantage. "If you'll step back, I'll be on my way," she said.

He held his position for an extra second. And then she saw it. A blistering hint of those communal memories drifted into his expression, a fading echo of the passion they'd once shared. Like an ember hidden deep within a banked fire, her touch uncovered the white-hot blaze of his passion. Alex felt something for her. Still. Some small trace of the hunger and desire they'd once shared lived within him. And then it was gone, the sweetness fading beneath the acrid burn of bitter discord. But it was too late. She knew. He'd managed to bury his reaction with impressive speed, but she hadn't mistaken it. The flame had been there.

Just as a matching flame burned within her.

As though aware of how much he'd given away, he stepped backward and gestured her in with a gracious nod. Both he and his sister, Alicia, had impeccable manners. Their mother, Carmen, who had also been the Huntington's one-time housekeeper, had insisted on it. Forcing herself to move, Rebecca swept past without giving him another look. Recovering her equilibrium was an entirely different matter. She could feel his gaze like a fine-tuned laser frying a hole between her shoulder blades as she continued on her way.

She made a beeline for the Texas Cattleman's Club Café, relieved to see that her luncheon date and best friend, Kate Thornton—now Brody—hadn't yet arrived. It gave Rebecca a moment to sit and pull herself together. The waiter, Richie, who often served her and who had memorized the preferences of all the regulars, brought over unsweetened iced tea and a dish of lemon.

He greeted her with a broad smile. "Lots of action today," he said in an undertone.

She grasped the topic like a lifeline—anything that would help erase Alex Montoya from her mind…and heart. "Interesting," she said, taking a long, refreshing sip of tea. "What sort of action?"

"Some sort of meeting among our newer mavericks. Maybe they're planning a coup to replace the old guard," he joked. He looked up in time to catch a reprimanding glance from the hostess and segued smoothly back into the role of waiter. "I assume someone's joining you?"

"Kate Brody."

"Ah, yes. Unsweetened tea during the summer, boiling-hot coffee during the winter. I think her husband is one of those participating in the meeting."

Rebecca shook her head with a grin, her tension easing. "How do you know so much about what's going on, Richie?"

He leaned in, keeping his voice low. "Pays to know, Ms. Huntington. Better tips. And sometimes I pick up suggestions on how to get ahead in life, like from Mr. Montoya." Richie's eyes shone with hero worship. "He's always helping out the staff."

She stiffened. "I…I didn't realize."

And she hadn't. Granted, she'd been out of the loop while living in Houston and learning how to run a retail business. But where had she been the past year since she moved back to Somerset? Working her fingers to the bone getting her lingerie shop, Sweet Nothings, established and in the black. And during her few precious hours off, she got together with her friends. If she were honest, she'd admit that she'd been careful not to listen to gossip about one of the TCC's newest members, especially since the other recent members—like the Brody brothers, Darius Franklin and Justin Dupree—were at odds with Alex. But maybe it was time to pay closer attention. Especially now that Justin was poised to become Alex's brother-in-law.

Kate appeared in the doorway of the café just then, scanning the tables for Rebecca. Tall and lanky, she was beautifully turned out in one of the chic pantsuits the two of them had selected on their Houston shopping spree. In one short day, her best friend had gone from country-bland to Southern sophisticate and Rebecca couldn't be more delighted, especially since it had led to Kate's then employer—now husband—tripping right over his tongue and into her bed.

Spotting Rebecca, Kate broke into a broad smile and worked her way around the blue-and-yellow floral-chintz tables. "So, what's got you all worked up?" she asked as they exchanged hugs.

Was it that obvious? Not good. Rebecca took a stab at innocent denial. "I have no idea what you're talking about. I'm fine."

Kate waved that aside with a sweep of her hand. "That won't wash with me, and you know it. Something's wrong and—" She broke off, her gaze arrowing across the room. "Okay, that explains it. I wondered when you two would finally bump into each other, and today must have been the day."

Rebecca didn't need to look to know precisely who Kate was talking about. Alex had returned to the club with a file in hand. He must have been on his way to his car to retrieve it when they'd run into each other. She could feel his presence like a low-level buzz of electricity. "Would it surprise you to hear that it didn't go well?"

"No," she retorted crisply. "The man is incredibly difficult. If Lance had his way, Montoya never would have been invited to join the club."

"Money talks."

Kate smiled thinly. "Well, he has plenty of that, doesn't he? Amazing, considering he used to be the groundskeeper here. I just hope the rumors aren't true."

Rebecca eyed her friend in concern. "What rumors?"

Kate hesitated. "You must know he has ties to El Gato."

"Paulo Rodriguez, sure. They're childhood friends." Understanding dawned and she inhaled sharply. "People think Alex made his money from drug trafficking?" She dismissed the suggestion out of hand. "No way. Not a chance. Not Alex."

"Not trafficking," Kate replied. "Shall we say…investing in some of El Gato's activities."

Rebecca shook her head, adamant. "Sorry, I don't

believe it. I can say a lot about Alex—plenty of it bad—but not that. Never that."

Richie arrived just then with Kate's coffee. Apparently, the crisp November weather had been the deciding factor on the choice of beverage. Based on Kate's appreciative grin, he'd chosen right. "You ladies ready to order? Our special today is the mahi-mahi with our homemade zesty dill pesto. It's really good."

"I'm sold," Kate announced.

"Make that two," Rebecca agreed.

"Coming right up." Richie jotted down a quick note and then gave a soft whistle. "Now there's a sight I never thought I'd live to see. Alex Montoya and Lance Brody shaking hands. Even weirder, the earth hasn't stopped spinning."

Startled, Rebecca glanced over her shoulder and saw that Alex had been joined by Kate's husband, Lance, his brother Mitch, and fellow frat brother, Kevin Novak. The three men were indeed shaking hands, though she could see the coolness and tension in their body language. As she watched, Justin Dupree and Darius Franklin joined the group, bringing all six of the newest, hottest TCC members together.

Rebecca couldn't contain her curiosity. "Okay, what's all that about?"

Kate frowned. Checking to confirm that Richie had moved out of earshot, she explained, "Some hush-hush meeting about the recent arson fires. Lance is there because the first fire was at Brody Oil and Gas. Since the other was at El Diablo, Alex needed to be present for the meeting, as well."

Rebecca stiffened. Of course, she'd heard about the fires. She wasn't that far out of the loop. And she knew that arson had been suspected. "It's been confirmed? They're certain both fires were arson?"

"That's my understanding. Why?"

Rebecca shot her friend an apologetic look, knowing how rough recent events had been on Kate's husband and his family. "Dad insists the fires were accidental, particularly the Montoya blaze."

"No offense, Becca, but how would your father know?" Kate asked. "Unless he's in on the investigation—and last I heard he didn't work for Darius's security firm—he wouldn't have anything to base his opinion on, other than secondhand information or gossip."

"Fair enough," Rebecca conceded, taking a cooling sip of her iced tea.

"Plus, they think they have a suspect."

Startled, she returned her glass to the table. "Who?"

Kate grimaced. "I was afraid you were going to ask me that. Lance told me the name." Her brow wrinkled as she struggled to remember. "Cantry?"

Rebecca froze. "Could it have been Gentry?"

Kate shrugged. "That's possible. Why?" She leaned forward and asked urgently, "Do you know this man, Becca?"

"I don't know anyone named Cantry," she temporized.

"But you do know a Gentry." It wasn't a question.

Rebecca nodded. "My father hired a new foreman a couple of years ago named Cornelius Gentry. But I'm sure it couldn't be the same man."

Kate's concern deepened. "Maybe we should make certain." She came to a decision and shoved back her chair. "Let me run over and ask Lance. If it is the same man, you and your father could be in danger."

Rebecca caught Kate's arm before she could put action to words. "Wait."

Everything inside Rebecca cringed at the notion of confronting Alex again. He and her father had a history. A very volatile history. If Gentry were the man they were after, Alex would find a way to draw her father into the scandal, something she'd do almost anything to avoid.

She leaned across the table and spoke in a low hush. "Kate, what if they want to question me about Gentry? What am I supposed to say to them? I don't have any information about the man other than he's been my father's foreman for the past two years." That, and he gave her the creeps. "Let's wait and get our facts straight. Then we can decide what to do about it. But I'd rather not interrupt them if it isn't Gentry."

Before Kate could respond, Richie arrived with their lunch. Rebecca stared at the beautifully plated food, but found she'd lost her appetite. She could only pray it wasn't her father's foreman. Maybe the name really was Cantry and her imagination was working overtime. That didn't change how she felt about the man. From the moment she'd returned home a year ago and first met him, she'd struggled against her aversion to his presence, trying to impose rationale and logic in the face of her instinctive reaction whenever he came around.

But just that morning she'd had a run-in with him. He'd blocked her exit as she'd been leaving her father's house for the club, standing too close and refusing to move back. In fact, now that she thought about it, it was identical to what had happened between her and Alex. How interesting that with one man she could have melted into his embrace, but with the other, every ounce of intuition had urged her to put as much distance as possible between them.

And he'd sensed how she'd felt. She'd seen it in the narrowing of his hard, brown eyes and the tightening of the fleshy mouth he'd twisted into a grimacing smile. "Miz Becca," he'd greeted her. His gaze had swept over her and his smile had pulled wider. "Don't you look the picture."

"Thanks, Cornelius." She lifted an eyebrow. "If you'll excuse me?"

He'd kept standing there, a knowing look in his eyes, before he'd fallen back a scant step. "Of course, your ladyship. Didn't mean for the hired help to get in your way. Don't want to lose my job the way the Montoyas did. Though it would be a sweet way to go."

Her uncontrollable outrage had only deepened his amusement. "I'm sure my father will be interested in your opinion," she shot back. "I'll be certain to share it with him."

"Feel free. Won't make a lick of difference." He bent

toward her and she couldn't help herself. She turned her head to the side, revealing a vulnerability she'd have preferred to keep hidden. "I'm here to stay, missy. Your father won't dare let me go."

"And then, of course, there's the discrepancy with the club accounts. That's caused an absolute furor among the boys," Kate was saying.

Rebecca came to with a start. "What was that? What discrepancy are you talking about?"

"You haven't listened to a word I've said, have you?" Kate asked in exasperation.

"Most of them." She offered an apologetic smile. "Some of them."

Kate sighed. "Darius noticed discrepancies in the TCC accounts when he did the billing for the Helping Hands women's shelter. Mitch agreed to do a fact-finding audit with Darius, Justin and Alex. Apparently, something's up. At least that's what Lance told me."

"But surely Dad—" She broke off, her nervousness increasing. She cleared her throat. "I wonder why Dad didn't catch the problem? He's been the club treasurer for years."

Kate shrugged. "Maybe it's a recent problem that your father hasn't noticed. It's probably some sort of glitch with funds going into the wrong accounts. I'm sure Mitch will get it straightened out."

Rebecca spared another glance over her shoulder. The six men had disappeared into one of the meeting rooms with the door firmly shut. More than anything she wished she could be a fly on the wall and find out just what the devil was going on. In the meantime, she could only pray her father wasn't unwittingly involved.

It didn't make sense that her father would have anything to do with the fires, but the irregularities of TCC accounts… That might be a different story. Hopefully, it really was a glitch and nothing that would pit her father against her friends. And then there was Alex. He despised her father. If a mistake had been made with the financial records, Alex wouldn't spare him. He'd do anything and everything to ruin her father's reputation.

Alex fixed his gaze on the five men, several of whom had, during his formative years, done their best to make his life a living hell. They stood together in a united front on one side of the room while he planted himself opposite them. Despite the animosity between them, he planned on enjoying the sweetness of his vindication today. Not only would he have the means to bring down an old enemy, but he'd be able to figuratively plant his fist in the face of the worst of the "frat brats" and his key nemesis, Lance Brody.

"Are we going to stand around and stare at each other?" he asked. "Or are we going to start offering apologies?"

"Sure, feel free to apologize, Montoya," Lance said with a grin that didn't come close to reaching his dark eyes. "I've been waiting a lifetime for you to apologize for your existence."

Alex took a swift step in his direction, only to be cut off by Darius who crossed the breach and held up a hand. "Easy man," he said in an undertone. "This won't solve anything."

"Maybe not, but it would make me feel a hell of a lot better."

Alex could hear his accent deepening, thickening, as it often did when he was angry or passionate. It only served to underscore the differences between them—differences in their cultures, their birthrights, their backgrounds. He was the son of a maid. And though some of the men present had worked for every dime they possessed, Justin Dupree and the Brody brothers had been born with silver spoons feeding them every elegant morsel they'd ever eaten. For the sake of his sister, Alicia, Alex would leave her brand new fiancé, Dupree, alone. In the past weeks the two men had established an uneasy accord. But as far as he was concerned, it was open season on the Brodys.

Alex addressed Lance. "You accused me of torching your refinery. Darius has evidence that proves you wrong. Are you man enough to finally admit it? Or do I need to beat the apology out of you?"

Amusement lined the other man's face. "You can try. I guarantee you won't succeed."

"It will be interesting to test that theory."

"Enough." Kevin Novak cut them off impatiently. "This isn't going to solve anything, and quite frankly, I'm tired of acting like we're still in high school." He turned his intense blue eyes on Alex. "We were wrong about you, and I for one would like to apologize."

He offered his hand and Alex didn't hesitate in taking it. "I appreciate it, Novak."

Lance groaned. "Oh, for the love of—"

"Shut up, bro." Mitch cut him off. "A dry well is a dry well. In our business, you have to know when to cut your losses. This is one of those times."

One by one, each man followed Kevin's example. Lance, the lone holdout, finally stepped forward and clasped Alex's hand, as well. Considering Brody was built like a tank, he didn't need to exert much pressure for Alex to feel the power behind his grip.

"I still don't like you," Lance said.

Alex inclined his head. "The feeling's mutual."

Lance's mouth kicked up in one corner. "But I do respect you."

The admission stunned Alex and it took him a second to reply. "I think we can both start from there and see where we end up."

"Fair enough."

"Now that we're through with the warm and fuzzies, let's get to work, shall we?" Darius suggested drily. He made a move toward the conference table and once everyone was seated, passed around copies of his report. "I need everyone here to understand that most of this is speculation. It's solid speculation, but we don't have enough to take to the cops. Yet. The one thing I can state categorically is that Alex is not responsible for the fire at Brody Oil and Gas. I have eyewitnesses and credit card receipts that place him well away from that location on the night of the blaze."

"So, what *do* you have?" Lance asked.

Alex took over. "If we examine the timeline of events, what becomes clear is that there is an interesting order to these incidents. From what Mitch has been able to discover in his review of the books, money has been siphoned off to the tune of three hundred grand."

Kevin emitted a low whistle. "How?"

"Just the way Darius thought. He's been using a company with a name similar to Helping Hands. When an invoice comes in from the shelter, two checks are cut. One to the shelter and a second one to 'Helping Hearts.' Every last one of these checks was cashed at the same bank." Alex eyed each man in turn. "And isn't it interesting that a year ago—right before the first check went through—the president of that bank was approved as a brand-new member of the Texas Cattleman's Club."

"Who put his name forward?" Lance asked.

"Sebastian Huntington."

Lance winced. "Oh, Kate's not going to like this. She and Rebecca are closer than sisters."

"It's our belief," Darius picked up the story, "that Huntington had his foreman, Cornelius Gentry, set the fires in order to pit the six of us against each other to keep us distracted long enough for him to replace the funds. Since he's the treasurer of TCC, he could tidy everything up so that no one was the wiser."

"*If* we'd remained distracted and fighting amongst ourselves," Alex added.

"How did you connect Gentry to the fires?" Justin asked.

Alex eyed his future brother-in-law. "The same way I was let off the hook is the way Gentry was put on it. He drives a pickup similar to mine. And the idiot stopped for gas a mile away from the refinery—fifteen minutes after the place went up in flames."

Darius shook his head in disgusted amusement. "Not the sharpest knife in the drawer, our Gentry." He tapped one of the points in his report. "The police also found identical boot prints at both the refinery blaze, as well as Alex's barn fire. Since they're two sizes smaller than what Alex wears, that's one more piece of evidence that points at someone other than Alex. If we can connect our man to those prints—and I think we can—we'll have something we can use. Connect Gentry to the fires, put some pressure on him, and I think we'll have Huntington."

Lance swore. "I don't like the man, I admit. He's a pompous, arrogant SOB. But even so, he's Rebecca's father and I flat-out adore that woman." He shot Alex a cold look. "Even if she doesn't always show the best judgment in men."

Alex tamped down on the fury sweeping through him. He didn't want to think about Rebecca. Not here, in the presence of these men. He'd thought he could handle seeing Becca again, deal with emotions that shouldn't still be edged with raw pain. But that combined with the animosity that lingered between him and the men in the room with him set his blood boiling. It wasn't just the Brodys' treatment of him during high school and the rivalry he and Lance had experienced on the soccer field. They'd made their disapproval keenly felt when he'd dated Rebecca in college. And when their affair had ended, they'd closed ranks and made his life a living hell.

"Let it go, Lance," Mitch urged.

But he wouldn't, Alex knew. Couldn't. "Say it, Brody," he taunted. "Don't hold back."

Old anger burst free. "You used her. You wanted to screw the daughter of your mother's employer and you did everything and anything necessary to coax her into bed before dumping her like so much garbage. Rumor has it, it was a bet. Is that why you did it? You and your old pal, El Gato, put money on which of you would be the first?"

"You have no idea what you're talking about." The words escaped in a flood of Spanish, but Lance got the gist. "Huntington filled her head with lies—lies she chose to believe."

"That's not the story we heard."

Alex forced himself to relax, using every ounce of the iron will and tenacity that had earned him his first million. He deliberately switched to English. "And we all know how trustworthy Sebastian Huntington is. Clearly, his word is solid."

An uncomfortable silence reigned for a full minute

before Darius tapped the sheaf of papers in front of him. "If we could focus on the matter at hand?" He paused until he had everyone's attention. "The one thing we do have is incontrovertible evidence regarding the embezzlement. And there's little to no doubt Sebastian Huntington is behind it."

"I've spoken with some of the other board members," Mitch offered. "Quietly. Privately. They all say the same thing. They want Huntington to step down as treasurer—"

Justin snorted. "You think?"

"—and replace the money. There's been some talk about his resigning from the club."

"Some *talk?*" Kevin responded indignantly. "You can't be suggesting there's any question about that."

"Apparently there is," Mitch replied. "He's been a member in good standing for decades. We may all consider him a pompous ass, but the old guard is closing ranks."

"Sounds familiar," Alex murmured. He released his breath in a sigh. He didn't know why any of this surprised him, but it did. "I'll speak to Huntington about replacing the money."

The Brody brothers exchanged uneasy glances. "I'm not sure—" Lance began.

Alex cut him off without compunction. "I don't care what you think or what you're sure of or not sure of. *I* will speak to Huntington. Deal with Gentry as you wish. Perhaps you can squeeze the truth out of him. If he points the finger at Rebecca's father, then you may choose how to handle it. I, for one, have no qualms about seeing both Gentry and Huntington locked up for the rest of their miserable lives."

"Regardless of what it'll do to Rebecca?" Lance asked.

Alex leaned across the table toward him, his gaze implacable. "He gave no thought to what it would do to the lives of my mother and sister when he threw us off his ranch. All because I had the temerity to fall in love with his daughter. As far as I'm concerned, my mother's death is a direct result of that man's actions. So, no. I'm not too concerned about Rebecca's feelings when I see to it that her bastard of a father is thrown in jail." He'd had enough. More than enough. He shoved back his chair and stood. "Are we finished here? If so, I have pressing business to attend to."

It was business that would eventually return him to Rebecca's orbit. As he left the meeting room, he glanced toward the café. She was still there, sitting with Kate and picking at her food.

She'd worn her hair up today, piling all that fire and glitter into an elegant little knot on top of her head. Did she have any idea what that hairstyle did to a man? She had a redhead's complexion, her skin the exact shade of rich cream. And her hairstyle exposed the creamy length of her throat and vulnerable nape of her neck to his gaze. When they'd collided earlier, it had taken every bit of control not to feather his fingers along that throat. To restrain from cupping the back of her neck and urging her upward so he could sample her lush mouth and discover if it still tasted as sweet. To watch those witch-green eyes go slumberous with passion.

As much as he despised the woman—as much as Rebecca Huntington had made his life a living hell—he still wanted her. And somehow, someway, he'd have her.

Only this time, it would be on *his* terms.

Two

Rebecca had planned to question her father at dinner that night. But when she entered the dining room, the housekeeper, Louise, informed her that he was dining with his cronies. It seemed ridiculous to eat in solitary splendor, but since the table had been set and the food prepared, there wasn't much she could do except enjoy the lovely meal that had been prepared for her.

Shortly after nine, Louise appeared in the doorway of the library where Rebecca was curled up reading. "There's a visitor to see Mr. Huntington. When I informed him that your father was out for the evening, he insisted on speaking to you."

Alex stepped around Louise and entered the library. "Thank you, I'll take it from here."

Rebecca shot to her feet, her book bouncing onto the floor. Louise stared wide-eyed from one to the other. Clearly, she'd heard the whispers regarding their romantic history and didn't know how to respond. "I'll deal with Mr. Montoya," Rebecca informed the housekeeper.

Alex waited until the door closed behind the woman before bending over and picking up Rebecca's book. He gave the cover a cursory glance before handing it over. "You always did enjoy science fiction."

She didn't bother with the niceties. Instead, she cut straight to business. "Why are you here? Louise said you wanted to speak to Dad."

"Texas Cattleman's Club business. Rather urgent business. Is he really gone, or am I simply *persona non grata?*"

"Both, actually."

He absorbed that with a smile. "When do you expect him?"

Dread gripped her. This must be about the meeting at TCC and the account discrepancy Kate mentioned. Rebecca had called her friend after dinner hoping to get an update, but had been forced to leave a voice mail. Now she wondered if there was a reason Kate elected not to take the call.

She faced Alex with what she hoped was a serene expression. Realizing that he was still waiting for a response, she shrugged. "Dad didn't say when he'd return. Perhaps if you phone him in the morning?"

He laughed. "Get real, Becca. He'd never take the call. I'll wait until he returns. I'm sure you don't mind."

Making himself at home, he removed his suit jacket and dropped it over the back of the nearest chair. His snowy-white shirt stretched across a physique every bit as impressive now as when he'd played soccer. In fact, she found it more impressive with the added heft and refined muscle the years had built into his frame. A silk tie in a deep, rich ruby was knotted at his throat while a gold tie tack and matching cuff links gleamed in the subdued lighting. He was a gorgeous man, fully in his prime. Intelligent. Confident. Wealthy.

And he knew it.

Unless she chose to throw him out—a laughable exercise in futility—she had no option but to surrender gracefully. "What's this about, Alex?" She waved aside the response she knew he'd make. "I know it's TCC business. What, specifically?"

He considered for a moment before inclining his head. "Since I'm sure Kate's already told you, I don't suppose it matters." She didn't bother to correct him, and he continued. "It's regarding an account discrepancy."

She fought to swallow against a throat gone desert dry. "What sort of discrepancy?"

"Some money has gone missing."

Oh, God. "How much?" she asked tightly.

"Three hundred thousand."

The blood drained from her head and she felt her knees buckle. He reached her side before she even sensed him moving. Strong, powerful hands closed around her arms and he ushered her backward the few steps it took to reach the sofa.

"Sit down." When she balked, his voice took on an impatient edge. "Don't be ridiculous, Becca. You're going down whether you sit or fall. Better to sit, yes?"

"You think he stole it, don't you? You think my father's responsible."

He eased her onto the couch cushions and took a seat beside her, his hands still on her. Touching her. Grasping her. Warming her. "I don't *think*." He instantly dashed her hopes by adding, "I *know* he stole the money. The proof is undeniable."

"There must be some mistake, some reasonable explanation—" she began, searching his expression with raw distress. "Please, Alex."

"You always do that." His gaze blistered her, pinning her in place with eyes the color of bitter dark chocolate. "You always defend him. It doesn't matter what he does, how despicable his actions, you always take his side."

"I don't want to discuss our past." She couldn't bear it. Even after seven long years, the hurt was as fresh as yesterday. "He may have fired Carmen, even though I begged him not to, but his actions weren't anywhere near as despicable as your own."

His expression hardened, assuming a ruthlessness she'd never seen in the Alex she'd known all those years ago. "You're talking about the bet."

She attempted to escape the couch, but he held her

in place, refusing to give her the breathing room she needed so desperately. "Of course I'm talking about the bet. The one you made with Rodriquez."

"I've always been curious." He tilted his head to one side while he studied her. "How, precisely, did your father learn of this bet?"

She stirred uncomfortably. "Word gets around, Alex. People…people brag."

"Meaning, I must have bragged, because I was so proud of having won this bet. So, first I coaxed you into my bed on a dare and then I boasted about my success when it proved so easy?" He ignored her flinch. "Yes, I see that's what you believe. Because that was the sort of man I was. A man who steals innocence and brags of his misdeeds. A man who lies and cheats to get what he wants."

"Don't do this, Alejandro."

But he didn't relent. "And because I was this liar, this cheat, this ruiner of all pure and wholesome, your father lashed out at—not just me—but my family, as well. As payback for having the audacity to touch you, he left my sister homeless and caused my mother to work herself into an early grave. This is the man you defend, *dulzura?*"

She would have covered her ears if she could have. But he continued to hold her, forcing her to hear each hideous word. "Don't. Don't call me that. You don't have the right. Not any longer."

It was the wrong thing to say. "I've never had the right, have I?" he demanded in a harsh voice. "Even though you took me into your bed, you still felt guilty. Tarnished."

"That's not true," she instantly denied. "I loved you."

"The housekeeper's son."

How could he think such a thing? She'd never felt that way. Never. "I didn't care. It didn't matter."

His eyes blazed. "You mean it doesn't matter *now*. Now that I have money and status and a ranch that rivals any in Maverick County." With a muttered curse, he ripped at the knot anchoring his tie as though it were strangling him, and removed the gold tie tack. Up close, she realized it was a beautifully scripted *M*. He slipped it into his pocket before leaning in. "And now I have the power to determine your father's future…as well as your own."

None of this made sense. Not any of it. "My father is renowned for his investment acumen. His business abilities are unparalleled. Why in the world would he need to embezzle money from the club?" Rebecca demanded. "Obviously, there's been some sort of mistake."

"You're right. There has. And your father made it. Even worse, he made it right in front of me, where I could have the pleasure of playing sheriff to his bank robber."

She moistened her lips while she struggled to find some answer to his accusation. In response, a flame of desire licked across his expression. Just like that, time slowed and her world tipped in a new and dangerous direction. It was as though all her senses grew more acute and intensely focused, consumed by her reaction to one man.

Alejandro Montoya.

Sound dampened. The only whisper slipping through was the labored give and take of their breath. She inhaled sharply, but all that did was fill her lungs with his unique scent, something crisp and spicy. Exotic. His hands tightened on her arms and she remembered how they'd felt against her skin all those years ago. Strong, when they swept her up and carried her to his bed. Tender, when he'd undressed her and caressed parts of her no man had seen or touched until that moment. Gentle, when he'd mated his body to hers and taught her a passion she'd only dreamed about.

Rebecca's surroundings melted and all she could see was Alex. He became her universe. He leaned in, so slowly she couldn't mistake his intent. So slowly, that she could have avoided the embrace if she'd truly wanted to. She didn't. She wished she could have claimed it was simple curiosity. But it went far beyond that. She needed to know, once and for all, whether the heat between them was real, or mere shadows of what they'd once shared.

"Dulzura…" he murmured.

And then he consumed her. How could she have forgotten how it had been between them? Or perhaps she hadn't forgotten. Living without him and what he'd given her had been too painful to bear, so she'd pushed the memories from her mind as an act of self-protection. Now those memories came crashing down, ripping her apart like shards of broken glass.

His mouth shifted over hers, firm and experienced,

with more assurance than ever. Where before he'd coax her lips apart, this time he demanded. She didn't want to resist, it seemed so pointless. So she didn't. Her mouth parted beneath his and she shuddered in the taking, the clever parry of tongue and nip of teeth, combined with the sweet, sweet flavor of him.

The sofa cushions caught her as Rebecca fell backward. Alex followed her down, settling angles over the soft give of her body, angles that had grown sharper and more defined with the passage of the years. While his hands coasted along her sides and swept upward beneath the flowing cotton blouse she wore, hers made short work of the buttons hindering her own path. At long last, she yanked apart the edges of his shirt and found the warmth beneath, reacquainting herself with every muscular knot and burl.

He followed suit and she shuddered at the sweep of the calloused ridges of his fingers and palms. He might be one of the wealthiest businessmen in the state, but at heart he was, and always would be, one with the land. El Diablo wasn't just a rich man's toy. It was a working ranch, and based on the calluses on his hands and the lean, sculpted expanse beneath her fingers, he worked it himself.

His hands stroked upward until they closed over her unfettered breasts, cupping the weight of them in his palms. "I could never get over the softness of your skin. It feels like velvet. But when I look at it...I swear, it's paler than moonbeams."

His thumbs drifted across the tips of her breasts in a tantalizing circle and the softest of moans escaped her. She couldn't help herself. She cupped his face, tracing the elegant contours. Sweeping cheekbones above shallow hollows. A wide mouth that begged to be kissed, framed by deep brackets of painful experience. A squared jaw with just the shadow of an indent, one she'd traced with her index finger on countless occasions.

She slid her hands into his hair to anchor him in place, taking private delight in gaining control of the embrace. Lifting upward, she nibbled at his lips, teasing at them until he groaned and sank back against her. She parted her legs to give him more room, running her bare foot along his calf, secretly amused as she pressed a series of wrinkles into the crisp material of his trouser leg. She wanted to take the urbane businessman and strip away the outer layer of sophistication, to reduce him to that elemental core that made him so unique and distinctive. To find again the pure masculine essence of the man she'd fallen in love with.

It was a moment out of time. A moment of indulgence. A moment that came to a shocking end when the door to the library slammed open against the wall.

"What the *hell* is going on?" Sebastian Huntington demanded.

Her father's arrival snapped her out of her sensual haze as effectively as a hypnotist snapping his subject out of a trance. She knew there was no point in trying to shove Alex off her. For one thing, he was far too heavy and strong, particularly if he had no intention of getting off—which she suspected was true in this case. Plus, the damage had been done.

Alex glanced across the room at her father and bared his teeth in a wolfish smile. "You're interrupting a private moment," he said. "Next time, you might consider knocking before you barge in."

Sebastian stared, stunned. "It...it's *my* house," he sputtered in protest. "I don't have to knock to enter a room in my own house."

"You do if you want to avoid scenes like this." Alex levered himself off Rebecca and shoved his hands through the hair she'd taken such delight in rumpling. Then he held out his hand and helped her escape the embrace of the sofa cushions. He took his time buttoning his shirt and tucking it into his trousers. He didn't bother to adjust his tie, but left it dangling. "I see you're still as arrogant as ever, Huntington. Let's see how long that lasts."

"Alex," Rebecca attempted to intercede.

He simply shook his head. "This doesn't involve you, Becca."

"But—"

He shot her a single look and she fell silent. Unfortunately, he was right. This was none of her business, other than the fact that her father was somehow involved. She wasn't privy to whatever information he had about the missing money, or what mistakes might have occurred that led Alex to believe her father had committed the crime. But she could stand beside her father and support him while he cleared up the misunderstanding.

"What are you doing here?" Sebastian demanded. He shot Rebecca a look of intense rebuke. "Other than attacking my daughter."

"Is that how it looked to you?" A genuine grin broke across Alex's face. "Well, whatever allows you to sleep at night."

Dull color crept up the older man's cheekbones. "I repeat. Why are you here?"

"I've been asked to come. The board of the TCC requested it."

To Rebecca's horror, every scrap of color drained from her father's face. His jaw worked for a moment before he managed to say, "I don't believe you."

"Discrepancies have been discovered in the club's financial accounts. Checks have been paid out to at least one bogus company." His mouth took on a taunting slant. "Checks you endorsed."

Sebastian's hands clenched into fists. "The only checks I've written have been in response to legitimate billing statements."

Alex folded his arms across his chest. "Like to Helping Hearts?"

Rebecca frowned. "Don't you mean Helping Hands?" she asked. "That's the women's shelter where Summer works. Aren't they part of an outreach program that the Texas Cattleman's Club funds?"

"Helping *Hands* is the outreach program we assist. I

couldn't tell you what Helping Hearts is," Alex replied. Though he addressed Rebecca, his gaze remained fixed on Sebastian. "But since your father cut several generous checks to them, I'm hoping he can tell me. Especially considering all of them were cashed at the same bank by none other than the president of that fine, upstanding institution—who, coincidentally enough, joined TCC shortly before the first check was cashed." He allowed that information to sink in. "So explain it to your daughter, Sebastian. What exactly is Helping Hearts?"

To Rebecca's shock, beads of sweat broke out across her father's forehead. "I'd have to check the records, examine the invoices, assuming they can be found."

"That's easy enough. I have a copy of the checks in question, all signed by you and approved by your banker friend, Rhymes. But the invoices are conveniently missing."

Sebastian's chin lifted. "Then I don't see how I can help you."

"All of the invoices for Helping Hearts are missing," Alex repeated softly. "Quite a coincidence, wouldn't you say?"

"It happens. They were probably misfiled."

"Or shredded, assuming they ever existed."

Sebastian shrugged. "If that's all…?"

"Not even close. There's going to be an audit, Huntington. And when it's done, you will be, as well. How much will they find missing? From what little we've been able to dig up, it's in the neighborhood of three hundred grand."

"Dad!"

Sebastian flinched. "You have no right—"

Alex stepped forward, his voice low and hard. "We have every right, you son of a bitch. You sit in your fine mansion and act as though you're somehow superior to everyone else."

"I can trace my birthright back to—"

Alex cut him off. "Who cares? You think that will matter to the board? Save it for your cellmates. Maybe they'll give a damn who your ancestors were and what they accomplished. Personally, I don't see a pedigree when I look at you. All I see is a thief."

Sebastian pulled at his tie as though it were choking him. "You have no proof!"

"How long do you think it'll take for me to get it? Do you think Rhymes will stand by you when we trace those checks back to him and accuse him of fraud? Where do you think he'll point the finger, especially if he's offered a deal?" Sebastian's breath quickened and he wiped his brow with a hand that trembled, but it was clear that Alex wasn't finished. "Just like Gentry is going to point the finger at you as the instigator when we pin him for torching Brody Oil and Gas and my barn."

"What?"

Sebastian stumbled and Rebecca darted to his side, helping him to the nearest chair. Then she hurried across the room and splashed a generous finger of whiskey into a tumbler. Returning to her father's side, she pressed the glass into his hands.

"Easy, Dad. Drink this."

"I swear to you, Rebecca," he said in an undertone. "I had nothing to do with those fires. I have no idea what Montoya is talking about."

She believed him. "Why would my father ask his foreman to set those fires?" she demanded of Alex. "What possible motive could he have?"

"We wondered the same thing," he admitted. "But considering how everyone's been running around like a bunch of crazed ants when their anthill has been kicked over, the motive became clear enough. Your father needed to keep the Brodys, me and several other key members of the TCC too busy to look at the accounts. To keep us fighting among ourselves while he covered his tracks."

"You're insane," Sebastian whispered. Then his eyes widened. "My God! You think I don't see what's going on here? You're behind the arson fires—assuming it really was arson."

Alex laughed in genuine amusement. "Why would I burn my own barn?"

"To implicate me." Her father's voice grew more assertive. "You're a fool, Montoya, if you think anyone will believe me capable of such an act. They'll all see this for what it really is—your petty stab at revenge for my having fired your mother all those years ago. I had nothing to do with those fires. Nothing."

She couldn't help but notice that he didn't deny dipping into TCC funds and her heart sank. "The money?" she asked tentatively.

He tossed back the whiskey, then closed his eyes and nodded his head. For a full thirty seconds, she couldn't move. Couldn't seem to process the truth. Then it all came crashing down on her. No. Oh, please, no. How could her father have done such a thing? *Why* would he?

Aware of Alex's intent gaze, she slowly straightened and faced him. "If—and I stress the word *if*—my father did contribute to some sort of accounting error—"

"So gently put." Alex's expression hardened. "It's called embezzlement, Becca. He stole the money."

She pressed her lips together to keep them from betraying her panic. "If he stole the money, will you give him an opportunity to return it?"

"I don't have it," Sebastian said wearily. "I invested it and the investment hasn't come through yet."

A small cry of distress escaped, despite her best efforts to control it. "Why? Why would you do such a thing?"

"Because he's arrogant." Alex answered the question before Sebastian had the opportunity. "Because he feels he's entitled."

"Because I'm on the verge of bankruptcy and thought this investment would turn everything around. Rodriquez swore it would."

Rebecca could literally feel the change in the atmosphere, the way it stilled and thickened. "Rodriquez?" Alex repeated. "Paulo?"

Sebastian shrugged. "Paulo. El Gato. Your old friend from the barrio. I didn't realize he was behind the investment opportunities until it was too late to pull out.

The first few ventures went well enough. We both made a modest amount of money. But then, it all went to hell. I realized I was in far deeper than I'd planned."

"How?" Alex demanded.

"He offered to let me pay a mere pittance of my actual stake, and foolishly I went along. When the deal went south, I had to come up with the balance of the money, fast. That's when I found out the identity of my new partner." He gave Alex a pained look. "I don't have to tell you that Rodriquez plays for keeps."

"So you stole the money from TCC."

"Yes. The plan was to replace it as soon as I received my return on our final investment."

"Only it didn't work out quite that way. That investment went sour, as well."

Sebastian's mouth twisted. "I see you know how it works. I should have figured it out long before I did and cut my losses. Instead, I borrowed—"

"Stole," Alex cut in.

Sebastian's head jerked up and he glared across the room. "You want your pound of flesh, don't you, boy?"

Alex took a single step in Sebastian's direction, but it was enough to make the older man shrink into his chair. "First, Huntington, I'm no longer a boy. I haven't been since the day you destroyed my family."

"You destroyed them yourself!" Sebastian fought back. "If you'd kept your hands off my daughter, none of this would have happened."

Alex continued as though he'd never been interrupted. "And second, you're right. I intend to have my pound of flesh. Every last ounce of it. I appreciate your making it so easy for me."

Sebastian rose to his feet, trembling with the effort. "Fine. I *stole*. Does that make you happy? I stole money from TCC and gave it to Rodriquez. He swore this last deal would finish the matter between us." He laughed without humor. "He was right. It has. I have no more money to give him—hell, I still owe him a bloody fortune—and I don't doubt that I'll soon hear that our investment met with tragic results."

"Count on it." Alex folded his arms across his chest. "So, if you're on the verge of bankruptcy, how do you plan to pay back the money?" He glanced around. "I suppose you could always sell your home, and the land that's been in your family for countless generations. Move to more modest accommodations."

A hideous silence settled over them, one that Rebecca finally broke. "I'll sell Sweet Nothings," she said quietly. "I own the building, as well as the business. There should be more than enough to cover what my father owes the club, and possibly El Gato, too."

"No," Sebastian and Alex said in unison.

If circumstances had been different, she'd have smiled at their unusual accord. But right now, she didn't find anything about the situation even remotely amusing. "Neither of you has any say in this."

"That's where you're wrong," Alex corrected her. "This is your father's debt and he'll pay it, not you."

"You can't stop me, Alex," she argued. "If I choose to liquidate Sweet Nothings, that's my business."

"And when word gets out about the reason for liquidating your shop?" Alex shot back. "Somerset's a small town. Do you really think your father will be able to hold his head up when everyone learns that he's a thief? That he allowed his daughter to bail him out? It won't be long before he sells, if only because he can no longer handle the whispers and looks of disgust. The sheer humiliation of it all. Who will welcome the Huntingtons into their homes?" He allowed that to sink in. "No one. You will be outcasts."

"You have a better suggestion?" Rebecca demanded.

"He sells his homestead to me. The money is replaced quietly, with no scandal. I'll handle Rodriquez. And then your father leaves Maverick County. I'll see to it that he has sufficient funds to keep him in comfort for the rest of his days—assuming he's careful and doesn't make any more risky business ventures. But Huntington Manor will become Montoya property from this point forward."

Three

"Get out!" Sebastian snarled. "Get out of my home, you vulture. I'll find my own solution to this mess. This land will never bear your name. Never, do you hear me?"

Alex just smiled. "You have three days to return the money to TCC or the board will be contacting the authorities. They've also relieved you as treasurer and appointed Mitch Brody in your place. Consider your membership officially suspended." He picked up his suit jacket from the back of the chair where he'd left it and shrugged it on. "I'll see myself out."

Rebecca spared a brief, anguished glance at her father, and followed Alex. She caught up with him in the foyer. "Wait."

He paused by the front door and turned to confront her. "You'd be wise to stay out of this, Rebecca."

So formal. So cold. Even so, she couldn't let him go. Not without doing everything within her power to stop events from moving any further along this path of destruction. It didn't matter if she had to swallow every last ounce of pride. If it meant a quiet and reasonable solution to her father's dilemma, she'd do it. "Please, Alex. There must be another way of resolving this."

He turned on her. "I've never met a woman who possesses even a tenth of the loyalty you display toward your father," he marveled. "It doesn't matter what he does to you, to the people dependent on him for a living, to casual bystanders who get in his way. You still defend him."

She shook her head in instant denial. "I'm not defending him. If he stole the money—"

Alex lifted an eyebrow. "If?" he repeated softly.

She hovered between crazed laughter and tears. "I know he stole the money." The wound was so new and raw, she couldn't even fully feel the hurt. But she didn't doubt for a minute that would change. And soon. "I guess I haven't digested it yet."

"I suggest you start. As of tomorrow, your life will take a dramatic change."

"My life?" She stared at him, not understanding. "It's my father—"

He simply shook his head. "You've lived in Somerset all your life and still you don't know how things work?"

he said with disbelief. "How many of your so-called friends will stand beside you when it's discovered that your father is a thief?"

It took her an instant to comprehend his words. "But they're my friends," she replied. "Why wouldn't they—"

He gave a short, hard laugh. "Grow up, Becca. Your father is already teetering on the edge of bankruptcy. He earns—earned—his living investing other people's money. Who do you think will invest their money with him after this? Do you think they won't wonder whether he somehow scammed them during one of their past associations? That they won't make accusations, if only to one another?"

A denial leaped to her lips, one she didn't dare utter. Until today she'd have sworn her father was as honest as the day was long, that his pride in his name and reputation and family honor meant everything to him. But she didn't know the man sitting in their library, a man who had confessed to a crime that her father had always taught her ranked just shy of murder.

"I see you're starting to understand," Alex said. "It's time to face facts, Rebecca. Your life as you knew it is over. Who will want anything to do with you or your father? Maybe his dishonesty is a genetic trait. Maybe you were in on it. And how delighted some will be that the mighty Huntingtons have finally gotten their—" He tilted his head to one side in consideration. "What is that antiquated phrase? Ah, yes. Comeuppance."

"Is that how you see us, Alex?" She dared to close the distance between them. "Is that how you see me? As the daughter of a thief?"

"It's what you are." He spoke the words—brutal, unkind words. They'd have wounded her beyond bearing if she hadn't seen the truth on his face. He didn't believe those words. Not even a little. Regret already glittered in the inky depths of his eyes. "Becca—"

"Tell me what we can do. Tell me what you want."

The regret vanished as if it had never been. "And you'll give it to me?"

"Yes. Ask and it's yours."

"Just to make all this go away?"

Her chin shot up. "Not go away. My father owes the money. If it takes us the rest of our lives, it'll be repaid. If it can be done quietly, fine. If it can't, it will still be repaid." She stepped even closer. "But he's not responsible for those arson fires. I'll never believe it."

"Yesterday, you'd never have believed your father was a thief."

"Help me, Alex." She couldn't believe she was asking, but what choice did she have? Once Alex set himself a course, he wouldn't be dissuaded. If she could focus that determination on his finding the true culprit for the arson fires, it would prove her father's innocence. "I'm only asking you to help me find the truth. Help me find out who's really responsible for setting the fires at the refinery and at your ranch."

"And in exchange, you'll give me whatever I want?"

"Yes."

He hooked a finger in the neckline of her cotton blouse and tugged her closer. "What if it's you I want, *dulzura?* How far will you go, and how much will you give me, if I make you the price for my help?"

She didn't hesitate. "All I want is the same thing you do. The truth. And I'll go as far as you want and give whatever you ask in order to get that truth."

"I was hoping you'd say that."

He cupped the back of her neck and took her mouth in a kiss that threatened to destroy what little sanity she retained. His mouth didn't just take hers, it possessed it, consumed it, set her on fire and then drove those flames into an inferno. And then he released her and stepped back. A late fall chill swept in, replacing the warmth from his embrace.

"You tempt me, *dulzura.*" He fixed her with an unreadable gaze. "Unfortunately for you, I'm not a man so easily bought."

And with that, he left her standing in the foyer, utterly devastated.

Rebecca gave herself a day. One single day to get her head straight, her heart protected, and her determination to a point where it outweighed her desperation, before confronting Alex again.

She wished it could be on her territory, or at the very least at a neutral site, but he made that impossible. He didn't show up at the Cattleman's Club, nor at work where she might catch him on the fly. Instead, she was forced to drive out to his ranch, El Diablo.

At the entryway to his gravel drive, she pulled her convertible to the shoulder of the road and climbed out of the car to gaze at his spread. It was an impressive place, rolling across a full hundred acres of windswept pastureland. The ranch house occupied the southeast corner of his property and from her viewpoint she could see several fenced paddocks and a large barn, which was currently under construction. The general noise of that construction drifted toward her, the sound of saws and hammers and the occasional shout borne to her on the chilly fall breeze.

The mansion—for it could hardly be called a house—stood crisp and white against a cerulean sky, the central portion a stately two stories, complete with porticos and balconies, while the sides sprawled outward in wide-flung wings like a warm Texan embrace. The sight filled her with dismay.

Seeing El Diablo in all its glory proved once and for all that this wasn't *her* Alex anymore. She'd known that. Known it for a very long time. But until this minute, she hadn't fully allowed herself to see him as the man he'd become, versus the younger, slightly less powerful version he'd been when they'd first fallen in love. Alejandro Montoya wasn't a poor teen from the barrio anymore. He was a male at his full strength and capability, a force to be reckoned with. He was also a rich, successful, influential man intent on destroying her father.

Rebecca's mouth firmed and she set her chin at a
defiant angle. Forewarned was forearmed. Somehow,
someway, she would get through to him and resolve this
situation, to their mutual advantage.

Returning to the car, she drove down the sweeping
drive and parked a short distance from the barn, where
she suspected she'd find him. Sure enough, he stood
near the main entrance, blueprints spread across a table
made from plywood and supported by a pair of saw-
horses. A hammer, a crowbar and a can of nails kept the
sheets of paper from rolling up.

"We need the rough on the plumbing completed
today, as well as the electrical," Alex was saying. "Make
sure he puts bibs here, here and here. The building in-
spector comes tomorrow and I won't be pleased if there
are any delays. Winter's not that far off and I want this
place finished before Christmas."

"Yessir, Mr. Montoya. That won't be a problem."

"Thanks, Hank." He looked up then, his gaze sharp
and direct beneath the brim of his Stetson. He didn't
appear surprised to see her. No doubt he'd been expecting this visit. "I'm honored."

Okay, color her surprised. "And why is that?"

"For the first time since I've taken ownership of El
Diablo, a Huntington has come to call."

"And yet, no brass band or groveling peasants," she
dared to tease.

His mouth twitched before he regained control with
characteristic ruthlessness. "I won't bother to ask why

you're here. I'll just tell you that you're wasting both your time and mine. You may have endless hours to fritter away. I don't."

"But you'll listen to my pitch, anyway."

He lifted an eyebrow at her confident retort, then jerked his head at Hank. The construction foreman took the hint and made himself scarce.

"Pitch away," Alex instructed. She'd never seen him look harder or more remote. A wall of granite would offer a softer embrace than this man. "Not that it'll do you any good. I have your father right where I want him and nothing you do or say is going to make a bit of difference. So you go right ahead, Ms. Huntington. Lob your best pitch."

She struggled to conceal her dismay. "Here?"

"I'm a busy man. And this has already taken more time than I can spare." He tugged off his leather work gloves and slapped them onto the makeshift table. Planting his palms on the rough wood, he leaned in her direction, the sheer, unadulterated essence of the man threatening to swamp her senses. "So it's here and now, or not at all."

"Okay, fine." She took a deep breath. "I'm asking you…begging you…to help me find out who started those fires. To find out who's really behind them. I know you think it's my father, but I'm telling you, it's not. He's guilty of—" She forced herself to say the words, no matter how acrid they tasted. "He's guilty of theft. But not arson."

Alex simply shook his head. "It's not my job to find who started the blazes."

She marshaled her arguments. "When you put your mind to something, you do it. You make things happen. Please, make this happen."

He was shaking his head again before she'd even finished. "There is nothing you can say, nothing you can offer, no inducement tempting enough for me to assist you or your father in this matter. Stay out of it before he takes you down, too."

She could see the strength of his decision in his set expression and the burning coldness of his gaze. Time to try a different tack. "We also need to talk about the repayment of the money owed to the TCC."

Even on this point he remained unrelenting. "That's between your father and the club."

Alex may have temporarily won their first round, but he wouldn't win this one. When it came to stubborn, she was his equal. "If we could just have a little time," she began. "I could make payments—"

"Forget it, Becca," he interrupted curtly. "Do you think the Texas Cattleman's Club is going to wait years for you and your father to pay back the money he stole? They're barely willing to wait days. If it had been left up to Brody, your father would be cooling his heels in a jail cell as we speak."

He couldn't have shocked her more if he'd slapped her. "Brody? Lance Brody? Kate's Lance?"

He didn't spare her. "That's right. Once he was in possession of all the details, your best friend's husband demanded that the board have your father arrested. But the board decided to give him the chance to repay the money. My offer to purchase Huntington Manor was his one shot at doing just that."

That stung. "I'd be far more appreciative if I didn't know that your motivation for doing so was to get your hands on our home," she shot back.

"Get my hands—" He broke off with a word that had color warming her cheeks. "Why the hell would I want Huntington Manor when I have El Diablo? Your home is a financial sinkhole. Who could afford to buy it, let alone maintain it?"

That shook her and she scrambled for understanding. "You want revenge. You want to drive my father out of Maverick County."

He didn't deny it. "I would prefer to do both of those things without having such an albatross hanging around my neck. Look around you, Becca. El Diablo is a working ranch. My import/export business doesn't carry this place. Far from it. I work hard to keep the ranch solidly in the black. Your father, on the other hand, plays at being a rancher. But I guarantee it doesn't turn a profit and hasn't for a long time."

"I don't understand. Then why...?"

"Why would I offer to buy Huntington Manor so your father can pay off the debt? Simple. I want him gone. He doesn't realize it, yet, but he's out of options. Either he sells to me or he sells to Rodriquez. But he will have to sell out. And soon."

"Rodriquez." Something her father had said the

previous night gnawed at the back of her mind. "Dad says he owes him money, too."

Alex nodded. "I'm sure it's more than either you or your father can get your hands on."

"But if you loaned us the money using Sweet Nothings as collateral, that would be enough, wouldn't it?"

He shrugged. "This isn't my problem, Rebecca. Don't put me in the middle of it."

"You came to us as the Cattleman's representative, remember?" she retorted. "You put yourself in the middle."

"It's out of my hands. Mitch Brody has taken over as club accountant. Talk to him."

"I already did. He needs the cash and we don't have it. But I do have this." She opened her purse and removed the deed to Sweet Nothings and centered it on the plywood between his widespread hands. "As I told you last night, I own both the building, as well as the business. Combined, they're worth well in excess of what Dad owes the TCC."

He made no move to pick up the deed. "We've already discussed this."

"We're discussing it again," she stated evenly. "I can't approach Rhymes for a bank loan using the property as collateral, since he's involved in whatever my father pulled. So, I'm asking you. Will you draw up a loan agreement using Sweet Nothings as collateral?"

He didn't even hesitate. "No. Ask the Brodys. They're your friends, not me."

"That's precisely why I can't ask them," she argued.

"They're friends. It would put them in an awkward position and I refuse to do that to them. But if you loan me the money, everyone will know it's on the up and up because you despise my father."

A humorless laugh stirred the air between them. "I have never understood your brand of logic, and I doubt I ever will." He rocked backward and thought for a moment. "Okay, I'll bite. How will the good people of Maverick county know it's on the up and up? I seem to recall we have a romantic history between us."

"A history that didn't end well," she pointed out. "You have every reason *not* to help us and damn few reasons to go along with this."

"Precisely."

He allowed the word to linger until she released a sigh. "I have two goals, Alex. The first is to help my father repay the money he owes. I guarantee *someone* will loan me the money. My second goal is to prove that my father is innocent of the arson fires and find the person who's actually guilty."

"Not a wise move, Becca. In fact, it's a downright dangerous one."

"Really? There's a way you can stop me." She tapped the deed. "Accept my offer and go with me to visit Darius so he can explain why he thinks my father is complicit in these fires. Help me figure out the identity of the guilty party. Otherwise, I'm taking my offer elsewhere."

His mouth carved into a cynical smile. "I thought you weren't going to approach your friends."

"I'm not. But since El Gato has a vested interest in all this, perhaps he'll be willing to help me."

"Absolutely not!" Alex bit out.

She could tell that the words escaped before he'd had time to think better of them, or he'd never have given her so much leverage in their little skirmish. She offered him a gentle smile and waited. It didn't take long. He snatched off his hat, flung it into the dirt at his feet and swore. She suspected that if he'd cursed in English, she'd have been quite shocked.

"I take it that means you agree?" she dared to ask.

He shot her a black glare. "Let me make myself clear, Rebecca. You are not going to ask Paulo Rodriquez for anything, particularly not a loan."

Interesting. She tilted her head to one side. "I don't understand. I thought he was your friend."

"He was. Is. We grew up together, were close childhood friends. Until recent events, I'd have said we were still friends. But since it was Paulo who helped put your father in his current predicament, you'd be wise to stay well away from him."

She didn't disagree. In fact, she'd deliberately used the name just to goad him. Now he'd roused her curiosity. "Why shouldn't I approach El Gato?"

His mouth tightened, a clear warning signal. "Because I don't know what he wants from your father. Until I do, it isn't safe for you to put yourself between them. And it sure as hell isn't wise to give Rodriquez leverage over you." His gaze swept over her, the sensation almost as tantalizing as a touch. To her dismay it elicited the same reaction, a deep welling of heat and desire, one it took every ounce of willpower to conceal from his discerning eyes. "Nor should you give me that sort of leverage."

"Just out of curiosity, would you use it to hurt me?" She couldn't resist the question, any more than she could deny her interest in his response.

"I'd rather not find out." He bent to pick up his hat, the set of his face making it clear he'd reached a decision. "I'll take you to see Darius. Maybe he can talk some sense into you. At the very least he can give you a general idea why we think your father is behind the arson fires."

"This isn't just about your vendetta against my father, is it?" she asked in dismay. "You really believe he's guilty, don't you?"

He didn't hesitate. "I don't doubt for an instant that he's guilty as sin."

After taking a few minutes to give instructions to Hank, followed by a call to Darius, eliciting the information that the security consultant was at the club, Alex gestured toward her car. "Shall we go together or separately?"

"Together," she decided.

That way she'd have time to further discuss the situation with him—or rather, argue. And if she were brutally honest with herself, she'd also admit that arriving together at the club as a couple would be far less traumatic than enduring the potential stares and whispers from the members if she arrived on her own. The uncomfortable thought gave rise to an even more uncomfortable realization.

She waited until they were clear of his drive before asking a question that left her feeling equally embarrassed and ashamed. "When Dad resigns, the board will want my resignation, too, won't they?"

Alex hesitated before replying. "I don't see why they would."

"You know why," she whispered, not daring to look his way.

"We'll worry about it if it happens."

We. That single word gave her hope. He wasn't totally immune to her or to what she was going through. Maybe she could convince him to help her, to get to the truth. If that proof led to her father, so be it. But she was certain, with every fiber of her being, that as guilty as her father was of embezzlement, he was innocent of arson.

The fact that his fate rested in the hands of men who would just as soon see Sebastian Huntington in jail as get at that truth, couldn't be taken lightly. But somehow, someway, she'd find a means to convince them to put aside their animosity and find the actual person responsible.

Nervous dread swept over her as they approached the entryway to the club. "What is Darius going to tell me?" she asked as calmly as she could manage.

"That your father is guilty."

She gave him a brief, searching glance. "I'm serious, Alex. What incontrovertible proof has Darius found?"

"He isn't going to share that with you, Becca."

"Why not?" she demanded.

"Because it would undermine the D.A.'s legal efforts to prosecute your father." He shifted in the leather seat, angling so he could look at her. "Fair warning. There isn't going to be any plea bargaining this down. When we get all the evidence we need, the guilty party is going to jail. End of story."

She understood on an intellectual level that Alex had good cause to feel that way. But this was her father, the man who'd loved and protected her, who'd comforted her when her mother had died. The man who'd raised her and taught her right from wrong. Tears pricked her eyes as she acknowledged his flaws, the incredible distance he'd stepped over the line between honesty and dishonesty, a line he'd once taught her was intransigent.

She refused to believe he'd fallen so far that he'd put the lives of men and livestock, who could have been injured by the blaze at El Diablo, in jeopardy. Parking the car beneath the shade of a wide-flung cottonwood tree she drew in a deep breath, fighting to find some sort of balance amidst the emotional seesaw she'd been on the past forty-eight hours. Was it only two days ago that she'd arrived here to have lunch with Kate? It seemed like an eternity.

"Are you ready?"

The sheer gentleness of the question nearly proved

her undoing. Tears flooded her eyes, tears she suppressed with single-minded determination. She kept her gaze fixed straight ahead while she struggled for control. She needed to put her emotions aside and remain focused on her goals. Otherwise, she'd fall apart and there would be no one left willing to lift a finger to keep her father out of jail. She snatched another quick breath and that's when she felt it.

It was the lightest of touches. Just a fleeting caress along the curve of her cheek. Memories swamped her at the familiar gesture. How many times in the past had Alex comforted her in just that way, lifted her during difficult times with a simple reassuring stroke of his hand? The fact that he'd offer it now, when they were so at odds, meant more than she could ever express.

Energy and sheer obstinacy flowed through her, lending her the strength she so desperately needed. Her chin firmed and she turned toward him, every scrap of grit and purpose concentrated on the goal at hand. "I'm ready," she told him. "I want to know just what we're up against."

She could see his conflicted response to her comment. Part of him—no doubt a reluctant part—wanted to reassure her, while the other intended her to understand the futility of her hopes. He blew out his breath in a sigh. "I'm afraid you're in for a world of disappointment."

"Let's find out."

To her dismay, his words proved prophetic. Darius didn't have any particular ax to grind. His approach was simple: What evidence had he uncovered, and what possible conclusions did that evidence allow him to draw? He took her through it with matter-of-fact precision, his attitude professional, logical, but with an edge of compassion that caused Rebecca to realize that Summer Martindale had chosen wisely when she'd eloped with Darius.

The proof he'd compiled against Cornelius Gentry was formidable. Even so, it wasn't direct or even circumstantial proof against Sebastian Huntington, as she was quick to point out. Gentry could have been acting on his own.

"That's possible," Darius conceded. "Though considering the nature of the man, it's unlikely. Until he's found, we won't know for certain."

"He's disappeared?" Rebecca asked in concern.

Alex didn't bother to hide his cynicism. "Most likely, he was paid to disappear."

She rounded on him. "And you believe my father paid him?"

"It would be in his best interest."

"That doesn't make sense." She'd gotten their attention with that simple statement. A twinge of hope stirred, along with a hint of relief. The more she considered it, the more certain she grew. "I'm serious. Think about it. My father, in effect, gambled away TCC funds by investing them with Paulo Rodriquez, right?"

Both men nodded.

"If he'd had any spare money, he'd have repaid the

club so he wouldn't get caught and accused of embezzlement. So where did he find the money to make Gentry disappear? I know the man." She couldn't conceal her shiver of dislike. "He would require some serious money to go away."

"What do you mean you know him?" Alex asked sharply.

She hesitated before admitting, "I've had a few run-ins with him." Both men fixed her with identical looks, and she caved beneath the joint pressure. "He was too familiar. Cocky. Arrogant. And when I gave him a verbal slap, he laughed at me. He told me my father would never fire him."

Darius groaned. "That doesn't help build a case for your father's innocence, Rebecca."

"The reverse, in fact," Alex added.

"What? Why?" she asked in alarm.

"Your father destroyed my family when I dared to touch you. I assume Gentry knew what your father had done to us?" Alex asked with surprising compassion.

She moistened her lips. "He knew. He said my father would never fire him the way he had Carmen."

The touch of pity in Alex's gaze totally unnerved her. "If Gentry was that certain of his position, he must have had something on your father. Something serious. If he set the blazes at your father's instruction, he'd have reason for that sort of confidence."

Four

It took Rebecca a moment to absorb Alex's comment. The instant she did, her breath caught in a gasp.

"No." She shook her head, adamant. "No, that can't be it. Gentry must have known about the money. Thought he could use that as leverage."

"How?" Alex persisted. "It's not likely your father would have mentioned it to him."

"Maybe he overheard a phone conversation between my father and Rhymes." She could hear the desperation in her voice. "There could be any number of ways Gentry could have gotten hold of the information. Besides, what possible motivation could my father have for setting fire to Brody Oil and Gas, or your barn, Alex?"

"I explained this to you the other night," he said, making his point with as much relentless logic as she'd used on them. "To keep all of us fighting among ourselves so we wouldn't notice the missing money until he'd had time to replace it. The fires were simply a delaying tactic."

"I'm telling you, he didn't do it." But their certainty roused another worry. "What happens if the police find Gentry and he points his finger at my father? It would be his word against Dad's."

He and Darius exchanged a brief, telling look before Alex responded. "The word of an embezzler against the word of his employee." He put it in terms that had her wincing. "Assuming Gentry doesn't have indisputable proof, it could go either way with a jury. But if I were Gentry's lawyer, I'd pound home the fact that Huntington is a thief, and a desperate one, at that. That in his position as employer, he brought considerable pressure to bear on Gentry to set the fires and promised to protect him with the Huntington name and reputation. Since the fires only caused property damage without harm to life, I suspect Gentry could get a reduced sentence in exchange for his testimony against your father."

Rebecca wondered if she looked as shell-shocked as she felt. On some level she'd thought she'd walk in here and discover it had all been a hideous mistake. That a simple conversation would clear the air. At the very least, she anticipated getting some idea of who might have done this. The fact that the evidence pointed

straight at Gentry would have been cause for celebration, if they weren't so determined to link her father to
his foreman.

"How do I prove Dad didn't do this?" she asked.
Again, the two men exchanged glances and her anger
sparked. "Look at it from my position. Assume he's
innocent. There must be a way of proving that."

"We won't know anything until Gentry is found,"
Darius replied with stark simplicity.

She shook her head, her desperation growing with
each moment that passed. "It might be too late by then.
He may have figured he could use Dad as his scapegoat
if he ever got caught. We need to have our own defense
lined up in advance."

"In that case, I recommend you and your father hire
the best lawyer you can afford."

Afford. The word impacted like a slap. She could tell
Darius had said all he intended. And though he radiated
patience and empathy, there was nothing more he could
do for her. In fact, he'd probably said more than he
should have, considering he was one of those building
a case against her father. She forced herself to concede
the inevitable. There wasn't any advantage to dragging
this uncomfortable meeting out any further.

"Thank you, Darius," she replied. "I appreciate your
frankness."

"No problem."

She would have left then, but Alex stopped her with
a touch of his hand and addressed Darius. "I've been

meaning to get in touch with you and Summer," he said. "I'd like to throw a small party for the two of you. I thought I'd invite the Brody brothers and their wives, Justin Dupree and my sister, and Kevin and Cara Novak. Since you eloped, none of us have had the chance to celebrate your marriage."

Darius regarded Alex with surprise and a touch of puzzlement. "That's very generous of you."

"But unexpected?"

Darius shrugged. "A bit, given your guest list."

Alex inclined his head in understanding. "I think we've all decided it's time to put the past behind us and move forward. Celebrating your marriage to Summer provides the perfect opportunity."

A huge grin spread across Darius's attractive features. "Thanks, man. I know Summer would really enjoy it. Just tell us when and where, and we'll be there."

"It'll be at El Diablo, and I'll call you with the exact date. But I'm thinking a couple weeks before Christmas? That'll make it more festive."

They all shook hands and then she and Alex returned to the parking lot. Without a word, he took her key from her hand and diverted her path toward the passenger side of the car. She didn't argue. All the fight had drained out of her. They didn't speak for the entire time it took to return to his ranch. To her surprise, he didn't turn down his drive, but continued on toward the back forty. He parked on a small hill that overlooked the bulk of his property, including the ranch house and newly con-

structed barn. Without a word, the two exited the vehicle
and wandered toward the rigorously tended fence line
edging the pasture.

"I don't know how to fix this," she confessed in a low
voice.

"It's not your problem to fix."

"I can't sit by and do nothing. He's my father."

"He's a strong, ruthless man who got himself into this
predicament. He can damn well get himself out again."

She shot him a look. "Is that what you did when your
mother was in trouble?" she asked drily. "When Alicia
had problems?"

"There's no comparison. My job was and is to protect
my family."

"Exactly. Just as it's—"

He cut her off without compunction. "You have it
backward, *dulzura*. It's your father's duty to protect
you, not the other way around."

"He has. He's protected me my entire life. It's my
turn now."

"You still don't get it." Anger underscored Alex's
voice. "He put himself in this mess. He caused it."

"The embezzlement, yes," she argued.

"And yet, even with that you're trying to take the
burden from him."

She turned on him. "What else am I supposed to do?"

"Walk away. Do nothing."

She dared to touch him. "Alex, please," she whispered. "Help us. Help me."

He stilled beneath her hand and she literally held her breath. Then he exploded into motion. Snatching her into his arms, he pulled her into an unbreakable embrace. "Just once I want you to touch me without an ulterior motive." His voice escaped, low and harsh. "Just once I want you to come into my arms without your father standing between us."

How could he even think such a thing? "My father isn't here now."

"That's where you're wrong. He's with us every minute." Alex's mouth twisted. "But you never understood that, did you? So be it. See if you understand this instead."

He bent his head and took her mouth, consuming her. Memories of the past collided with the actions of the present and merged into a confusing blend of what once had been and what now existed between them. There was sweetness from their long-ago affair. The bitterness of its ending. The lingering passion that ripped through them whenever they came together. And something else. Something more. Something new and tentative.

It was as though the fall wash of colors had grown more vibrant, filled with the promise and joy of the season. Sensation grew more acute. She became attuned to the quickened sounds of his breath and the sharp, crisp fragrance that clung to him, a combination of leather and sawdust and some incredible masculine scent she'd always associated with him. Her lips parted beneath his and she sank inward with the softest of sighs.

She'd exchanged kisses with other men. Passionate kisses. But no one had ever stirred her the way Alex did. Nor did any other man have the ability to arouse her to such heights with just a single brush of his mouth. And his hands... With typical assurance he unbuttoned her blouse. An errant breeze caught at the edges, flipping them backward and exposing the lacy bit of nothing covering her breasts.

He dragged his mouth from hers and his breath escaped in a gusty sigh. "Ivory."

She stared at him in bewilderment. "Ivory?"

His fingers drifted across her silk-covered breasts. "The color. It's been driving me crazy wondering." Before she could respond, he lowered his head and feathered a string of kisses along the edge of her bra. Her head fell back and he groaned. "I've never seen skin like yours. Like velvet cream."

His mouth drifted upward along the line of her neck until he once again delved between her parted lips. As his mouth took hers, his hands swept blouse and bra straps from her shoulders. Before the chilly air had time to bite, he cupped her breasts, the combination of cold and warmth causing them to peak against his palms. She moaned, the helpless sound a half plea. He responded by dragging his calloused fingers across the aching tips until all she wanted was to slip to the ground and complete what he'd started.

He must have felt the same because he surged against her, everything about him growing more demanding. His determined touch. The aching tenderness of his kiss. The growing need that communicated itself in every taut line of his body. No matter how much he tried to deny the fact, he wanted her. Just as she wanted him.

But almost as soon as the thought slipped into her head, he was adjusting her clothing. "There's not enough privacy," he said in response to her questioning look. "Some other time and place."

She wanted to protest his assumption, but didn't dare. If he'd taken their embrace one step further, she'd have followed. Willingly. Joyfully. Instead, she asked the first question to pop into her head, anything that would give her time to recover from what had just happened.

"What about my father?" she inquired. "Will you help me?"

It was the wrong question at the worst possible moment. All expression vanished from his face. "No." The word escaped, blunt and uncompromising and unadulterated.

She could tell he wouldn't be swayed. Couldn't be. Still, she had to try. "Alex—"

He cut her off without remorse. "Enough, Rebecca. Let me make this clear. The money is due tomorrow. If your father can't pay, he's going to jail. And I will be all too happy to put him there."

By going in person to Huntington Manor to attempt to collect the money due the TCC, he was rubbing salt in the wound, Alex decided—both his and Rebecca's. Not that his tiny epiphany stopped him.

As he turned toward the manor, a sleek black McLaren shot around the corner toward him and disappeared almost as fast as it had appeared. But even those few seconds was more than enough time for him to identify the driver.

Paulo Rodriquez.

An ice-cold fear raced through him. Rebecca had warned that she'd find someone to help them out of their predicament. Had she settled on Rodriquez, despite Alex's warning? And why wouldn't she? Since he'd turned her down, she'd have moved on to other, more fertile possibilities. And the minute she asked those other possibilities for help and received the inevitable doors slammed in her face, she'd have realized her choices were limited. Rodriquez might have seemed like the perfect solution, despite his warning.

His knock on the door was once again answered by the housekeeper, Louise. This time he was shown directly to the library where he caught the fragments of a heated argument between Rebecca and her father.

Sebastian broke off the instant Louise knocked. "What is it?" he asked, ripe impatience implicit in the question.

The housekeeper opened the door a crack. "Mr. Montoya wishes to speak with you, sir."

Sebastian swore. "Of course he does. Come on in, Montoya. Why shouldn't you put the cap on the end of a perfect day."

Alex gave Louise a sympathetic smile before entering the room. He waited for the door to close behind him before speaking. "That bad?" he asked his nemesis. He didn't wait for a response. There wasn't any point. "Allow me to put you out of your misery and make this short and not so sweet. Do you have the money to reimburse the Texas Cattleman's Club or not?"

"That depends," Rebecca responded before her father had the chance.

To Alex's private amusement, both he and Sebastian swore in unison. "How many times do we need to have this discussion, *dulzura?*" he asked. "This conversation is between me and your father."

It came as no surprise to either of them that she didn't listen. Despite the fact that she looked unbearably exhausted and stressed, she regarded them both with a strength and determination that won his reluctant admiration. Now that he considered the matter, everything about her roused a grudging admiration.

She wore a dress in the exact same shade of ivory as the undergarments from the day before and he couldn't help but wonder if it were more than mere coincidence. Her dress was elegant and deceptively simple, almost bridal in its feminine chastity, yet wickedly flirtatious in the manner in which it caressed her curves. It made his hands itch. Worse, it roused a fierce protectiveness when he realized Rodriquez had seen her looking like this.

"Will you loan us the money, Alex, and use Sweet Nothings for collateral?" she asked.

He was so preoccupied with her appearance that it took a moment for her question to sink in.

"I forbid it," Sebastian said at the same time that Alex offered a terse "No."

She lifted an eyebrow and waited a beat before filling the thundering silence that followed their outburst. "I didn't discover that El Gato came to call until after he left. I'm sorry I missed meeting him. But maybe I should get in touch with him and see if he won't loan me the money we need," she retorted calmly.

This time the two men reacted and spoke as one. "No!"

She simply lifted an eyebrow and folded her arms across her chest, waiting them out.

Alex swore again, this time in Spanish. When he'd managed to regain most of his composure, he glanced at Sebastian before returning his attention to Rebecca. "Would you mind fixing some coffee so we can discuss the situation?" he asked with formal politeness.

"I'll ask Louise to bring a tray."

"You will wait for the tray," Alex instructed. "I wish to have a private moment with your father."

He could tell she wanted to argue. Clearly, her exhaustion worked to his advantage. The fight drained out of her, leaving her pale and drawn, her only color the intense glitter of her dark green eyes and the fiery sweep of hair surrounding her ghost-white face. She gave an abrupt nod and without another word, exited the room.

Alex didn't waste any time. He turned on Sebastian. "I saw Rodriquez leaving as I drove up. What did he want?"

"That's none of your business," the older man retorted, reverting to type.

There wasn't time for this. Alex cut through the other man's bluster without hesitation. "Either make it my business or I'll leave you to deal with this mess on your own." His tone underscored his determination. He'd had all he intended to take from the Huntingtons. "You either give me the information I'm requesting or I walk out of here and leave the pair of you to learn just how ruthless Paulo can be." He shot Sebastian a hard look. "Well?"

The antagonism escaped Sebastian like air from a leaky balloon. "He wants it all," he whispered. "The manor, as well as Sweet Nothings. In exchange he'll pay off what I owe the TCC and wipe our debt clean."

"I'm not surprised."

"Because you're in on it, aren't you?" Huntington accused, working himself up into a new rage. "Because you put him up to it."

Alex stared in disbelief. "Have you lost your mind? Why would I do that?"

Huntington replied without a moment's hesitation. "You want revenge for my having fired your mother."

"An interesting theory. And though I won't deny that I'm capable of it, that isn't what happened. Rodriquez doesn't have any interest in turning Huntington Manor over to me." He paused a beat. "Any more than he's interested in owning Sweet Nothings. You do realize what he's really after, don't you?"

Sebastian turned gray. "That won't happen."

Alex merely cocked a skeptical eyebrow. "Won't it?

How much are you in to him for, Huntington? I'm guessing it's a hell of a lot more than three hundred grand."

"Closer to a million," Sebastian confessed.

"A million." Alex fought to tamp down his fury at the man's stupidity. "Where are you going to get that sort of money? How are you going to stop him from taking this house?" He drove his point home with the cruelest question of all. "What if he goes after Rebecca?"

"He wouldn't."

Alex stared at him in disbelief. "You can't possibly be that ignorant. Paulo Rodriquez is ruthless. He will stop at nothing to get what he wants. And what he wants is Huntington Manor, and now Sweet Nothings. What's next on his list? Or should I say…who? What if he adds to his demands? As far as I can see, the only question that remains is whether you're going to give him what he wants."

"Never," Sebastian said fiercely. "Not him. And not you. The manor is mine and it stays mine. It's off-limits to both of you. As is my daughter."

Alex looked at him skeptically. "I assume that means you have the money to pay off your debts?"

The answer was written in every crevice of the older man's face. "I'll find it," he bluffed, his spine as ramrod stiff as ever. "I'll take out a mortgage. People in this town owe me. They'll help tide me over."

Alex released a short laugh. There was no point in wasting his breath. Sebastian Huntington lived in a fool's paradise and only time and those people who "owed him" would be in a position to change that. "Good luck with that. It's clear you don't need my help. Let me know when you have the money. We'll expect you at the TCC first thing in the morning."

He started for the door, only to have Huntington stop him at the last second. "Wait." And then Alex caught a word he never thought he'd hear from Sebastian Huntington's lips. "Please, Alejandro. Please, wait."

It was the name his mother used whenever she'd addressed him. Hearing it come from Huntington filled him with a deep grief, chased by an even deeper anger. If not for this man, his mother might still be alive. "Last chance, Sebastian."

"Can you keep Rodriquez away from Rebecca?"

Alex turned. "I can try."

"Will you take Sweet Nothings from her?"

"I have no interest in your daughter's boutique."

"And…and the manor?"

"You would have to turn it over to me. In exchange, I'll pay off Rodriquez."

Huntington struggled with his pride before asking his final question. "Would you…would you consider allowing me to remain here? You said you have no interest in living here yourself. But this is the only home Rebecca has ever known."

"She'll get over it."

Desperation took hold. "I…I could rent it from you."

"You can't afford to rent it from me." Alex shook his head, adamant. "I want you gone, Huntington."

Huntington's hands collapsed into fists. "At least give me time."

"Time for what?"

"Allow me to remain here. Give me a year to raise the necessary funds to pay you back." Alex's expression must have been answer enough, because he waved that aside. "Fine. Six months. In the meantime, accept Rebecca's offer. Let her believe that she convinced you to loan us the money using Sweet Nothings as collateral. If I can't raise what I owe you for paying off the debt to the TCC and Rodriquez—plus interest—in those six months, the sale becomes final. You hand the deed to Sweet Nothings back to Rebecca, I'll sign the final papers giving you ownership of Huntington Manor, and I'll leave Maverick County for good. But if I manage to raise the money, you return both the manor and Sweet Nothings to us and then stay out of our lives."

Alex's eyes narrowed in suspicion. "Why involve Rebecca and her shop?"

"I don't want her to know about our deal." Huntington's mouth twisted. "She won't believe me if I tell her you simply handed over the money out of the goodness of your heart."

Alex couldn't help smiling at that. "True. She knows me too well to buy that particular fairy tale."

"Which means I need to come up with something plausible that she will believe. Her pride demands that we give you some sort of collateral in exchange for the money. And she won't give up this crazy crusade of hers if it's Huntington Manor. She'll continue to try and find another option rather than see me thrown out of my home. I can't risk her going to Rodriquez. But if she thinks you're willing to take Sweet Nothings, and that it's enough to pay off both debts, she'll back off."

Understanding dawned. "She doesn't know how much you owe Rodriquez, does she?"

"No. She believes that any money from selling Sweet Nothings—or obtaining a loan for its value—will be sufficient to pay off both debts. And I don't intend to explain otherwise."

Alex considered his options. "You realize that if Gentry implicates you in the arson fires, I won't lift a finger to help you? In fact, I'll make that a condition of the loan. If you have anything to do with those fires, the manor is mine. And nothing Rebecca says or does will change my mind."

"Since I'm not guilty I have no problem with your making that a condition of the loan," Huntington responded with impressive dignity. "Right now my main concern is paying off my debts. Are we in agreement on that score, if nothing else?"

Before they could complete the negotiations, Rebecca returned with a tray. The two men remained stoic beneath her searching gaze. While she poured coffee for the three of them, Alex gave Huntington the slightest of nods, signaling his agreement to the deal. Once the beverages had been poured and served, Rebecca stood with her saucer held in a white-knuckle grip.

"Well?" she asked.

The single word was uttered with a casual air, but Alex caught the strain welling beneath it. Carrying his coffee to the couch where they'd shared their passionate embrace just a few nights previously, he took a seat. "I've agreed to listen to your offer," he said.

"And consider it," Huntington added pointedly.

"Don't push your luck," he retorted. He didn't want to make this appear too easy or Rebecca would never buy it. "I said listen, and that's what I meant."

"It's a simple business proposition," Rebecca jumped in before her father had an opportunity to reply. "And one I hope will be to your advantage in the long run. I put up Sweet Nothings as collateral in exchange for a loan that will pay off the Texas Cattleman's Club—" She darted a swift, apprehensive glance in her father's direction. "And I'm hoping the value is also sufficient to cover my father's debt to Paulo Rodriquez, as well."

"You're asking a lot."

"I realize that." She hesitated. "Dad, would you mind if I talk privately to Alex now?"

Alex almost laughed at Huntington's expression. He had to commend the man, though. He held himself in check. Refraining from allowing the spill of words to escape, he restricted himself to a warning look before exiting the room.

The minute her father disappeared, she turned on him. "Okay, Alex. What's going on? Something's up. I can see it in both your faces. What aren't you two telling me?" she demanded.

Five

Alex offered a bland smile. "I have no idea what you're talking about."

Rebecca set aside her coffee and joined him on the couch. "You're sitting here, aren't you? Why? Yesterday you were determined to see my father go to jail. What's changed?"

Okay, he could give her that much information without her figuring out the rest. "Rodriquez."

She pinned him with a searching look. "He's that dangerous?"

Paulo might be his friend, but that didn't make Alex blind to his faults. "Yes," he replied simply. "He's that dangerous."

"This sudden willingness on your part, the fact that today you're considering my offer, it isn't about my father, is it?" she guessed with characteristic shrewdness.

"No," he conceded. "Despite my constant warnings, you keep threatening to turn to Rodriquez without realizing what sort of risk you're taking. If you go to him, you play right into his hands. Your father can't protect you from Paulo. I can."

"Why?" she whispered.

"Why am I willing to help you?"

"That and…" Her brows drew together. "Why is Rodriquez after us? What have we done to him?"

Alex chose his words with care. "Paulo's gone to a lot of trouble to dip his fingers into your father's pocket. Thanks to Sebastian's arrogance, he can't pay off both debts with what little cash he has on hand. Paulo would know that. In fact, he's probably counting on that fact. He's also not going to be happy if someone else steps in and pays off those debts after he's set everything up so he can take Huntington Manor from your father."

"You still haven't answered my question."

Fine. He'd give it to her straight. "Paulo wants status. Huntington Manor will give him that, or so he undoubtedly believes. He also wants Sweet Nothings in order to tie your hands and prevent you from using your business the way you intend to—as collateral to get your father out of debt."

"He asked Dad for Sweet Nothings, too?" Rebecca asked, appalled.

"He probably would have been willing to settle for the manor if you hadn't put yourself in the middle. I'm sure he's heard about your efforts on your father's behalf and this is his way of circumventing them."

"I couldn't sit by and do nothing."

"Actually, you could have." He waved her silent before she argued the point and placed his cup and saucer on the coffee table in front of them. "All of this is pointless to discuss. The bottom line is that both Paulo and the TCC need to be paid off or there will be consequences for both you and your father. If it were just your father, I wouldn't lift a finger to help. But for you…"

She bowed her head. "I thought you hated me."

"I'm willing to agree to your proposal. That's all that should matter to you."

She looked up at him and he could tell from her expression that she'd darted off on another path of concern. "Will Rodriquez come after you if you help us?"

"Paulo and I go way back."

She caught her bottom lip between her teeth. "Once again, you haven't answered my question. Will he come after you?"

"Are you going to put yourself between the two of us now?"

She offered a short laugh. "Apparently."

"Don't. In fact, I think I'll have my lawyer put a clause in our agreement that you'll stay away from Rodriquez or I have the right to call the note due."

Her eyes widened. "Is that even legal?"

He shrugged. "That's why I hire a team of very expensive lawyers. It's their job to make my wishes legal."

This time her laugh came more easily. Some of the strain eased from her face. "Then we have an agreement? You'll loan us the money to pay off both my father's debts, and use Sweet Nothings as collateral?"

"Yes. There might be the odd 'and, if, or but' to figure out. But we can sort that out at a later date."

She nodded. "Okay." She drew in a slow breath. "Thank you, Alex. I know this isn't what you'd either planned or wanted."

"No, it isn't."

"But I'll find a way to make it up to you. I promise."

"You can start by staying well away from Rodriquez."

She offered a small, calm smile, one that had always succeeded in driving him crazy. Unable to resist, he leaned in and cupped the back of her neck, drawing her closer. His mouth played over hers and he felt her instant surrender. With the softest of moans, she opened to him, gave as thoroughly as she received.

They drifted back against the couch cushions and he accepted this moment out of time as sheer indulgence on his part. It couldn't continue, not now that they'd agreed on the loan. But today, for this brief interlude, he'd accept what she so generously offered. As though afraid that he'd call a halt to the embrace, her fingers threaded through his hair, anchoring him in place. Unable to resist, his hands slid downward over bridal ivory, cupping the generous weight of her breast in his hand. She moaned again, just a sweet breath of sound that he drank in as though it was the most precious of nectars.

He couldn't get enough of her, wanted to discover all the ways in which she'd changed since he'd last made love to her. He swept downward over the narrow dip of her waist, the flare of her hip, to the flirtatious hem of her dress that had somehow managed to creep up toward her thighs. Slipping beneath, he found the silken length of her spectacular legs and inched upward in tantalizing circles until he reached the scrap of lace protecting the heated core of her. She gasped when he penetrated the barrier and pulled her mouth free from his.

He froze at the desperate longing gleaming in her eyes, and the full weight of his actions crashed down on him. Did she want him because she had feelings for him, or because he'd agreed to loan her father the money he needed? Carefully, he eased back, feeling a distinctive chill replace the blazing heat of only seconds before.

"Why are you doing this?" he asked suspiciously.

She stiffened, disbelief stealing away her cloak of passion. "You can't seriously believe that I'm offering you some sort of down payment on your loan?" she demanded.

"You think our affair was the result of a bet. Why wouldn't you also believe I'd expect more from you than just your business as collateral? After all, I'm keeping your father from going to jail. So why wouldn't I make you part of this devil's bargain?"

She studied his face for a long, thoughtful moment, then shook her head. "I would hope you have too much integrity to do such a thing."

"Unlike before? Tell me what's changed, Rebecca."

"You've changed. I've changed. People change, Alex."

"And then, of course, there's the fact that I have money." He pulled free of her arms and stood, regarding her coldly. "Others will suspect you're paying me off with your body. You realize that, don't you?"

She sat up and adjusted the clothing he'd left in such delightful disarray. "I've never concerned myself with what others think."

He released a humorless laugh. "You will. When word of our arrangement gets out—and no matter how careful we are to keep it quiet, it will get out—we'll see how long you continue to feel that way." He walked to the door and paused. "My lawyers will be in touch. But I'm warning you, Rebecca. If you go anywhere near Rodriquez, the deal is off." And with that final warning, he left.

How had she done it? How had Rebecca managed to take his thirst for revenge and quench it with a single kiss? Alex climbed into his Jag, put it in gear and flew down the Huntington drive. The stately oaks lining the drive passed in a blur of deep autumnal russet.

He'd clearly lost his mind. Here was his perfect opportunity for revenge and he was allowing the woman who'd helped destroy his life—and the lives of his family—convince him to give it up. Again. Of course,

Sebastian Huntington had played a big part in that, since it was through him that Rodriquez had managed to get so close to Rebecca, which had forced Alex to act.

None of that changed the bottom line, he reassured himself. He had his plan in place. Granted, it was a new plan, but the end results would remain the same. When Huntington finally realized that his friends had deserted him and he wouldn't be able to finagle his way out of his current predicament, he'd be left with one choice. To sign over the deed to Huntington Manor and leave town. In the meantime, Alex would make sure the embezzled funds were returned to the TCC with interest. Then he'd clear off any outstanding Huntington debts, including Paulo Rodriquez's. He frowned at the reminder.

Paulo.

He'd have to talk to his onetime friend and find out what the hell was going on. He couldn't remember the last time they'd touched base. Maybe once in the past year, when he'd asked his old friend to keep an eye on Alicia after the arson fire. Even then, it had been by phone. But the fact that Paulo had chosen to go after Sebastian Huntington raised red flags. It was time for a face-to-face reunion.

To his surprise, he found Paulo waiting at El Diablo. He was leaning against the black McLaren he'd been driving earlier, a sleek machine that must have set him back a cool mil. He grinned when he saw Alex pull in and lifted his hand in greeting.

Alex climbed out of his own vehicle. He crossed to Paulo's side and gave him a hard hug. "Good to see you, man."

"My address hasn't changed any more than I have." He lifted an eyebrow. "Maybe it's you who's changed, eh? Maybe the barrio isn't good enough for you anymore?"

"You know that's not true."

They'd just chosen different paths in life. Paulo's wasn't one Alex cared to follow. He's always assumed they'd both understood that fact and made peace with it. Now he wasn't so certain.

Paulo let the comment pass and inclined his head toward the barn, still in the process of being rebuilt. "Problems?"

"Nothing I can't handle." And it wasn't. Once Huntington's complicity in the arson fires had been proven beyond a shadow of a doubt—and despite the man's protests, Alex suspected it would be—there would be retribution. And it would taste sweet, indeed. He deliberately changed the subject by gesturing toward the McLaren. "I see you've bought yourself a new toy."

It was the perfect distraction. "It's just in. I think I own the only one like it in the entire state." Paulo's avid gaze ran over the sleek lines of the car, examining it with more passion than he would a woman. "Make my day, Alejandro, and tell me you aren't just a little envious."

"Maybe a little." Alex smiled. "Though I'd think you'd choose something a bit more subtle, something the cops don't instantly peg as belonging to you."

Paulo clasped his hand to his chest. "You wound me, *amigo*. The cops have no reason to stop me. I'm a legitimate businessman these days."

"I gather that includes your business with Sebastian Huntington?"

An expression of amused delight appeared on Paulo's face and his grin flashed white. "I wondered when you'd figure that out. Accept it as a gift from an old friend."

Alex stiffened. "Tell me what you've done."

"Consider it payback for what Huntington did to you, little Alicia and *Tía* Carmen."

"You scammed him."

Paulo gave an impatient click of his tongue. "He was easier to train than a dog. I said, 'roll over' and he asked how many times. Even after the first deal went bad, he came back begging for more. He made it easy. Too easy."

Damn it. Damn it. Damn it! Alex forced a smile to his lips. "Come inside and have a drink while we discuss it."

"Nothing to discuss." Paulo rubbed his hands together. "Soon, you and I will both own big Texas homesteads. You will sit in your El Diablo, while I am lord of Huntington Manor." His eyes took on a frenetic glitter. "And when I submit my application to the TCC, you will get me approved. You and my beautiful new wife."

Alex didn't like how this was going down. Not even a little. "Congratulations. I didn't know you were engaged."

"Oh, I'm not. Yet. But I have a feeling Rebecca Huntington will do almost anything for her dear *papá*. Especially if it keeps him out of jail, yes?"

"Becca?" he said, stalling. It confirmed his worst suspicions.

"I've wanted a taste of her for a long time." Paulo's eyes narrowed. "You wouldn't deny me that taste, would you, *mi amigo?* Not considering I was honorable enough to keep my hands off her while you took your fill a few years back."

"Honorable."

The word tasted like acid in his mouth while fury burned in the pit of his stomach. The mere idea of Rodriquez putting his hands on Rebecca had the most base and brutal instincts ripping through him. The bitter irony tore him to shreds.

His friend was right. Chances were, Rebecca would do anything to save her father. Hadn't she all but offered herself to him in exchange for his help? And hadn't he taken advantage of that fact not even an hour ago? How did that make him any better than the man standing before him? At least Paulo was honest in his desires, while Alex had wrapped his up in the pursuit of revenge and justice.

"There's only one problem, Paulo," Alex found himself saying. He could only pray he could pull this off without incurring his old friend's wrath. "I've agreed to pay Huntington's debts. If you'll tell me what he owes you—"

"Have you lost your mind? This is the man who made your life a misery. The man who destroyed your family. The father of the woman who—" He stopped dead and swore. "Of course. The woman."

"It's done. Let it go and walk away."

"*No!*" Paulo cut him off with a slicing sweep of his hand. "That's not going to happen. I've worked too long and hard to allow that *cabrón* to escape vengeance."

"He didn't do anything to you. It's not your revenge to take."

"Don't you understand?" Paulo's retort bit sharp in the quiet night air. "I'm doing this for you. I'm doing this for your sister. For your mother."

Alex refused to allow the lie to stand. "You're doing this because it's the only way you can force Rebecca into your bed."

Paulo's expression turned ugly. "Do not interfere, *hombre*. We have been friends a long time. But no one, not even one I consider *mi hermano,* takes what I regard as mine."

"Rebecca Huntington isn't yours. She never was and she never will be." Alex stepped closer, ignoring the way Paulo's hand shifted to the back of his jeans. There was only one way to get through to a man like Rodriquez. "The lady belongs to me. Her father belongs to me. Huntington Manor belongs to me. And I will protect what is mine."

Rage swept across Paulo's face, ripping apart any remaining shreds of civility. "You are making a mistake, Montoya." He tore open the door of his McLaren and slid in, gunning the powerful engine. "A big mistake."

Hitting the accelerator, he forced Alex to jump to one side as he sent the car screaming down the drive, a

rooster tail of gravel kicking up in his wake. Getting the
nicks and scratches out would cost him a pretty penny,
which wouldn't help his mood any. Alex glanced across
the yard, surprised to see his foreman, Bright, standing
on the portico of the sprawling ranch house, a shotgun
leveled in the direction of the retreating taillights.

"He had a gun," Bright called. "Tucked in the back
of his belt."

Paulo always had a gun tucked in the back of his belt,
but Alex didn't bother to explain that fact. He lifted a
hand. "Thanks, Bright. Everything's fine."

For now. But for how much longer? Not only did
Alex have to deal with Paulo Rodriguez, but he'd now
committed himself to paying off the TCC debt—along
with whatever Huntington owed Rodriquez. Even more
pressing, he needed to make a decision about Rebecca,
as well. Was he going to prove he was as savage as
Rodriquez by sacrificing his honor and taking what
she'd offered? Or was he going to do what his mother
would have considered the "noble" thing and help the
woman he'd once loved?

His intellect strained toward noble. Unfortunately,
the rest of him wasn't listening.

Rebecca unlocked the front door of Sweet Nothings
and flipped the discreet sign in the window from "Please
visit later" to "Please come in!" She'd already started
the coffee percolating on the vintage serving table that
separated the retail area of the store from the section

containing the cozy sitting area and the dressing rooms. And she was literally counting the minutes until the freshly ground beans finished brewing. She'd managed two whole hours of sleep last night and it showed. Thank God for makeup, since it managed to hide most of the damage.

She couldn't decide whether to be relieved or dismayed when the morning started out dead slow. At least it gave her time to put out a shipment of new inventory and catch up on her billing. She was on her third cup of coffee when the bells above the doorway released a light, sweet chime, signaling her first customer of the day. To her delight, it was Kate.

"Thank goodness it's you." Rebecca headed for the silver service and topped off her own coffee, then poured a second helping into another delicate Lenox cup and saucer. She handed it to her friend. "All I've gotten whenever I call is your voice mail."

Kate accepted the coffee with a grateful smile. "I know, I know." She took a sip and moaned. "I swear you make the best coffee in the entire county. Maybe the entire state."

Rebecca took a restorative sip and then handled the situation the way she always did—confronting it head-on. "Okay, what's up? I can tell when you're trying to avoid something, and you have avoidance written all over you." She mentally braced herself. "What's going on? I've left a thousand messages. Why haven't you gotten back to me?"

Her friend winced. "I'm sorry. Things got crazy after lunch the other day."

"So, you have been ducking my phone calls."

Kate held up a hand. "Only until Lance got his facts straight. Plus, I wanted to be with you when we spoke."

Rebecca stared in dismay. "It's that bad?"

Sympathy swept across Kate's pretty face. "Yes," she stated bluntly. "It's that bad."

"If this is about the TCC accounts…" It took every ounce of resolve for Rebecca to meet her friend's eyes. "I know about it and it's true."

"Oh, sweetie!"

"The money will be replaced," Rebecca stated emphatically. "Every last dime. Alex has agreed to loan us the money in the meantime."

"Alex?" Kate looked as amazed as Rebecca felt.

"See what you miss when you don't return my calls?" Her flash of humor died and she met her friend's gaze. "I'm determined to see he's paid back as quickly as possible, even if I have to take on a second job to do it."

Kate caught her lip between her teeth. "There's something else you should know. I'm not really supposed to tell anyone, but you should have some warning."

"It's about the arson fires, isn't it?"

"Yes." Kate caught Rebecca's arm in hers and guided her to the divan adjacent to the tea table. "Sit before you fall down."

"He didn't do it." Tears welled up in Rebecca's eyes and she blinked fiercely to hold them at bay. She wasn't a crier, but between her father's confession, the interludes with Alex and the lack of sleep, her self-control was pared down to a mere thread. "I swear, Kate. Dad's admitted to taking the money, but he swears he had nothing to do with the refinery fire or Alex's barn. And I believe him."

"Of course you do," her friend said in a soothing voice.

"I know he's not the easiest man to like," Rebecca confessed with difficulty. "He's hard and…and arrogant. And he's made mistakes. But he wouldn't endanger lives."

"Darius Franklin is looking into it. I trust him. He's a good man. He'll get to the bottom of everything."

"I spoke with him the other day and I agree with your assessment. He is a good man. He…he advised we get a lawyer." Without warning, Rebecca dissolved. Her cup rattled against the saucer and Kate rescued it before the fragile porcelain could shatter. Without a word, the two embraced and rode out the storm. At long last, Rebecca pulled back and wiped the tears from her cheeks.

"I'm—"

"Don't you dare apologize," Kate said in a fierce voice. "After all the times you stood by me while I wept over Lance, don't you dare. You hear me?"

Rebecca managed a watery smile. "I hear." Behind them, the bells above the door sang a gay greeting and she flinched. "Will you cover for me while I fix my makeup?" she asked in an undertone.

"Of course." Kate spared a quick glance over her

shoulder. "Oh. It's Alicia Montoya. She and Justin will be tying the knot soon, won't they? She's probably here to pick out something for her wedding night."

"Let's hope that's all she's here for," Rebecca murmured.

Not waiting for a response, she hastened into the back to the small powder room. She groaned when she looked in the mirror. Black mascara tracks streaked her face and left crescent moons beneath her eyes. She looked like a zebra, her face dead-white in between the black stripes, while her eyes and nose were red and swollen. The downside to being a redhead. Everything showed on her face.

She took her time washing up and reapplying her makeup. Then she loosened the formal knot of hair and allowed the auburn strands to flow loose around her shoulders. Better. If Alicia looked closely, she wouldn't be able to miss the hint of red that lingered around Rebecca's eyes. But with luck, it wouldn't be readily apparent. Taking a deep breath, she exited the powder room and returned to the front section of the store.

Kate and Alicia had their heads together, deliberating between two nightgowns. Kate held the first, a sexy little black number that revealed far more than it concealed. Alicia clutched the second, a deep ruby gown that gave an extra luster to her lovely olive complexion.

"Is this for your wedding night?" Rebecca asked as she joined them.

"Yes, it is." Alicia gave her a shy smile. "I've wanted an excuse to buy lingerie here for a long time."

Rebecca returned Alicia's smile with surprising ease, probably because the other woman had a knack for making people feel comfortable. "Yes, I remember you telling me that when you were in here a while back with Cara. But you didn't have anyone special to wear it for." She gave a wide smile. "Until now. Congratulations."

"Thank you." She returned to deliberating between the two choices. "I just can't decide whether to go full-out sexy with this black one, or more modest with the red."

"If you're asking my advice…"

"Yes, please!"

"Go with the red. The black may look sexy, but it's too blatant for a wedding night. One look and all your secrets are revealed. You want more romance. More mystery. And watch…" She draped the material over Alicia's arm. The feather-light material clung, while the light seemed to sink into the gown, turning the silk almost transparent against her skin. "Justin will be able to see through the gown just enough to drive him crazy."

The next hour passed in a flash. Helping Alicia choose lingerie for her wedding and honeymoon proved a delightful distraction. Afterward, while Rebecca rang up the stack of purchases and Alicia looked on with a shell-shocked expression, Kate discussed wedding details.

"Have you decided whether or not you're holding the wedding at El Diablo?"

"That was our original thought, but after the incident with the barn, Alejandro has changed his mind. We've decided to marry at the mission church."

"Just because of the fire?" Kate asked in concern. "Is he worried about another incident?"

"Not since Darius installed security. But after the fire, Alejandro's housekeeper quit and he's had a terrible time finding a replacement." Alicia shrugged. "It just made more sense to switch the venue to the church. Besides, it's a beautiful old place, all stone and timber. And we've decided to have the ceremony on Christmas Eve after Eucharist."

"I can't think of anything more perfect," Rebecca said with all sincerity.

She finished ringing up Alicia's purchases, then wrapped them in tissue and placed the lingerie in a series of elegant boxes. But all the while her brain spun in circles, replaying that one sentence over and over again. *Alejandro's housekeeper quit and he's had a terrible time finding a replacement.* An idea formed. A crazy, impulsive, outrageous idea.

The minute Alicia left the shop, Rebecca turned to Kate. "I know the perfect person for Alex's housekeeper. And the best part about it is that it will kill two birds with one stone."

Kate stared in utter bewilderment. "What in the world are you talking about?"

"Not what. Who."

"Okay, I'll bite." Kate smiled indulgently. "Who would be the perfect person for Alex to hire as his housekeeper?"

"Me."

Six

Alex tucked his hammer into his tool belt. Stepping back from the barn, he settled his Stetson more firmly on his head to shade his eyes from the late-afternoon sun and stared up at the towering structure. Almost done. Soon, no one would ever know there had been a fire here.

He always found hard physical labor satisfying. It also had the added benefit of easing some of the pent-up anger and frustration from his encounters with Huntington and Rodriquez. The temptation to allow the two men to destroy one another was overwhelming. He'd actually consider it, except for one thing.

Rebecca.

Desire continued to rip through him after his latest encounter with her. He'd hoped that working on his barn would ease it. Instead, a bone-deep hunger gnawed at him, warning that this wasn't an emotion he could expunge from his system through sweat and determination. It would require far more than that. Even so, his labors had clarified one thing.

Sebastian Huntington would pay for what he'd done. And Rebecca was going to end up back in his bed—but not in order to settle her father's debt.

"You've got company," one of his hands said, inclining his head toward the gravel drive.

Sure enough, a faint plume of dust rose in the distance. A few minutes later, a sporty convertible pulled into the sweeping circle fronting the ranch house. It didn't take much guesswork to figure out who sat behind the steering wheel.

He took his time joining Rebecca. She stood with casual elegance beside the door of her Cabriolet and waited him out. She wore a sexy little dress in a stunning bronze that made the most of her figure and showcased a pair of legs that were among the prettiest he'd ever seen. The setting sun caught in her hair, turning the rich red to a halo of vibrant color around her face. She wasn't wearing sunglasses and the vividness of her green eyes hit like a shock as he approached. She stared at him, as proud and indomitable and self-assured as ever. Well, that made two of them, both too headstrong for their own good.

He shoved his Stetson to the back of his head. "I'm almost afraid to ask, but what are you doing here, Becca?"

She straightened, facing him with a determination that made him instantly wary. "I've come to solve two of our most pressing problems."

Hell. "If this is about your father—"

"It's about my father's debt, to be exact."

"By all means, let's be exact."

He might as well have saved the sarcasm. She brushed it aside the way she would a pesky mosquito. "Alicia came into my shop today and mentioned that you've been without a housekeeper ever since the fire."

He took the odd turn of conversation in stride, merely folding his arms across his chest and cocking an eyebrow. "So?"

"So, you'll be relieved to know that won't be an issue any longer."

The comment caught him by surprise. In order to give himself time, he stripped off his gloves and hooked them in his belt. Then he leveled the playing field by closing the short distance between them and tipping her face up to his. "What are you up to, *dulzura?*"

If he hadn't been near enough to see the hint of alarm flashing through her gaze or to hear the slight hitch in her breathing, he'd have thought her unaffected by his touch. "Meet your new housekeeper," she informed him. "I'll accept whatever wages you were paying your former live-in and I'll stay until my father's debt is paid off."

He couldn't help himself. His mouth twitched into a broad smile. "You're joking."

She pulled free of his grasp and reached inside the car to push the trunk release. "I'm also giving you my car. That should put a small dent in what's owed. I bought an old pickup as a replacement since I'll still need to get to the boutique." She circled to the rear of the car and wrestled the first suitcase free, dumping it on the gravel drive. "I'm afraid I'll have to spend part of each day at Sweet Nothings, but my assistant is well-trained and I can arrange my hours to suit your convenience. I'll also get up early to take care of the main housekeeping duties and then finish them off after work and whenever the store is closed."

"Enough, Rebecca," he insisted with a hint of impatience. "I don't know what game you're playing, but I'm not amused."

She whipped around with a ferocity that shocked him. "This isn't a game. Nor is it funny. In fact, I find nothing about the events of the last twenty-four hours the least bit amusing."

"I'm not hiring you."

She must have anticipated that small hurdle, because she had her counterargument already lined up. "You won't be able to resist, Alex. Just think how delicious it'll be, telling everyone that Rebecca Huntington is your new housekeeper. Where once your mother was housekeeper to the Huntingtons, now the last of the Huntingtons is housekeeper to you." Turning her back on him, she hauled out the rest of her possessions, stacking them neatly on the ground. "Now, if you'll show me to my quarters and give me a rough idea of my duties, I'll get some dinner on the table for you."

She bent to gather up the first load and he snatched the suitcases from her hands. Son of a bitch! They weighed a ton. What the hell had she filled them with, rocks? "You're not staying, and you damn well aren't going to play at being my new housekeeper."

She stepped in front of him to prevent him from returning her suitcases to her trunk. "I intend to pay off my father's debt one way or another. I'm going to hand over every spare penny from the shop and work the rest of it off here, Montoya, one day at a time, until the debt is paid in full."

"That's Mr. Montoya," he shot back. "My employees address me as *Mister* or *Señor,* or even Alex. But they all address me with the proper respect or they find a job elsewhere."

She inclined her head with a dignity and grace that was an innate part of her. The fact that it also filled him with a bizarre combination of pride and desire left him at a loss for words. "You're right. I apologize, Mr. Montoya."

He swore in Spanish. "This is ridiculous." She'd realize just how ridiculous if she knew the full extent of the debt. "I can't have you working for me, Becca. You must see how it'll look. What people will say?"

"Let them talk," she retorted fiercely. "They're going to, no matter what I do. As you've already pointed out, my reputation is in tatters. And I don't see how my presence can possibly hurt yours."

Didn't she get it? He spelled it out for her. "People will say you're my mistress, not my housekeeper."

Her eyes blazed like emeralds. "But I'll know the truth. My friends will know the truth. You'll know the truth. As far as I'm concerned, that's all that matters."

He hesitated.

When Rodriquez had left the previous night, he'd been furious. He'd also been determined to make Rebecca his. At Huntington Manor, she was vulnerable. Here, where he could keep an eye on her, she'd be safe, or reasonably so. Granted, she'd still have to go into town each day and work at her shop. But he didn't think even Paulo would have the nerve to do anything to her in broad daylight within the confines of a busy store. And wasn't her safety paramount?

As a rationalization, it barely passed muster. But he couldn't quite get past the image of Paulo's face when he'd spoken about Rebecca. There'd been no mistaking the man's intentions, just as there was no mistaking one simple fact.

Alex would do anything to keep Rebecca out of Paulo's hands.

He gave it two full seconds of careful consideration. "Fine. You're hired."

She didn't bother to conceal her triumph, though that would be short-lived. The minute he explained the full extent of her duties, he expected her to pack up her overstuffed suitcases, chuck them into the trunk of her car and scurry off down the road as fast as her fancy little sports job would take her.

When she reached the steps leading to the front door, she paused and he caught the first hint of vulnerability. She turned toward him. "Maybe we should start the way we intend to go on," she said.

"What are you talking about?" He shot her an impatient look. "Could we move this along? These suitcases aren't getting any lighter."

"I'm your housekeeper, Alex." She gave a quick shake of her head. "I mean, Mr. Montoya."

"Alex," he said sharply.

"Housekeepers don't usually enter through the front door," she pointed out. "Your mother never did. Not after the day you first arrived."

"Oh, for the love of—" He tromped up the steps, juggled the suitcases and managed to drop one on his toe. He practically kicked open the door. "In," he ordered.

Beside him, Rebecca opened her mouth again, no doubt to argue some more. "But—"

"*Madre de Dios!* You don't have the first clue how to be an obedient, respectful employee, do you? Is it your intention to argue over every single request I make?"

She stared at him, stricken. Then a hint of laughter crept into her eyes and her lips quivered into a full-blown smile. "Not if they're requests."

He dropped her suitcases in the foyer and succeeded in avoiding his toes this time. He slammed the door shut, sealing them in the dusky interior. Without a word, he swept Rebecca into his arms, intent on proving to her in the simplest, most straightforward manner available the sheer insanity of her idea.

"You know what they'll call you, don't you?" he warned.

She didn't struggle. Nor did she sink against him. "I believe you said I'd be labeled the daughter of a thief."

"Now they'll call you Diablo's mistress."

She met the ferocity of his gaze with surprising equanimity. "We'll know the truth."

"And what truth is that?"

She stood within the warmth of his embrace, their heated breaths mingling, their hearts beating as one, and said, "That I'm just your housekeeper, nothing more."

He took her words as a challenge. And then he took her mouth, intent on proving her wrong. This was a mistake, Alex conceded an instant later. Rebecca had only been in his home for thirty seconds and already he had his hands on her. Hell, all over her. He was practically eating her alive. Not that she resisted. She should have slapped him. Instead, she slipped her fingers into his wind-ruffled hair, knocking his Stetson to the parquet floor, and secured him in place so that their mouths melded, one to the other.

He couldn't get over the flavor of her, the delicious appeal that was so distinctly hers. His hands swept downward, sliding over territory he'd spent bitter, lonely years dreaming about. The shape of her had changed since those long-ago days. Subtle changes that had transformed the girl he'd once known into the woman he now held.

Her breasts still filled his palms, but her body had grown leaner, more honed and better defined. Her hips flared beneath the narrowest of waists and her backside had just the perfect amount of curve to it. He wanted to slip his hand beneath her skirt and discover whether she wore another sampling of the sweet nothings that gave her lingerie shop its distinctive name. Sultry black bits of nothing or maybe siren-red. Perhaps she'd chosen the same sort of dainty ivory scraps of sweetness he'd seen before. Silk and lace that melted against her creamy skin and set off the blazing nest of curls between her thighs.

The image his brain created threatened to unman him. He didn't want to take her here in his foyer, though if they didn't find a suitable arena for their activities, that was precisely what would happen. More than anything, he wanted to carry her to his room and spread her across his bed while he stripped her down to those delicate morsels of feminine finery and find out just what color she'd chosen to wear today.

Intent on turning thought into deed, he eased back in order to sweep her into his arms. Instead, he gave her just enough breathing room to come to her senses. With an exclamation of disbelief, she ripped free of his embrace.

It took her a moment to regain her breath enough to speak. "This has got to stop," she informed him. "I'll be your housekeeper and do the best job I know how. And I'll even deal with any gossip that occurs as a result. But I'm damned if I'll become your mistress in anything more than imagination."

"Too late, *dulzura*. We're both damned already." He leaned in. "And you will become my mistress. It's only a matter of when."

God help him, but she was beautiful, especially when angry. She glared at him with those witch-green eyes. The deep, lustrous red of her hair spilled around her face, emphasizing the creaminess of her skin and underscoring the flush that rode the sweeping arch of her aristocratic cheekbones.

"If you'll show me to my room?" she asked in her best lady-of-the-manor voice. "I'd like to unpack before I start dinner."

"Yes, ma'am," he said in his driest tone. "This way."

He headed for the back of the sizable ranch house. Near the kitchen, he opened the door to the suite of rooms that had belonged to his former housekeeper. He carried her suitcases through to the bedroom and set them on the floor near the bed. He glanced up in time to see an odd look on her face.

"What?" he asked warily.

"This can't possibly be the housekeeper's quarters," she said.

"That's exactly what they are."

Her expression turned unreadable as she walked through the pair of bedrooms, each with its own bath, and then into the generous-size living area. When she finished, she looked at him with eyes gone dark with pain. "These rooms weren't at El Diablo before you moved in, were they?"

"No."

"You had them built specifically with a housekeeper and…and whatever family she might have in mind." She didn't wait for his confirmation. "This is because of Huntington Manor."

He flashed back on the single room that her father had grudgingly split in two so that he, his mother and sister wouldn't all have to share a single bedroom. There'd also been a living area, but it had been so tiny there'd barely been space for one, let alone two teenagers and their exhausted mother.

It hadn't taken long to figure out that the only reason Huntington had accommodated them with even that much was to avoid any whisper of gossip. Image was everything with Sebastian Huntington. Image. Reputation. Appearances. It wouldn't do to have someone accuse him of mistreating the hired help, particularly since Alex's mother had cleaned most of the homes in Somerset at one point or another and was well-liked by all. But that didn't change the fact that the spaciousness of Huntington Manor stopped short at the servants' quarters.

Another flush swept across her face, this one deeper than before and having nothing whatsoever to do with passion. "I'm sorry, Alex," she said. "I'm sorry for what my father did to you and to your sister because of our affair. But I'm most sorry for what he did to Carmen. It was wrong."

He folded his arms across his chest. "I'm surprised you're not defending him, or at the very least offering a string of excuses. Isn't that part of your role as his daughter?"

She sighed, revealing a hint of weariness. "Not in this case."

Now that he looked closer, he could see the exhaustion in the paleness of her skin. Dark smudges underscored her eyes, intensifying the color. It gave her a vulnerability that made him long to take her in his arms again. But he didn't dare. Not here. Not when her father's actions still stood between them.

"Take the night to get situated. You can start work in the morning."

Her shoulders straightened and her spine snapped into an unrelenting line. "That's not necessary. Just tell me what you want."

He took a single step in her direction. "You already know what I want."

Alarm flared for a brief instant before a hint of humor replaced it. "I'll be happy to check in the refrigerator, but I can say with some degree of confidence that that particular item isn't on tonight's menu."

"Put it on the menu," he advised. "Soon."

He exited the room before he put it there for her. He forced himself to keep walking, to stride out of his home and return to the barn. Once there, he'd put in another solid hour or so of hard physical labor. Maybe then he'd be too exhausted to think about what awaited him back at El Diablo and what he'd like to do to and with her when he returned. His mouth compressed. Who was he kidding?

He'd never be that exhausted.

The evening rapidly went from hideous to total nightmare in the space of two short hours.

Rebecca stood in the monstrous kitchen of El Diablo and faced facts. The few cooking skills Carmen had taught her during her teen years had totally deserted her. Lack of practice, no doubt. She'd aimed to serve Alex a simple but filling dinner of Texas-size steak, charbroiled on the outside and still mooing when sliced. A large salad. Baked potato. And homegrown beans with almond slivers. The only part of what ended up hitting the table that remotely resembled her game plan was the salad.

The steak hadn't been charbroiled, but crispy-crittered. The potato was stone-cold in the middle, and hard as a rock. And the beans were great alps of green mush with almond chunks clinging to the mountaintop like jaw-breaking boulders. Alex had taken one look, closed his eyes and muttered a prayer beneath his breath before digging in. Five minutes later, she noticed that he'd added a generous serving of whiskey to the menu to help wash the mess down.

Rebecca surveyed the endless stack of dishes still to be scoured and fought an overwhelming urge to weep.

Enough of that! She'd chosen to do this and she'd succeed no matter how difficult. She refused to quit. She refused to back down. And she absolutely, positively refused to fall into any bed but her own.

Searching through the various drawers and cupboards, she located an apron and rubber gloves and set to work. She'd check with Alex once she finished and get a list of the chores his previous housekeeper had covered. In order to get them all done and still arrive at her shop by nine in time to open the doors, she'd have to get up early. Very early.

She was just loading the final dish into the dishwasher when Alex appeared in the doorway. "Thanks for the meal," he offered.

She sighed. "That's generous of you, all things considered." She turned to face him and tugged off gloves. "Do you have a minute to give me a list of my duties?"

"Won't take even a minute. Clean the house. Keep up with the laundry. Fix breakfast and dinner. Don't worry about lunch. I usually eat out."

"I assume you also need me to do the grocery shopping?" When he hesitated, she planted her hands on her hips. "Did my predecessor do it?"

"Yes."

"Okay, then."

"Becca—"

"Please, Alex," she whispered. "I have to try. Give me a chance."

The mouth she'd taken such delight in kissing compressed into a hard line. "You know as well as I do that you can't do an adequate job around here and still run Sweet Nothings. It's too much for one person."

"I can manage until I get the debt paid off."

He shook his head in disbelief. "Do you have any idea how long that's going to take?" he demanded. "We're not talking about a few weeks or months. We're talking about years."

"Not necessarily. The shop provides an excellent income. You should be able to get a decent amount for my car. It may be used, but it's been gently used."

"You're living in a fool's paradise, Rebecca. You won't be able to keep up this pace for a month, let alone years. Face facts."

Rebecca struggled to regain her footing. Maybe she'd have a better shot at it if she weren't so tired she could barely see straight. "You think I haven't? You think I don't know how much we owe you?" Struggling for control, she pulled out a chair at the kitchen table and sat as carefully as though the least careless movement would shatter her. She moistened her lips before continuing. "I'm not quite the fool you take me for, Alex."

He studied her warily. "What do you mean?"

"I realize that if you hadn't agreed to use Sweet Nothings as collateral that you'd now own Huntington Manor." She waved a quick hand through the air. "You, or someone other than my father. Someone like Rodriquez. Dad would have been forced to sell in order to cover his debts and lawyer fees."

"Probably."

"It could still happen," she whispered. "Couldn't it?"

He started to reply, then broke off with a shrug. "Don't worry about it."

"Alex?" she pressed.

"Let's just say this mess is far from over." His expression was more grim than she'd ever seen it. "Until it is, stay away from Rodriquez, Becca," he ordered. "If he contacts you, refer him to me, and then call me immediately."

"Is my father in danger?"

"Madre de Dios!" Alex forked his fingers through his hair. "Paulo is dangerous to *you,* Becca. That's all that should concern you. Your father made his bed. Let him learn to sleep in it."

"Is that the attitude you'd take if our situation was reversed and Carmen was the one at risk?" she dared to ask.

He made a valiant effort to control his temper, which impressed the hell out of Rebecca. "As I've pointed out before, that's not a fair comparison and you know it. First, my mother would never have put herself in the position your father is in. There were times when she couldn't put sufficient food on the table, but she never resorted to stealing so much as a penny from any of the fine mansions she cleaned, even though they could well afford it and would never have missed the odd bits and pieces that would have made the difference between filling our bellies and going hungry."

"Oh, Alex," she whispered, her heart breaking for him.

His head reared back. "I'm not asking for your pity," he said in a cutting voice. "I merely state fact."

"Let's say that your mother had borrowed money from Rodriquez to tide you over, and was then unable to repay it. You'd have stepped in before he could harm her." There wasn't a doubt in her mind. "How is what I'm doing any different?"

He crossed the room in a half dozen swift strides and plucked her from her chair. "The difference is that your father is well able to look after himself, even if he now chooses to hide behind your skirts. The difference is that my mother was a kind, loving, humble woman, while your father is an arrogant bastard who thinks he can do whatever he pleases without taking responsibility for his actions or suffering the consequences for them."

She wished with all her heart that she could deny any one of his points, but she couldn't. As much as she loved her father, she wasn't blind to his faults. That didn't mean she wouldn't stick by him and do her best to help him out of his current predicament. The full enormity of the task pressed down on her like a crippling weight. Paying back the TCC—or rather, Alex—had seemed tough enough. But now that he'd explained about Paulo Rodriquez…

"Enough," Alex announced. "It's clear that you're at the end of your rope, and I won't have people saying that I'm responsible for driving you into the ground."

She started to wave that aside, letting out a gasp of surprise when he swung her into his arms and carried her out of the kitchen and into her private quarters. He didn't pause, continuing straight through to the bedroom. There, he dumped her onto the mattress and cupped the back of one ankle, and then the other, in order to slip her shoes from her feet.

"I can undress myself," she informed him with a dry smile. It was either that or weep. "I've been doing it for more than two decades."

"And here I thought you had servants to take care of that, as well as grant your every other whim."

"Funny." She pointed toward the door. "I believe I've made it clear where my duties end. And it's on the other side of that door."

He continued to hold her ankle for a long moment. His fingers drifted over the narrow bones, teasing the sensitive skin until she shuddered with the effort to control her reaction. To her profound relief, he didn't seem aware of how close she came to tugging him down on top of her and allowing desire to overrule common sense.

"A pity." Alex released her ankle and stepped back. He paused halfway to the door and glanced over his shoulder. "You will remember to call me if Rodriquez contacts you in any way?"

It wasn't worth arguing about, not when every instinct she possessed urged her to do just that. "I promise."

"Sleep well." His mouth tugged to one side. "God knows, I won't."

Seven

The next week proved one of the most stressful Rebecca had ever experienced. Exhaustion dogged her every step. It wasn't just getting up at four each morning in order to take care of her housekeeping duties before racing into town to open Sweet Nothings. She hadn't taken into consideration the sheer manual labor involved in keeping a mansion the size of El Diablo in pristine condition.

Well, if she looked at the bright side of things, she could cancel her gym membership. Her daily workouts there were nothing compared to what she received cleaning and dusting the endless rooms that comprised Alex's home. She just had to give herself time to adjust. And she needed time to learn the most efficient way to clean.

Until this week, she'd never considered her shop a place to rest and relax. But now she treasured every precious hour she spent there, especially knowing what awaited her back at El Diablo. It wasn't that she minded the physical aspects of the work, despite how exhausting they were. It was the quiet forbearance with which Alex regarded her efforts.

He ate her under-over-badly cooked food with a stoic air. He didn't complain when she bleached the color out of his shirts or tinted unexpected color into them. He didn't do more than sigh when his boots stuck to the polish she'd spent hours applying to his wooden floor. But with each incident, she felt less and less capable and more and more as though she were taking advantage of him. He shouldn't be paying her. She should be paying him for all the damage she'd inflicted on him and his home.

Rebecca forced herself to her feet with a heartfelt sigh and proceeded to unload the latest shipment of lace and silk delicacies. Though the beginning of the week had been as busy as ever, the past few days business had slacked off. She suspected the recent cold snap was in part to blame. Who wanted to purchase silk lingerie when the weather screamed for fleece?

Behind her, the bell tinkled merrily and a customer wandered in, someone Rebecca vaguely recognized from high school. "It's Mary Beth, isn't it?" She greeted the woman with a friendly smile and gestured toward the section of the store she'd just finished organizing.

"The items on the rack beside you are just in. In fact, you're the first to see them."

"Probably the last, too," she said in a cool voice.

Rebecca stared in confusion. Maybe if she hadn't been so tired, she'd have caught on sooner. Instead, she offered a puzzled look. "Excuse me?"

"Business a bit slow?" Mary Beth ran careless fingers over the latest shipment, knocking several of the garments off their padded hangers. "It's only going to get slower now that all of Somerset knows the truth about you mighty Huntingtons. Who's going to want to buy sleazy underwear from someone like you?"

Rebecca froze. "I don't know what—"

Mary Beth cut her off with a wave of her hand. "Oh, please. It's all over town. Your father. You working for Montoya." She made annoying little air quotes around the word "working." "And won't we all just have the biggest laugh while we watch you tumble off your pedestal." She gave the store a dismissive look. "Enjoy your Sweet Nothings. Without customers, that's precisely what this place will be. Nothing."

She swung toward the exit, just as the door opened. A man standing there ran an appreciative glance over Mary Beth. *"Señora,"* he murmured, flashing a brilliant, white grin at her.

She returned the look with interest, then stepped into the November chill. Rebecca could only pray that she didn't appear as shell-shocked as she felt. Gathering her self-control, she offered the new customer her most professional smile. Now that she looked at him, he seemed vaguely familiar, as well. Dread swamped her. With luck, he'd prove to be a legitimate customer and not some curiosity seeker reacting to the rumors that had apparently begun circulating about her and her father.

"May I help you?" she asked warily.

His mouth curved upward in an oddly satisfied smile. "In more ways than you can count," he murmured in a lightly accented voice. Aware that his comment had thrown her, he gestured toward the interior of the store. "I'm looking for something special. For my future wife," he clarified.

"I can help you with that."

"I'm sure you can."

His comment caused a visceral reaction she couldn't explain, but one that sent warning alarms clamoring. She did her best to conceal her concern and moved toward the front of the store, rather than the back. "Could you give me some idea what you're looking for?"

He gave it a moment's consideration. "A nightgown. For our wedding night."

"And your fiancée's coloring?"

A slow smile lit his face, one that didn't quite reach his hard, black eyes. "Why, she's a redhead, like you."

Okay, she knew when someone was playing games with her. And this guy was definitely a player. And then it hit her where she'd seen him before. It had been a brief glimpse several months ago. He'd been talking to her father, the two in a rather heated discussion. When she'd asked her father about the incident, he'd brushed it aside. Now the incident took on greater significance. If she were a betting woman, she'd lay odds this was the infamous Paulo Rodriquez, which could only mean one thing.

Trouble.

As casually as she could, she picked up her cell phone from the counter by the register and bounced it from hand to hand in what she hoped appeared to be a restless, unconscious habit.

"Hmm. Well, black always looks—" She blinked, as though in surprise. "Hang on. My phone is vibrating. Damn. It's Alex. If I don't take this…" She broke off with an irritated shrug.

Before he could react, she flipped it open and hit the 1 key assigned to automatically dial Kate's cell. At the next opportunity, she was going to program Alex's private number into her phone. To her profound relief, her friend picked up almost immediately. "Yeah, Bec. What's up?"

"Yes, Alex. I'm fine." She rolled her eyes in an exaggerated manner. "You worry too much."

There was a beat of silence. Then, "Something's wrong, isn't it?" Rebecca could only thank God that she'd picked smart friends. Kate wasn't slow in putting two and two together and coming up with "Help!"

"You said Alex. Is he there? Is he causing the trouble?" she asked.

She could only hope the note of irritability she forced into her voice would cover up her fear. "No, no. I'll be home at the usual time."

"No, of course not. That wouldn't make sense. You wouldn't have used his name if he were there with you," Kate muttered. "That can only mean you want me to call him."

"Yup, that's it. Listen, I'm with a customer and I don't want to keep him any longer. So stop calling me."

"I'm out at Brody Oil and Gas. I'll call Alex. And then Lance and I are on our way."

"Whatever. Goodbye, Alex." For some reason, just saying his name out loud helped steady her. Unfortunately, it had the exact opposite effect on the man flicking through the rack of nightgowns. She took a deep breath and asked brightly, "I'm so sorry. Where were we?"

"Ah, yes. This." He held up a sheer baby-doll nightie in blazing red. "This will look beautiful against your skin."

"Your fiancée's skin," she corrected with a smile. "And if she has hair similar to mine, that particular shade of red will clash."

He returned the bit of silk and lace to the spiral rack. "A shame. I am quite fond of this particular shade. Perhaps something in green." He plucked an emerald-green costume at random and slowly approached. "To match my soon-to-be fiancée's eyes."

Rebecca froze. She edged backward, but the man moved with lightning speed, putting himself between her and the exit. He flicked the lock on the door and then casually picked up the welcome sign and reversed it. Then he smiled in a way that sent a wave of terror pouring through her veins.

"Paulo Rodriquez, I assume," she managed to say.

"It is a pleasure to finally meet you, Señorita Hunting-ton." His cold smile flashed. "But considering how close we're about to become, why don't I call you Becca?"

"Because only my friends call me that. And you're not one of my friends."

"I could be." He glided toward her, trapping her against the counter. "I *will* be."

"What do you want?"

"Your father owes me a great deal of money. I think it's time I was paid a small down payment." He closed in. "Let's call it…an interest charge."

Alex hit the sidewalk outside his office building at a dead run. It was faster to walk—or run—to Sweet Nothings than to drive there, Alex decided. Plus, he didn't want to alert Paulo to his presence until he walked through the door. He didn't know how Lance Brody had become embroiled in whatever was going on at the lingerie shop, but he owed the other man for calling with the warning. It was a debt that wouldn't easily be repaid.

The small placard in Sweet Nothing's window read, "Please visit later" and drove a shaft of fear straight through the core of him. From what he could see of the interior through the tinted glass, the inside stood dark and silent. Gathering his self-control, Alex tried the door. It was locked, but he made short work of that. Even after all these years, some of his less-reputable skills came back with amazing swiftness. Opening the door, carefully so the bell wouldn't give his presence away, he walked in. For an instant, he didn't see or hear anything. Then a muffled cry came to him from the small divan in the sitting area of the store.

He didn't recall moving. One minute he was in the front of the shop, the next he was in the rear with Rodriquez on the floor, bleeding. He glared at Alex through a rapidly swelling eye and ran his tongue across his split lip.

"You shouldn't have come," Paulo said.

He'd switched to Spanish, no doubt to keep Rebecca from understanding what he said. Alex decided to accommodate him. "I warned you not to touch what belongs to me. You should have listened."

Paulo shifted and Alex stepped closer, shaking his head. With a groan, the other man settled back on to the floor. "And you should have listened to me, Montoya. I will do whatever I must to have the woman. To have her home. To have the status that once was hers." He smiled, despite the pain it must have caused him. "To have her in my bed, heavy with my child."

The image burned like fire in Alex's mind, no doubt as intended. He forced himself to ignore it, not to allow it to distract him. Just as he forced himself to ignore Rebecca. If he looked at her, he'd lose it. Big-time. "She's in my home now. In my bed. And that's where she's staying. If you want payment for Huntington's debts, I'm the man to see."

"You would really pay off his debts, after all he's done to your family?"

"Yes." Alex smiled coldly. "Like I said, Paulo. You can't win. Now get out before the lady presses charges."

"She won't do that." He tossed Rebecca a knowing look. "There's been enough gossip. If anyone hears about this… Why, they might just wonder whether the lovely Becca is helping her father pay off all his debts. And in a tradition as old as time. Eh, Alejandro?"

"Basta!" Alex ended the conversation by hauling Paulo to his feet and swiftly disarming him. "Where are your men?"

"I'm alone."

Alex dismissed that with all the contempt it deserved. "You haven't been without bodyguards since you were twelve. I repeat. Where are your men?"

"Out back." He fingered his lip and winced. "Next time I will post them at the front door, as well."

"There isn't going to be a next time, Paulo. Now get out and take your men with you before I call the cops."

Paulo shot a lingering glance in Rebecca's direction before exiting the shop. The instant Alex deemed it safe, he crouched down in front of her and gathered her ice-cold hands in his, rubbing her fingers to warm them. "Are you okay?"

It took her a nerve-racking moment to respond. "Shaken, rattled and rolled. But I'll survive."

Her stab at humor would have been more reassuring if her face wasn't bleached white and her eyes weren't so frantic. They'd turned a green so dark they reminded him of an impenetrable jungle wall, closed off from light and easy ingress. In fact, now that he looked carefully, he realized she had closed down.

He continued to rub her hands and talk to her in a low, calm voice. All the while, he examined her. The attack had been brief, if terrifying. The first two buttons of her blouse were ripped, exposing the plum lace of her bra. Her skirt was hiked up to her thighs, but he knew that had occurred when she'd kicked Paulo while Alex was dragging him off the divan. He noticed a few bruises marring her pale skin, one on her neck and one on her knee. The rest of the damage was psychological, rather than physical.

He had no idea how long he crouched there. Behind them, the bells above the door tinkled in alarm and she jumped, panic stricken. Lance and Kate slammed into the shop.

"Is she okay?" Kate demanded. "Bec?"

She flew to her friend's side and wrapped her up in a tight embrace. Alex slowly rose, feeling impotent and angry. He spared Lance a quick look, surprised to catch an expression of sympathetic understanding in his dark eyes.

"She was attacked?" Brody asked in a low voice.

Alex nodded. "Rodriquez," he answered quietly. Leaving her in Kate's capable hands, he shifted toward the front of the store where Rebecca couldn't overhear their conversation.

"Were you in time?" Lance asked.

"Yes. Though he left plenty of damage in his wake."

"This doesn't sound like a problem that's going away anytime soon." Brody frowned. "How are you going to handle it?"

"I haven't quite decided," he admitted. "But I won't have Rebecca put at risk."

Lance planted his fists on his hips and studied the floor. "Are the rumors true?" he asked bluntly. "About you and Becca? Is she living with you now?"

"She's my housekeeper, nothing more."

Lance swore beneath his breath. "That's low, Montoya. Even for you."

"Do you think I had any choice?" he shot back. "She showed up on my doorstep, bags in hand."

"You could have—and should have—sent her packing."

"As it turns out, El Diablo might be the safest place for her."

"Not likely. She's fast becoming a laughingstock. Her reputation is in shreds. And the fine, upstanding 'ladies' of our fair town are talking about boycotting Sweet Nothings."

It was Alex's turn to swear. "She's just trying to pay off her father's debt."

"It's how she's paying it off that has people talking."

Alex glared at Lance. "You've wanted a piece of me for a long time now, Brody. Keep poking and you'll get your wish."

He waved aside the offer. "Calm down. I'm not saying anything that isn't flying all over town. Becca doesn't deserve this. And I'm telling—*asking* that you fix it before any serious damage is done."

"I'll handle it, Brody." But right now he had something else to handle. He crossed to where Kate and Rebecca were huddled. "I'm taking you home, *dulzura*. We can either close the shop or call your assistant. Which would you prefer?"

"That bastard isn't going to win. I refuse to shut my store down," she stated in no uncertain terms. Her ferocity relieved him as nothing else could have. "I'll call Emma and ask her to cover for me."

"Why don't you come and stay with me and Lance?" Kate offered. "Just for a day or two."

It took every ounce of willpower for Alex to keep his mouth shut when he wanted to simply step in, sweep Rebecca into his arms and carry her back to El Diablo. It wasn't his choice to make. If staying with her friends would make her feel better, then he'd pack a bag for her himself and send her on her way.

"Thanks, anyway," Rebecca said. "I'll be fine at Alex's."

"She'll be more than fine," Alex stated. "I'll see to it, personally."

"Besides," she continued. "I'm behind on my housekeeping. This will give me a chance to catch up."

Two sets of accusing eyes ripped into him. Alex simply shook his head. "That's not going to happen. You need time to recover from your shock."

"No," she corrected firmly. "I need something to

keep my mind occupied so I'm not sitting around dwelling on it."

"We'll argue about it later." He urged her to her feet. "My car is back at Montoya Imports. Do you think you can walk that far?"

"I wish you'd all stop treating me like an invalid. Of course I can walk that far," she snapped.

By the time they arrived at the ranch, she'd recovered both her color and, along with it, more of her fight. "I really do need to get some housework done, Alex."

"As your employer, I forbid it."

"Forbid." She blinked as she absorbed the word. "Did you really just use the word 'forbid' with me?"

He shot her a quick grin. "Only as your employer."

"Seriously, Alex. What do you expect me to do?"

He pulled into the sweeping circle and parked by the steps leading to the front door. If he could have driven right up onto the porch, he would have. "I expect you to relax. You've worked very hard this past week. You've earned a day off."

Alex exited the car and circled around to open the passenger door. Rebecca climbed out. To his concern, she appeared pale again. Shadows smudged the delicate skin beneath her eyes like faint violet bruises. In the unrelenting glare of the late fall sunshine, he could see the exhaustion that shrouded her. His mouth compressed. He should have stepped in long before this. She couldn't keep playing at being his housekeeper and manage Sweet Nothings. It was too much for any one person.

"Come inside." If the words sounded more like an order than a request, he didn't give a damn. Whether Rebecca liked it or not, she needed rest and he'd see to it that she got it. "I don't know about you, but I could use some coffee."

Her eyes brightened at the suggestion. "That sounds perfect. I'll make some."

"You brew excellent coffee, but I plan to add something you don't."

"What's that?"

"Wait and see."

Together, they headed for the kitchen. He pointed to one of the chairs and waited for her to reluctantly take a seat. Once she'd complied, he slipped off his suit jacket, rolled up his shirt sleeves, and started the coffee. While it brewed, he poured a hefty dose of whiskey into a pan and gently warmed it until it was piping hot. Then he carried mugs, brown sugar, the heated whiskey, and the coffee to the table where she sat.

"Okay, I'm intrigued."

"Forget intrigued. Prepare to be impressed."

He poured coffee into each of the mugs, added the sugar and stirred the mixture. Inverting the spoon so it faced downward, he slowly poured the hot whiskey over the curved back. When he finished, he crossed to the refrigerator and pulled out whipped cream, topping each drink with a healthy dollop.

"Irish coffee," he informed her, nudging one of the mugs in her direction. *"Sláinte."*

"What does that mean?"

"It's Gaelic for 'to your health.'"

Her eyes glittered with laughter, chasing the shadows away. "Okay, I'm officially impressed."

"You'll be even more impressed when you taste it. Give it a second to cool and then see what you think."

He'd sparked her curiosity. "That good?"

"Better."

With a laugh, she buried her nose in the mug and took a cautious sip. "Oh," she murmured. She lifted her head and gazed at him, wide-eyed. "Oh, my."

He chuckled at the sight. Reaching out, he swiped a smear of whipped cream from the tip of her nose. How was it possible that she could look so beautiful? The lingering traces of fear and panic had left her pale and drawn. The whipped cream added a bizarre element of silliness to the contours of her face. And yet, she still took his breath away. She appeared almost ethereal in her aspect, especially with the blaze of red hair that tumbled to her shoulders and the impossibly green eyes glittering in delight. If she hadn't been so strong-willed and passionate, he'd have thought her a delightful pixie who'd decided to drop in for a dram of the whiskey he'd slipped into the coffee.

"How in the world did you learn to make this?" she asked.

"My previous housekeeper was Irish. She taught me."

Rebecca grimaced. "You must miss her, especially considering that her replacement doesn't come close to matching her high standards."

"I'll survive," he said with lazy assurance. He sipped his own coffee. "But you're right. I do miss her. Mrs. O'Hurlihy was a gem."

Rebecca released her breath in a gusty sigh and put a serious dent in her coffee before responding. "I know there's a lot of room for improvement, but I am trying."

"I'm aware of that. And to be honest, I can't think of anyone better suited to organize the party I'm planning to celebrate Darius and Summer's marriage. As I recall, you used to put together some rather spectacular events for your father."

For some reason, she withdrew ever so slightly. The smile she offered appeared strained and tight. "I'd be happy to take care of it," she said. "Though I would like to suggest you hire caterers, if you don't object. I'm not sure my cooking is quite up to par for what you have in mind."

"I would have hired caterers even if Mrs. O'Hurlihy were still with me. I just need you to decorate and oversee everything."

"Of course." Her nose disappeared into the mug again. "Who…who do you plan to invite?"

"The usual crowd. The Brodys, Alicia and Justin Dupree. Mitch and Lexi. Kevin and Cara Novak. Maybe a few others, too."

"Will this be a formal dinner?"

"No. Let's keep it casual. I'll arrange for you to have some strong backs to help with the Christmas decorations and the tree. I'm thinking we should serve dinner buffet style." Collecting her empty mug, he crossed to the stove and put together another round of drinks, making sure he gave Rebecca a generous helping of whiskey in the hopes it would further relax her. He set the drink in front of her, pleased when she immediately picked it up and took a sip. "This place actually has a big fancy ballroom. I think I've set foot in it once. But see if it won't work for the party."

"I'll get on it first thing in the morning."

Something in her voice sounded off and he studied her in concern. "Okay, what is it? What's wrong?"

She tossed off the question with a shrug. "Nothing. Just tired."

Guilt flooded through him. He was a selfish bastard. Here he was dropping a huge party on her after she'd just been attacked. What the hell was he thinking? He took her mug from her hands, surprised to find she'd already emptied the contents.

"Bed," he stated emphatically.

Not giving her time to argue, he swung her into his arms and carried her through to her living quarters. She rested against his chest and for the first time he realized just how fine-boned and downright fragile she felt against him. Easing her onto the mattress, he started to pull back when her arms tightened around his neck. Then she lifted her face to his and feathered a kiss across his mouth.

"Stay," she whispered. "Please, Alex. I don't want to be alone."

Eight

Rebecca clung to Alex, tightening her hold when he started to pull away again.

"Please, Alex," she said again. "Don't go."

"You don't know what you're asking." His voice sounded rough.

"I know precisely what I'm asking."

"It's the whiskey talking. And the reaction to what happened with Rodriquez."

She shook her head and held on, soothing the tension rippling across his back and neck with a gentle kneading motion. "Don't bring him into this. Not here. Not now. This is just for the two of us to share."

"There is no 'us.'"

"Who are you trying to convince, me or yourself?" She laughed softly and caught his bottom lip between her teeth. Ever so gently she tugged. "There's always been an us, from the first time you walked into Huntington Manor." Old, sweet memories flooded through her. "You came swaggering in, this tough, angry teen from the barrio, and I knew my life would never be the same."

He sank against her, the smallest of surrenders. "You were just a kid."

"I'm only two years younger than you. I was…" She searched for the appropriate word. "Teetering."

"Teetering?" His smile flashed white in the duskiness of the room. "Sweetheart, you were all woman, even then. Slender, graceful, that incredible hair of yours a silken waterfall of deep rose. You stood along the second-floor railing, looking down at us in the foyer. A princess inspecting the peasants."

"Never," she instantly denied. "I never felt that way and I never will. I remember looking at you and thinking… Why, there he is. He's the one."

"And I remember looking at you and wondering if your skin really was that white or if it was just a trick of the lighting. And thinking how much I wanted—" His smile faded. "That's when your father told us that the help didn't use the front door. We were to go around to the back."

"Oh, Alex," she whispered, feeling his pain. "I know there's nothing I can say to make up for his attitude."

"Don't even try."

"I don't intend to. In fact, I don't intend to say much of anything. Instead, I'd rather act."

She lifted upward and captured his mouth with her own. Slowly, she drew him closer until he fell heavily into her embrace, his weight a delicious pressure. For a long time, she indulged herself in a thorough exploration of his mouth. His kisses had always been intoxicating, but now they were even more potent than the whiskey he'd poured into their coffee.

He'd changed in a number of ways since they'd last been together, she realized. His shoulders were broader and the muscles across his back and along his arms harder and more sharply defined. He'd also filled out, his torso wider and more solid than the whipcord leanness she remembered with such clarity. Even his face was different. Distinctive brackets were etched into either side of his mouth and laugh lines crinkled at the corners of his eyes. Though his features had never possessed a particularly youthful aspect—at least not in all the time she'd known him—when last they'd been together, he hadn't quite attained the mantle of command that now cloaked him.

Intent on familiarizing herself with this new Alex, she took her time, allowing her fingers to wander over his face, to skim across the furrows and climb into the shallow indent dividing his chin. All the while he studied her, his expression watchful, his eyes the exact shade of bittersweet chocolate. Memories flitted there, some that allowed tenderness to slip through, others that held him at a distance. She accepted it. Understood it. After all, didn't she feel the same?

Rebecca lifted upward again, her mouth following the path her fingers had taken. She had a choice. She could give him a final kiss and send him on his way. And he'd go. She didn't doubt that for a moment. Or she could listen to the dictates of her heart and finish what she'd started. It took no thought at all.

She didn't know when—or if—this opportunity would ever present itself again. Chances were excellent that morning-after regret would prevent a reoccurrence. But just for today, she couldn't bear to turn him away. Their romantic interlude wouldn't lead anywhere. She knew that. Too much stood between them. But they could have right now. They could have this brief time together. And when it was over, she'd deal with the fallout. She'd even walk away, if he insisted, because she'd still have the memories to take with her.

The instant she reached her decision, she stroked her hands downward, finding the buttons of his dress shirt and releasing them one by one. His skin felt warm against her own, and the firm, steady beat of his heart seemed to gather within her palms of its own accord. Slowly, she pushed the crisp cotton from his shoulders and down his arms. He stopped her before she could remove it altogether.

"Are you sure?" he asked. "No regrets afterward?"

She offered him a teasing smile. "Of course there'll

be regrets, on both our parts. But I'll deal with them. And so will you."

"You've had too much to drink. It's been a traumatic day for you. I should—"

"You should tell me whether you still keep an emergency condom in your wallet."

She saw the answer in his eyes and smiled in a way that had him swearing beneath his breath. He shoved his hand into his back pocket and pulled free his wallet. She took it from there, removing the foil packet before tossing his billfold to the floor, followed by his shirt. Then she reacquainted herself with every inch of him, memorizing anew all the corded ridges and smooth, rippled expanse of him. When she grazed his belt buckle, he toed off his shoes, allowing them to drop to the floor with a decisive thud, signaling his unconditional surrender.

"You strike me as a woman who's a bit overdressed for the occasion," he informed her.

"Maybe you should do something about that."

"My thoughts exactly."

He channeled his energy into remedying the situation. With the ease of experience, he had the zipper of her skirt undone and the lightweight wool following the path of his shirt and shoes. She lay beneath him clad in the silk and lace products of her trade, a delicious advertisement for him and him alone.

"I wouldn't have thought you could wear that shade of plum. Not with your hair. But it works." He shot her a slow grin. "It really works."

"So I noticed."

She made short work of unfastening his belt and unzipping his trousers. He eased back and she reluctantly let him go while he removed the last of his clothing. Then he returned to the bed and ran a finger along the low-cut edge of her bra.

"Still overdressed," he observed.

"Still waiting for you to do something about it," she retorted. "Or shall I?"

She didn't wait for him to decide, but wriggled out from under him and stood. Taking a swift step backward, she evaded the arm he shot out to snag her. She crossed to a nearby chair and lifted one foot onto the seat. Deliberately taking her time, she released her stocking from her garter and rolled it down her leg. A low groan emanated from the direction of the bed. She turned her attention to the next stocking before removing the garter altogether and draping the various pieces of sheer femininity over the back of the chair.

"Come to bed and let me finish that," Alex demanded.

"Don't get up," she insisted with mock solicitousness. "I'll take care of it."

One by one, she lowered the spaghetti straps of her bra, which seemed to drift of their own accord down her arm. Then she released the catch at her back and inch by excruciating inch allowed the lacy scrap to fall free. Alex released a harsh exclamation and exploded from the bed. In one swift move, he had her off her feet and falling through the air onto the mattress.

Sunlight stroked her skin, and then it was Alex stroking it. Her. She tilted her head back and closed her eyes, reveling in a touch that combined tenderness with a tormenting aggression. He cupped her breasts and then took possession of them with lips and teeth and tongue. She arched beneath him, wanting more. And he gave it to her.

His hands plied across the softness of her belly to the final triangle of silk still covering her. She felt the delicate waistband snap and the next instant, the silk had been torn away, leaving her completely open to both his gaze and possession.

Sunlight danced along the auburn nest protecting the heated core of her. Murmuring in Spanish, he slid his splayed fingers into the curls, arousing her even further with a probing touch. Ever so carefully he spread her, teased her to the very brink. She clung to her sanity just long enough to rip open the foil packet he'd given her earlier and slip the contents over him. And then he was breaching her, sliding inward with a single, deep thrust.

"Alex!"

"I'm right here, *dulzura.*" His breath escaped in a hot gust. "I'm with you all the way."

She closed her arms and legs around his powerful form and clung to him, rode with him, melded with him. The sunlight around them intensified, so bright it blinded her to all but the man within her arms. He became her everything, filled her with all that he was. And she gave up to him, surrendering every bit of what she felt within her heart and body, until there was no more to give.

And in that final moment of climax, they became one, no longer separated by the past, but joined by it. Until that instant she'd truly believed that their connection had ended a long time ago. But as she tumbled toward bliss, Rebecca realized that the love she'd felt for Alex had never truly died. It had simply waited dormant for this time and this place and this man to rise again, like a phoenix from the ashes. The love she felt for him hadn't gone away.

And in that incandescent moment, she realized it never would.

She didn't know how long they slept. It was dark when she awoke, disoriented. She no longer lay in Alex's arms, though the warmth from his body lingered, indicating he'd only recently left her. From the depths of the room she caught the quiet movements as he gathered his clothing.

"Alex?" she murmured.

"Go back to sleep, Rebecca."

The formality dismayed her. He'd called her Rebecca. Not *dulzura*. Not even Becca. He'd thought she'd be the one with regrets the morning after. It would seem that he'd beaten her to it, and it wasn't even morning yet. She lifted onto one elbow.

"Are you all right?" she asked gently.

He froze, then released a sound that was part sigh and part laugh. "I believe that should be my line."

"Probably," she conceded. "But I'm not the one sneaking out."

"I wasn't sneaking," he instantly denied. "I was trying not to wake you. There's a difference."

"Mmm. Only a man could come up with that sort of distinction." She swung her legs over the side of the bed. "You're sorry this happened, aren't you?"

She caught the shadow of his head turning in her direction. "Aren't you?"

She considered for a brief moment. "I'm sorry that I've become a cliché," she admitted. "But I'm not sorry we made love."

"And only a woman could make that distinction."

"Probably." She released her breath in a sigh. "Would you prefer we pretend this didn't happen?"

She sensed his sudden stillness. "You're joking, right?"

"No, I'm not."

She wrapped the sheet around herself and switched on the bedside lamp. A soft pool of light enveloped her. Dragging the sheet from the bed, she stood and faced Alex. To her disappointment, he regarded her with a wary, remote gaze. Where was the man who'd shared her bed, who'd made love to her with such intense passion? Long gone, apparently.

"Look…" Alex ran a hand through his already rumpled hair. "It happened. We're both adults. We've been here before."

"And will again?" she dared to ask.

He shook his head a bit too promptly. "There's too much between us, Becca. It wouldn't be wise."

Well, at least he was calling her Becca now. A slight

improvement. "In case you hadn't noticed, wisdom isn't my strong suit."

"We can't go back."

He made the statement with such gentleness that tears pricked her eyes. "I'm aware of that. I was actually thinking of moving forward. You know." She lifted her shoulder in a shrug, catching the sheet before it could slip to the floor. "We're at a crossroads and all that. We can't go back, but we can go forward. It's how we move forward that's in question."

"I won't turn you into a town joke. If we start an affair, people will pick up on it. They'll see it in the way we look at each other. Or speak. Or touch." He bent and snagged his wallet off the floor where she'd dropped it and tucked it into his back pocket. "Alicia didn't have to say a word and I knew she and Justin were together just from how they interacted."

"I don't care about gossip."

"I do and you will."

He stated it with such implacability that she knew no amount of argument would sway him. "All right. We won't make love again."

"You'll see. It's the right decision," he said. "The only decision." Picking up his shoes, he crossed to the bedroom door. There, he paused and glanced at her over his shoulder. "You okay?"

She smiled reassuringly. "I'm fine."

He took her at her word and left. The instant the door closed, her smile faded. Well, what had she expected?

That he'd fall at her feet and declare his undying love? That he'd beg her to marry him and have his babies? She sank onto the edge of the mattress and closed her eyes. Damn.

His babies.

Once upon a time, it had seemed not just a possible dream, but a likely one. Now it was as much an improbability as her reaching for the moon and plucking it from the nighttime sky. Curling into a ball, she reminded herself that she wasn't going to have any regrets. If all he could give her was this one night, then she'd thank heaven above for the memory and be grateful she'd been given that much.

Unfortunately, she hadn't planned on falling in love with Alex again. Too bad she hadn't considered the likelihood of that beforehand—not that it would have made a difference. If she lived to be a hundred, the memory of this one special night would bring a smile to her face whenever she thought of it. And she planned to think about it a lot. With that final thought, sleep claimed her. When it did, it was with a smile on her lips.

And a tear on her cheek.

Everything changed over the next week. Alex turned into her employer—a real employer. And Rebecca found keeping a smile on her face more difficult than she imagined possible. When he scheduled a formal meeting with her in his office to discuss the upcoming party, Rebecca was determined to prove to him that she could handle the aftermath of their…

She hesitated to call it an actual affair. A one-night stand? Whatever the term for it, one thing was certain. Alex was determined to hold her at a careful distance.

"I want to discuss the Franklin reception with you," he said when she joined him in his office. He waved her toward the chair in front of his desk and folded his hands on the tidy teak surface while leveling her with a detached stare that buried all hint of emotion. "You've handled these sort of affairs for your father, haven't you?"

"I've organized them, yes," she agreed cautiously.

He lifted an eyebrow. "Okay, I know a 'but' when I hear one."

She hesitated. "In the past, I've always hired a caterer."

"Which I've already given you permission to do," he replied with an edge of impatience.

She sacrificed tact for honesty. "I'm not sure I can handle all my normal responsibilities in regard to maintaining the house in addition to covering everything that needs to be done for the party, especially since you want the place decorated for Christmas."

"Got it." For the first time, a hint of emotion slipped through his impassive demeanor. The fact that it was amusement she took as a good sign since it returned them to a more companionable footing. "You have my permission to hire extra staff if you need it. You can supervise staff, I assume?"

She grinned. "I excel at it."

He returned her smile with one of his own and that's when she saw it—a blistering flash of desire that came and went so quickly she thought maybe she'd imagined it. Right until she saw his fingers tense. And for the first time since their night together, she felt a resurgence of hope.

"Fine. Your new job is to take care of the party." He shoved back his chair. "If you'll excuse me, I have to get back to work."

She stood, as well. When he made to pass her, she touched his arm. Just that. He paused, staring down at her with keen regret. "We can't, Becca," he informed her gently. "It won't lead anywhere good."

"Funny. I thought our night together was pretty darn good. More than, if you want my opinion." This time he didn't reveal any amusement. Instead she caught regret, and that more than anything filled her with sorrow. Without another word, she let him go. "Right," she whispered when he was no longer within earshot. "I get it."

It wasn't until she was in the middle of discussing the meals with the caterer that she saw her conversation with Alex in a far different light. Rebecca had worked successfully with Angie, the owner of the company, in the past, but her new position as Alex's housekeeper seemed to change Angie's attitude toward her. There was a slight hint of discomfort that Rebecca was finally forced to confront.

"Okay, Angie. What's going on? You and I have worked together a dozen times in the past. What's the problem?"

Angie sighed. "I'm sorry, Rebecca. It's not your fault. It's mine."

"Is it because I'm Alex's housekeeper?" she asked bluntly. "Or is it because of my father? What's the deal?"

"I can't pretend I haven't heard the rumors, but I know you. If your father did something unethical, that's on him," Angie replied just as bluntly. "I don't hold it against you."

Rebecca blinked in surprise. "Thanks. I appreciate it. But...if that's not the problem, what is?"

"It's Montoya. Rumors are flying all over Somerset about his forcing you to be his...housekeeper," she spoke the word with a telling edge to her voice, "in exchange for helping your father. I'm just not sure I want to work for someone capable of doing such a thing."

"Is that all?" Rebecca said with a relieved laugh. "Then let me reassure you. Alex didn't force me to work for him. If anything, it was the other way around."

It was Angie's turn to blink. "Come again?"

"I showed up on Alex's doorstep and told him I'd work as his housekeeper until my family's debt is paid. He did everything he could to talk me out of it." She grimaced. "If what you're saying about the rumor mill is accurate, I'm beginning to understand why he was so reluctant to take me on. I had no idea people would think he'd forced this on me."

"I have to tell you, this certainly puts a different light on things."

"Good. I'm glad." Rebecca smiled. "Alex is really a great guy. Maverick County is fortunate to have him living here."

"Fair enough," Angie said, though a hint of doubt remained in her voice. "But won't it be weird for you?"

Rebecca shook her head in confusion. "I don't understand. Won't what be weird?"

Color darkened Angie's cheeks. "Won't all your friends be at this party?"

"Most of them, sure. So?"

"Well, won't it be weird being one of the hired help instead of a guest? I'd think it would be really awkward. For you *and* them."

Rebecca couldn't believe the thought hadn't occurred to her before this. It would be awkward. She spent the rest of the day considering it and trying to find some way out of her predicament. Maybe she could arrange for the extra staff she'd hired to cover for her.

Then she shook her head. The party was her baby and hers alone. Dumping the job on someone else wasn't fair to Alex or his guests, particularly Darius and Summer Franklin. Besides, everyone would only be uncomfortable if she made them feel that way. If she treated it as par for the course, so would they.

She hoped.

Rebecca considered calling Kate and explaining the situation, but feared her friend would end up leading a protest that would ruin the party. She'd feel awful if a reception meant to celebrate the Franklins' marriage turned into something unpleasant. All of which meant that she needed to rely on every ounce of poise and good humor to carry off the evening.

The next few weeks flowed by while the house took on more and more of a holiday aspect. Fresh greenery, poinsettias, vases of fresh-cut winter flowers and swags in winter-green and burgundy festooned the house. With the help of a workforce of willing backs, the ballroom became a winter fairyland that delighted everyone who saw it.

The day of the party, she took extra pains to make sure everything was set up properly. Angie arrived with her catering staff and began to prepare the dishes for the buffet. Toward the end of the day, Alex passed her in the hallway on his way to his room and paused long enough to compliment her on how beautiful the house looked. He even surprised her—and himself, she suspected— by planting a fleeting kiss on her lips.

"Thank you for all your hard work. The place looks amazing."

"Thanks."

He drew back, though she could see it was a struggle to revert to the role he'd assumed over the past few weeks. "Guess I'd better get showered. Guests arrive soon."

"I think that's my cue to get changed," she said lightly. "I'll meet you back here in forty-five."

Hastening to her room, she debated over her choice of clothing. She didn't want something that looked too much like a uniform. No point in rubbing people's faces in it. But at the same time, she didn't dare wear anything that smacked of a cocktail dress. She needed to draw a subtle line between staff and guest without causing tension. Finally, she settled on a simple black skirt and black silk blouse.

Precisely fifteen minutes before the first guests were due to arrive, she stationed herself in the foyer where she could greet Alex's guests and escort them to the ballroom. She carried a tray of champagne to offer each couple as they arrived and was in the process of finding the best place to position it when she heard Alex's footsteps on the sweeping stairway behind her. He halted halfway down. She turned to smile up at him, but to her alarm, he stared at her in outrage before finishing his descent.

Crossing to her side, he grabbed her arm, jarring the tray. "What the hell do you think you're doing?"

Nine

Rebecca struggled to hang on to her dignity, but she could feel fine cracks forming, expanding with each second that passed. "I'm getting ready to serve your guests," she replied, amazed at how calm she managed to sound.

He snatched the tray from her hands and slammed it onto a nearby table. The crystal sang in protest at his rough treatment and champagne splashed over the edges of the fragile flutes. "I don't know what game you're playing—"

"Game?" To her shock, fury shot through her, a fury she didn't even realize she felt until that moment. "I'm not the one playing games. I'm your housekeeper.

You assigned this job to me. I'm simply doing what you pay me to do."

He glared at her in open affront. "I am not paying you to offend our friends and neighbors by acting the part of a servant. Go change into an appropriate outfit and then join us for the celebration."

"Why?" she insisted. "So I won't humiliate you? I'm not ashamed of my job. Why are you?"

His eyes narrowed dangerously. "Is this your way of getting even? Is this because I haven't pursued a relationship with you after we made love? You feel the need to wear sackcloth and ashes because you've become, in fact, what people are calling you behind your back?"

She could feel the blood drain from her face. "How dare you?"

"How dare *I*? How dare *you* put me in such an embarrassing position with people who are more your friends than mine? Who have spent the last decade barely tolerating my presence in the community?"

Understanding crashed down on her and she began to realize she'd made a terrible mistake. That somehow, maybe because of what Angie had said to her, she'd misunderstood his intention. And now she'd insulted him. Truly, deeply offended him.

It had never occurred to her that he felt so uncomfortable around people who had been her friends for most of her life. And it should have. Hadn't she seen how difficult the Brodys had made his life through the years? How he'd been treated by some of the more elitist of those with whom they'd gone to school, who would have considered it beneath them to associate with the son of a housekeeper? In that moment, she saw herself through his eyes and felt incredibly small and petty even though she hadn't been deliberately trying to embarrass him.

"I'm sorry, Alex. I swear I never meant to put you in such an awkward position."

"And yet, here you stand," he snapped, "on the verge of shredding my reputation."

She stared at him in utter bewilderment. "Excuse me? How would this affect your reputation?"

A mask fell over his expression, cold and forbidding. "How do you think my guests will react when you answer the door dressed like that? If you play servant to my lord of the manor? They will take one look at you and walk out of my home." He thrust a hand through his hair. "Don't you get it? My reputation is all I've ever had. Whatever I've earned has been through that and sheer hard work. Endless days and nights of it. And I won't have you or anyone else destroy in one single night what I've spent decades building."

"That wasn't my intention," she said stiffly.

"In that case, you have a choice, Rebecca. You can retire for the evening, or you can put on a dress, along with a pleasant expression, and join your friends while they celebrate Darius and Summer's marriage. Or are you so determined to show everyone what a total bastard I am that you'll go to any length to prove it?"

A knock sounded at the door and before either could answer it, it opened. One look at the Brodys' expressions and it was clear they'd heard the argument right through the solid-oak partition. Their gazes slid from Rebecca to Alex and back again. Horrified understanding dawned in Kate's expression as she took in her friend's attire.

"Oh, no," she whispered, her grip tightening on her husband's arm.

Lance had taken in the situation with a single glance, as well. "Problem?" he asked coldly.

"No problem at all," Alex responded, keeping his gaze fixed on Rebecca. "A small misunderstanding that will be cleared up momentarily. Please come in and help yourself to some champagne." He addressed one of the catering staff who'd appeared in the doorway and indicated the tray. "Would you greet our guests as they arrive and show them to the ballroom? We'll join everyone in a minute."

He didn't wait for a response, but simply snagged Rebecca's arm and towed her in the direction of her quarters. Once there, he immediately went to the closet and removed the first bit of color and sparkle he came across, tossing it onto the bed. It pooled there in a brilliant lake of emerald-green silk.

"Strip," he ordered.

He wasn't surprised to see her mouth drop open in disbelief. "Have you lost your mind?" she stammered.

He managed to control his temper, but it was by a

mere thread. "Take off what you're wearing and put this dress on and do it within the next thirty seconds," he instructed, "or I swear by all that's holy, I'll do it for you."

Something about his implacable expression must have convinced her of his sincerity. She removed her blouse and skirt without a word of argument and in less than thirty seconds had exchanged it for the dress he'd chosen.

She lifted her chin and faced him. "Satisfied?"

"Not even a little." He regarded her critically. "Jewelry?"

Crossing to her dresser, she opened the top drawer and pulled out a rolled-up silk case tied with a tasseled string. After removing a few discreet pieces, she put them on. Pearls and gold gleamed softly against her earlobes and throat. "Now are we done?"

"One last thing." He came toward her, trying not to feel offended when she fell back a step. "Relax, Rebecca."

Reaching behind her, he removed the clip that held her hair in a tidy roll. The strands rained down to her shoulders, flashing with fire. He ran his fingers through the length, the silky texture tempting him almost beyond endurance. The emerald-green dress matched the color of her eyes and complemented the richness of her hair. Her anger had given her cheeks a healthy flush and made her beauty all the more startling.

"Now we're done," he informed her in a husky voice. "Let's go greet our guests."

"Your guests," she dared to correct.

"Our friends," he offered as a compromise.

She sighed. "I'm sorry." She rubbed her temples with her fingertips. "I guess I'm tired. I didn't mean to spoil the evening. It's just—" She broke off with a shake of her head. "Never mind. It doesn't matter."

He stilled. It should have occurred to him before that there was more going on than Rebecca being contrary. Or he would have if his anger hadn't gotten in the way. "Just what?"

She hesitated before admitting, "Someone said something to me about the party and about my role in it. I thought you expected me to show up as your house-keeper rather than a guest." She trailed off with a shrug. "Obviously I was wrong."

"Yes, you were. As was the person foolish enough to put the thought in your head. You should have asked me." He shook his head with a smile. "Or did your pride get in the way?"

"A Huntington flaw, it would seem." She returned his smile with a rueful one of her own. "One of many, in case you didn't notice."

"Can't say that I did," he lied diplomatically. He offered his arm. "Shall we?"

"My pleasure."

When they entered the ballroom, it was to find the rest of the guests had arrived and all eyes were fixed on them. For the first time in more years than he could recall, he felt the old awkwardness he used to experi-ence when he'd been an angry outsider, new to a high school rife with the cream of the social select. Rebecca took one look at the expressions on the faces of her friends and offered an abashed grin.

"Sorry, guys. My fault. I misjudged the time I would need to change and get ready for the party."

Rebecca kept her hand firmly on his arm as she approached Darius and his wife, Summer, both of whom radiated the joy of a couple deeply in love and exquisitely blissful. She hugged first one and then the other. "Congratulations, you two. I couldn't be happier for you."

And just like that the entire atmosphere changed from charged to celebratory. The party continued on until the candles guttered and the caterers had long gone. Finally, sleepy couples offered their thanks and farewells, and just as the one day ended and the next began, the party drew to a close.

"That went well, don't you think?" At her nod of agreement, he gestured toward an unopened bottle of champagne. "Would you like a final drink before we turn in?"

Rebecca stifled a yawn. "Okay. Why don't we have it in the living room? I want to show you the tree we put up."

He poured two glasses of champagne and together they wandered into the room, a spacious area with a plush rug and thirty-foot ceilings trimmed in juniper. Floor-to-ceiling windows reflected the huge Christmas tree positioned in front of them. Alex let out a low whistle.

"I think that's the prettiest tree I've ever seen."

Rebecca smiled, amused to feel a blush warm her cheeks at the compliment. "Thanks."

"No." He turned to face her. "Thank you. You made this evening one of the most enjoyable I can remember in a long time."

"My pleasure."

He tossed back the champagne, all the time studying her. "What the hell am I going to do about you?"

She stilled and he saw her give the question serious consideration. Then she set her champagne aside and turned to him. Everything about her was vibrant and glowing. But it was her eyes that gave him the answer long before she spoke the words. "Love me," she whispered. "Make love to me right here and now."

"I've been giving that considerable thought," he admitted.

"And?"

"And no matter how hard I try, I can't keep myself from wanting you. From touching you." He placed his flute on a nearby table and gathered her into his arms. Then he lowered his head until their mouths were no more than a breath apart. "I can't keep from doing this…."

He kissed her, giving free rein to all that he'd kept under such tight control these past weeks. Her arms entwined around his neck and she shifted closer. From the very start she'd brought a delicate grace to their mating dance, melding their bodies with a slow, delicious rhythm so distinctively her own. It had always stunned him how she opened herself to him, completely and utterly, allowing him to know her at her most vulnerable. Gifting him—heart, body and soul—

without reluctance or reserve. And so it had been from the start.

The knowledge humbled him.

Without a word, he undressed first himself and then her, stripping away all artifice until all that remained was the bare essence of them both. As one, they sank onto the plush rug in front of the Christmas tree. The soft glow from the lights caressed her alabaster skin, sliding over the lovely swell of her breasts and setting aflame the burnished curls between her legs. Gently, he reached for her, the contrast between her paleness and his own bronzed skin tones adding to the dichotomy between masculine and feminine.

She was all light and brilliant color. A soft place to rest. He was made up of darkness, with the strength and determination of stone. He'd never been a soft place for her to rest and he doubted he ever would be. They were opposites in every way, coming together in brief, sweet interludes before fate pushed them apart again.

"Don't," she whispered.

He hesitated. "Do you want me to stop?" he asked, amazed by the depth of despair the request caused him.

She smiled. "Not that. Stop thinking. Stop analyzing." Her touch was one of infinite tenderness. "Stop trying to protect me and simply love me."

He didn't require any further prompting. Lowering his head, he worshipped her with mouth and tongue and teeth. He felt the warm tide of desire sweep across her skin like a sun-drenched wave, and he

cupped her breast, feeling her heart beating for him
and only him. She flowed against him, her hips lifting
to mesh with his.

He took her with a slow, easy stroke, drawing the
moment out. But the night wasn't meant for slow. A
hunger burned between them, a demand that compelled
them toward something harder and more urgent. Fierce
heat melded with a fluid softness and he drove into her.
Her breath escaped in a frantic plea as she lifted herself
to him, matching his rhythm until they were both driven
to a peak beyond anything he could recall ever experi-
encing before.

They teetered there for an instant. But it couldn't
last, couldn't do more than hold them there for a brief,
incandescent moment before they took flight, soaring
together, forever bound. He surrendered to the woman
in his arms, surrendered all he'd worked so hard to
protect. Surrendered his body and heart.

Surrendered all that he was to the woman he loved.

The next morning Rebecca awoke to find herself in
her own bed. She stretched, feeling happier and more
deeply in love than she could ever remember. Anything
and everything seemed possible. Life was perfect—or
so it seemed—right up until she arrived at the Texas Cattleman's Club to have lunch with Kate. She caught a
buzz of excitement the instant she stepped through the
doors, one that increased when she walked into view.

For some reason, she was the center of attention and

it made her extremely nervous. It only strengthened when she caught a glimpse of her friend's broad, excited grin. Kate flew to her side and threw her arms around Rebecca.

"Congratulations! All I can say is that it's about damn time."

"What? What's happened?"

"Don't play coy. Not with me. Come on." She held out her hand in a demanding manner. "Let's see it."

Rebecca shook her head in genuine bewilderment. "I don't have a clue what you're talking about. See what?"

"The rock Alex put on your finger last night."

Rebecca's mouth dropped open. *"What?"*

Kate froze, her eyes widening. Hustling Rebecca into the club library, she dragged her to a secluded reading alcove. "You need to level with me, Bec. Are you or are you not engaged to Alex?"

Rebecca's throat closed over. "Not."

"Well, your father is here having lunch with some of his cronies. Someone made some crack about your serving Alex's guests at the party last night and your father told everyone within hearing that you and Alex are engaged."

"No." Rebecca shook her head, her voice taking on an air of desperation. "No, that's not true."

"Well, you better get it straightened out and fast. Like, seriously fast."

"Why? Oh, no. Tell me Alex isn't here, too."

"Not yet. But the guys are meeting so Darius can update them about the arson investigation. And if he hasn't gotten wind of this yet, he will the minute he steps foot through the front doors."

Rebecca shot to her feet. "Where's my father?"

"He's just finishing lunch at the café."

She left the library without another word and caught up with her father just as he was exiting the restaurant. Grabbing his arm, she drew him away from the avid gaze of the other patrons. "Kate just told me you announced to everyone that I'm engaged to Alex. Where did you hear such a thing, Dad? It's not true and you have to tell everyone it's not."

"It will be," her father retorted calmly. "Montoya can't very well back out now that it's public information, not without looking like a total bastard."

"You set us up? Deliberately?" Rebecca demanded in an appalled undertone. "How could you do such a thing?"

His jaw assumed a stubborn slant. "I've only told everyone what I had to in order for us to continue holding our heads up in this town."

"Have you lost your mind? After everything Alex has done for us—"

"What he's done for us?" her father repeated in an irate undertone. "What he's done is turn you into a laughingstock. He's forced you to become both his housekeeper and his mistress."

"In case you failed to notice, I've chosen my own path in life, Dad, just as you have. Alex didn't force me to do anything. *I* went to *him* and told him I'd be his housekeeper until I paid off your debt. He didn't want me working for him and for good reason. I'm a terrible housekeeper. And if I ended up in his bed, it was because that's where I wanted to be."

He waved her comments aside as though they didn't matter. "You're a fool, Rebecca. You could work for that man for the rest of your life and never come close to putting a dent in that debt."

"What are you talking about? Three hundred thousand is a lot, granted, but I've already paid down a decent portion of that."

"It's not three hundred thousand. It's one-point-three *million*. My debt to Rodriquez? It's a million dollars, Rebecca."

Her mouth dropped open and she could only stare, stricken. To her horror, Alex chose that moment to appear, his expression one of unmitigated fury. He could barely bring himself to look at her.

Focusing on her father, he said, "I'll deal with you in the morning when I'm not tempted to put an end to your miserable life. And in case you've forgotten, your membership was suspended. I suggest you leave before I have you thrown out." He still refused to so much as glance her way, even when he addressed her. "Rebecca, we're leaving. Let's go."

He didn't bother to see whether she followed. Before going after him, she addressed her father in a harsh undertone. "Fair warning, Dad. When Alex is done with you, I intend to have a go at whatever he hasn't chewed up and spat out."

"It was for your own good."

Rebecca refused to let him get away with that one. "No, Dad. It was for yours."

She caught up with Alex just as he exited the club and addressed him in a breathless voice. "I'm so sorry. I promise I'll straighten it out. I had no idea he planned to do that."

"We'll discuss it back at the ranch."

They covered the miles in a painful silence. His anger was so great he practically vibrated with it. She could only hope the time it took to reach El Diablo allowed his infamous temper to cool somewhat. It was a forlorn hope. She joined him as he pounded up the steps of the porch and entered the house. He made a beeline for his office where he poured several fingers of whiskey into a tumbler and downed it in a single swallow.

"Madre de Dios!" he swore. "I have had about as much as I can stomach."

"I'm sorry," she said again. "I promise I'll take care of it."

He poured two drinks this time, then rounded on her. "How do you intend to do that?" He handed her one of the glasses. "'My mistake, everyone. Alex didn't propose. My father just claimed he did because he couldn't bear the idea that I've become both his housekeeper and mistress.' Is that what you plan to say?"

"Something like that." She took a gulp of the whiskey and winced. The potent liquor burned her throat and caused tears to fill her eyes. She much preferred whiskey when it was disguised as Irish coffee. "I may leave out the housekeeper and mistress part of the explanation," she managed to gasp.

"Do not attempt to humor me. I don't find any part of this the least bit amusing."

She released a tired sigh. "I don't, either, Alex. But considering all that's happened over the past few weeks, a sense of humor is just about the only thing left to me." He started to speak, but she waved him silent. "What does it matter what I tell people or what they think of me? They can't think much worse than they already do."

"But they can think worse of me."

It took her a moment to puzzle through that one. And then it hit her. "And they'd think worse of you if you married the daughter of a thief and arsonist, wouldn't they, Alex?"

She must have hit pretty close to the truth because he swore again, this time a virulent string of words in Spanish. All the while Rebecca fought to breathe. To pretend that his attitude toward her and her father hadn't wounded her to the very depths of her being. To her relief, fury came to her rescue.

"Let me make sure I understand this," she said with impressive calm. "You're not upset because of what my father did, but because you're—" she struggled to find the most appropriate word "—because you're disgusted at the idea of being romantically linked to a Huntington? Your business would be harmed? Your precious reputation? Your honor?"

His head jerked up as though scenting danger. Took him long enough, she thought. "Rebecca—"

"Just answer the question, Alex." She tossed back the whiskey, this time ignoring the alcoholic burn, and slammed the glass onto his desk so hard she couldn't believe it didn't shatter. "On second thought, never mind. You've already made your feelings crystal clear."

He studied her without expression. "It's not you. You understand that, don't you? It's your father."

"No, I got it. I'm good enough to bed, so long as no one finds out. But you wouldn't dream of marrying me."

He cocked an eyebrow. "Is that what you were hoping would happen? I'd take you to bed and fall in love with you again? We'd marry and your father's debts would be miraculously forgiven?"

"In other words, did I seduce you as some sort of nefarious plot so you'd pay off our debts and save my father from jail? Sure, Alex. Have it your way." She closed the distance between them. "Now let me ask you a question. When I approached you about taking over as your housekeeper in order to pay off our debt, why didn't you tell me it was an impossibility? A one-point-three-million-dollar impossibility? Or would that have spoiled your fun at having the opportunity to turn the tables on the Huntingtons and get a little payback after all?"

"Your father told you?" At her nod, he sighed. "Interesting, considering I promised him I would remain silent on the issue. I did warn you the debt couldn't be settled anytime soon."

"There were alternatives to telling me, Alex. If you'd flat-out refused to hire me, there's not much I could have done to force your agreement."

He shrugged. "I thought having you stay at El Diablo might protect you from Rodriquez."

It made a hideous sort of sense. "So it had nothing to do with wanting me back in your bed?"

He didn't answer that, but she could see the truth in his eyes. He wanted her. He'd always wanted her, just as she'd always wanted him. What a sad pair they were. Exhaustion swamped her.

"I'll pack my things and be out of your life first thing in the morning." A bit melodramatic, but maybe he'd put that down to the amount of whiskey she'd consumed. She paused by the door, but couldn't bring herself to look at him again in case she burst into tears. "You know…I find it interesting that you've always held my father in such contempt when you've spent your entire life turning yourself into an exact replica of him. And just in case you were wondering, tonight you completed the transformation. You're just as much a snob as he ever was."

And with that, she walked out.

Ten

The ringing of her cell phone woke Rebecca from a groggy sleep. Sitting up in bed, she looked around her room in a daze while the events of the previous night crashed down on her. At some point in the midst of her packing frenzy she must have fallen asleep, leaving the evidence of those crazed hours strewn around her. Clothing was piled half in and half out of suitcases. Dresser drawers hung open. And the closet door stood agape, with the hangers stripped bare.

The cell phone continued its annoying chirp and she cleared her throat as she fumbled to answer it, praying it was Alex calling with a change of heart. Though why he would call instead of simply joining her in bed…

"Yes, hello?"

"Good morning, señorita. I trust you slept well last night?"

She hesitated for a full ten seconds before moistening her lips and replying. "Paulo?"

"Very good," he responded with warm approval. "You've come to recognize my voice. An excellent step forward in our relationship. Soon you'll learn to listen to my every word, and of course, always do exactly as I tell you."

Was he kidding? "That's not likely."

"Really?" His laughter sent a chill of dread coursing through her. "I think it's not only likely, but inevitable. Why don't we test my theory and see. Are you listening, *muñequita?*"

She vaguely recalled that meant *little doll,* but suspected it had a slightly different connotation the way he chose to use it. "I'm listening."

"See, already part of my prediction has come true." His voice lowered, became more sinister. "Let's see if I can't make the rest come true, as well. Shall we try?"

Her palms grew damp, making it difficult to hold the cell phone. "What do you want?"

"I want you to come to Huntington Manor. Alone. When you get here, you will join your father and me for a little…conversation."

Her heart leaped. "My father?" she repeated.

"Is right here with me. Shall I put him on?"

"Yes. Yes, I want to speak to him."

"Very well. I will allow it. This time."

There was a momentary pause and she could hear men's voices conversing in the background. Then her father came on the line. "Gentry's here! Find Alex. Tell him—"

Her father broke off with a groan and then Rodriquez spoke again. "If you are very wise, you won't listen to your father. He's an old man. He can't handle pressure well. Such pressure could do him serious harm. Do we understand one another?"

Terror filled her. What had he already done to her father to cause him to groan like that? What more was he willing to do if she didn't follow his instructions? Injecting a docile tone into her voice that was only partially feigned, she said, "Don't hurt him. Please, Paulo."

To her relief, it worked. "Much better. I like how you ask so nicely." He paused a beat before continuing. "It's time for you to come home. Get into your car and drive over here. Then the three of us—"

"Don't you mean four?"

He chuckled. "Very well. The *four* of us will have a brief conversation while we determine the future direction of our relationship." The amusement faded from his voice. "Under no circumstances will you call Alex. Besides, I've arranged for him to be well occupied at his office with strict instructions not to be disturbed. He won't be able to help you, even if he were so inclined. Do you understand?"

"Yes."

"Excellent. See? I told you that you'd listen and obey me. I'm very pleased at how quickly you've learned. You won't keep your future husband waiting, will you, Rebecca?"

She gritted her teeth. "No, Paulo," she answered dutifully.

"See that you don't."

The instant he disconnected the call, she began to punch in Alex's number, then hesitated. She'd never been a good liar and doubted she could fool Paulo if he asked her whether or not she'd disobeyed him. But she hadn't promised she wouldn't call someone else. Unfortunately, this time she doubted anyone could save her from what Paulo had planned.

Again, she started to use her cell, but thought better of it. Allowing instinct to drive her, she called Kate using Alex's landline. Precious moments passed while she argued with her best friend, finally hanging up in a panic when she realized how much time was passing. Running flat-out for the pickup truck she'd purchased to replace her Cabriolet, she turned the key in the ignition and prayed that the stubborn engine would turn over. To her relief, it caught on the first try. Grinding it into gear, she bumped her way down Alex's gravel entryway.

The drive from El Diablo to Huntington Manor seemed interminable. When she finally arrived everything looked perfectly normal, with the exception of a powerful black vehicle squatting on the grass in front of the house like some predatory cockroach. No doubt cutting across the lawn was Rodriquez's quaint manner of marking the territory he intended to claim. Gathering her self-control, she climbed the steps and entered the house.

She suspected she'd find her father entertaining their "guests" in the library. Her guess proved accurate. She entered to find her father seated at a desk with his ex-foreman and Paulo Rodriquez standing over him while he scratched his signature on a piece of paper.

Rodriquez looked up at her entrance and offered her a look of cool approval. "Join the party, *muñequita.* We've been waiting for you."

"What's going on?" She focused her attention on the wad of papers in front of her father. "What is my father signing?"

"Just a few unimportant documents."

Right. Sure they were. "Let me guess. Unimportant documents that transfer ownership of Huntington Manor over to you?"

He grinned and shook his finger at her. "I can't fool you, can I?" His smile faded and he approached, holding out his hand. "Your cell phone, if you don't mind."

Her fingers tightened on the strap of her purse. "I do mind."

"Do not attempt to play with me, señorita. I am most displeased with you right now."

She attempted to swallow her fear, but her throat had gone bone dry. Removing the phone from her purse, she passed it into Rodriquez's keeping. "Why do you need my cell?"

He flipped it open and pressed a series of buttons. "I wish to see who you've phoned since we last spoke." He nodded in approval. "Very good. No calls were placed after mine."

"Satisfied?"

"Not yet. But soon. Come." He waved a hand toward the couch as though he were the host and she his guest. "Make yourself comfortable. You won't be going anywhere for a very long time. You and I... Let's just say we have plans to discuss."

Her sense of dread increased and she forced herself to bury it beneath an air of casual inquisitiveness. "What sort of plans?"

He deliberately waited a beat, no doubt in an effort to increase the apprehension she'd failed to conceal from him. "Why, wedding plans, of course."

"I'm going in there and nothing any of you say or do is going to stop me," Alex stated implacably.

"Don't be more of an idiot than you can help, Montoya," Lance Brody argued. "That's precisely what Rodriquez is counting on. Then he'll have all of you."

Alex stared at Huntington Manor, standing tall and stately in the distance while he remained tucked out of sight like some timid mouse cowering before a hungry cat. "I'm not going to allow Rebecca to remain in there unprotected."

"Will he be armed?" Darius cut in.

"Without question."

Darius lifted an eyebrow. "So, what? You're just going to stroll in and tell him to let your woman go? Once he has the two of you together, he'll use you against each other."

Lance took up the argument. "I know Becca as well as anyone. You would put yourself in harm's way to protect her—she'll do the same on your behalf. And you damn well know it. Think. You can't give Rodriquez that sort of leverage."

"I have to."

"You're not in this alone," Lance maintained. He nodded toward the rest of the men grouped around them. His brother, Mitch, had his back. Alex's future brother-in-law, Justin Dupree, had positioned himself on one side, while Kevin Novak had taken up the other. "We're all here for you. Every last man."

Alex found it difficult to reply. He'd been alone for so long, it was hard to accept that was no longer the case. "Thank you," he said simply.

"Here's the deal," Darius said, laying it out. "If we storm the place, chances are someone will get hurt. Or Rodriquez will claim he was there at Huntington's invitation. We don't have any evidence to prove differently. We sure as hell don't have any evidence that he's guilty of any crime. There's no proof that he scammed Huntington. No proof that he intends anyone any harm. He'll walk."

"Then what am I—are we—supposed to do?" Alex demanded in frustration.

Darius grinned. "I thought you'd never ask."

* * *

Rebecca glared at Rodriquez. "You can't honestly believe I'll agree to marry you?"

"You will unless you want to see your father put in jail as an arsonist."

She switched her gaze to Gentry. "He can't testify against my father without implicating himself."

Rodriquez waved that aside. "Cornelius is about to take a long, restful trip. But before he goes, he'll leave behind more than enough evidence to convict your father of the charges." He approached the couch and ran a finger along the curve of her cheek, his mouth tightening at her involuntary flinch. "Soon you will not just welcome my touch, but beg for it."

"Take your hands off her," Sebastian roared from where he sat behind his desk. He half rose, but Gentry shoved him back into the chair.

Rodriquez shot him a look of disgust. "Shut up, old man. You have your own problems to worry about." He took a seat beside Rebecca and gathered her hands in his. "Don't look so tragic, *muñequita*. We're going to have a perfect life together. We will be a happily married couple and share this estate. I will stamp my own name on the history of the Huntingtons, improve on what your father began. You will fall madly in love with me and be the most beautiful bride anyone has ever seen."

She shook her head, tears gathering in her eyes. "No. Never."

He ignored her, speaking with surprising tenderness.

"Can't you picture it, my sweet? We will start our own dynasty, one to rival all others in Maverick County. People will see how we live and envy us. Envy all that I have managed to acquire. Me, a poor nobody from the barrio, now the richest, most powerful man in the county." His hand settled low on her stomach, splaying across her abdomen in a possessive gesture. "In time, you will grow heavy with the first of our many children. Children who will go to the finest schools and have friends among the most elite in Somerset."

Before she could tell him just what she thought of his insane dream, someone cleared his throat. Jerking free of Rodriquez's hold, she saw Alex standing in the doorway, leaning against the doorjamb. Her heart leaped at the sight, while her stomach twisted into knots. She'd known by calling Kate that she risked Alex storming Huntington Manor, but she'd hoped he'd show more sense than to play into Rodriquez's hands by simply walking right in.

"Am I interrupting something?" he asked with seeming casualness.

Rodriquez shot to his feet, his hand darting behind his back where she saw the butt of a sleek, black gun. "What the hell are you doing here, Montoya?" he demanded. His infuriated gaze switched from Alex to Rebecca. "I warned you not to call him. I warned you!"

She looked him straight in the eye and spoke the God's honest truth, praying he'd believe her. "I didn't. I swear I didn't."

"You can believe her," Alex said in a calm voice, drawing the other man's attention. "I'm only here to deliver the rest of Rebecca's belongings. We had a... I guess you could call it a falling-out last night. Bottom line is, she quit. Since Her Highness was taking her sweet time getting her backside out of my house, I thought I'd help move her along."

"She was leaving you?" A hint of uncertainty threaded through Rodriquez's voice. "Why would she do that?"

"Let's just say she refused to fulfill all her duties as my housekeeper and I got fed up waiting for her to change her mind."

To Rebecca's amazement, Rodriquez bought it, his expression one of sheer elation. "She wouldn't sleep with you?"

Alex shrugged, and a hint of irritation drifted across his face. "It happens."

"But the rumors around town..."

"I have my pride, Paulo," Alex snapped. "People thought what I wanted them to think."

"You son of a bitch!" Sebastian burst out. "How dare you ruin my daughter's reputation?"

"And how dare you tell everyone we were engaged," Alex shot back.

"Enough," Rodriquez interrupted. His suspicious gaze darted from person to person before swinging back in Alex's direction. "You've delivered Rebecca's belongings. Feel free to leave, Montoya."

"No problem." Then he hesitated. "Although..."

"Although what?"

A deep scowl blossomed on Alex's face. "I've been thinking about what you said when you came to visit me the other day."

Rodriquez bristled. "You mean when you tried to take all of this away from me?"

Alex gave a chagrined shrug. "Foolish, I know. I've never been able to beat you at anything. I don't know why I even bother trying."

Clearly mollified, Rodriquez nodded. "It's time you learned how pointless it is."

"You're right. So, it's only fair that I—" he grimaced as though the words left a bitter taste in his mouth "—congratulate you for a game well played."

Rodriquez smiled. "You never saw it coming, did you, *amigo?*"

A hint of admiration gleamed in Alex's eyes. "You must have had this planned a long time to pull it off so successfully."

To Rebecca's horror, El Gato stiffened. "I have no idea what you're talking about. I've planned nothing."

Alex crinkled his brow in bewilderment. "What? Oh, I don't mean…" He gestured toward her father and the papers strewn across the desk. "Whatever you have going on there is none of my business. If I could have figured a way to fleece Huntington with no one being the wiser, I'd have done it myself. No, I'm talking about Rebecca."

"The woman?" Rodriquez glanced her way and wet

his lips before jerking his attention back to Alex. "I have wanted her for a long time."

"I didn't realize how much or I wouldn't have interfered." He advanced into the room, just a single pace, his hands at his sides, his shoulders slightly hunched in defeat. "But you couldn't take her when she and I first started dating, could you?"

Rodriquez shrugged. "Not so long as she was with you." His chin lifted defiantly. "I stuck to the code. You can't claim otherwise."

"True." Alex's mouth tightened. "You wouldn't have taken her from me. But if you could trick us to part ways…"

"That's a different story, isn't it?"

"So you told everyone that I'd seduced her as part of a bet."

"You figured that one out, yes?" Rodriquez's smile widened in delight. "One of my more clever ideas, I must admit."

"But you also knew she'd need a little incentive to fall into your arms. That's when you hit on your investment scheme. As much as I hate to admit it, it was brilliant." Alex's scowl returned. "In fact, I wish I'd thought of it myself."

To Rebecca's relief, aside from a low growl, her father remained silent. She shot him a warning look.

"As I told you before," Rodriquez said. "The greedy pig couldn't get enough. Even when the investments went under, he came back for more. It was so easy to set up."

"Serves him right," Alex murmured.

"Exactly! He deserves everything coming to him." Rodriquez gestured around him. "Soon all his possessions will become mine, including his daughter."

"You were right, you know," Alex admitted. "If I hadn't been so preoccupied with having Rebecca again, I'd have been on board a lot sooner. Just think of it, Paulo. A pair of *hermanos* from the barrio owning two of the richest spreads in all of Maverick County. We'll be members in the same club, rubbing elbows with people who years ago wouldn't have given us the time of day."

"And the woman?" Rodriquez demanded through narrowed eyes. "What of her?"

Alex grinned. "She's all yours. You've earned her as your reward."

Triumph glowed in Rodriquez's dark eyes. "Yes, I have, haven't I?"

"There's just one thing I don't get." He gave a self-deprecating shrug. "I guess my mind just doesn't work like yours."

"It never did."

"And never will," Alex conceded.

"Tell me what you don't understand. I will explain it to you," Rodriquez offered expansively.

"I just don't get the arson fires. Why the hell did Huntington have Gentry set them? Were they just a distraction, so all the club members would be at each other's throats?"

A flash of anger exploded across Rodriquez's face and Rebecca went perfectly still, terror creeping up her spine. "You think that *cabrón* has the intelligence to plan something like that? You insult me!"

Alex's eyebrows shot upward in amazement. "*You* planned the arson fires? You had Gentry set them?" His anger rose to match Rodriquez's. "You burned down my barn? What the hell for?"

"To set Huntington up. To give me extra leverage when the time came to close my trap around him." Paulo attempted to placate his friend. "I apologize, *amigo*. I wouldn't have done such a thing to you if it hadn't been absolutely necessary."

Alex steamed for a few seconds before shrugging it off. "I suppose if you can let bygones be bygones, so can I," he said grudgingly.

"Agreed." He wagged a finger in Alex's direction. "I did not like being at odds with you. Don't let it happen again."

"You're right. My mistake." He closed the distance between them and offered his hand. "What do you say we start over."

Paulo grinned and gripped Alex's hand. "I'd like that."

The instant the two men connected, Alex's left hand plowed into Rodriquez's jaw, the movement so fast it was little more than a blur. El Gato's eyes rolled into the back of his head and he dropped like a stone, out cold. Before Gentry could do more than jerk to attention, Sebastian snatched the burl wood lamp off his desk and smashed it over the top of his ex-foreman's head. Then he turned to glare at Alex.

"I hope to hell you're wearing a wire, Montoya."

"That's Mr. Montoya to you. And yes. I'm wearing a wire."

Sebastian's jaw worked for a moment then to Rebecca's shock, he nodded. "Mr. Montoya. I'm man enough to admit when I've made a mistake. I've been wrong about you and wrong in my treatment of you and your family." He crossed the room and stuck out his hand. "I know I don't deserve it, but I hope you'll accept my apology."

Alex hesitated for a split second before taking Sebastian's hand in a firm shake. Then he turned to Rebecca. For a long moment he simply looked at her. Then he opened his arms. With an inarticulate cry she exploded from the couch and threw herself against him. He held her in a grip that spoke of pain and love and relief, all wrapped up in one.

"I'm also man enough to admit when I've made a mistake," he whispered against her hair. "I'm sorry, *dulzura.* I was wrong the other night. About everything."

"And the bet? You never had a bet with Rodriguez?"

"Never." Tenderness filled his expression. "I could never do such a thing to you."

Tears filled her eyes. "I should have known. Maybe if I hadn't been so young and foolish, I would have."

Suddenly the room was crowded with people. "You do know you're still being recorded, right?" Darius Franklin asked drily.

Alex never took his gaze off Rebecca. "So long as you have Sebastian Huntington's apology on tape and make me a half dozen copies, I don't give a damn."

And then he lowered his head and kissed her. Kissed her world right. Kissed his way home. Kissed her with all the passion of a man who understood where his heart lay and with whom. When they finally pulled back, it was to discover the room deserted.

He cupped her face, his thumbs sweeping away tears she hadn't even realized she'd cried. "I love you, Becca. I have since the moment we first met."

"And I love you." She hesitated, one final cloud casting a shadow on her happiness. "You realize your reputation will be linked with mine and my father's?"

"I was a fool," he said simply. "And I'm more sorry than I can possibly express. I'd be honored to have my name linked with yours and be part of your family."

It was all she needed to hear. With a contented sigh, she surrendered to the inevitable…a life with Alex, filled with laughter, passion beyond imagining and a love that would last them for the rest of their lives. "Take me home, Alex."

He swept her into his arms, allowing love to wash away the bitterness of the past and provide a pathway toward their future. "I thought you'd never ask."

Epilogue

The small mission church was crowded to capacity, the beautiful stone building decorated for the Christmas Eve wedding ceremony in fresh greenery and red and white roses that combined their perfume with the delicate scent of candle wax. A soft prelude echoed off the walls and rafters as Alicia and Justin's bridal party made its way down the aisle.

Cara, in her role as matron of honor, reached the altar just as the sweet herald of the Trumpet Voluntary sounded. And then Alicia appeared, glorious in a fitted ivory gown that swept into a long train. She clung to her brother's arm, tears glistening from beneath the beautiful lace mantilla-style veil that framed her exquisite features. Beside her, Alex looked more handsome than Rebecca had ever seen him. While all eyes were riveted on his sister, his gaze never wavered from hers.

Once he'd given away the bride in traditional fashion, he crossed to where Rebecca was seated in the front pew. As the clock edged from Christmas Eve toward Christmas Day, the ceremony proceeded at a stately pace.

Through it all, Alex held her hand, their fingers interlaced. It couldn't have been more perfect. While Justin and Alicia exchanged their vows, their love for one another unmistakable, the other couples who'd recently found a love just as deep and enduring exchanged looks of joy and passion. And then it was over. The newly married couple shared a lingering kiss while tears of happiness glistened in the eyes of those who watched.

Trumpets began the recessional, the familiar strands of Ode to Joy accompanying the bridal party's departure. While the guests began a general exodus of the church, Alex gathered Rebecca into his arms.

"It's been a long, hard road for us, hasn't it, *dulzura?*"

"At times," she conceded.

"Maybe because it's been so hard, it makes this moment so much more meaningful."

She smiled and asked, "This moment? Why this moment?"

"Listen." Around them the bells tolled the midnight hour. "It's the first minute of Christmas and my final responsibility to my family has been discharged." He took her hand in his and slipped a ring onto her finger. "I can't think of a better time to tell you that I love you more than life itself and to ask if you'll marry me."

A gorgeous diamond solitaire captured the flickering candlelight and threw it outward in rainbow rays of hope. "Oh, Alex." It took her a moment to gather her self-control enough to respond. "I've loved you since the minute I first saw you."

His gaze grew tender. "Is that a yes?"

She answered him with a kiss, a kiss that held all the passion their life together would bring and echoed the love that had filled the church that evening. When she pulled back, the expression in her eyes was beyond anything he'd ever see before.

"Yes, Alex. It's definitely a yes."

* * * * *

Snow, sleigh bells and a hint of seduction

Find your perfect Christmas reads at
millsandboon.co.uk/Christmas

MILLS & BOON®

Why shop at millsandboon.co.uk?

Each year, thousands of romance readers find their perfect read at millsandboon.co.uk. That's because we're passionate about bringing you the very best romantic fiction. Here are some of the advantages of shopping at www.millsandboon.co.uk:

* **Get new books first**—you'll be able to buy your favourite books one month before they hit the shops

* **Get exclusive discounts**—you'll also be able to buy our specially created monthly collections, with up to 50% off the RRP

* **Find your favourite authors**—latest news, interviews and new releases for all your favourite authors and series on our website, plus ideas for what to try next

* **Join in**—once you've bought your favourite books, don't forget to register with us to rate, review and join in the discussions

Visit **www.millsandboon.co.uk**
for all this and more today!